Our Lives for Others

A novel

By

Shay M. Wills

For Meg, Eva, and Samuel,
Their love sustains me.

Rand and Will

July 5, 2008

In the shadows, beneath a purple, pre-dawn sky, the two warriors rose from the stone lined pit, and, while one of them removed the griddle from the campfire, the second kicked dirt over the flames. Disturbed dust and smoke shrouded the two men. They coughed and squinted. Both snuck glances at the silent, seemingly empty Winnebago parked nearby. The warriors collected their trash, plates, cutlery, and mugs, and they packed them into a green milk crate. Finished, both men gazed at the Winnebago while they stood near the now cleaned campsite. Within that Winnebago lay their first two vanquished enemies in a war that would rid the world of stupid people.

"Did you leave the index card with the question on it?" asked the one who kicked the dirt over the flames.

"Yep."

"Where?"

"I put it on the guy's chest."

"You wore the gloves?"

"You saw me put them on."

"Yeah, I guess I did."

"Are you okay?" said the one who had picked up the griddle.

"Fine," said the kicker of the dirt.

"You can't be weak."

"I'm not."

"Remember, this is a war."

"Don't tell me about war. I know about war. More than you'll ever know." Defiance sharpened his voice.

"All right." The other calmed the air with his free hand. They shoved the green milk crate into the back of their station wagon. Finished, the taller of the two, who had handled the griddle, slammed the back hatch shut. They stared at each other. The taller of the two was Randall, but he had everyone call him Rand, after one of his favorite authors. Not only was Rand taller than his companion, he was thinner, had blonde hair and blue eyes, and was thought attractive by women. He dressed in well fit jeans, his t-shirt tucked in to accentuate his narrow waist and show the crotch of his jeans. He never smiled, he smirked, always to the right. He was quick to talk. His companion, who spoke second, was shorter but had a stocky, muscular build. He outweighed Rand by twenty five pounds, easily. His name was

William, Will, and he had acne scars that he often probed with his fingers, but he was resigned about this, though he envied the way girls held their breaths and widened their eyes at Rand. Will joined the US Army out of high school, and was medically discharged after a four year stint. He used the GI Bill to go to college. His college roommate was Rand, four years his junior. Rand said, "This is our first operation too. We've done it."

"Yeah."

"It was exhilarating," Rand looked to the RV. Will bowed his head, his eyes on the dry dust at their feet. "Don't you feel it too?"

"I'm tired. Do you mind taking the first shift driving?" Will said.

"No, I don't mind. Are you okay?"

"Mm hm."

Rand reached and shook one of Will's shoulders. "What? Didn't you sleep all right?"

Will shrugged out of Rand's grip and looked him in the eye though his head was still bowed. "I had a dream."

"Oh, yeah? You and Martin Luther King. What was your dream about?" Rand stepped back, inclined his head, and scrutinized his fellow warrior.

Will hunkered his shoulders and dug his fists into the pockets of his loose jeans. His jeans were loose by necessity, his legs too muscular to allow him to pull on anything as tight as what Rand wore. He looked down the trail, which led away from this camping site, and noticed the way the sunlight knifed between the rib-like tree trunks. It was dawn now. Were witnesses hidden in the shadows between those stabs of light? "We should get moving. What if someone comes along?"

Rand shook his head. "No one comes to a campsite first thing in the morning."

Will returned his gaze. "Except park rangers."

Rand pursed his lips. He nodded. "Okay. That's possible. Let's get out of here. Do we have everything?"

"Yeah. Did you wipe it all down inside?" Will turned to take a last look at the silent RV.

"Remember, I wore the latex gloves."

"Yeah." Will reached to one cheek and dug at a particularly large pockmark.

Rand said, "People have to know why. We have to also be teachers. How else can we make the world better? People need examples to follow. They have to think of principles so they can act accordingly."

"I suppose so." Will nodded slowly as if their actions of the night before were still up for reconsideration.

Rand became agitated. He put his fists on his hips. "What do you mean, you suppose so?"

Will's eyes were on the woods around them. Every shadow was a possible threat. "What?" He'd forgotten the thread of their talk. He shook his head to clear away his anxiety about witnesses. "Yeah, definitely. That's right, but we got to get out of here. Now."

Satisfied that Will was not having second thoughts, Rand dropped the disapproving stance. "Come on. Let's go."

Rand marched to the driver's side and jumped behind the wheel. The station wagon cranked, caught, and came to life. Will scanned the shadows along the trail side again. He saw no one. No movement. Not even animals were around except for an invisible chorus of birds. Perhaps the fresh corpses marked this spot in the world as taboo to all living beings? Still unconvinced that they were safe, he continued his surveillance as he felt his way to the front passenger door and got in. Seated, with his belt on, Will said, "Hurry."

"Right." Rand pulled the car forward, turned the wheel, reversed, turned the wheel the opposite direction, and they left. Rand put speed under them, and stones ricocheted in the wheel wells. He checked the rearview mirror several times though no one could follow them from the dead end of the campsite. There was no one alive to do so. "What was the dream?" Rand asked.

Will reached and opened the glove box. The Browning 9mm hopped around as the vehicle bounced along the rutted and rocky route. "There was a man chasing me in the desert. I had been running a long time, and I couldn't run any more. My chest and legs were on fire. I pulled up and spun around. He was practically on me, maybe ten yards behind me. I drew my Browning." He took the pistol from the glove box and gripped it with the butt set on his knee. "I aimed and fired. I saw the bullet hit. The guy jerked. Blood popped from his sternum, but he kept coming. I unloaded on him, and every shot was in the center of his chest, but the fucker wouldn't fall. His heart must've been shredded. But he was alive and coming to kill me. I saw it in his eyes. He leaped at me, his hands ready to choke the life out of me. I couldn't believe it, you know?"

Rand nodded. They hit the main branch of the trail and headed for the exit from the camping grounds. Rand kept the speed up. The stones machine gunned the wheel wells.

"When he landed on me, we toppled backwards, and his hands got around my throat. He was too strong, like Achilles or Hercules, I couldn't break his grip. That's when I woke up."

"That's a freaky dream."

"Yeah." Will watched a river, clear except where the sun's light glinted coldly on its rippling surface, rush past. He thought of Hemingway and yearned for peaceful times to come, but this was a war and they had to win. That was what he and Rand had agreed. They were soldiers in a war to change the world. Pacifists never changed anything. History forgot them as war after war tilled their bodies into the earth. It would be nice one day to return here and go fishing though, after the world was a better place. Were there trout or perch or catfish here?

"Ah, dreams don't mean shit anyway," Rand said.

"No, I guess not," said Will as the road veered from the course of that clear bottomed river. "Let's hope." He craned his head to track the river a while longer as it emerged from the shadows of a copse of spruce.

"It's not like it's a premonition." Rand laughed at him. Why was Will so spooked? "I mean, no one can get shot a baker's dozen times in the heart and lungs and keep coming at you. Right? It's just a dream. Why are you letting it bother you?"

They raced past a large wooden sign that showed all the various trails cut like termite tunnels into its face. Fifty yards ahead was the state route and a smooth black top. Both men tensed a little more at the nearness of their escape.

"Here we are. Home free," said Rand as he feigned cheerfulness. He glanced over and saw the pistol in Will's grip. "Hey, put that away will you? What if someone sees?"

Will nodded and stowed the weapon in the glove box. They struck the state route and headed west. Rand maintained a speed that was just above the posted limit but which would not attract the attention of police looking for speeders. After an hour, they merged with an interstate and continued their westward passage. At close to noon, they hit a gas station, refueled, bought food, used only cash, and Will took Rand's place at the wheel. They drove a Subaru Forester station wagon. It was a perfect vehicle because of its all-wheel drive, good ground clearance, and interior storage space so that their gear was both out of the weather and accessible to them even as they drove. They purchased the three year old used model by pooling their savings. Both men worked throughout college and the week after graduation, after much searching, test driving, and debating, they chose their war chariot. In the back of the station wagon, the pair had a wide array of equipment for camping, eating, fixing the car, and killing. There was a two man pup tent, two sleeping bags, and two rolled foam cushions. They had a saw, a hatchet, an ax, and a folding, entrenching tool from Will's days in the service. There was a plastic bin of food with cereal, cans of beans and other vegetables, a loaf of bread, pancake mix, jelly, peanut butter, coffee, and other edibles. There were two one gallon jugs of drinking water, one for each man. There was another bin with a skillet, coffee pot, and a sauce pan. There was a hard plastic Craftsman tool box with standard and metric end wrenches and sockets plus an array of drivers and extensions. They also had purchased and carried with them two gallons of antifreeze, five quarts of oil, an oil filter, two quarts of transmission fluid, a full set of spark plugs and plug wires, extra windshield wipers, air filters, and belts and hoses. They each had a Browning nine millimeter pistol with two hundred rounds each and four magazines each. And on their hips, sheathed, were the survival knives they had used to make their first kills the night before, July 4, Independence Day, 2008.

Will drove and ate a peanut butter and jelly sandwich that Rand made in his lap as the car vibrated and hummed along at close to eighty. They spoke very little. There was little need since they had become men of action, warriors, now. Along with his sandwich, Will ate a bag of pretzels then an apple. Rand ate a banana and a bag of potato chips with his sandwich. Rand gathered their trash into a Ziploc and put it on the floor by his feet. At their next stop for food and fuel they would toss it in the garbage.

When they crossed the state line, later that afternoon, Rand said, "Well, I guess we can breathe easy."

"Yeah."

"Are you still thinking about it?"

Will shrugged, checked his blind spot, and changed lanes to pass a Winnebago similar to that other they slept by last night.

"You know, they say the first is always the hardest."

"Only this wasn't my first."

Rand eyed his friend with envy. "No."

Will steered back into the slow lane.

"I feel like I'm on a high." Rand smacked his thighs.

"Adrenaline."

"Maybe." Rand began to beat a rhythm on his thighs, somewhat like the call to charge for cavalry. "I think it's really just that we're doing what we've talked about for so long. We're committed now. This is our war. The deeds we do now will mark us for greatness."

Will nodded slightly. "Thanks, Raskilnikov."

"Come on. After more than a year of talking about it, and months of planning it, we've finally begun our war. Isn't it amazing? Aren't you caught up in the spirit of it? Where's your enthusiasm? Why aren't you gung ho?"

"It doesn't seem real somehow. I don't know. Those two almost seem like ghosts, shadows, not-people, if you will."

"That's it. You've noticed it too. I thought it was just me. Last night feels like a dream now, but it really happened. I think maybe it has to do with those two. Remember what Plato said, 'The unexamined life is not worth living.' Well, those two had never examined their lives. They hadn't lived, and they hadn't lived well either. Their lives were worthless. That's why they don't seem real." Rand raised his hands and examined them. "But that wasn't a TV knife in my hand. I've really done it."

"Yeah." Will braked as they caught up to traffic.

"I did it." Rand stabbed the air in front of him with his hand shaped around the handle of an invisible survival knife. Quickly his face changed though, and he looked around as if he meant to catch something in flight. His hands dropped into his lap. He shifted in the seat. "I'm sorry about what happened though."

Will's eyes flicked to Rand then returned to his concentration of the movement of cars ahead and behind. "It's all right."

"No, I'm really sorry. It could have been a disaster. I mean, I missed. I hesitated. That was stupid. Our first time in action and I damn near blew it."

"You won't next time."

"What if I do though? That could give them the chance to fight back or, worse, to run."

"Like you said, they say 'the first time is the hardest.' It was just nerves." With a shrug, Will showed his friend that he was unconcerned.

"But I hesitated. That's why I missed his heart."

"Forget it."

"You didn't miss."

"Like I said, that wasn't my first."

"Yeah, I know." Rand reached with one hand to his hip, pushed his shirt up and drew his survival knife. He raised the knife and examined it, turned it around to eye both sides. He leaned close. There were small dots on the handle and the hilt. Blood. "I missed some."

Will glanced and saw the knife. "You're making the same mistake I did earlier. Sheath that, will you."

"Yeah." Rand did so.

"Besides, you're not going to lose that somewhere, are you?"

"Only when I die."

"Then don't worry about the blood." Will accelerated as they broke clear of the traffic.

"Did you use a knife before? You know, back when you were in the service?" Rand twisted in his seat so that he faced Will more fully.

"No, my M-4."

"So it was at long range with a rifle."

"Hardly. About fifty yards."

"Oh."

"Close enough to see the blood and the expression on his face as he slid off the wall where the rounds planted him."

"Wow." Rand imagined a turbaned Taliban soldier thrown against a sand colored wall. His AK-47 spiraled from his grip to clatter in the floury sand where a plume obscured it. The expression of shock and agony in his face drained away as the body slid to a sitting position, but it did not stop there because death pulled him over to one side until he too landed in the dust that rose instantly to reclaim him back to the origin of all life, the earth. Rand beamed with pride and envy. "How did you feel afterward?"

"Scared shitless."

Rand blinked several times, the glory of the kill dispelled. "Why?"

"It was combat. Anybody that tells you they aren't scared shitless by combat is a liar. Besides, about twenty of them popped up from a draw on our left flank. My platoon was pinned down, taking fire from a hill to our front, when out came those twenty guys."

"How many did you get?"

Will shook his head. "Two, three, I don't know. That one for sure. I guess it was three. One KIA and two wounded."

"Three?" Rand breathed heavily.

"Mm hm."

"You never told me that before."

"It's not stuff I care to talk about, you know."

"Uh hunh, yeah, you know, a lot of vets, like those World War Two guys, they didn't talk about the combat unless they were with other vets. They always said that civilians couldn't understand what they went through." Rand nodded as he recalled what he had read in a few of Stephen Ambrose's World War II histories. He felt so intimate with Will right now. He reached and patted Will's shoulder. This was one of the best days in Rand's life, maybe *the* best. "Yeah, you're like that, but you don't have to worry. I understand. Okay? You can tell me everything. All right?" Rand left his hand on Will's hard deltoid.

Will nodded, but he refused to look at his partner. Rand removed his hand when Will let the silence stretch like the string on a bow. There were no cars in close proximity to them so he let his eyes travel from the asphalt and out to the land they drove over. Will felt reassured because they headed west to where mountains and canyons dwarfed a man's ambition to pursue anything, especially two soldiers on a mission.

A year before, Rand burst through the front door along with a blast of Tucson's desert heat and parching sunshine. He chucked his keys at the dining room table and they scraped halfway across before their momentum was spent. Will slouched on the couch with a book close to his face. A pencil was in one hand and index cards lay in his lap. Rand headed for his room.

"How was Scrugg's class?" Will asked, still behind his book.

"We started discussion of Machiavelli." Rand slung his backpack to the floor and kicked his flip flops into opposite corners of the room.

"I never get tired of *The Prince*."

"Nietzsche will be soon."

"He's another. Endlessly fascinating, particularly *On the Geneology of Morals*."

"I want to skip Rousseau and read ahead. By the way, I had the best idea ever."

"Your parents called."

"Fuck. What did they want this time? Did you talk to them?" Rand stamped into the living room and stared at Will.

"No, it was before I got home. I just saw that there was a voicemail, so I checked the number." Will drug the fingers of his left hand down his cheek and, with each pockmark that a nail dug into, that finger caught and stayed for a second before the weight of his palm unglued it and then it slid to the next divot in his flesh.

"I don't want to listen to it. I'll delete it later."

"Okay."

Rand went back to his room. "What've you got?" He meant the book.

"*The Social Contract*. Due next Tuesday, remember?"

"Yep." Rand returned with his copy of *The Social Contract* in hand, and he slapped it on his thigh with every thud of his heels. "Why do they have to call so fucking much? Don't they have their own lives to live? Can't they just enjoy all the money and bullshit they own and just leave me the hell alone?"

"At least you have parents."

Rand crossed to the easy chair and stopped. He ground his teeth. "Sorry," he said through his locked jaw.

"I wish I had parents to bug me."

"I know. I'm sorry." He dropped into the chair. "But would you really want my parents?"

"They're not mean. They didn't beat you or tell you that you were worthless. I don't understand why you hate them so much." Though Will had his book up, he had not read a word since Rand entered.

Rand shook his head in response. "You can't understand. You can't." He slapped the arm of his chair with his book. "Hey, enough about those a-holes. Don't you want to hear about my idea?"

"Sure." Will scanned the text to find where he had left off.

Rand tossed *The Social Contract* onto the coffee table. "Put it down."

"What?" Will peered over the top of the paperback at Rand.

"The book. What else have you got in your hands? Toss it." Rand nodded to indicate where his own book lay.

Will dog eared the page and then leaned forward to lay the book face up on the coffee table. He set the pencil along the book's spine, and then index cards atop the book. Rand shook his head. "The edges aren't aligned." He smirked.

Will just glared.

Rand bounced in his seat like a toddler. "Are you ready?"

"Okay." Will sat back and crossed his arms and then his ankles. "What's this amazing plan?"

"Do you believe that there is such a thing as a justified war?"

"Historically?" Will asked. Rand nodded. "World War Two was justified from the Allies' point of view. The American Civil War. The Revolutionary War. They both were." He pondered it, his eyes circling with the thoughts that wanted to coalesce in the air near the ceiling.

"Why were those wars justified wars?"

"The US was fighting against oppression and aggression."

"Don't you think they were ideological wars as well?"

Will's head rocked from side to side as if he was panning for gold, bringing the gold dust to light with the swishing of logical reason's water. "Which ideologies are you thinking of?"

"Democracy versus totalitarianism, for one."

"Aren't those just methods of governing? Forms of controlling the population?"

"No, not necessarily. How a leader rules a population of a nation tells you about their view of humanity's capacity for decision making. It explains whether the leader believes that people are good, evil, or blank slates. Economic policies are also demonstrative of underlying philosophies. Laissez faire implies that people can choose to buy what they want, that they are free to govern prices, business relations, and their inner, personal greed."

"Which never works in practice, only in theory." Will pointed at him.

"Well." Rand shrugged to dismiss that argument. "Anyway, the point is that wars are duels between opposing philosophies."

"Modern wars are, I think. When the world was only divided up by kingdoms, I see war as nothing other than land grabs and kingly squabbles."

"Then it's a good thing that we live in the modern world, hunh? My point though is that wars are now justifiable as a means to determine which philosophy will dominate in the future."

Will rubbed one cheek then the other. "Except that there are still a number of wars that are ethnic cleansing. 'We hate them because they're different than us,' they say. That's the prevalent attitude. I don't think those are defensible wars from any ideological point of view."

"I disagree. Usually, those ethnicities are also of different religions, and thus they have different philosophies regarding human nature, governance, and the meaning of life, all those things I was just talking about. I think the term 'ethnic cleansing' is used by first world nations to morally frown upon wars by third world nations that are just as brutal as the wars of those first world nations. The difference is that the media machines and politicians of the first world nations are better at cloaking the destruction as being beneficial for a higher, moral purpose. In the third world nations, naked aggression is still seen as a legitimate means and not something that needs to be dressed up into a moral, messianic narrative." Rand held out his hands to offer the truth to Will who jutted his lower lip to give tacit support to this argument, but only until he read or reconsidered on his own that there was a flaw to Rand's ideas of war.

"So that's your idea?" Will asked.

"No, no. I'm just laying the groundwork."

"Ah. To what?"

"A war."

"A war?"

"By us."

"Us who?"

"You and I. And maybe others if we can teach them the ideas behind what we do."

"And who would we be fighting?"

"Do you think the world, well, society, maybe civilization is the right word, is moving in the right direction?"

"Right direction?"

"Progress, man. Do you think that we humans have progressed? And maybe progress isn't the right word either, but how about improved? Yes, do you think humans have improved over time? We're certainly not just a step above our genetic cousins the apes any more, are we?"

Will shrugged. "Where's this going? Jump to it. So how are we going to war?"

"We'll kill stupid people."

Will blinked several times. "What? Are you for fucking real?"

"You know how we always say that it should hurt to be stupid?"

Will shrugged and nodded at the same time.

"Well, we'll just take it to the next logical step."

"By killing stupid people?"

"Right."

"I've got one, well, actually, I have a lot of questions, but the first one is this: how do we know who the stupid people are? It's not like they're branded on their foreheads, 'Stupid I Be.' And we can't just look at them and decide they look stupid."

"Ah, well, I haven't quite figured that part out, but I'm working on it."

"Okay. Then I've got another one for you to figure out. This is murder. Make no mistake about it. That's how the police would see it. It's just murder."

"Is that what you thought during the war?"

"I don't know." He preferred to imagine that his time in Afghanistan was a vivid, unforgettable nightmare. Will's hand folded over his brow. What had he thought during the war?

A day later, suddenly, Rand stepped into Will's doorway and, without preamble, asked, "You see the problem, don't you?"

"The problem?" To Will, at that moment, as he read Rousseau's final pages, the problem seemed self-evident. "People don't learn. Our education system is geared toward making people useful to society. That type of learning does nothing for them when it comes to living a life. We've given up philosophy and even religion both of which are grand attempts to struggle with and answer the toughest problems we humans face, such as 'Why should I or should I not kill you?'" Will wacked his thigh a few times with the Rousseau. His other hand twirled his pencil around. "In place of that the schools today teach facts such as math and science and history. Facts that are not to be questioned only accepted and regurgitated for tests." Will stopped.

Rand leaned on the door frame, his eyes agoggle, and his jaw askew. "Wow. You sure sounded off on that one. Given it some thought?"

"A bit."

"Well, all right."

"Did you have something else in mind?"

Rand finally reset his jaw and nodded. He grinned, stepped across Will's room, and sat on his bed. "Stupid people have diluted the population's gene pool because they're protected by laws, armed forces, governments, and so forth. When the world was tribal, people died if they weren't smart. Maybe they ate the wrong, poisonous plant. Maybe they strayed from the tribe's territory and were killed by hostile neighbors. Maybe they walked in a dry river bed while it was raining and a flashflood swept them away. I'm sure there were more ways to die, but you see my point. And quite often nonproductive children, say those with mental retardation or whatever, were euthanized at the outset or just left for dead."

"Kind of brutal, don't you think?"

"Hey, what good was a member of the tribe that couldn't hunt and gather and defend the tribe? Why keep around a person who sucked up resources but could never contribute to the survival of the tribe, not to mention their personal survival? In times of famine and war, you'll look at that idiot retard and wish you had someone who could step up and do his duty for the family and the tribe. You resent that useless mouth and stomach."

Will turned from Rand's hard features, but he conceded the validity of this ruthless point. He said, "That would be a hard decision to make."

"The hardest if the baby was yours. Even if the baby doesn't have Down's Syndrome or autism or cerebral palsy or some such thing, the fact is that you will value the smarter, stronger child, the one that can help itself, the family, and the tribe over the one that is perceived as a burden. You know?"

"I guess so. I just hate to think like that."

"The hardest decisions to make are the ones that have an impact for a whole lifetime. Having a religion or a philosophy to guide you in this regard is essential. You know what needs to be done in the case that I was talking about. When the task is completed, you console yourself with the iron-clad belief that you acted not only in the right but in the best interests of all who are affected by the deed, including that baby I've been using as an example."

"Do you think it's that easy? Do you think there is no angst at all?"

"None. Just the same as you feel for those guys you shot in the war."

Will scratched his chin. Rand always brought his time in the war back to haunt him as an example to drive home his point. "You really like to carp on about my time in the war. What the hell? Do you think I was wrong to go?"

"No, rather the opposite." Rand scribbled with his finger on the bedspread. "I'm envious. I feel like I missed out on something that was powerful and worthwhile. I don't mean from an historical perspective. The impact of an event like a war on your own person is colossal. I don't have anything comparable. I've been sheltered by my upper class parents so that I'm now a baby in a man's shell. You see?"

Their conversations and plans took place over months, always prompted by Rand, who piped up with ideas randomly, seemingly as the inspiration struck. People can learn. People cannot learn. People can learn, but they refuse to do so. They debated human nature back and forth. What was the best way to teach? By real world example, by force, by simple suggestion a la books? Can you hold a gun to someone's head and make them change? Would they agree with anything to keep from dying? People need to change. Most people have no idea that the problems of their life are fixable if only they applied their minds to what the problem was and what solutions were available. Ultimately, both Rand and Will agreed that humanity's ultimate issue was that it refused to draw fully upon its greatest resource, the mind. Most people were taught how to behave, how to think, how to live or love or hate. How many people questioned the absurdity of the situations they then found themselves in? Even if they did question their predicaments, they believed themselves to be stuck because they were inured to their circumstances, totally plugged into a perceptual framework they received from parents, family, friends, teachers, and society. They were incapable of leaping onto the missile of a radical idea that might improve their lives. What was the course of action then?

This last question was posed by Will as they sat eating heaping bowls of fettuccini topped with meat and vegetables in a store bought marinara. Rand had shrugged. "We could kill them." He twirled noodles onto his fork.

"But why?"

"Because if you can't unplug these people from the matrix of their society's and their family's beliefs then they'll perpetuate the same closed mindedness by passing it on to their children."

"But killing someone isn't the easiest thing in the world. Even if it was legal, I doubt most people would kill despite the expediency it might provide in getting what they want. Trust me when I tell you that it affects you in profound ways. You begin to battle with yourself. What kind of person are you? You ask. And you can't answer anymore. You literally lose your sense of self."

One weekend, Rand asked, "Can you show me how to fire a pistol, you know, like they taught you in the army?" Will acceded to this. They went to the Santa Catalinas outside Tucson. Among the foothills, off a dirt road between scrub brush, sage, and barrel cactus, Will hammered lengths of 2X4 into the hard caliche, each with a paper target nailed to it. They spent a day out there. Will had a Browning 9mm Hi-Power that they practiced with. They fired five hundred rounds that first day of training. Rand's aim improved with each successive run through the kill zone. "Shouldn't we have earplugs?" Rand asked.

"I want you to be conditioned to the sound of a real shot. Makes you jump, hunh?"

They trained physically by lifting weights and running. The running ached Will's back after only a mile. They pushed each other to go as far as they could, usually about three miles. Often he sat with a bag of ice sandwiched between his shrapnel scarred back and the chair when they returned home. The university rec center was packed with nautilus and free weights. They alternated the styles of weights to always keep the muscles from being relaxed or overly familiar with the exercises. Both men, individually, when they stepped from the shower and stood before the mirror, admired their developing musculature. "Man, I'm getting ripped," Rand said more than once as he emerged from the steamy bathroom with a towel tied around his waist. Will wished that he could have abs as muscular as those. There didn't seem to be an ounce of fat there. The muscles stood out in hard squares. Will's own abs were rounded bulges, and there seemed to be a permanent layer of softness packed over them. Rand seemed to be barely contained muscles over bone.

They challenged each other to competitions over who could do more push ups, wall squats, sit ups, jumping jacks, and so on. Will won those exercises that required strength like the push ups and squats. His larger muscles could power past Rand's leaner body. That gave Will some satisfaction and pride. Besides, he was the one who set the tasks, he was the drill instructor. Rand was in Will's boot camp. Will said, "Jump," and Rand, even as he began to jump, answered, "How high?"

They came home with DVDs one Friday night to last them through the weekend. Rand was particularly insistent about watching one of them immediately when they came home. It was an old film, directed by Alfred Hitchcock, titled *Rope*. The movie starred Jimmy Stewart and Farley Granger. Granger and his roommate murder a classmate for intellectual thrills. Rand sat entranced during the entire film, and, unlike his usual predilection, after the movie, he went straight to his room and to bed. Will was wired after the movie. For a while he prowled the apartment and hunted for something to do. He rinsed the dinner dishes and aligned them in the wire racks and prongs of the dishwasher. He locked the front door. When he entered his room, his eyes rested on his bookshelf. He scanned the titles, arranged in alphabetical order by the author's last name. It was the black spined copy of Nietzsche's *On the Genealogy of Morals* that caught his eye. He had read it the previous semester for Dr. Sherry. In *Rope* Granger's roommate, played by John Dahl, referred to the philosopher as a justification for killing inferior beings. With the book in hand, he stood in the middle of his room and opened it to the first page he had dogeared when he studied it. He read the passage he had underlined. Interesting, though it was not what he sought. He methodically proceeded through the book with his earmarks as a guide. When he came to the passage that spoke of the nature of the eagles and the lambs, he blinked, and stopped. This is it. He lay on his bed to read. The author's concern regarded the nature between the strong and the weak. The strong naturally dominated the weak, just as eagles killed and ate lambs. You could not transmute the natures of eagles and lambs, nor could you alter the natures of the strong and the weak. Will read the passage a few times. He became electrified by it. The words became louder in his mind's voice each time he reread it, until the final read through had the volume of trumpets and drums, blaring and pounding, martial music that made him want to take up arms. He had to share this passage, these brilliant words, this inspiration to be what was best inside of him with Rand. He almost vaulted from his bed to burst into Rand's room and read what Nietzsche had written for them more than a century before. That was a moronic idea. Rand was asleep. He could share this with him in the morning. There was no rush. This passage might be just the truth they were looking for in the idea of their war against stupidity, but they were not about to embark on their mission tomorrow or, for that matter, at any definite date. Everything was hypothetical and embryonic. So Will relaxed on his bed, though he did not want to, and reread the passage. He went back a few pages to follow the train of Nietzsche's argument as it led to this idea, and then he read beyond the crux, deeper into the meaning. When he halted his determined eyes, he felt calm and satisfied. He laid the book, open to the key page, face down on the floor by his bed. It was four in the morning and way past the time to sleep. The rush of his brain stopped so that he fell right to sleep when he closed his eyes.

"Teach me everything," Rand said.

For Spring Break, they camped in the White Mountains. When Will rocked in hysterical laughter at Rand's clumsy attempts to erect a tent, Rand threw the ropes on the ground. "I've got to fucking learn this."

"Why?"

"It matters."

"It matters?"

"Yeah."

"Because you'll be doing a lot of camping in this war?"

Rand propped his hands on his belt and stared at the collapsed olive drab canvas. He squatted and resumed his travails. Slowly, he propped the tent. Finished, he stepped back, and tugged on the front rope. Will nodded. "Good job."

"I did it."

"Yes, sir. Feel better?"

"Yeah."

"If I was a DI, I'd make you break it down and do it again."

"DI?"

"Drill Instructor."

"They really do that kind of thing?"

"You had better learn or they will definitely take a shit on your parade. That's called motivation."

They hiked from after breakfast until an hour before sunset with a break at midday for lunch. Will taught him how to compare the ravines, ridges, and valleys they saw with the topographical map they carried. Will taught him to use a compass. He pointed to the constellations and explained their movement, their relations to each other, and how to determine direction. "Just like the ancients." Rand scratched his scalp in wonder.

It was during yet another evening of study, as Will worked through *The Republic* for the second time in his college career that he said, "Why don't we ask people a question?"

"Who?" Rand was caught off guard this time. Though he was reading the same book for the same class he'd been contemplating the excitement he would feel if he had the ring of power that made him invisible and was then able to move with impunity through an unsuspecting population. Oh, the deeds he might perform!

They were in a café on the north side of the University called Bentley's so Will felt it wise to lean across the table and whisper, "For the war. People we might, you know, dispose of. The stupid and inferior." He referenced the movie *Rope* again.

"Oh."

"So we ask them a question about a philosophical problem, let's say, what's the meaning of life, or if there is such a thing as free will, or, maybe, where do we acquire morals. The possibilities are endless."

Rand settled back in his chair. His mind whirled. He nodded. "Yes, yes. That's the right idea. A test of sorts that determines your fitness for survival." He nodded. "That way it's not really up to us. We're just another part of the world that could potentially kill. It's not us. We're tools. Warriors wedded to a higher goal. Yes. That's it. Don't you think so?"

"Yes." Will's voice. "They have the opportunity to save themselves. If they answer well, we just congratulate them on how intelligent and thoughtful they are. If they answer poorly . . ."

"Then it's their own stupidity that dams and condemns them to the judgment by the . . ."

"Higher principles, which they failed to search for and educate themselves about. It's their own fault. They chose . . ."

"To stand on the wrong side of a line drawn in life. On one side are the intelligent, curious, educated, those who seek to raise themselves above the mere nature they inherited, and on the other side . . ."

"The ignorant, lazy, weak, who need constant prodding and governing so that they do what is right and good instead of whatever moronic, infantile, and greedy desire pops into that neglected gray mass they call a brain."

"Yes."

They laughed. They were heated and jittery. Their feet tapped and their hands hunted for a productive outlet for their energy. If only they could start now. Both men spied the crowd around them in Bentley's. They wondered who in this café would be intelligent and who would be dead.

And months later on July 6, they awoke in their sleeping bags at a campsite somewhere in the western US. Their first kills were more than a day dead. The Plato Warriors had struck their first blow against the widespread tyranny of the thoughtless and disingenuous.

July 8, 2008

Each of the previous three days they drove a few hundred miles until they located a camping site. They hiked and fished. They saw no one, and they figured they were eluding the law quite well. They went to a Wal-Mart in a small town in Wyoming. Like all Wal-Marts there were thousands of fluorescent bulbs lining the ceiling designed to make everything visible. No shadows or darkness was permitted in the shopping experience of Wal-Mart. And the size of the place was identical to every other Wal-Mart in the USA, you could plop a city block within its boundaries. The identical nature of the building was meant to inspire a sense of familiarity in the consumer. The summer heat was probably nosing up to one hundred so when they slouched into the store the air conditioning felt perky. Into a shopping cart they loaded a few necessities: cans of tuna, beans, corn, and peas. Then they spied a teen girl dressed in jean shorts that showed the bottoms of her butt cheeks and a tank top that revealed the top halves of her boobs. She kept looking furtively around.

Will said, "If she's not up to something, no one is."

"Yep."

Neither was surprised when she slipped a pair of pink panties from a lower shelf down the front of her jean shorts as she leaned over the display to dig about in the items on the top shelf. Her head jerked around, left and right, as she looked for signs of someone alert to her deed. Will pretended to talk to Rand, who kept his back to her, but this allowed Will to witness her moves by looking just past Rand's ear. Over the next five minutes, a matching bra, a white tank top and a pair of sunglasses disappeared either into her red purse cinched up into her armpit or under her clothes.

"She seems quite practiced at the art of shoplifting," Will said.

"Definitely not her first time."

"Too bad we're not cops."

"Too bad for her we're better than cops." Rand clapped Will on the shoulder. "Should we 'bust' her?"

Will eyed her again as she surveyed the watches. Was Rand making the obvious pun about their not being police who were about try and possibly execute her, or was he referring to her large breasts that Will desired to fondle and suck on? "Maybe we should just turn her in?"

Rand chuckled. "She would just blame someone else." He adopted a feminine voice. "'Oh, it's not my fault. I've got no money. I got fired from my job. My parents don't give me money. It's society's fault that I'm poor.' Whatever. I think she needs the kind of confrontation with ethics that we can give her. We warriors of truth and virtue need to battle against people like her."

Will gave a nod. "Let's go then."

They closed in. Five yards out, Rand said, in an over loud voice, "Could you even imagine the chaos of a society without morals? It's simply not plausible. There would be no society."

"It's against the nature of man," Will said to further the illusion. "Morals are the frame in which society occurs."

The girl glanced at them and the hand that had selected a nice gold watch, forty dollars, fell away to her thigh.

"Hi," Rand said to her. "How are you?"

"Uh, fine." She turned to escape them.

"Hey, wait up a sec." Rand reached as if he could halt her with his willpower alone, the mere force of his hand raised.

"Say, I hope you won't mind if we involve you in a friendly debate?"

"Um, like, well, okay." She shrugged, and her eyes jerked left and right with fear disguised as impatience.

"You see, we're curious about why morals are important."

"Morals?" Her eyes still had not focused exclusively on them.

"Yes, you live by morals. We all do. But why do we have them? How does having morals shape our life?" Rand said.

"Which morals do you feel that you live by?" Will asked.

"Uh, morals? Well, you mean like the Ten Commandments and such, right?" She switched her weight from one foot to the other as if she had to pee, or maybe those panties stuffed down the front of her low cut jean shorts were not seated properly.

Rand nodded. "If those are the morals that you live by, then yes."

"Well, I don't know. I think I've, like, broken most of those."

"You have? Why?" Will rolled the cart back and forth and imagined that he charged her and slammed her into the rack of sunglasses behind her. Would she scream or just crumple like paper?

"Well, there's like that sex before marriage one, and I broke that before I was like sixteen." She rubbed her hip and set her head at an angle as if that was the pose she adopted toward all men, coquettish. Rand half rolled his eyes and Will cocked an eyebrow.

"Hm. And how old are you now?" Will asked.

"Like nineteen."

"You either are nineteen or you're not. There's no such thing as 'like' nineteen," Will said.

She looked like a scolded child and shot a glance left and right for impending arrest. There was no one else around.

Rand said, "I guess that's not one of your morals then. What morals do you have then? That's what we're interested in right now."

"Oh. Well, like, I don't know. I mean, I've stolen before."

"What did you steal?" Rand's eyes went in a quick review of all the spots on her person where he knew she had Wal-Mart merchandise.

She looked guiltily around. "Clothes, food, magazines, I don't know."

"Why did you steal? What made you do it?" Will rocked the cart once more.

"I couldn't pay for it so, like, I just took it."

"But why? Did you not have clothes?" Will's eyes looked to the front of her jean shorts where the panties were stuffed without making a detectable bulge though her body was packed into the fabric in an alluring display not of fashion but of teen lust. "Were you starving? And when I say that, I mean had you not eaten in days because you didn't have food?"

"No." She glanced at the coveted watch and shook her head.

"Was it to rebel against the inequalities of our capitalist, consumer driven society?" Rand offered his hand as if maybe she might take it and demonstrate to them that she had a conscience.

"Uh, I don't think so. Nah, I just wanted those things so I took them."

Both men nodded. Will's mouth pulled to one side in complete disapproval. He said, "Well, don't you have any morals at all? Isn't there something you wouldn't do? Come on, are you telling us that you would even kill someone?"

"Kill someone? Oh, God, no. I'd, like, never do that."

Rand's eyebrows rose. "Why not?"

"I doubt I could, like, do it." She took a step away.

"Care to elaborate?"

"What?"

"Explain," Will barked. "Can you explain why you wouldn't kill someone?"

Rand glanced at his agitated friend. Will wouldn't shoot her here, would he? He seemed wholly offended by her casual stupidity.

"I just couldn't do it. I, like, faint at the sight of blood. I'm such a wimp. There was this one time. . ."

Both men failed to listen. They turned to each other, and Will gave his head a shake while Rand rolled his eyes.

Rand cut her off. "So it's not that you wouldn't kill someone, it's that you physically couldn't tolerate the act. It's not a moral issue for you then?"

"Um. Well, like, I don't know. I never thought about it." She turned her eyes to the front of the store where the exits were.

"Never thought about it?" Rand repeated.

She shook her head. "Nope."

Will's hand agitated his acne scars. "You've never thought about the right or wrong of it?"

She shook her head again and shrugged. "No."

"You probably never thought about the right or wrong of those other things then either. The stealing or the sex before marriage." Rand's hand travelled to his pistol beneath his shirt but quickly resisted because it would be obvious what lay beneath the thin fabric if he lodged his hand on the grip.

She reached and touched the plastic box that held the forty dollar gold watch that she coveted. Her eyes latched onto the item as well.

Rand said, "You're good at satisfying your body, but you never worry that brain of yours about the things of the mind. You just let it be empty, just be thoughtless."

She ignored their eyes and words as she concentrated on the watch.

Will said, "You can't have morals if you don't think about them." Nothing was sinking into that empty head. Not a word. The men knew it, and they both concluded that no amount of effort would be of avail to provoke her to any greater intellectual understanding. They broke off the conversation without apologies, and, after they abandoned the cart of items, they shadowed her outside. Rand wrote the note on an index card as they tailed her. When she came to her car and opened the door, Rand said, "Hey." She froze. Will did not slow his stride as he came right to her and shot his fist out and punched her in the soft belly beneath .those firm breasts. She collapsed. Her purse spilled. Objects rolled under her car and the other car she lay between. Will drew and aimed. Rand slipped right up beside him, drew, and aimed. Both men fired as her mouth stretched into a scream that never came. Rand tucked the index card into the front of her jeans. For the briefest flash, he savored the soft warmth of her belly. She might have been fun to screw, but a terror to talk to if you had any brains. They sprinted to the Subaru.

July 12, 2008

They had been in Boise, Idaho, valley city of two hundred thousand, for three days trying to engage someone in a full-fledged debate. On the first day they accosted two college aged guys. One of them had a basketball under his arm. They tried to persuade the guys to discuss the importance of government, but the guys, after strutting one block and with barely any kind of answer to all the queries, burst through a gate and into the bustle of several games at an open air city court. That first night, while at an Italian restaurant, they wanted to converse with a married couple dressed to the nines on an anniversary date, but, after two questions, the couple begged to be left alone so they could enjoy two hours of bliss without their children. Rand started to embark on a third avenue of debate on the curriculum for an ideal education, but the couple asked to be relocated to another table. Will ordered Rand to shut up. They ate silently. And so it went. People ignored and frustrated them. By the end of day two, seven refusals resulted.

That third morning, they ate a breakfast of bagels and cream cheese with green grapes in their hotel room. They sat and gazed at CNN news stories repeated every half an hour. "Let's go out for lunch," Will said from his torpor.

"And then what?" Rand's funk was deeper and darker. For him, the refusals by all those people to engage in a sporting, philosophical debate was a sign of the pathetic state of early twenty first century culture. Everyone in the nation switched their brains off in their fanatical pursuit of God-money. Maybe it would be more productive if he and Will destroyed all the ATMs in the nation.

"We'll blow this town. Maybe it's Boise. They're all dipshits."

"Yeah, maybe." Rand shrugged. He imagined a hydrogen bomb detonation. No more Boise.

"Where do you want to go?"

"How about the coast? Say Seattle?" Rand wanted to see the rain. Like any desert dweller, the rain held a magical spot in his imagination: cool, cleansing, life-giving, yet dangerous.

"No, I meant for lunch." Will turned off the TV with the remote that was bolted to the nightstand.

"I don't give a shit." He sat up and pivoted on the bed so that he could clomp his feet on the floor.

They packed, toted their gear to the Subaru, and went to the front desk to pay and check out. As he passed the key to the clerk, Will asked, "Are there any Mexican restaurants around?"

Two miles later, they went into a small establishment where, to their surprise, a complement of Mexicans bustled among the tables as waiters, bussers, and hostesses.

"Who'd have thought?" Will shrugged.

The hostess led them to a small square of a table beside a similar table where a fat, fiftyish woman with a sack of a floral dress, several gold bracelets rattling on each wrist, and a gold crucifix on a gold chain hung from her neck sat.

Will said, "So I presume that you would agree when I say that morals are *a priori* to human existence."

Rand, whose eyes had crossed the menu from the top and were now half way down, stopped what he was doing to look at Will with a quizzical expression.

Will's eyes directed him to the lady beside them. Rand sighed. He played along. They asked the woman if they could speak to her as part of a thesis project in a class they were taking.

"Okay." She wiped the salt from her lips after she crackled a chip into her throat. "Don't you need to take notes?"

"Don't worry. We both have very good memories." Rand tapped his temple. "What one of us forgets, the other won't." He smirked.

"All right then."

"Which came first morals or God?" Will asked.

She seemed surprised. "Well, God, of course."

"Why do you say, 'of course?'" Rand took a chip and dipped it in salsa. He wedged the whole chip in his mouth.

"Because God is the creator of all things, morals included." She ate a chip too.

Will asked, "So there was nothing before God?"

"That's right. He is the Creator after all," she said from around the baked corn detritus on her tongue and teeth.

"The Bible says that?" Will waved a chip in the air.

"Yes." She nodded with vigor.

"What denomination are you?" Will bit off half his chip. A drop of salsa splattered on the tablecloth.

She said. The answer did not matter to either man, they did not note it or process it.

"Have you always been a part of the church?" Will finished his chip, this time with one hand below the chip to catch any stray salsa. "Have you always been Christian?"

"Yes. Yes, that is the true religion and the one God. There is no other. Jesus Christ was His Son who came to earth to redeem all of the fallen people who would listen to the true teachings. I listened. I go to a lady's Bible study once a week and services every Sunday morning. My husband, a police officer, comes with me on Sundays."

Will asked, "Have you ever actually attended a service by another religion?"

"No."

"Ever read the Koran or the Torah?"

"Absolutely not."

"'Absolutely not.'" Rand snickered.

The lady's face transformed into a grotesque scowl. "I don't appreciate being mocked. If that's the way you're going to act then I won't speak to you anymore." Her penciled in brows gathered like an inverted chevron.

"I'm sorry." Rand bowed his head.

"It's rude of you."

Will said, "He apologized."

"I'm taking time out of my day to talk to you, understand?"

"Yes, ma'am." Rand nodded like a little school boy intimidated by the teacher who was twice his size.

"I don't have to do that for your survey." The waiter brought her food.

"Right. You don't have to," Rand said.

"Your research can go on without me." She thrust a huge portion of a burrito in her maw.

"Oh, no, you're just the kind of person we need to hear from for our survey." Rand smiled and forced himself to reach and pat the back of her hand as it lay on the table. "A true believer. I really am sincere in my apology, but I'm afraid that I have a fiendish sense of humor. I must be a kin to Puck."

"Who? What?" She finished her Coke, flagged a waitress and tapped the brim of the plastic red cup to indicate that she needed more.

Will said, "Puck was the name of a mischievous fairy in Shakespeare's *A Midsummer Night's Dream*. Have you ever read it?"

"No. I think I read a Shakespeare when I was in high school, but I don't remember which."

"Oh, I know." Rand came off his seat for a second.

The lady and Will stared at him. How could he know which she read?

"I was curious." Rand held up his hand. "What level of education did you reach?"

"I got my associate's degree."

"Oh, very nice. And what do you do?"

Will thought Rand was having too much fun. That stuff about Puck was too much, and now he was getting off on a tangent with this stuff about her personal history. Why did any of that matter?

"I work as a stenographer for the city court."

Will's mouth hung. What a perfect coincidence. Rand turned to Will and winked, luckily with the eye that the lady probably could not see.

"That's perfect."

"Excuse me?" she said through a mouth swollen with beans and tortilla, lettuce and tomato, and who knew what else. Will looked away.

"Oh, it's just that here you are, a perfect candidate for our research, and we came upon you by sheer accident." Rand spread his arms like the master of ceremonies at a circus.

"What I think he means," Will said. "Is that because you believe in Christ, you are familiar with the laws of Heaven, but you are also, as a stenographer for the city court, more than aware of the laws of Man."

"Oh, I see." She swallowed. "They're not the same you know."

"Precisely." Rand poked the air between them with another chip. "And it's that contrast which prompted our previous question about which came first morals or God."

"But how can that be a question? I told you that God created everything." To put the period on her axiom, she took another wallop of burrito in her mouth.

"Well, yes, but let me ask you a tricky question." Rand dropped the chip in the bowl, wacked his hands together to shed the salt, and then planted his hands on his thighs. "If god created everything, morals included, then he could make the morals be whatever he wanted. So, for instance, he might decree that murder is a good and not an evil."

She coughed and spluttered around the bite in her mouth. When she stopped, she said, "He most certainly did not make murder a righteous act."

"I know, I know, but-"

"And he never would have considered such a thing. That's Satan's province. He's the begetter of evil."

"This is just an example. I'm not saying that he did create evil, I'm just saying-"

"To think such a thing is unbelievable, it's practically an evil itself."

"Please, please." Will felt the dialogue was careening off in desperate ways. "He didn't mean to suggest-"

"I don't think I can sit another moment and listen." She shoved away her mostly finished plate and gathered her purse and cell phone.

"No, no," Will held up his hands to placate her. He looked to Rand.

Rand smiled and said, "Who created Satan?"

The woman went as still as the table and chair, just further furniture.

"What?"

"It's a shocking question, isn't it?" Rand said. "There's only one possible, and thus troubling, answer, too."

"Are you saying . . ."

"So God created Satan, who was an angel that fell from grace, fell from Heaven. Right?"

"Yes." She narrowed her already heavily encumbered eyes.

"Why? Why did God create Satan? Surely you've talked about that in your Bible Study or in a service."

"God gave us the choice. We have free will. He gave us free will to test us, to see if we were true to Him and His teachings."

"But why?"

"Well, to test us. We have to be tested in order to show our virtue."

"But why give us the choice? Why test us? Why not make us good only? Why create evil as a possibility at all? And if you create evil as a choice, then why be wrathful and vengeful towards those who choose evil? And so many have chosen evil throughout all times and throughout all places. In fact, so many have disobeyed the word of God, His laws and teachings, that it seems that humans are born to be evil. Our sins outweigh our saints. So why damn humans to Hell because they chose wrong?"

"Because they chose wrong!" She gaped at Rand.

"Yet they would've been better off if they'd never been given the choice. Some people are forced to confront the choice of good and evil over and over, while others go their whole lives without that sinister choice ever coming to distort their bliss. Why?"

Her lip quivered even as her jaw rose up and down with her respiration, and the stuck gears of her mental machinery jerked back and forth, unable to advance or retreat.

"Or, let me put it this way," said Rand. "You doubtless learned that you cannot know the mind of God. That was taught in the Book of Job. If we cannot know God's mind, and if so many people have chosen the path of evil, then who is to say that what we conceive of as evil is really such? What if we got it wrong? What if murder, rape, robbery, lying, adultery, and all the other sins are what is truly good? And that is why most humans succumb to its whisperings and taunts?"

The poor woman was on the verge of a cardiac arrest. She panted, her eyes bugled from their sockets, her left hand groped about atop the large hemispheres on her chest, and her right hand performed a head lock on her purse.

"What if murder is good?" Rand asked.

"It can't be. That's a sin. It's evil, evil only. Why would you say that? How can you sit there and say that? It's a sin to think that way even. You, you-"

Will rose and made for the front door. It would be time soon. She could no longer think. She was a believer, not a thinker. She accepted, she never questioned. As Will passed his comrade in arms, Rand said, "If God created evil, then he created it to do some good. The good must come by testing us. Is that possible?"

"No, never. That can't be the way it is. No. God isn't like that. He's good. He can't make evil. What you say isn't true. It's a lie. You're, you're-" She was stuck on the next word, the next condemnation.

Rand scanned the nearby tables and perceived the animosity of those other patrons. They were alarmed by what he had said. He was in a pinch now. "Maybe I'm wrong. Thanks for your time." Their food had never come, but he rose, teased a twenty from his pocket and flipped it onto the table. "Bye." He left.

When the poor lady lumbered several minutes later out of the restaurant and toward her sedan, with one hand to her forehead to massage the headache that they gave her, the two of them popped up from behind the Subaru, pistols already trained on her. They fired. For an awkward, gut wrenching moment, not a second, though it seemed to be forever, she stood with the two bullet wounds, one above her right eye, the other through one of her breasts, and then she dropped to the pavement. "Go," Will commanded. Rand sprinted to the woman's side and shoved the notecard with its question into her purse. They leapt to the Subaru's doors, and banged them open into the parked cars beside them. Will drove. The tires screamed and, when the car lunged from the space, he gunned the engine and they roared away.

July 20, 2008

In Seattle, an unfamiliar part of the world for them as it was moist and cloudy, Rand and Will went to a joint called the Dog Bite Bar and Grill. There were two rectangle rooms set with their long sides adjoining and connected by two door-less entry ways. The street door opened on the room with the bar along the back wall and a door to the kitchen in back. There was the usual window behind the bar where food could be passed through to be served. The place was brightly lit by canned bulbs in the ceiling. It smelled of cheap beer, grease, and the acrid smell of old, masculine sweat. It was four in the afternoon, before a college aged crowd might come in to dominate with scents of seduction and sex, perfumes and lotions, and hair treatments and soaps. This was the daytime crowd of wrecked men, some employed and some not, who came to escape a harder world outside the bar while they enjoyed the diversions of alcohol, pool, darts, and talk with other men who would sympathize with the unfairness of life and society. There were no women.

The place was drafty though there were no windows, and Rand and Will were happy they had their flannel shirts on. They were the youngest men there, and, though everyone in line of sight to the door glanced at them, the dozen or so pairs of eyes set in crinkled skin with red in the irises did not betray anything like contempt, resentment, or any other negativity. To these men in this bar, Will and Rand did not qualify as interlopers. Rand breathed lightly at this realization. He and

Will had not shaved since they embarked on their war more than two weeks earlier. It was only the night before, at their motel that Rand had shaved his patchy beard into a mustache and goatee. Will had just let his thick beard go. To Rand, that tangled growth on Will's face was miraculous. So often, Will was the more virile of them. Rand enviously stroked the bristles on his chin.

The two young men perched on stools at the bar and, from the stout bartender, who wiped the bar top off as they sat, they ordered two burgers with fries and beers, a black and tan for Will, and a Guiness for Rand.

Their survival knives and Browning pistols were one on each hip beneath their flannel shirts. When their plates were a desert of crumbs and ketchup smears, they ordered a second round of beers and took them to a pool table that had opened. After two matches amongst themselves, a couple, about their ages, but dressed in torn jeans, t-shirts, and scuffed combat boots, each with visible tattoos and piercings, and brightly colored hair, his blue and hers pink, sat at a table and began to watch. These two did not belong here. All the men, these hard workers, hard livers, hard drinkers, they glowered and gave the couple a once over of disgust. What were they doing here? Rand sided with the men in this establishment. They knew who belonged and who did not. Rand gave a slight nod and a cast of his eyes to indicate the couple to Will, who nodded in affirmation. At the end of their third match, Rand asked the couple, "Would you like to join us?"

Sure, was the answer. The boy and girl found decent cue sticks from a rack on the wall, chalked them up, and stood ready. The boy said, "Your table, your shot."

Will racked the balls. Rand leaned in and took aim. He slammed the cue ball to a standstill and the sixteen balls ricocheted around it. The nine and thirteen sank. "Stripes," Rand called. He took his next shot and sank the fifteen. From the time Rand turned twenty one, he and Will had played pool in the bars around Tucson. It was fun, they could drink a few brews, and they could talk about the people they saw, who were all opaque curiosities, unknowable. "Hey, uh, do you mind if we involve you in a little philosophical debate that my friend and I were having?"

No, the couple shook their heads.

"We're curious about what the meaning of life is." Rand chuckled and set up for his next shot. "You see, we were watching that Monty Python film—have you seen that one, *The Meaning of Life*?"

The boy smiled, nodded, and said, "Oh, yeah, man."

The girl shrugged.

"Well, anyway," Rand said, and then intentionally missed a bank shot. "Damn. Your shot. Who'll go first?"

The boy stepped up, took his stance, and aimed for a shot on the seven in the far pocket. The stick whacked the cue ball into the seven, but both balls went wide and stumbled and clicked around with the other balls on the green felt. Nothing fell. This kid sucked as a pool player.

"Partner." Rand nodded to Will. "So, like I was going to ask, what do you all feel the purpose of your life is? I mean, for me, I believe that I need to teach people to be better. My silent friend here," Rand motioned to Will as he pegged a stripe into the side pocket and set up a shot into the reverse pocket too, "Well, he feels that he should make the world a better place than when he left it. Now mind you, both of these simple ideas create numerous questions about the methods to be used, which have to be answered too, and so on. You follow?"

Will sank another stripe. He decided to run the table and be done with the match. Rand could do all the talking. That was his thing, not Will's. Besides, this couple seemed pretty dim.

"Wow, man, I dunno. I thought the whole point of life was just to live it," the boy said.

Will sank his third shot in a row, and, from this bent, shooting stance, he glanced at Rand, who scowled.

"That's it?" Rand asked.

"Sure. I mean we're all just animals, like, you know? And it's like what we gotta do is survive despite all the ways there is to die, see?" The boy motioned with his arms as he spoke, his black clothes, slack on his lanky frame, slapped loudly even over the music from the Sirius radio station on the bar's speakers.

"Uh hunh." Rand nodded as his thumb and fingers worked at the end of the cue stick to see if it was loose.

"I like to watch the nature shows on cable. We're just animals, man. We fuck and pee and shit. We eat and sleep and fuck. And we breathe and our hearts beat and we fuck. I like the fucking part best. Can you tell?" The boy grinned.

"Yeah, he does," the girl said as she tugged the waist of her jeans and wiggled about so as to get them to hang just so on her bony hips that everyone could see below the hem of her t-shirt.

"Eight ball far corner," Will said with apparent disinterest in the conversation, and he sent it home.

The boy blinked several times at the half empty table. "Whoa."

Rand worried the rubber stopper on the end of his stick with his thumb. "Oh, yeah, my friend Will is quite a pool shark." Rand turned the cue stick upright and let it slide through his fingers to bounce on the floor like a gavel. "Why don't you just say that the point of life is fornication? I assume that the primary role of reproduction isn't what interests you. You don't have lots of babies at home do you?"

"Nah, man." The boy shook his head and slapped the girl on the ass. She gave a little hop and said, ooh.

Will growled just loud enough for his own ears, racked the balls, and the losers broke.

"So you think that the point of life is sexual gratification?" Rand asked.

"Sure," the boy said.

"What happens when your dick goes limp when you're old?" Rand laid a hand on the side of the pool table and leaned his hip into the table.

"Hey, man, you mind?" The boy nodded at Rand's pose and imposition upon the pool table.

"What?"

"Well, you know, I don't think you're supposed to lean against the table like that when someone's trying to take a shot." The boy smiled good-naturedly. Rand stared. The boy blinked. Across the table the boy's eyes caught onto Will's cold glare as he too set a hand on the bumper and leaned. The boy blinked and slowly bent into his shot. His head down, he said, "But it's okay. Maybe I'm wrong about the rules." He took his shot, missed, opened his mouth to gripe, but he saw the unflinching faces of Will and Rand, stepped away from the table, and left his gaze on the green felt.

"Yours or mine?" Rand asked.

"Yours." Will moved back from the table.

"Right." Rand measured the distances of all the balls on the scratched green felt. "Well?"

"Hunh?" the boy asked.

"Is life going to be all about sexual pleasure once your dick doesn't rise?"

"Hey, man, that's what Viagra's for, right?"

"You're just a walking dick, I guess." Will held his cue stick like a baseball bat. He even swung it once.

The boy swallowed and muscled up a smile.

Rand said to the girl, "What do you think the purpose of life is?"

"To be happy," she said as she checked her black eye makeup in the glass of a framed photo on the wall.

"But how do you define happiness?"

"Whatever makes me feel good."

"What if it's at someone else's expense?"

"I don't know. Too bad for them, I guess." She checked her teeth and ran a black painted fingernail between two of her lower teeth.

"That doesn't bother you that someone else might be miserable on account of your happiness?"

"Well, maybe they need to make themselves happy."

"What if it's at your expense? What if it makes you miserable?"

"No, that won't happen. I'd just leave."

"Leave?"

"Sure."

"What if it's your job that makes you miserable?"

"I've quit a lot of jobs."

"How many?"

"Um, seven, no, nine, I think."

"Do you quit relationships at the first sign of unhappiness?"

"I've been through lots of relationships. Lots of boyfriends. Even a couple of girlfriends too."

"Lots?" her boyfriend asked with narrow eyes.

Rand shrugged to the boy. To her, he said, "At the first instant, at the slightest twinge of unhappiness, you bail? That's what you're telling us?"

"You don't think that there's more to life than that?" Will exploded. "You only do things to make yourselves happy?" Will's voice rose in agitation. "What about sacrifice? What about the happiness and the good of others? Is there anything beyond you and you?" He pointed to one then the other of them with the cue stick like a rifle. There was nothing in those two heads. He imagined them as balloons, human colored balloons that he could shoot with a rifle and score points, like at a carnival. What would be the prize?

Rand shook his head. These two could never think their way out of a wet paper bag with a knife and a flashlight. They probably did drugs too, as some kind of escape. How utterly pathetic. It was bad enough that they refused to utilize their brains, but to burn up brain cells with drugs was reprehensible. They finished the game, and Rand said, "We have to go." Will said nothing. They went outside and waited in the Subaru as a squall came from the Pacific and extinguished the summer sunset. The city went gray and purple. The lights waited to turn on at their appointed time.

"Patience is a virtue, hunh?" Rand snorted.

"Remember, we get within five feet, then put one in the heart and one in the head."

"Roger Dodger." Rand liked to say that because Will once said it.

After an hour, out stumbled and shuffled the boy and girl. He walked behind her, with his hands shoved down the front of her jeans. She was nonchalant, went along as best as she could with the impediment of his body glommed onto hers.

"Go." Will opened his door. The two men drew their pistols as they exited the car, left the doors wide, marched into the lane between the painted lines where there were only a few vehicles, and concealed their weapons behind a leg as they came to confront the young couple.

"Uh, hey, wow, look, it's the guys we played pool with." The boy stopped and clung to the girl's crotch even as she tried to take another step. He was now half bent forward and still concealed by her. Rand moved to their flank so that he could maybe get a clean shot. Will was within the specified range when both of his arms flew up, the left caught the right as it held the pistol, his aim was sure, and he fired once, aimed again, fired twice. With the movement quick and done, the pistol went behind his leg again.

Rand slowly took aim at the boy, who now clung to an inert body, and shot him in the head first. The body went to its knees, sprung part way up, released the dead girl, and dropped to its left away from Rand. He took three huge strides to gain the side of the body, and he fired at the sternum. The body gave a jerk. He aimed a third time and made the boy a eunuch. Rand smirked at Will, but his partner had placed the note in the girl's pants pocket and was already halfway back to the Subaru. Rand rushed after him. Will took the driver's seat, to Rand's surprise. When Rand got in, Will cranked the car and tore from the parking space. They passed the two inert forms in the middle of the lane. There was a slight bump as the left wheels crunched over some body part. Will slowed only slightly as they came to the street. Both men leaned to the dashboard as they sighted the clearance for their escape. A set of lights approached but was far enough down the street for them to make their turn. Will gunned it and swung the Subaru to the right.

"Get the map. We got to get to the interstate and get down the road. At least one town away," Will said.

"All right. Yeah, you're right." Rand still held his pistol in one hand.

"That safety better be on."

"Oops."

"Jesus fucking Christ. Here you are waving that thing around with the safety off. What the hell?"

"Sorry." Rand flicked the safety with his thumb.

"'Sorry' don't cut it if you shoot me. 'Sorry' don't cut it if you shoot the car."

"I'm . . . I know."

"How would we explain it to a cop if he sees us with a bullet hole in the window? What are you going to say?"

Rand holstered the pistol.

"Use your head. Get a procedure. As soon as we're done with the action, that safety's on. Got it?"

"Yeah."

Will's voice rose. "And then you holster the pistol. Okay?"

"Yeah, I get-"

"Because if you don't and you accidentally discharge that weapon, where do you think that'll land us?" Will thumped the dashboard between them with his fist.

Rand opened the glove box and thumbed at the stack of state maps. "Jail." He could not look at Will. Where was that map? Arizona, California, Colorado.

"Laziness, inattention, and sloppiness get you killed in a war, soldier. Do you read me?" Will boomed like a drill instructor.

Montana, Nevada, New Mexico. Will alphabetized them apparently. The proper map must be at the bottom. "Yes."

"You've got to be clean, hard, and sharp. Situational awareness at all times. That means that you don't do something unless you've thought about it or it's drilled into you as an instinct. Got it?"

Rand nodded. He found the Washington map and unfolded it.

Will's voice returned to normal volume. "Does it have a Seattle inset?"

Rand checked one side, then flipped it. He could barely read the lines and symbols as night was full upon them. "I need the light."

"Go for it, but be quick. And what was that third shot for? I said only two."

Rand grinned with wickedness as he pored over the multiple routes inked in yellow on the map. "I blew his dick off."

Will said nothing. Why would Rand be that cruel?

July 21, 2008

Last to arrive in the conference room was Special Agent Christopher England. He was fifteen minutes late because of the call from Quantico. "Is this everyone?" the Seattle lieutenant of detectives asked with a peeved tone. The room was jammed with detectives and investigators from multiple city, county, state, and federal agencies.

Christopher nodded. "Sorry, lieutenant." Christopher replaced a spot at the table that a fellow FBI agent had held for him. "Thank you." He nodded to the junior agent.

The briefing began. No witnesses to the crime, though the young couple earlier in the evening played pool with two men who had left before the couple. "The men were Caucasians, both bearded, wearing jeans and flannel shirts."

"That's not much," someone muttered.

"No."

"Height?" Christopher asked.

The lieutenant scanned his notes. "Quote, 'One was taller than the other by a few inches,' end quote. Average height, some other witness said."

"Weight?"

"Slender and athletic builds."

"We're not getting anywhere with these descriptions." Christopher took notes on a legal pad, but he already wanted to chuck his pen against the opposite wall. "Ages?"

"Mid to late twenties."

"Well, that's something," someone else groused.

"Eye and hair color?" Christopher prompted the SPD lieutenant, who had just shot a stern glance toward the grouser.

"The bartender had the best description, but not of much use still. According to him, one had light eyes, the other had brown."

"Did you have him talk to a sketch artist?" an officer from the sheriff's department asked.

"Here they are. Why don't you pass those around?" The lieutenant nodded to his nearest detective who held a vanilla envelope with papers in it. The detective took out the sheaf of papers and handed them to the officer next to him. When the pack of photocopied sketches reached Christopher, he paused to look at the two faces represented there. They could have been any two young white guys. He took one of the copies, passed the others along, but then laid his copy face down on the table top to let everyone know that he did not think much of what was there. The two men could have been brothers. While he was ostensibly there because SPD had called the FBI to help solve a particularly motiveless crime, Christopher had just hung up with his boss who told him that there was a similar murder in Idaho a few days earlier with possibly two more cases in addition. Christopher asked, "Is there a press conference after this briefing?"

"Yes."

Christopher related how his boss felt it judicious to request that certain evidence, like the existence of a note and the connection to another murder two states away, be hushed to avoid public panic. At the mention that there was a similar murder only a few days earlier, the room erupted with whispers and murmurs of shock and swearing. After Christopher let that die away, he explained that they would use the guise of the quote 'this was an ongoing investigation' to facilitate it. Christopher further argued that since there was a note it was best to not let the killers have their sick words end up all over the media to their delight. "Serial killers have delusions of grandeur and these men are no exception."

"Does that explain this note then? 'Question: What is the meaning of life? They died because they had no meaning of life. They wanted happiness, not for others or even each other, but only themselves.' What kind of shit is this?" The SPD lieutenant raised the note in its clear plastic evidence bag for all to contemplate.

Christopher nodded. All heads turned to him. "Yes, these men believe they are engaged in a messianic crusade. They believe they are the messengers and enforcers of a new world order. It's a fanaticism that feeds off feelings of importance. If the newspapers and other media outlets play up their acts, if everyone runs around talking about them, then this proves how great they are. It's a smart cycle that benefits the killers, not us and not the victims. I think it best if we try to limit the press conference to information about our two vics, particularly their names—repeat them often—their ages—they're quite young—and the fact that they went to that bar just to have a good time. If you have any other biographical info on their lives, share that too. As for the killers, let's release the sketches and the physical stats. Quash the info on the note and that this murder has a connection to another murder in Idaho."

"What exactly is the connection?" A sheriff deputy raised his hand.

"The MO. Now," as he said that, Christopher's eyes went to that evidence bag still in the SPD lieutenant's grasp, but he plowed on before someone could ask for any more. "Lieutenant, I'll be happy to accompany you to the press conference," here he rose from his seat and bowed his head slightly to show his subservience in this matter, "but I defer to you and your authority in your home court."

July 22, 2008

Christopher hopped from the immaculately kept, park ranger SUV, along with the local sheriff and the ranger who had discovered the RV with its interred dead. Christopher strode about and gazed at the wilderness. Idyllic. His cell vibrated, he pulled it out, checked the number, and decided to call his wife back later. He asked the sheriff and park ranger by the SUV, "This was when?"

"We found them on the fifth. They were killed the night before around ten or so, the coroner estimated," the sheriff said in his gruff voice. Christopher turned. The park ranger's eyes were very white. He seemed to re-experience the moment of discovery as they stood there. Poor guy. The sheriff came over to Christopher's side and set his fists on his belt. "They'd been laid out on the bed inside, hands on their chests, like a funeral. A note was atop the man's chest."

"Stabbed?"

"Yep. The man had three wounds, the woman had one."

"Where were his wounds?"

"One was in the arm, another in the abdomen, and the third to the heart." The sheriff pointed to his own body part in turn.

"She was probably killed first, then he struggled. Same knife used to kill them both?"

"All the wounds, on both of them, came from the same blade."

Christopher nodded and tried to recreate the struggle in his mind. "And the note, what did it read?"

The sheriff's brow furrowed for a moment. "What it said was that the two could not define what the good life was."

"The good life?"

"Mm hm."

"What's that mean?"

"Beat's me. That's what you're here for."

Christopher kicked the gravel of the campsite around. "I guess tire marks are out of the question with this surface."

"Not only that, we couldn't tell how many tire marks there were. How many vehicles, I mean."

Christopher didn't have much reason to be here. He had come because he had to see, though what he would learn would be negligible, and was. The mountains around them loomed green and slate into the sky. He wished he could stay and hike them. Solitude. No murder on them. Death was accidental up there on those peaks, caused by the shifting of stones beneath hikers. Death did not come from a pistol or a knife used by someone who interrogated you because of your beliefs, or lack thereof. The park ranger slapped both hands over his face and gasped. The sheriff went over and spoke to him for a few moments to calm him. Christopher ignored them. He went and climbed back into the spotless SUV and waited. What was the 'good life?' He had never heard such a phrase before. Do they mean a life where you are good to others? Do the killers ask that question and wait silently for their victim to stammer out an answer? Why? What's the purpose of asking such a question? How do they get their kicks from such a thing? Maybe their kicks come from watching the fear in their victim's face as they face a gun and a question they've never thought of before. What psychological need is served by the question and the answer? Why not just kill their victim straight off? Because toying with their victim like a killer whale tosses around a seal amuses them, the sick bastards. Christopher shook his head at that, while the sheriff and ranger finally clambered into the SUV.

July 25, 2008

The five of them appeared to be members of a street gang, and they went down the concourse of the mall two by two by one. They wore baggy pants and sports jerseys and ball caps, a few of which were cocked off at odd symmetries to their faces. They strutted and slouched and shuffled along, while they glared and glowered, chips on their shoulders and feelings of superiority in their attitudes. They were stereotypes, real people, and enigmatic individuals all at once.

Rand begged Will for the challenge of trying to engage them in dialogue. Will acquiesced, but he was cautious and insisted that he speak. He opted for the cover that he and Rand were involved in a University of Oregon sociology graduate school program and that they were tasked with interviewing minorities.

The five young men halted, but two of the gang had stony expressions that Will recognized as similar to what fellow soldiers he knew back in Afghanistan had shown. Those expressions meant that they wanted to kill Will and Rand. Two others of the gang appeared receptive to answering because they chattered their opinions about everything. The fifth, the one at the tail of their column, did nothing but stare at girls who giggled and gabbed and loped past. Without preparation, Will decided to ask if the men thought it was more important to be an individual or if it was better to be a member of a group, a community, or some other large social entity.

"What's he on? You think we in a gang or somethin' cuz we what? Niggas?" said one of the two who looked like he would shoot Will and Rand for kicks.

Will's heart pumped furiously, his chest swelled, and he swallowed the cold, metallic taste of adrenaline. He explained again, with greater false elaborations, that they had to ask people like them, African Americans, because that was what their professor expected of them. "Believe me, this isn't some kind of racist profiling by us." Will gestured to himself and Rand, who stood by with a dead smile on his lips. "We just need to know if you think it's more important to be an individual or a member of something greater than just yourself. You see?"

"Think he still disrespectin' us," hissed a tall guy with his hat askew by forty five degrees from his face. He actually placed a hand at the front of his waist.

Rand said, "You know, if you don't want to talk to us that's fine. We understand. It's a tough question no matter who you are. I mean, here you are with your peers, and we drop a question on you about whether you want to be with them or on your own. It's kind of unfair." Rand tapped Will's chest with the edge of his hand. "Why don't we just let them go?"

So they did. The five young men set their jaws and shoved past them, two of them shouldering right into Will.

"What the hell?" Will asked Rand.

Rand smirked. "It's all good in the hood. Come on." They set out after them. "I'll talk this time, but be on guard. I think they have inflated trigger dreams." He guffawed at his own words, though Will only scowled. He did not like Rand's sudden swagger. As they marched after the gang, Rand wrote on an index card the question that Will had asked. "Couldn't you think of something better?"

"I tried to make it relatable to their lives."

"Good job. It was so relatable to them they resented us for asking it."

The pair followed the quintet to the parking lot, down a lane, and to a lowered Cadillac Sedan with tinted windows. There, the tall guy with his hat skewed forty five degrees sighted their pursuit and nodded for his four comrades to confront Rand and Will, which they did. As Rand and he closed the distance, Will fell a few steps behind and drew his pistol. This was going to end in murder, and he would be damned if it would be his or Rand's murders. He thumbed back the hammer. Instead of staring at one, he unfocused his eyes. He tried to see them all, to observe and react to any movement at all. All five gang boys stayed motionless.

Rand said, "Hey, guys, sorry, but we need to try this again."

"Hey, muthafucka, ya just keep up yo lippin,'" said a different member of the quintet, whose hat was turned sort of backwards and who wore sunglasses though it was dusk. This guy whipped an arm behind his back. That arm swung in a huge arc back around.

Rand froze for a split second until he understood the motion and what was coming. The gangbanger's piece was a snub nosed revolver, and he set his sights on Rand. Rand slid his hand up his hip to his pistol with his thumb pulling the shirt up and his other four fingers curled to take up the pistol grip. He drew. Bang. The gangbanger jerked and fired, bang, but now the revolver was aimed a few feet high. Rand flinched as the shot whined above him. He had his pistol out and aimed but the gangbanger flew and sprawled over the car behind him. Rand reset and shot the tall guy who had spotted Will and him. A shot, Rand's shot, two more shots. Rand saw Will rush past him at a low crouch. He popped up, sighted, and fired. Rand did the same. Two more shots. A third. Rand came around the last car before the Cadillac. Three bodies lay over the parking space's white line. Will rushed around the front of the car. Rand shot each body in the heart. On the other side of the car, Will did the same. Rand squatted over the would-be driver and stuffed the index card into his open mouth where a gold tooth shone on the top left. What a fucking stereotype these guys were. Why did they have to be like that? Could they have been otherwise? They had brains. Why didn't they use them?

They drove well into the night, jumped off the interstate onto a two lane state route, pulled over, and spent the night in the Subaru, parked on a dirt road, under some pine trees. Will suspected that it was a logging route. Too tired to pitch their tent, they slept with the front seats reclined and a blanket over each of them, their pistols under their thighs. Despite the evening of duress, the gunfight with the quintet of gangbangers, they both slept heavily and well. They dreamed.

Will came down a mountain where he had just experienced something momentous, though he could not remember what. As he travelled, his mind was quite clear. He stumbled and slid. He dropped to one knee and a hand. The going was treacherous, but he hoped to be down the mountain soon. For some reason he thought that he moved toward something, though he did not recognize the valley below. Down from the rocks, into the trees, pine and spruce, he maneuvered and grappled. He maintained a vigorous pace, and, as the slope leveled and the forest thickened, he drove himself faster. He found a canyon with a stream, and he drank from its clear waters. His thirst slaked, he splashed the frigid water on his face and rubbed it down his neck and around his collar. He stood, felt lighter, and knew something was missing. He wore his old Army ruck still, and he tugged the straps and adjusted the weight on his shoulders. He set off, still uncertain about what it might be that he left behind on the lonely mountain top. His clenched fists pumped the air as he jogged with gravity's aid through a canyon. The stream was his guide now. The songs of cardinals, sparrows, and finches passed over him as he gained ever more momentum, which propelled him toward the valley floor that he no longer saw through the trees. Now, in his sight, there was only the mountain opposite of the one he descended. The mountain's peak was high and knuckled with clouds like a raised fist set to club an unsuspecting traveler. Between the brown and red trunks of the forest, he spied deer, rabbits, even a fox, and none of these wild animals were startled at the sight of his quick motion, the sound of either his blowing or his clumping boot steps, or the scent of his sweat. They accepted his travel, observed it, and then ignored it as they worked on their own survival.

He reached the valley floor, soon exited the forest, and came to a junction of the stream with a river that rushed by with torrential speed. The winter snows had melted and swelled these waters. He halted and shucked his pack from his shoulders and let it thud to the ground. He rolled his shoulders and pressed his hands into the small of his back. Now he realized what the missing weight was. He checked anyway. He patted his waist at the back, his ankles, beneath his arms, and throughout the pockets of his backpack. He knew where it was. He had left his pistol behind, up there on the distant mountaintop. He would not climb the mountain to retrieve it. Partly the distance was too far, but mostly he felt he no longer needed it. He closed his ruck and stood. With his hands at his hips, he looked across the river.

How long had she been there? Among the tall grass she stood, a woman about his age, and she showed him a knowing and welcoming smile. She held his gaze, and he held hers until the world dimmed around him, as if he had stared too long at the sun and everything was now dark in comparison. Then she turned and sauntered away. It was the first time he noticed anything but her face. The long flow of hair and the sun dress rippled as she moved. He searched up and down the banks for a way to cross the torrent because he knew he must follow her. And just to seal his commitment, she paused and glanced over her shoulder and gave him a smile which he believed meant that she knew all he thought and felt, all he had done, and all he had survived.

How do I cross? He shouted.

She beckoned with a wave of her arm. Or maybe she indicated that he should swim with a free style stroke. Neither up nor down the river was there a narrow point, an obvious shallow place, or a bridge. Should he leave his pack? Maybe he could sling it across? Or he could just wear it. She continued to stroll away, and now she did not look back until she came to the edge of the forest on the other bank. How could he cross? The river whipped past. Fish darted by. A broken tree branch came into view upstream, borne by the current, and was gone downstream in a flash. Will barely had time to turn his head to follow its motion before it swung around a bend in the river's course. It was impossible to swim this river without drowning. He could not cross. Her dress flashed and disappeared, over and over, as she moved among the trees. He swore that she still looked back for him. Though she would not wait or offer a solution to the problem of how to cross safely, she wanted him to follow, expected him to follow, and would be there somewhere in that forest for him to find whenever he could follow. He ran up and down the river. How do I cross, he called to her from between the funnel of his hands. He sprinted along the river, but could not find a way to cross.

In the driver seat, Rand had his own dream. He stood at a podium in the middle of a stadium. The eyes of the crowd, hundreds of thousands, maybe even a million in number, stared at him and their bodies did not fidget. They were mesmerized by him! They were a nation there to listen and to witness what he said. Rand was at the end of his oration and he began his summation. He said, "And that is the new world order that I bring to you, you who need rules to feel secure, to govern yourselves, to keep peace between yourselves. That is the reason for laws and governments. They are for your benefit, your survival, and, otherwise, you would fight each other, steal from each other, and not be able to settle your disputes. So I have come to be your philosopher king."

There was an ear drumming sound as the audience rapped their knuckles on the arms of their chairs. That colossal thunder swelled

Rand's chest and throat. The crowd knew that what he said was right, and they approved of him and adored him. He felt powerful, sublime, godly. He had them right where he wanted them: bound to their chairs at the ankles, waist, wrists, and head, unable to move or look away from him because their eyelids were spread by metal clips, and they were in perfect harmony. He was their leader, their master. They agreed with him, they had to agree with him. They were his people, his kingdom.

Front and center, in that audience, were his parents. He turned and extended his arm to show the man who would be his second in command, his trusted aide de camp, Will, who sat in a chair just like those of the audience, ankles, wrists, chest, and head, all held in place with metal clamps. Only Will did not rap his knuckles on the arms of his chair like everyone else. He held his survival knife in one hand and in the other hand his pistol aimed at Rand. Rand stared into the deep, unfeeling blackness of the barrel. He thought he saw the flash.

He woke up. He drew his pistol from beneath his blanket and turned to Will, but Will's seat was empty except for his blanket. Outside, the stars were gone and the sky was painted like a hemorrhaging membrane. Rand twisted and whipped his head about. For three hundred and sixty degrees there was no sign of Will. Where was he? Rand flung his blanket into Will's seat, yanked at the door handle, but found it locked. When he finally leaped from the Subaru, he dashed down the rutted, dirt road sixty or seventy yards. He stopped, spun, and suddenly shivered from how cold it was. His breath erupted in white explosions that hindered his view. He was alone. Will had abandoned him. Had he? He spun again, bobbed, now sprinted back to the Subaru. From behind a tree, not ten yards from the car, appeared Will.

"Hey," said Will.

Rand skidded to a stop on the rocks and dirt from the road. He aimed the pistol right at Will's face, the right eye.

"Whoa!" Will threw up a hand in front of his face and began to reach for his own pistol though he halted halfway. "Rand. It's me, man. What's up?"

Rand shivered so hard the sights on the pistol bounced everywhere.

"Rand, lower your weapon. It's me. What's wrong?"

Rand's arms dropped to his sides and he slouched. The shivering made his teeth clatter like tank tracks.

Will stepped slowly over. His hand was now on his pistol butt though he did not draw. "What's wrong?"

"I didn't . . . didn't know where . . . you went where?"

"Uh hunh." Will thought Rand was delirious. "I couldn't sleep so I went for a hike." Will was in his thick, heavy coat. He did not appear to be cold though his nose was red and his cheeks above his beard were pale which made the acne scars stand out even more. "You need your coat on. Or you need to get back in the car." Will was within a yard. He settled a hand on Rand's shoulder. "Come on, let's get you warmed up or properly clothed. All right? Why were you running around out here?" Will guided him to the Subaru.

"I couldn't find you. I didn't know what happened."

"Well, I'm right here." Will, though worried about the pistol loosely dangling in Rand's grip, did not attempt to relieve him of it.

Rand covered his face with one hand. "I'm crackin.' I don't know. I had a crazy dream."

"You told me dreams don't mean shit."

"They don't, but it still freaked me."

"So what happened?"

Rand debated how to answer. The truth? "You deserted me."

"Why would I do that?"

The image of Will, bound just like every other person in that crowd, wrists raw and red where the metal bit and chafed, came to Rand. Rand shook his head. "I don't know."

"Well, I wouldn't worry about dreams. They have a logic all their own, and it doesn't pertain to the reality that we know." They were back at the Subaru, though on the passenger side. Will opened the door, tossed first one and then the other blanket into the backseat, and then motioned for Rand to sit. Rand did as commanded. Will began to shut the door, looked in the back seat, and then went ahead and slammed the door. He jogged to the driver's side and got in. Quickly, he started the vehicle and turned on the heater full blast though the air was cold. Rand shuddered violently and circled his chest with his arms. His hands burrowed into his armpits. Will reached and brought forward one of the blankets. With all solicitation, he tucked it around the pale and shivering Rand, whose lips were purple like dead livers.

"As soon as the car warms up, you'll be fine." Will stripped off his heavy coat and put it also over Rand, though it slumped into his lap, less than effective. Will began a monologue about how they needed some R & R. Too long in the field will do a soldier in. It's the strain, the threat of death that wears hard on a soldier. That's why the army rotates units in and out of the front line. Everyone needs relief. No soldier can endure steady warfare. The mind cannot absorb it, neither can the body. "It's okay. I think we should spring for a hotel, a nice one. Take it easy for a while. Yeah. What do you say?"

"Okay." The adrenaline leaked away, and a meek Rand plummeted into a dreamless sleep.

July 26, 2008

Christopher was at the FBI office in Los Angeles. In the morning he had emailed every police agency at every level he could find an address for in the western US to ask if anyone had any unsolved murders that involved the MO with its one specific tell-tale, the index card with a hand written philosophical question on it. It was now eleven seventeen at night. The APB on a dark colored Subaru Forester had only turned up a lot of stops by highway patrol officers but no winner. Christopher was in the office of a profiler, Agent Sammy (Samantha) Rialto. Sammy finished reviewing the file.

"Well?" Christopher asked. "Who are they?"

"You believe that there's two of them?" Sammy said.

"Without a doubt. The young couple in Seattle had slugs with different bore marks. The casings had different strike marks. Other victims had the same. I'd say there's no doubt."

"It could be one man with two pistols."

Christopher patiently sat still.

Sammy acknowledged his belief with a nod. "Not likely, I guess, but I wouldn't exclude it if I were you."

"Fine. It's not excluded, but the fact is that the couple in Seattle shot pool with two men before their deaths. My assumption is that those were their killers. The woman in Boise sat by two men who talked to her and greatly upset her by what they said. Again, my assumption is that those were her killers. And let's not ignore the statements of yesterday's shootout in the mall parking lot. So, let's get back to my question."

"Well, they're good shots, aren't they?"

"Ex-military crossed my mind."

Sammy spread the copies of the notecards out on her desk. "Possibly. That would explain the steadiness of their aims. Look, these are ideological murders. These victims did nothing to their killers. The killers were total strangers. That's an emotional detachment that makes the steeliness of these murders understandable."

Christopher rubbed his face in exasperation and exhaustion. She was telling him nothing he had not already come up with, but it was his boss's idea that he work with the younger profiler. Perhaps as training, perhaps as an extra set of eyes to catch something he missed. He needed some coffee.

"You okay?" Sammy glanced over the tops of two of the notecards with their philosophical questions.

"I'm beat."

"Would you like some coffee?"

"Yeah."

"The pot's over there," she said. Christopher's face came from his hands. Sammy smirked at him. She swung back and forth a bit in her chair. "Just teasing." She rose, the notecards still in her hands and crossed to the file cabinet where a small machine was set up with a pot half full. Christopher watched her from the waist down as she went along. She wore gray slacks, the kind called boot cut, fitted around her hips and butt. God, she was hot. He looked up at her face, and blinked when he saw that her eyes were on his. He pulled a nervous grin and avoided her steady gaze. His hands came together in front of his face, his right over his left and he tried to concentrate on where the murderers might be.

"When was the last time you ate?" she asked.

Instead of an answer from his brain about where the murderers might strike next, his stomach spoke up with a howl. He covered his gut with one hand.

Sammy snickered. His cell vibrated in its holder on his hip. Without looking at the screen for the number or name, he answered, "Special Agent England."

"Where will you sleep tonight?" A woman's voice asked.

Christopher's eyes went to Sammy who stood inches away, the coffee cup held in front of his face. He took the cup and nodded his thanks. For a long moment, he could not recall whose voice this was. So familiar.

"Are you there? I know that wasn't your voicemail greeting."

Finally, he had it. "Hey, hon, what time is it?" He checked his watch by raising his arm like a man defending his face, and tried to read the numbers. His wife ought to be asleep.

"It's not late, it's early. You said you would call back."

"I know, I know, but I haven't moved from where I was when we talked."

"I see. I would say you have roots, but we both know that isn't so." The resentment was strong and heavy in her voice.

"Look, this isn't the time." He glanced half way across the desk to where Sammy had reseated herself, but his eyes retreated. He rose from the chair, his knees creaked from sitting there for so long and he tottered around the chair so that his face was hidden from Sammy.

"Never is." Her tone was meant to injure.

"You knew," he said.

"I thought I did, but I hadn't experienced it. Now I know."

"This is what I do."

"It's who you are too."

Christopher sighed and his head drooped. Was she as upset as that? He couldn't tell over the wires and atmosphere where their signals zipped invisibly. After only one year of marriage he was in the same place that he had been with his first wife. "I'll be home soon." He offered what he thought she might see as a lifeline. His stomach howled again. "We'll go somewhere special this weekend. We'll go-"

"I don't want to go. I want to stay. And I want you to stay too."

"Okay." He wanted to comfort her. She was alone in their house, a space that she wanted to have children in. That was her dream, and he wanted to give it to her, but she wanted it all now. That seemed too soon to him.

"But it won't be for long will it? You'll take a few days off, but then you'll be back in the field again, on the hunt again."

He wanted to lie, but she would never believe him.

"Why don't you stay home? Why don't you change departments or whatever it is, and stay home with me? Why don't you want to be with me? Don't you love me?"

"Of course, I do. You're-" What? Wrong? He sympathized with her, but he did not want a different job. He knew that Sammy's eyes bore into his back. A conversation with his wife should not be in front of her. He felt pinioned by these women. "You're tired," he finally continued. "Get some sleep. This isn't the way to talk about this, all right? We should talk face to face. Not this way. We can't do this when we can't see each other. Okay?"

"Okay." Her voice was deflated.

"Go to sleep. I love you."

"I love you too." He thought she would add more, there had been no drop in her tone to indicate a full stop.

"I'll call later. Good night."

"Bye."

He closed the phone and slipped it into the case clipped to his belt, only after that did he turn around. "That was my wife."

Sammy nodded. "Sounded like it. Problems?"

"No."

"Liar. And you should know better than to lie to a woman. For that matter, you shouldn't lie to someone in our line of work either."

"Very true." Christopher's head drooped.

"Let's get some food in you. Food helps everything. In my family the women always shove food into the men."

"Does that solve things?" Christopher asked. Sammy stood, took her jacket from her chair back, swung it on, and said, "My family's Mexican. That food, plus copious quantities of beer, will put you to sleep. What problems do you have then?"

Sammy drove him to a bar where the grill and kitchen were still open for orders. He ordered a burger, she had a grilled chicken sandwich, and beers for both of them. She began her life story. Rialto was from San Diego, Barrio Logan. Her parents had illegally immigrated from Mexico. Being skinny, having taped together horn rimmed glasses and large upper front teeth made her socially shunned, shy, and, as a result, a great reader and student at a school where the white teachers were either apathetic or frightened of their Hispanic charges. Since both of her parents worked, and she did not want to go home to the empty house, Sammy went to the school library. There was always a teacher there to act as tutor though rarely did anyone ever venture to take advantage of the free service. Sammy did. The teachers, though impressed by the girl's love of reading and her presence in the library at all, never encouraged her when she asked questions about what she could do when she grew up, or what kind of job she could have where she could read. Every one of the teachers told her that she would grow up to be just what her mom was, a housekeeper and nanny for a white family in La Jolla. Her dad was a janitor at her school, and she had to hear the other kids make fun of him. The kids threw garbage on the floor to force him to clean more. She did not want to do what her parents did. Her body developed at a glacial pace compared to all the other girls. Her breasts took forever to grow from her chest. She had no butt, just long legs. She had no hips. The boys ignored her and the girls only wanted the attention of the boys. Sammy read her books. She read the whole library at her high school by her junior year. She earned straight A's. She applied for college, UCSD, and was not only accepted but given a scholarship set aside for a Hispanic female who showed particular academic talent. That year the scholarship went to Sammy. Her parents were proud for their daughter who had done what they had not. Their plates arrived. They ate silently. He devoured his burger and fries. He felt better, but he wished that he had ordered more. She suddenly asked, "Who is she?"

"Who?"

"Your wife. What's her name?"

He told her.

"She's not in the Bureau?"

He shook his head.

"She doesn't approve of your job?"

He looked up from his beer, eyed her, and tossed back the last of his beer. The bartender came over. He ordered another, this one with a shot of bourbon.

"She doesn't understand you."

That statement by Sammy, along with the shot, caused him to open up about all the pressures on him to quit, change jobs, and make babies. "I feel like a sperm dispenser," he quipped.

"I don't have a need for sperm." Sammy smirked. She rocked her head from one side to another and she leaned closer, her knees rubbed against his. "I have a need for men though."

They paid their bill, went to her apartment, and slept together.

As they dressed in the morning, Christopher sat on the edge of the bed with his wrinkled slacks in one hand and said to Sammy, who leaned against her bathroom counter to apply her female camouflage half dressed in a satin blouse, her bra, and panties, "Could you answer one of their questions?"

"What? Whose questions?" She worked at brushing mascara on her lashes.

"These killers we're hunting." He flipped the belt buckle, still fed into the pants loops, back and forth with his thumb. "If they came up to you with guns drawn or whatever, and they asked you 'What was the good life?' could you give a cogent answer?"

Finished with her lashes she screwed the cap back on the mascara, and sighed. "Sure."

"'Sure?' Okay, what's your answer? Mind you, this is a life and death situation. If your answer doesn't satisfy their requirements, you take shots to the head and chest. Do you really think you have an answer?" He snapped his slacks in the air so that the legs, when they hit the floor, spread before him, flat.

Sammy now had her lipstick. She applied it to her upper lip then sucked both lips in and there she was with bold maroon lips.

"You going to answer? Stalling for time?" He stood. One then the other of his legs rustled into the slacks.

"I don't have a meaning of life for everyone."

"Okay."

"I have my meaning for my life. I'm not about to dictate terms to other people because that's the reason I have the meaning of life that I do. All those teachers I had in school who wanted me to be just like my parents, to grow up to be a housekeeper, a nanny, or a janitor, they wanted to limit the meaning of my life to this tiny, brainless existence." She came to the doorway and took up a defiant, tough stance with her fists on her slender, bony hips. He wondered if she realized how sexy that pose was, still only clothed in the metallic colored blouse and the black panties. "I busted my way out of their meaning. I went to college. I went to grad school. I joined the FBI. The meaning of my life is an all-out effort by me to redress injustice. Why? Since I was treated unfairly, since I stood up for myself and I refused to be penned in by those stupid gringos, I have to help those who are getting screwed up like they tried to do to me." She marched to her closet, and stared at the selection of suspended slacks, pulled out two, held first one, then the second to her waist, appraised the chromatic combination with the pre-selected blouse, and decided on the first pair of slacks.

"That's pretty good." Christopher buckled and zipped up his pants as he lost sight of her smooth thighs when she hopped into her slacks. "Where should we go for breakfast?"

"Aren't you going to answer the question now? Or do you not have an answer?" She took a pair of shoes from the rack that hung on the inside of her closet door. She slipped them on as she leaned against the doorframe. He didn't answer as he tugged on his socks then his shoes. "Who's stalling now?" She taunted.

"I guess I am."

"You don't have an answer?" She strode to the nightstand and picked up her Browning .380 in its holster and attached it to the waistline of her pants off her right hip.

"That's all you carry? Kind of a light piece. Most agents who have those, have them as a backup on their ankles or something."

"That's all I carry." She scooped up her cell and clipped it to her left hip. "There's a Starbucks on the way to the office where we can get eats and caffeine. That all right?"

"All right," he echoed.

She went to her closet and whipped out a short black jacket, dressy yet light, and in a deft motion reached her arms in. "Ready."

He clipped his holster and cell to his belt. "Okay."

"While I drive you can come up with an answer. Okay?" She grinned deviously at him. "It might bother me to work with someone who has no purpose to life. After I kill you, I'll say it was a mercy killing. You asked for it."

"Really funny, but I don't know if I have an answer. I don't know what I believe, what I think."

July 31, 2008

In Hollywood, on Rodeo Drive, Rand and Will parked among the Rolls Royces, Mercedes, Jaguars, and Land Rovers that had never seen mud splattered on them from heading off the pavement. Rand and Will stepped onto the sidewalk in their jeans, combat boots, sweat stained t-shirts, and beards. Rand had let his go, scraggly though it was. The foot traffic immediately gave them a wide berth. They grinned at each other. The sneers they drew, the gasps they elicited, fully justified their decision to travel to this part of the country.

"We should just get a U-Haul truck full of fertilizer," Rand said. Over the past two days he had returned to his old self. The dream of Will shooting him forgotten.

"After McVeigh and the Oklahoma City bombing they changed the composition of fertilizer so that no one could ever do that again." Will shook his head.

"But there's always a way."

Will shrugged a shoulder. "Sure."

Rand gestured at two haughty women strutting side by side toward them. Each woman held three or four bulging shopping bags overstuffed with overpriced garments, shoes, and jewelry, and to an ear they each gripped a cell phone that they yapped into. Neither stuck up woman paid attention to the other, nor to anyone else in the world. They wore oversized dark sunglasses that fully hid half their faces. Both had to be in their forties but their lips were swollen like ripe plums and their jawlines were hard with tight skin. Their V-neck blouses barely hid the stiff balls of their augmented breasts. What else was fake about them? As they passed by Rand and Will, the nearest woman popped her bags into both men's knees.

"Hey! Watch it!" She shrieked at them, then went on with her phone conversation in which she continued to end every phrase with an exclamation point. Will and Rand looked at each other.

Will nodded quickly. "How long do we have to talk?"

"Talk about what?" Rand started after the two haughty women.

Will stepped after him and kept pace. "You know, listen to them after we ask our question."

"Do you really want to talk to them?"

"No, but we can't just. . ." Will nodded to one side as if it was a matter of heaving them over the side of a boat.

"Why not? I mean, why can't we?"

"I like to think that we both agree that people are innocent until proven guilty."

"How in the hell can they be anything other than guilty of being one of the thoughtless? Like I said, we could just set a bomb down here and be pretty damn certain that we'd do the world a load of good by ridding it of the people who are here."

Will stopped in his tracks. "You're that certain?"

Rand motioned for him to catch up. "Come on. If you want to continue the debate between us, that's fine, but I'll take five to one that those two won't even give us the time of day to ask our question let alone debate about it."

Will trotted after Rand, though he shook his head. "Maybe, maybe not. They still have to have that chance though."

"Fine, you give them that chance. Shit." Rand scowled and stopped dead in his tracks as the two haughty women with their bags that clapped together like an appreciative audience to their wealth approached a Mercedes SUV parked on the street. "To the car."

They sprinted, cut between people, received shouts and curses, and made it to the Subaru in time to see the Mercedes SUV jerk away from the curb and cause a passing vehicle to slam on its brakes. The Mercedes SUV sped off. Rand drove. He cut the wheel hard and squealed into the traffic.

"Let's just shoot them," Rand said.

"No, we have to ask our question."

"They won't answer, and, even if they did, they would have nothing intelligent to say."

"They have to have the choice to not answer."

"Fine."

A stop light was yellow, but Rand romped on the gas, and they rocked back in their seats as they shot past the line at the red light.

"Oh, shit." Will twisted in his seat because of the black and white squad car that idled in the line waiting for the green. The cop was two back from the front of the line. As Rand and Will reached the other side of the intersection, the squad car's red and blue lights began to flash. "Cops," Will said.

Rand spotted a space in the line of parallel parked cars. He ripped the wheel hard, stamped the brakes, and ran the Subaru diagonal into the curb. "Follow me." He leaped out of the car and left the door open.

Will followed. "We can't run away!"

The squad car squelched to a halt and blocked the Subaru in its space. Two cops hopped out and loped one around either end of the Subaru, to the curb. Rand stopped a foot from the parking meter, raised his arm, and pointed right at Will's nose.

"I can't believe you sucked him off!" Rand screeched. "He's such a hideous, gargantuan sloth. I can never trust you again after you blew him." Rand's eyes enlarged and became weepy. Will blinked and it registered that Rand's voice was altered, pitched higher. Will turned and scanned the faces of the nearest people, shoppers with their voluminous paper bags and the names of chic stores printed on the sides. Behind Will stood the two uniformed police men, with bemused grins, hands on their big belts with the batons, handcuffs, pistols, and extra clips. Rand shrieked. "I let you move in with me, and this is how you repay me?"

Will shrugged at the cops in exasperation. He scuffed his shoes as he turned back to Rand. "It's not like I had . . . sex with him." He tried to play along, but this was a stretch for him.

"How can I believe you when you betray me like that? You had nothing until you met me." Rand crossed his arms, took a quarter turn, and stamped a foot.

Will searched the faces of the cops and the spectators. "Look, we're not in a place where we can discuss this. How can I disclose my . . . conflicted emotions when we have an audience? This isn't theater. It's our . . ." Will gulped and closed his eyes. "Our relationship." He offered his hand for Rand to take. Rand, playing this queer role to the hilt, scraped his boot across the sidewalk to draw a line between them, but he stared at Will's hand and pretended to long for it. This was too much, Will wanted to holler. He would kill Rand for this ludicrous display. "Take it," said Will through his gritting teeth. Rand looked up, reproachful. "When we leave," Will softened his voice, "I'll explain everything to you. It's not like you think." Rand took his hand. They turned and headed to the car. Will crushed Rand's hand in his grip, and Rand winced and whined. They approached the cops.

The cops asked who was driving, explained that Will and Rand had run a red light and were now parked illegally. Rand whimpered and wept, partly for the role and partly because of the crush that his hand felt from Will's grip. Rand blubbered how it was there as they were coming to the light that Bill, referring to Will, casually and meanly told him of his little fling with one Howard, an obnoxious fairy of a wedding planner. Will could not look at any of them. He stared at the car and tried to demolish Rand's hand. The cops told Rand to calm down. They gave them a warning. One cop asked that Will drive. Okay. The cops strolled away to their cruiser, shook their heads, and their shoulders trembled as they scoffed at the quarrels of "fags," a word one of them hissed to the other as they opened their doors. Will's whole arm shook as he tried to smash Rand's hand. The police left.

"Let up." Rand reached with his other hand to relieve the pressure.

"Get in." Will slung Rand's bruised hand away. "Bastard."

"I had to."

They got in, this time Will assumed the driver's seat.

"Don't ever fucking do that again, you fucking freak," Will said.

"Chill the fuck out."

"Fudge packer."

"I had to get us out of that. Those guys were going to peg us. Do you want to be frisked with your gun and your knife on you?"

Will backed away from the curb and set off down the boulevard. The police cruiser escorted them to the next intersection then turned and disappeared.

"Do you think they would've let us go without a lot of questions?" Rand said. "I did the right thing." Rand massaged his glowing, red hand. "I got us out of that. What was your plan? Shoot our way out? That would've gone bad. We'd have had all of California on our asses within ten minutes. I kept us from dying. I kept us in the war, kept us free to continue with our offensive. Being chased by the police would cause us to lose the initiative, to be on the defensive. You didn't have a solution. I didn't hear you come up with a better idea. I'm the one who can think on his feet and get us out of the shit. I can improvise. I'm the leader. You're just a soldier. You can follow orders, but you can't give them because you have no strategy, you have no mind for the grand design. Do you? Well, do you?"

Rand glared and dared Will to refute the facts. Will said nothing. He drove on in silent defeat. Was Rand right? Was he just a follower? Was he just Rand's soldier? He found I-40 eastbound and put them on the path back toward Arizona.

July 31, 2008

"I called this in a while back."

"That stuff in Seattle and Portland got our attention first, since those were fresh events."

"They was gang members, wasn't they? The ones in Portland?"

"They were." Christopher sat taller and stressed his proper English grammar as he spoke to the sheriff of this shit heel town.

The sheriff snorted. "Good riddance, in my estimation."

Christopher glared at him. "Those boys had mothers too."

"Who shoulda done better by 'em in raisin' 'em."

Christopher looked around the room and swallowed a huge draft of air to extinguish his rising ire. Racist. Why didn't this hick sheriff just call those five boys niggers to his face? He was just an uneducated man who had learned it was wrong to spread his opinions at least, though he hadn't changed those opinions.

"Did anyone get a good look at the perps?" Christopher asked.

"If they did, they didn't come forward."

"What am I supposed to look for? Tall? Short?"

"Average."

"Average."

"Those who saw the fellas that were talking to the Rivers girl that mornin' said they was of average height."

"So they're about five feet ten?"

"Uh hunh."

"Hair color?"

"They had on ball caps."

"You can still see-"

The sheriff shrugged.

"Eye color."

"Nope."

"None of the employees took notice of them? Come on, it's a Wal-Mart."

The sheriff shrugged again, and Christopher and he stared at each other across the desk.

"What am I supposed to look for? If you don't mind?"

"They left this on young Casey's body."

The sheriff held up a sealed evidence bag with a note inside. Christopher leaned from his chair, reached over the desk, and took the bag. He looked at the blank side first, held it up to the fluorescent lights, and then turned it over to read. "Why are morals important?"

"Like nothing I ever heard of," the sheriff said. "You?"

"May I keep this?" Christopher recognized the handwriting.

"I called you in so you could take this off my desk. I damn well don't know what to make of this. Not at all."

"Were there shell casings?"

The sheriff looked in a vanilla envelope and pulled out a smaller evidence bag with two spent shell casings inside and offered it across his desk to Christopher. "There were two. Both nine millimeter, but they were from different guns. The firin' pins made different strikes. See?"

"Well, that's unusual." Christopher dangled the bag in front of his face and twisted it to inspect the shells.

The sheriff's face crunched down on itself until his eyes disappeared. "How's that?" His voice was a low growl.

Christopher looked up. "I was being ironic. There are tons of murders with nine millimeters involved. The caliber of choice these days."

"Mm." The sheriff sat back and laid his hands on his belly. "How'd you know there'd be more than one?"

"Because there are two killers. They work as a team. Neither of them ever sits out. They both kill their victim. I suspect that they believe if one of them sits out then that person can claim innocence if they're ever caught."

"Will you be taking this on?"

"Yes."

Christopher reread the note in the bag. "Why are morals important?"

"Uh hunh. Can you imagine it? Talking to some fellows and then they ask you that? And if you don't have an answer they like, well, they kill you."

Christopher shook his head once as he examined the handwriting, print, not cursive, struck hard into the notecard's fibers.

"What kind of man is it that thinks it's okay to kill someone because he can't answer a question like that? I don't know how I'd face that predicament. Have you an answer if it came down to it?"

After their meeting Christopher sat in the rental car in the parking lot. The sheriff had offered to escort him to the crime scene, but Christopher had declined. What would he find? Zip, zilch. A Wal-Mart parking lot where scores of cars had driven through. No, thanks. He would drive back to the capitol and fly to LA where he could try to collate the evidence for some kind of lead as to where these two would strike next. It all seemed so random, meaningless.

August 1, 2008

In Yuma, on the border of Arizona and California, the pair holed up in a Holiday Inn for a week. Both men enjoyed being able to take a shower each day. They swam laps in the pool early in the morning to avoid the families that arrived usually in the late afternoons and evenings. The exercise felt awesome, and they discussed buying some free weights, dumbbells and the like, but they decided that they would be unable to transport them in the already heavily loaded Subaru whenever they thought it was time to move on. Instead they did push ups, dips on a chair in the room, sit ups, and jogs in the evenings after sunset. They made sure to park the Subaru backwards so that the license plate faced a wall. They bought groceries from a market a few blocks away, which they walked to, and they ate in the room. Everything they did was a maneuver to stay inconspicuous. They felt sublime, cocky, and reinvigorated from a full week of R & R after their first extended offensive campaign. They read the national news to obtain intelligence about where the police stood in their investigations. In a way they felt secure and a little arrogant from what they read. The police had published a set of sketches based from evidence given by the bartender in Seattle. Will worried that the sketches would tip off the hotel staff. Rand shoved him in front of a mirror with the newspaper held next to his face. It looked only a little like him. Still, it was only a small comfort. Will suggested they use disguises. Rand countered that using hats had so far protected them from high angle security cameras. What they ought to do was make continuous though subtle changes in their actual appearances. They both shaved their beards. Rand shaved his head too.

August 3, 2008
Dear World,

We are writing this letter because we know that our actions are currently misconstrued and misrepresented by the media, police, and by you. We are not mindless in what we do. Everything is planned and because there are two of us there is little chance that our motives are purely based on emotions such as hate, fear, or desire.

We see ourselves as warriors embarked on an offensive that will restore certain traits to humanity that are now lost, though they once held dominance.

We are young men educated at one of the state universities of our once grand nation. We studied philosophy, history, and the classics. While we do not pretend to be masters, we are not novices. If we do not have a thorough knowledge of the above topics, neither do we have a viewpoint that is framed and boxed in by one line of thought. Our youth—perhaps it might be argued as overly impressionable—is still not hardened to disallow new ideas and approaches. So we feel that we are situated, and thus presented, with an opportunity of which we have to take advantage.

We do what we feel we must in order to better humanity, whose population bomb continues to explode forth a high number of members that are thoughtless, uneducated, and uninterested in the important questions, answers, and meanings that define human existence. We are hopeful that you will see us for what we are and not for what we are portrayed as by the police, namely, mindless, psychopathic, and motivated by hate. We did not and do not hate our victims. We attempted to illuminate them so they could move beyond the intellectual impasse in which they were stuck. We interviewed them, challenged them with questions in a Socratic style dialogue so that we could hold up their answers for cross examination. Unfortunately, we found that people stubbornly adhered to their wrong headedness. They pretended to be mountains when they were dust motes, without significance or greater meaning.

Sincerely,
The Plato Warriors

August 8, 2008

The mother with her three daughters just happened to sit beside them at the snack area in the Target. It was time to leave Yuma. Their supplies of food and water bottles were loaded in the car already. Rand initiated the conversation, but in a way that disturbed Will.

"Hi. How are you? We've been reading about those Plato Warriors in the news, and we were curious if we could confidently answer questions like what those guys would ask. Have you heard about them? Would you have an answer for their interrogations?"

Will's jaw hung.

"I have heard about them, but I haven't paid too much attention to it all. When you're busy like I am, the news just seems like a bunch of silly gossip. Who cares about the infidelities and lies of politicians or Hollywood stars?"

"I know exactly what you mean." Rand nodded with his customary smirk.

Will set his iced mocha down from a long drink, which he had taken in order to swallow his disbelief at Rand's introduction. He was practically telling her that they were the Plato Warriors. "There are more important things in life," Rand said. "If you don't mind my asking, what's the meaning of your life?"

"It's my job to raise these girls."

Will asked, "Are you going to have more?"

"Possibly. I've talked to my husband about that."

Rand said, "What if he doesn't want more?"

"Then maybe I'll become part of Big Brothers and Big Sisters to help out children less fortunate than mine. I come from a big family. There were six of us. Four girls and two boys."

"Are you of a particular religion?"

"I was raised Catholic, but I don't care for that church." She seemed about to say more but did not. She stroked the heads of two of the girls while her mind tried to suppress something. "I can't be a part of any religion now, especially not that one."

Will and Rand exchanged a glance. This woman was intriguing.

"It's my job to raise these girls and make them smarter, more thoughtful, and more caring than I was, more than what I was raised to be."

"Your job? That's the second time you've used that word. Do you mean it the same as a duty or an obligation?" Will asked.

"Yes, those are better words. I wish I'd thought of them."

"And how did you get this duty? Who gave it to you?" Rand rubbed his chin where the skin was very sensitive from having shaved off his goatee.

"I did."

Rand's eyes widened, and Will nodded in obvious approval.

"When did you decide that?" One of Will's fingers burrowed into a pock mark.

"I knew it as soon as my little Avery here was born." She rubbed the back of the oldest girl. "Did you know that?" She now spoke to Avery. "When you came out of my tummy and Daddy cut your umbilical cord, which attached you to me, and the nurse cleaned you up a bit and swaddled you, I held you first and looked into your brave eyes that are just like your Daddy's." Here she brushed the girl's cheek. Rand rolled his eyes and turned to Will, but found his comrade smiling as he basked in this apparently well-worn recitation. She said, "You reached and grabbed my finger as hard as you could, and I knew it right then. I knew that I had to be the best mom that I could be. I spent all of your first year and a half holding you while I read every book your daddy would let me buy on how to raise happy, healthy children." She nodded and smiled. "I studied it as well as I could."

"So you read as many books as you could? Seriously?" Will asked.

"Yes. I was always a good student. I just lacked direction. But when I had Avery, man, did I get all the focus I needed."

"You think you're a good mom, then?" Rand asked.

She seemed taken aback by this direct question. "Well, I work hard to be. Am I perfect? No. No one can be. Besides, children aren't like making a thing, like a TV or chair or something. They're never finished. Their whole lives are the only measure of whether their parents did a good job or not, and so talking about their first couple years doesn't seem worthwhile when they could make huge mistakes as adults and then there you would be, a bad parent. See?"

Rand drummed his fingers on the table. "You believe that parents are the ones directly to blame for how a child ends up as an adult?"

"Who else is there to blame? The TV? The society?"

"What about free will?"

"Too much is determined. We may have choices, but it's a finite set of choices. We're not as free as we might think."

"You don't think we're born as blank slates?"

"Neither of you has kids, do you?" They shook their heads. She got a sly look to her eyes and she smirked. "You're not a couple are you?"

"What?" said Rand.

"No," said Will.

"Absolutely not." Rand shook his head.

They both looked down, measured their propinquity, and scooted away. They chuckled the question off as well as they could.

"Oh, I don't think there's anything wrong with that. Homosexuality is fine by me," she said.

"Mommy, what's homosetsunanity?" the oldest girl asked.

"I'll explain later."

"So, uh, we asked about kids being blank slates. You said you didn't think so," Will reclaimed the thread of their conversation.

She shook her head at them with a smile. "Yes. That's right. Kids are too much like their parents. Haven't you ever heard your own family say about you that you're just like so-and-so? Maybe it's your dad or granddad or it's your mom or your aunt that you're like. That stuff's not an accident. A lot is passed through the genes, you know, like whether you'll be an introvert or an extrovert, a chance taker or someone who always plays it safe, or whether you're artistic or a math whiz, all that's pretty well laid out for you when you come into the world. Don't you think so? And if it's not coming to you through your genes, then it's from you watching and imitating the people around you, usually unconsciously."

Will nodded then dug at a pockmark, but Rand rubbed the sensitive skin on his chin with an air of being unconvinced. "What about good and bad?"

"You mean good and evil?"

"If that's how you want to say it."

"Well, I'd say that children have to learn to be good, to share and to cooperate. One of their first words is always 'mine.' That selfishness isn't evil though, that's survival. You have to make sure that you have enough for yourself, that your needs are met. Evil is taught, unleashed might be a good word. You have to learn how to dominate others, to work at making their needs go unmet while yours are totally fulfilled. Children are unaware that anyone else even has needs, so they can't manipulate others through their desires to fulfill their own."

Will's face held the expression of wondrous epiphany. Yet something about what she said seemed too clever by half to Rand. What was it that was off though? He could not put his finger on that. It all seemed so pat. Maybe it was somebody else's thoughts that she appropriated? He racked his brains about whose philosophy might be the origin for what she had said. Definitely not Nietzsche. Nor was it one of the ancient Greeks. She was too humane for them. Was it some reorganization of Christian values? No, Christians are always of the either/or camp. You are either evil or good at birth. Well, now wait. She did seem to point to people being good at birth and then corrupted by experience. Maybe she was at heart a Christian ideologue. The whole time that Rand sat there in contemplation, his chin now very sensitive from how his knuckles ran back and forth over his newly hairless chin, Will and the mother had talked. Rand glanced at Will and was confounded by the enamored look on his friend's face. Why was he fawning at her? He looked as if he had met Mother Theresa, Helen of Troy, and the woman he wanted to marry all wrapped into one. What had she been saying? Was her voice like one of the sirens that Odysseus heard that nearly drove him mad?

"You know," she said with a glance at her cell phone's clock. "I really need to be going. My youngest needs to have her nap." In fact, the youngest was leaning against her mom's side with slowly blinking eyes.

"We all have to be going sometime." Rand smirked with a malicious curl of his lip. Will gawked at him. Rand slid his right hand along the surface of the table and jerked his head to the side to indicate without words that they should take them out and kill them. Will gravely shook his head. Did Will really not intend to take her out? Was he going soft?

As if he heard those questions, Will said, "She's answered, and probably better than you could."

"Says you."

"Yep."

Rand's hand now sat atop the butt of his pistol beneath the thin fabric of his washed t-shirt. He and Will glared at each other.

"No."

Rand ground his teeth.

"Mommy, you're holding me too tight."

Both men turned their heads. The woman's eyes were wide in recognition and horror. She had her three girls clutched to her. "It's you." That was all she had to say.

"Go." Will jerked his chin. "He's not going to do anything." Will switched his calm gaze to Rand. "I'm not going to let you. She's not one of them." Will's hand now, with no pretense of hiding what it was doing, went to the pistol beneath his shirt. To the mom, he said, "Go, now. It's okay. He won't do a thing to you or your girls."

Rand's lip curled. Who the hell did Will think he was? Why was he going to let her go? The mom staggered from her chair. Her three girls gripped to her sides stumbled as they tried to keep up with their mom's longer, frantic strides. Will and Rand watched them clatter against chairs and tables as they fled.

"God damn it," Rand growled at Will.

"We need to go. Now." Will kicked his chair back and stood. Rand followed suit.

Since they left Yuma that morning, Rand sat with a surly look on his face while at the wheel. He was still galled by the disappointing encounter with that mother and her brats. Why had Will been so sentimental? She was no one to him. Her ideas were derivative. Why hadn't he wanted to eliminate her? True, there had been the three brats with her. That would be tough. Obviously, they would have let them go and given them the chance to be better than their mom. They wouldn't kill children. That was only proper, then they could learn from the failed example of their mom. Why had Will not gone through with it?

In the glaring glass city of Phoenix, Will requested that they stop at a Barnes and Noble. "I miss reading," he said. "These long stretches of the road get boring." Will rapped his knuckles on the window.

"I guess I'm boring." Rand feigned pain. He wasn't sure he cared.

"Yep." Will grinned. He was not serious, but he did miss reading. It was one of the activities that had sustained him for years, and they had not made time for that since graduation, when their plans shot them like bullets from a gun into nonstop activity, a trajectory they had yet to descend from. They hit the store. Rand picked up a copy of Sartre's *Nausea*, which he had always heard of but not read. He sat in the Starbucks café area and began to read while he sipped a double espresso. An hour, two, then three passed. Rand ordered and ate an onion bagel with cream cheese. After, he placed his dirty plate on the counter. The evening had come. Cars used their headlights to catch pedestrians in mid-movement like photographs cut from the fabric of the night. He went to locate Will, whom he discovered on the floor in an aisle, seated cross-legged with a small pile of books, about ten in all, beside him.

"What're you getting?" Rand asked.

"These." Will patted the stack without looking away from the one in his hand, the way someone pats the nearest body part, say a knee, shoulder, or back, of a best friend or lover.

"Well, let's get going, hunh?" Rand had his key ring on one finger, and he spun the keys as if to simulate the anticipated motion of the Subaru's wheels. Almost two hundred dollars later, paid on a credit card Will did not think he would need to worry about repaying, they were out the door. Rand glanced at the titles on the spines as Will balanced them against his body. He had refused a bag from the cashier. The selection was wildly eclectic. Lincoln, Thoreau, Emerson, Paine, and Camus. Several books by Camus. Rand only knew of Camus's name in connection with Sartre.

"Aren't we men of action now?" Rand asked as he opened the driver's door and pitched *Nausea* into the back seat. "I thought the time for learning and contemplation had passed."

Will struggled to balance the books with one hand beneath them as the other tugged at the door handle to the back seat. With the door opened—he only just managed to avoid dinging the car next to them with the door by halting its swing with his hip—Will squatted and set the stack of books in the back floorboard. Rand got in, started the car, pulled his seatbelt across him, lowered the emergency brake lever, and stopped. Will remained, squatted beside the Subaru with the back door open.

"Uh, are you getting in?" Rand twisted to check on what his friend was up to.

"Yeah, hang on."

"What are you doing?"

"Picking out a book."

Rand shook his head and turned around. He drummed his fingers on the steering wheel. This was damn irritating. "Come on, fellow man of action, let's boogie."

"Where are we going?" There was a soft thump, Will rose, shut the door, opened the front door, and hopped in. "To the discothèque? Maybe we can do a little dance, make a little love, get down tonight, get down tonight."

"While we're staying alive, staying alive, ah ah ah ah, staying alive."

They both chuckled. Rand steered through the busy parking lot. "What did you pick out?"

"Eric Hoffer's *The True Believer*."

"What's it about? Jihadists?"

"No, no. This was written back in the fifties, I think."

"Commies, then."

"I guess so, but probably also about Nazis."

"How'd you hear about that book?"

"I just saw it on the shelf, pulled it, and read the back plus the first few pages."

"Did you do that with all those?"

"Yep."

"No wonder what took you so long."

"I guess." Will patted his gut. "I'm hungry."

"I ate."

"Oh." Will's voice sounded slightly hurt. He unbuckled his seatbelt, shimmied into the backseat, and rummaged through their supplies for dinner.

August 11, 2008

At an Ace Hardware, where they stopped to pick up a new rope, they met a man who had four packages of mason jars stacked in a shopping cart.

Rand asked, "What are you going to do with all those?"

The man said, "I'm going to use them for my collections."

"Collections?" Will rocked onto his tiptoes to see if there was anything else in the cart. There was not.

"What are you collecting?" Rand asked.

"Everything. I'm trying to make a full account of the world I experience." He was an anxious, little man with specs and a small patch of white hair behind his left ear. He dug a knuckle at his brow where half of one eyebrow was white too. Rand and Will both towered over him.

"Why?" Will asked.

"I can't know anything except for the world I live in, and the only way that I can make sure that I know it is by documenting it in full, a full account, you see." He tapped his temple to indicate sight and thought.

"Uh hunh." Rand laid a hand on the cart because he didn't want to let this fellow go.

The little man rocked onto his toes as he spoke. When he dropped back to his heels, it gave his voice a little jolt upward in pitch, like a hiccup. "Yes, yes, I keep journals where I document the temperatures at six AM, twelve noon, and six PM. I step out to the street in front of my house and use my panoramic camera to take a photo of the world around me, every day at the same time. I record my dreams and moods at different times of the day."

"But why?" Will waved his hand to test the temperature and humidity of the air in the store.

"Well, how else can we *know* something unless we take a serious scientific approach to our world?" The man pulled his hand through his hair. It looked as if a clump might come out because of the way he yanked on it.

Rand said, "What about dreams? You said you record your dreams. Can you say that they bear up to scientific scrutiny?"

"Of course. What was Freud's greatest book? *The Interpretation of Dreams*. Science has turned its piercing gaze on every aspect of existence, and if we don't have every answer we at least gather data and ask questions so the raw material is there for when someone smarter, in another generation or more, can follow our inquiries and determine the answers. Mankind's greatest gift to its children was in its writing, where the greatest storehouse of our knowledge resided."

"So what are the jars for?" Will asked.

"Oh, goodness, all kinds of things. I've used these for soil, leaves, rocks, urine, feces, shells, pinecones-"

"Urine?"

"Oh, yes, bodily fluids are very important to understanding physiology, diseases, nutrition, and so on."

"So it's your urine?"

"Naturally."

"Naturally." Rand caught Will's eye. Not even Rand was certain if he himself was ironic, awed, or disgusted by the man's mammoth need for totality in his life's project. Rand probably felt a mix of all three.

"I've even," he peeked around and leaned toward the two men to include them in his conspiracy of knowledge, "preserved dead things. Oh, don't worry. I didn't kill any of them. I tucked them into a jar and preserved them with some formaldehyde."

Rand managed to get an "uh hunh" past his gaping jaw. Will merely gawked.

Seated in the Subaru, without it turned on, after minutes of meditation on the strange man they had met, Rand, in the driver's seat, said, "Wow." It was all he could manage. He felt as if he had just met some wild sage who contemplated the scriptures of the world found in every atom of the Great Existence and had come down from the mountains to enlighten lesser mortals.

"Yeah." Will stared at the textured plastic of the dashboard ahead of him.

"You don't want to, you know . . ." Rand shaped his hand like a gun.

"Absolutely not."

"Good. Weird guy. Probably off his nut is what other people would say."

"Yeah."

"I liked him a lot."

"Me too."

Rand drove. Will turned and pulled a book from the stack behind the passenger seat. Rand felt that he was alone again. Will always had a book in front of his face now, as if the world no longer mattered, as if their war no longer mattered. Why had he changed?

The book in front of Will's face was a deception, his mind was still in the Ace Hardware, face to face with that little professor. Could he make a full account of all he had done? Would he want to? He would be ashamed. Will glanced from his book. His eyes floated around, but he could not settle them anywhere. It was if he sought to look at something in particular but could not locate the object of his search. Eventually his eyes fell on the visor folded to the car ceiling, but that was not quite the sought-after-something either.

"Maybe we should do that," Rand said.

"What?" Will had no clue what he was referring to.

"Keep a full account of our war."

"No." Will shook his head vigorously.

"That was a fast answer. Why not?"

"If it ever fell into the hands of the police it would be used as evidence against us. Enough evidence to send us to the chair or the needle or whatever they do with you now."

"So what? I don't plan on being caught. I'm not going to go quietly." Rand slapped the steering wheel. "I'll take as many of them with me as I can, damn it."

Will's jaw hung. Was Rand insane? He blinked a few times and said, "Well, whatever. The other point to remember is that we've already missed out on a fair number of engagements. We can't go back and fully detail them now."

Rand, driving with one hand now, stroked his stubbly chin.

August 22, 2008

Rand checked the dash clock. It was time. He had been at the wheel five hours now, and it was time to shove Will behind the wheel. Will had stuck his nose into his latest book by Camus as soon as they got in this morning, and he had only spoken to read quotes that he thought were remarkable but which Rand thought were drivel. They had not engaged in any action in at least a week, maybe almost two. Rand began to think hard about it. When was the last time? There had been at least two attempts: that crazy little genius who collected everything around him, and then the mother with her three daughters that Rand would gladly have killed, but that was foiled by Will. Could it be three weeks then? Since they were in California? Could it really have been that long? Rand shook his head. Will still had his book in front of his face and didn't notice that shake of the head. They weren't doing anything to improve the world now. They were not educating people to be better, more thoughtful, and conscientious. They were not engaged in the action they agreed the world needed. Rand pulled off the interstate, slowed as they came down the off ramp, and pulled up at the stop sign. A car approached from the left, and he waited. Honk! In the rearview mirror was a big, white Lincoln Continental that filled Rand's entire view. The front grill was not visible because the bastard who drove that aircraft carrier of a car was so close to their tail end.

"Hey, check out this asshole." Rand jerked his thumb. Will turned and looked out the back window. Rand said, "He's close, isn't he?"

"So what? If he rear ends us it's his dime for the repairs." Will faced forward and shrugged.

"Yeah." Rand was still piqued.

Honk! The approaching car passed, and the way was clear. Rand turned right and immediately pulled into the gas station located there. The Lincoln bucked over the incline into the station too, whipped past Rand and Will, and skidded to a halt at a pump on a different island. "Can you believe that jerk?" Rand asked.

Will had his nose back in *The Rebel*. "Hm?"

"Never mind. Go back to your book." Will was so useless lately. Rand turned off the car. He checked his back pocket for his wallet then for his holster and sheath with his two weapons. Everything was there. "What's so great about that book anyway? What's Camus rebelling against anyway?"

"It's a treatise against political violence."

Rand looked to the opposite island. Out of the aircraft carrier car came a shiny cowboy of Texas with his immense straw hat, his tight jeans, a bollo tie, and aviator sunglasses. An oil man, maybe? He ambled to the pump and dug into his back pocket for an oversized leather wallet. Should he confront him? No, this was just not the time. Or was it? Will seemed to not be taking notice of anything right now.

Rand pulled the keys from the ignition. "Against, you said? What? You mean he thinks it's wrong to kill on account of political ideology?"

"Mm hm."

"If that's the case." Rand opened the car door. "Then what we're doing is wrong."

"That's his point of view."

"How can you read that?"

"If we bring others into dialogue and condemn them on the basis of their answers, then we ought to engage ourselves. Who knows that we may not run into someone who's read Camus and then where would we be? Besides, I liked the last book I read by him, *The Myth of Sysiphus*, which was against suicide."

"Well." That was just a word, a way to say something in reply. Rand put his ball cap on. "Put on your cover and go pay."

"Please, would be nice." Will laid aside his book after he dog eared a page.

"How about, please, now?" Rand got out. He should just clock Will once. The cowboy oil man with his giant hat set on what Rand now saw was a huge head, had started his gas. He strutted up to the garbage bin where there was also a small tankard that ought to hold a squeegee to clean windows, but the squeegee was gone so he stood and swiveled his big melon head to locate where the squeegee was. Rand opened the small metal door in the side of the car, unscrewed the gas cap, pulled the pump handle off its cradle, and plugged the nozzle into the receptacle. The sound of Will getting out of the car caused Rand to look his way. Will stepped out with his ball cap on. He went toward the store where he could pay the attendants. A voice rolled like a barrage across the station's lot.

"Well, hurry yourself up. I got a need for it too, and I can't wait on no donkey to get the deed done. You hear me?" The cowboy oil man stood with his fists on his hips. A little woman, middle aged, unattractive, and forty pounds overweight, scuttled around her mini-van, and swiped at the windows with the squeegee, while she cast flummoxed glances over both shoulders at the big, cowboy oil man. Rand saw the digital numbers on the gas pump display flash. He selected the grade and set the handle so that it filled on its own. He strolled to the garbage can on his island with its small tankard of soapy water and a squeegee. When he came to the side of it, he stopped. Already half way there was the cowboy oil man. Rand eyed him square in the face then reached and took the squeegee out.

Cowboy oil man stopped. "Hey. You gonna use that, boy?"

Rand gave the squeegee a shake that sent a splatter of excess water onto the ground like a thrown gauntlet, then he turned, went to the Subaru, and worked methodically on the windows. He heard a muttered curse but did not look again at the cowboy oil man. Will returned. As Will opened the car door, Rand asked, "What, no drinks?"

Will woke from his daydream. "Oh. Oops. I forgot. I had to go to the bathroom."

Rand stared at Will until he cowered and slipped inside the car. The pump shut off. Rand finished the windows. He went and recharged the squeegee with water from its tankard. He snuck a peek and saw that cowboy oil man now had the squeegee from the woman. Cowboy oil man scrubbed ferociously at the front windshield as if it was impossibly soiled and only his muscles could remove the insect carnage there. Rand cleaned the headlights. Then he plunked the squeegee into its murky tankard. He jiggled the pump nozzle so that no stray drops would fall on the pavement as he replaced the handle to its cradle. He screwed the cap back on and shut the fuel door. Cowboy oil man marched to the store.

Rand opened the car door. "You want anything?" He did not lean over and put his head inside. Instead, he stood tall and marked his target.

"Uh, a drink. Sounds childish, but a-"

"Chocolate milk?"

"Yeah."

Rand nodded. Sometimes he seemed older than Will. Will drank chocolate milk every day. He liked his sweet treats. "I'll be back. And it's your turn to drive when I do." He slammed the door.

Rand strode so fast, his body jerked with each heavy boot step. The middle aged woman in her mini-van pulled out and made for the highway. As soon as that mini-van left another mini-van took its place. The joint was hopping busy. Located only five miles from the Podunk town that the interstate bypassed probably way back in the fifties, this gas station was perhaps the one economic bright spot for the local inhabitants. The station was connected to a Taco Bell by a passage that had another hall which split at a right angle from it to allow for two large restrooms, one for men and one for women. All this was visible through the front windows. There were two islands with three gas pumps on each. Every time a car left, a new one took its place. It was a hot, sunny day, and everyone seemed to go inside for a drink.

As cowboy oil man entered the convenience store, he shouldered his way straight through a teenage boy with pimples that must be what Will looked like when he was that age. The kid's face was dead shocked. Nor did cowboy oil man hold the door for the mother and young girl who tried to come inside behind him. Cowboy oil man did not apologize to any of them. Rand held the door as the mother and girl went inside. Next, he went to the bank of refrigerator doors and found the chocolate milk for Will and an OJ for himself.

Cowboy oil man cut in front of yet another middle aged woman as she went toward the coffee. He filled a large paper cup, stood there with his hand still on the pot so that no one else could take it, gulped half the coffee down, and then refilled it. Finally, he strode away, and the nasty look of that woman was lost in the air behind him because he did not acknowledge her existence. Rand noticed that cowboy oil man's eyes only rested on his objective and nothing else. When he had come inside to get his cup of coffee, his eyes located the drink station and the pot on its warmer but ignored everything else. Now that he obtained his coffee, his eyes were set on the cashier so that he could pay. Rand easily found in his vocabulary the one word definition for this man, solipsist. Even over the noise of the other customers, the electric beeping that came from behind the registers, the talking, and the intermittent roars and purrs and growls of car engines that swept inside with each entrance and exit that the doors yielded to,

Rand heard cowboy oil man's snake skin, cowboy boot heels attempt to stamp his mark on every inch of the world that he trod. How could the linoleum in here resist his impressions?

Cowboy oil man approached the queue at the counter, bypassed his rightful place at the end, and strode on up to the front. "Here." Cowboy oil man flung a worn dollar bill at the cashier. "Keep the change."

"Hey, what the-" said the cashier, a pimply girl with a watermelon for a pregnant belly, as she spread her arms to request the attention of others to his disrespectful behavior. Cowboy oil man marched through the store to the corridor that ran along the front of the building, and turned into the hall for the restrooms.

Rand paid for his drinks and asked for a plastic bag to hold the two bottles. This man was abominable, as bad as those wenches back in Hollywood that he and Will had missed. The world was clotted by the misery a man like this spread to others. No one would miss him, especially none that had met him today. They all could have been saved from being irked by him today if he never existed. Maybe rudeness was only the tip of the iceberg for this guy, like a symptom of far larger moral depravities. And could he account for it in any way? Most likely not. His rude behavior was reflexive, thoughtless, much like the hard manner in which he dug his heels into the world. One less asshole could only make the world a better place. Rand loathed this man. It was a moral imperative to kill him. Oh, so justified. Rand turned into the hall with the restrooms. At the door he checked for anyone following him. He entered.

As Rand went in, there were the faint smells of urine and flatulence. There was a small wall that he moved along to the left, around its corner to the right, and here was the restroom in full: two sinks, cowboy oil man's cup of coffee on the counter between the sinks, three urinals, and two stalls. Cowboy oil man leaned into the first urinal with a wide stance. Rand moved forward, crouched, and crab walked to see beneath the stall walls, saw no other feet, and straightened. As he passed behind cowboy oil man, he said, "You're quite the asshole."

Rand drew his survival knife from the sheath and tapped each of the stall doors open just to make sure there was no seven or eight year old boy sitting in there with his legs straight, balanced over the wide hole of the toilet seat while he did his business. There was not.

"What in the hell did you say, boy?" Cowboy oil man's voice boomed. He was overloud. How did he get to be like this?

Rand doubled back. "I'm curious to know how you square your behavior with your conscience, you know, how you're such a jerk to perfect strangers." He kept his eyes on cowboy oil man's broad back.

"You snot nosed boy, I don't take no bull from no one." He began to shake his prick to be rid of any late drops of urine.

"You done?" Rand came to a halt an arm's length directly behind cowboy oil man, who had the young man by almost half a foot of height.

"You just wait. I'm going to deal you out an ass whoopin' you'll never forget." Zip. He spun about with his dukes up.

Rand stabbed the blade into the sternum clear to the hilt, while his left forearm came across cowboy oil man's throat. With all his strength, he shoved cowboy oil man into the urinal. Eyes widened in recognition, pain, fear, and desperation. Rand twisted the blade and peered into those shocked eyes that ranged out from the shivering flesh as if they might lunge at him in a counterattack. For a long moment they hung suspended, before Rand felt the tremble in cowboy oil man's body. Rand whipped free the blade, stepped back, shifted his arm, reset his hand a few inches above the bleeding wound, and then rammed the knife into the throat where it bit and scraped the vertebrae and crunched to a halt. A strange rattle shuddered past cowboy oil man's lips. Then the dead man dropped and took the knife and Rand with him to the floor. Rand managed to catch himself with both hands before he landed on top of the dead man and the incriminating, staining blood of the wounds.

Get up. Get the knife. Get out. Rand obeyed, though he paused to wipe the blood from his blade on the jeans of the body. He sheathed the knife as he raced out. At the door he decided that he needed time to get to the car, start it, and leave. Put cowboy oil man in a stall, lock the stall door, and no one will notice he's dead at least for a little longer. Rand went to the body. He staggered as he drug the huge, inert form by the hands. He meant to take him to the farther stall, but the effort to get the body to the first stall had him huffing and grunting. "To hell with it." Rand struggled to turn the body. He wobbled. He maneuvered the giant lug into the first stall. Rand had thought before that cowboy oil man was figuratively a big asshole, but now he realized how huge he was. The body must be two hundred and fifty pounds. He worked his way along the arms to raise the upper body so that he could get him on the toilet. With his arms under the arms of the body, making sure to avoid the blood, he locked his hands behind the head, and he tugged him up onto the toilet. Luckily, there was not a lot of blood. The front of the shirt was crimson, but blood did not gush. He was sweating. With his sleeve, he wiped his forehead. Hopefully, no one will come in now. The worst thing might be that someone who comes in would see two sets of legs and assume that there were queers in the stall. Just so long as they did not guess the truth.

As he came back for the drinks, he remembered that he needed to leave a message. He stood still. He had to hurry. The longer he stayed, the sooner he would be discovered. Cowboy oil man's coffee cup sat on the counter too. Rand dug in his pockets and, luckily, found a pen. He scribbled on it, not a question to cowboy oil man—since he had not really asked one—but the philosophical issue. He wrote as succinctly as he could.

Half an hour later, Rand said, "God damn, the more we drive the quieter you get." Rand finished off his second sandwich.

"You're hungry."

"Oh, yeah." Rand twisted and dug in the back floorboards. The iron taste of the adrenaline was gone finally. "So?"

"So what?"

"So why are you so quiet?" Rand turned back around with the mostly eaten box of doughnuts that remained from breakfast. He flipped it open and selected one of the two chocolate doughnuts. More than half of the doughnut disappeared in the first bite. Will drove, his eyes ever on the alert as they roamed from rearview mirror, out the windshield, to the driver's side mirror, to the front again, and back to the rearview mirror, and so on, over and over.

"You know, we used to have some hellacious talks in the beginning of our war. Now it seems like I can't get you to say anything at all. So what's up with that?" Rand finished the doughnut.

"I've just been thinking a lot."

"No kidding?" Rand stared at the last doughnut as he weighed his belly. "So tell me what about."

"What's our victory?"

"Hunh?"

Will scowled and his eyes settled just on the road ahead. "How do we know if we win? I mean I know that our immediate objectives are to make the world a better place by teaching everyone to seriously think about life, you know, all the big questions, but we can't just keep going indefinitely. How many is enough? What if no one even knows?"

"What do you mean, what if no one knows?" Rand tossed the doughnut box in the backseat.

"What if the police never release the notes with our questions on them?"

Rand scowled and covered his mouth with one hand. What if?

"How do we know if we're teaching anyone anything because the cops are sitting on the notes?" Will said it a different way.

"Shit." Rand knew that Will was right. "The letter went to the papers though. We saw that in print."

"Yeah, but without the questions to go with the letter, it doesn't make much sense."

Rand's appetite was gone. What now? How could they win? How could they make the world better? He did not have these answers.

August 23, 2008

The door to the men's restroom was blocked open, and there was yellow police tape across the frame in an X at shoulder height. Christopher stooped beneath and entered. Behind him came the town's police chief, a thirty seven year old woman who had just had her first kid a few months earlier. Christopher stopped well away from the bloody drag marks and waited for her. The area had not been cleaned since the murder yesterday and the reek of urine and flatulence was potent.

The police chief huffed when she came up beside him. "Phew. Does it always stink like this in the men's john?"

"I guess some guys aren't very tidy." Small smears of blood on the floor denoted where the victim was drug. Christopher stood astride the trail. "So what's the story?"

"Well, the old boy was standin' in the nearest of the two stalls when the perpetrator attacked."

"He was stabbed."

"That's correct. A thrust to the sternum that cut the heart nearly in half, and then a second to the throat. He was dead 'ere he hit the tile." She paused and glanced at Christopher to see how he was taking it all. "The ME that come from the state office said he had bruisin' across his throat, as if the perp done laid his arm there and held him as he stabbed the heart. Also there was some bruisin', on the old boy's back, the impressions of which match up with the urinal's shape."

"How come you had the state's ME look at him?"

"We got a funeral director in our town only. Our town only has natural deaths save for whenever a hunter or rancher comes across a wetback out in the hinterland."

Christopher ground his teeth at the racial slur. "Then the vic was drug to that first stall," he said to hurry this interview along.

"Yep, he was then propped onto the commode and left. The perpetrator closed and locked the stall door so it wasn't until late in the afternoon that one of the employees found the body when he came to give the john a cleanin'."

Christopher stepped close to the wall to again avoid the bloody smears. "No one thought the blood was unusual?"

The police chief had not moved. "Well, it seems the restroom gets a mopping every four hours, and, as it happens, it was done only minutes 'afore the attack occurred at high noon."

"Dumb luck."

"Yep."

"And worse luck that no one interrupted the murder."

"Might a proven fatal if someone had."

"I guess. Does this place have cameras?"

"Not the restrooms. No, sir. That's indecent."

Christopher turned from his contemplation of the empty stall where a small pool of blood sat dull and dried on the gray tile to look at the police chief's disgusted face. Did she really believe that was what he meant? Cameras in the restroom? She probably thought that he was some perverted city nigger, he decided. "No," he said with force enough to make her flinch and blink. "I meant in the store proper. And also out by the islands. I want to know if we can find the vehicle that the killers drove."

"Killers? I told you that it was but one man."

"How do you know it was only one?"

"There was only two sets of prints on the cup."

"The cup?"

"The old boy brung his coffee cup in here. Then the perpetrator wrote his note on it."

"Wait. The note was taped to the cup?"

"Not taped. Written straight on it." She dug her fists into her waist above her belt.

"No index card? There wasn't a philosophical question written on an index card?"

"No. Were you expectin' for there to be one?"

"Where's the cup?"

"You want to see it?"

"The handwriting. I need to have the handwriting analyzed and compared to the other notes."

"Just how many other are we speakin' of now?"

"Seems like more every other day."

"And you b'lieve there's more than one of 'em."

Christopher came away from the stall and stopped by the police chief. She was tall for a woman, pushing five feet nine, but he still had a few inches to look down on her from. She held her turf and her authoritative stance, her fists still above her thick, black belt, the kind Christopher was glad as an FBI agent to never wear. She was the kind of woman usually called a bitch by men because she would not put up with crap from men. Instead of respect, she probably earned derision. Christopher understood that only too well. He held up two fingers to enforce his belief that there were two killers though. "I need to see all the videos. Was the cup from here?"

"Yep. He purchased a large cup of coffee 'ere he came to his end in here."

Christopher took a step then stopped. "What was written on the cup?"

"I was wonderin' when you'd ask." She grinned as if she felt superior to him. "It read, 'This man could not explain why he was an asshole to everyone.' End quote." Christopher nodded and the police chief followed suit. "'Magine bein' called to account like that, while you're peein'. I wonder if the old boy knew that the Maker's judgment had come for him."

Hadn't he heard that recently, or something similar, Christopher wondered.

The police chief took him to the back office. The manager was none too happy when Christopher demanded to watch the videos and then told the police chief to escort him from his own office. As the police chief guided the manager by one arm, she tried to console the peevish, bald man, but, when they turned the corner, Christopher heard the manager mutter, "Who's he think he is anyway? The damned nigger." Christopher did not hear the chief's response. He rolled his head around two times clockwise. Let it go. Yes, maybe, but people won't change unless they are shown how wrong they are. Maybe. A young, local cop was seated in a chair at the table where two TVs and an equal number of VHS players were arranged. The cop looked scandalized, scared, and uncertain.

"They don't have DVD?" asked Christopher.

"No, sir."

Christopher pointed at the TVs. "Has anyone watched any of this?"

"I dunno. I don't believe so."

Christopher nodded. That police chief did not know what to do because, as she had said, she had never had murders in her town. So, of course, no one had watched the video. "How many cameras?"

Christopher and the officer pored through the videos. It seemed to take forever. The longer they took, the farther off their quarry had moved. A license plate, a clear image of a face, these were all they needed to corner these men. It was the difference between saving lives and losing more lives. And yet, for a small town service station set by the interstate, the place was hopping busy. Within the half hour of time, fifteen minutes before the murder and fifteen minutes after the murder, Christopher felt they should only have seen a few cars with a few young men, but they saw dozens. Thankfully, the officer knew several of them as locals. Any local could be eliminated because they had not traveled the distances to kill in Seattle or Oregon without being missed by the townspeople. And then he caught him. A young man checked out at the counter three back from the victim. He wore a ball cap which obscured this face from the camera, not accidentally. He glanced over his shoulders in the direction of the victim who by now had to be going toward the men's room and his doom. The young man paid cash. He turned and went toward the men's room also. Several minutes later, he walked out to a Subaru. As he stood in the passenger door, one foot inside, the young man surveyed the station. Christopher understood. The young man was asking himself whether anyone was following him or staring at him. It was a look to insure that the coast was clear. He hopped in and pulled the car forward. "Slow that down," Christopher directed the officer. There it was. The license plate was from California. The numbers were clear. "Can you get me a shopping bag? All these video tapes are evidence."

"Yes, sir," the officer said. "We got him, don't we?"

Christopher stared at the license plate, a small doubt spreading like a pool of blood: what if they swapped license plates regularly?

September 1, 2008

Will set down his copy of *Walden*. He gazed out the window at the woods and mountains that whipped past at fifty five miles an hour. "I could stop right here." They were in the Rocky Mountains of Colorado. "I could hop out of this car, shoulder my pack, and just roam out into that wilderness. That's what I want right now." He dripped his fingers across the warm glass. The tall, deep ranked, fir trees closed around the road, and they drove on in shadow.

"That's what you want?" Rand's hands flexed on the wheel. He seemed to always be the driver now. He was a soldier in a glorious war and Will seemed to be nothing but a burden, some malnourished orphan, too weak to walk, that Rand had to lug around on his back, when he could be rushing into combat and carrying the battle to the enemy.

Will saw between the trunks the spaces where pine needles were woven into brown mats. "It would be nice to disappear out into that. I bet that forest floor is soft to walk on. Even to sleep on, that would be a great place to unroll my sleeping bag. It just, you know, it looks like Heaven to me. Maybe I could find a place back in the mountains and passes, just off from a stream where I could get fresh water. Maybe I could plant some crops to feed myself. I'd build a log cabin. I could hunt deer or smaller game. And I could fish. I'd have to have some provisions to see me through to the harvest, of course, but eventually I might be able to gain self-sufficiency."

"Why?"

"What?"

"Why in the hell would you want to live like that? The simplicity of it?"

"I guess I'm tired."

"Tired?" Rand thumped the dash with the heel of his hand. "How the fuck can you be tired? All you do now is sit there and read. Maybe you drive a couple of hours, but, as soon as you can, you jump back over here to read."

"I'm sorry. I just . . . I don't know what it is, but I . . . I'm tired. That's the only way I know how to say it. I felt this way after I came back from being deployed."

"Tired? That's all it is? So go to fucking sleep."

Will sighed and looked at the dark comfort of the woods where he could disappear. "It's not sleep that I need."

"So what? You want to quit? What about our war? What about your need to change the world and make it a better place? Have you forgotten that? Are you giving up on that?"

"No," Will whispered. "But I don't know if . . ."

"If what? What do you think you can do? Just walk away from this?" Rand unconsciously sped up. Sixty miles an hour. "This was your idea too."

"No, it was yours."

"And you trained me."

"I don't think I thought it through."

"And you came up with how to do it and what we would need to do it. The equipment, the supplies, and the vehicle." Sixty five miles an hour.

Will's head shook. "It seems so long ago." His head hung on the weak stalk of his neck. "It seems like another person who said those things, who did those things."

"Well, it fucking wasn't a different person. It was you." They hit seventy and the tires squealed as they tried to make a curve, but they still went into the dirt and gravel along the roadside. Will's head snapped up. The trees loomed near Will's window. The trunks were so solid and deadly.

"Slow the fuck down. You're going to kill us!" Will's hands braced against the dash and the roof.

"Here." Rand stomped both feet on the brake. The car slid. Its tail end drifted to the right. One of the back tires bit into the loose earth and stones by the road.

Will ground his teeth. His eyes rounded into white globes with only small continents of color in their centers. "Oh, shit," Will cried out.

Rand straightened the vehicle as it screamed to a halt. The noise of the tires was like the anguish of a violent death. Will jerked as the momentum of the car died. "You want to be done," Rand said. "Then get out." He pointed to the trees. "Get your stuff and get out.

We'll see how long you make it." Rand glared at Will, who still sat with his arms braced for impact. "Go. Get the fuck out. You're done." When Will still had not moved, Rand jammed the shifter into park, ripped off his seat belt and leaped out. Will's arms relaxed, but his breathing was hard and quick with fear and adrenaline. He heard the back hatch open and the rustles and flumps as Rand yanked out Will's backpack and threw it to the ground. Will twisted so that he could see the side of the road where his backpack already lay followed in quick succession by his fishing rod, one of the two crates of food, and his sleeping bag. The hatch slammed. The rear passenger door opened. Will's books flew. They landed like dead birds in the dust. That car door whammed shut. Rand flung open Will's door.

"You're out. You want out, so get out," Rand said. He stood there, with fists on his hips and his feet apart. His expression was one of clenched rage and poised authoritarianism.

Will unbuckled his seatbelt. He stepped out, moved towards his few forlorn possessions that lay chucked into the dust, stones, and pine needles along this no name road in the wilderness of the nation he had fought to protect, its power to project, and its way of life to extend or share. The car door bammed shut behind him. By the time Will pivoted in his steps, Rand was around the front of the car. Rand got in without a glance in Will's direction. The Subaru had been idling this whole time, and Rand shoved it into gear and kicked the accelerator to the floor. The tires squalled and the Subaru jumped away. Within seconds, Rand was gone down the road and out of sight around a bend.

Rand was only a mile down the road when he removed his foot from the accelerator and allowed the Subaru to coast. "A body in rest or motion will stay in rest or motion until acted upon by another force." Rand repeated Sir Isaac's law in his head as he watched the speedometer's orange arm glide counter clockwise. Forty, thirty five, thirty, twenty five, twenty, fifteen. He steered as Newton's law whispered to him a third time. What was he doing? Where was his head? Will deserved to be left behind. What kind of action had they done in the last month? They had lost the initiative. They were not yet in a position of defense, but that would be next unless they took the battle to their enemy. Ten, five, stop. The Subaru idled in the right hand lane. He sat there with his hands still on the nine and three o'clock positions of the steering wheel. Could he really do this on his own? He could hardly drive the distances necessary to evade the police after he made an attack. He needed another set of eyes when he was selecting which enemy to strike and another mind to cross examine the thoroughness of the philosophy. Two minds are better than one to steer clear of cul de sacs. Yes, of course, two minds are better.

Rand looked behind him on the road. No cars, no one. He pulled the car into a three point U-turn. He would get Will. If Will didn't want to do the heavy work, well, he could still be of use for the logistics and planning of engagements. Rand raced up to fifty five miles an hour. He would see Will any moment. Maybe he would just be standing there by the shoulder of the road, or he might be gathering his books from the dirt. Rand shouldn't have just tossed them into the dirt like that. Books are perhaps the greatest invention of human kind and should be treated with great respect. Why had Rand felt the need to pitch Will's books into the dust like that? No, that wasn't right of Rand. He had been furious at Will for that crazy talk about living like a hermit in the mountains, but throwing all his possessions into a heap on the side of the road was unforgivable. Why would he want to do that when they had the opportunity to do such momentous acts that would alter the course of human history?

Rand screeched to a halt. There, much as he had thrown it out, were Will's belongings without Will. Rand again did a three point U-turn and pulled the car over just ahead of Will's possessions. He switched off the car and jumped out. Where was Will? Rand glanced at the Subaru as if he expected to discover his friend had never been out of the car at all. No, Will was not in the car. Rand stepped among the pines and firs to glance around the red and brown trunks. Where the hell was he? Rand's heart revved.

The trees stood tall, cut shadows this way and that. The sun snuck through the branches and illuminated slices of the forest in irregular patterns. He needed Will. He could not have gone that far. Rand had driven only a mile or so just now and then come right back. He slalomed between the red brown trunks. He used his hands and arms to guide him as if he was blind, but, no, he saw the world as nothing because he sought some sign of his only friend, his comrade in arms, the man he had gone to war with, shared a tent with, swapped all his aspirations with and memories with, like that time when he was twelve and asked Jenny Haversack to show him hers and here was his and for days after no matter where he was at school or in his room or at the store with his parents it was all he saw all he desired to see and to place his hand or his penis on because the latter became painfully engorged when he thought about Jenny and that curious cleft in Jenny's body that had a wild puff of gold hair that matched the color of her hair on top of her head, and, now, his heart went chaotic and rumbled like an earthquake because he needed this man, Will, in his life more than anyone, more so than even a girl, his parents, his entire family, even his cousin Turner who taught him how to use a bow and arrow when they went sneaking through the fields out behind Turner's house in Ohio where there grew crops higher than their heads and they crouched among the tall stems or stalks of whatever it was that grew and devised a system of hand signals to communicate silently as they set ambushes on animals and family members like Uncle Fred, and, now, he sprinted and shouldered past the trunks of the pines, and their pungent scent was all he inhaled like the menthol of the vapor rub his mom caressed onto his chest when his sinuses pulsed and closed tight so that his nose felt like a heart laid on his face to smother him and he gasped for air and gazed at his mom who sat on the edge of his bed in a silk robe that she wore at night and he wondered if she was naked beneath but that was wrong to ponder and he wondered if his dad touched his mom at night while they lay under the sheets and that was confusing and troubling to consider and did he take her robe off and make her naked, and, now, he caught sight of a movement that must be Will. There to the right maybe seventy yards away was Will as he hoofed his way into the wilderness with anger and resentment and bitterness at Rand, who had screwed up. He pounded his way up to Will who refused to stop and turn and face Rand.

"Stop, damn it."

Will stopped but he did not turn. "I can't . . . not anymore . . . I feel so tired."

Rand caught up, and he came to Will's side so that he saw his face. "You still having dreams?"

"Every night."

Rand put his hands on his knees and panted. They had not had much chance to work out since they departed for their war, and Rand had never felt so out of breath from a few hundred yards of running before. After a moment, he straightened and said, "You just need a break. That's all. We've been pushing hard now for weeks, driving everywhere, and . . . you know." He waved a hand around to indicate the speed and motion of time. "And that leads to a wallop of stress."

"You seem fine." Will shook his head, and Rand was unsure if that was to admonish him or if it was to admire him. "I felt this way at the end of my rotation in Afghan. I'm just so thin."

"Just a break, like a leave, that's all you need." Rand laid a hand on his friend's shoulder, but Will's side that he touched seemed to collapse like a sand castle. Will staggered. He almost dropped to the ground, and Rand reached for him in alarm. "Come on. We better get back to the car before a highway patrol or sheriff spots it and thinks that it's abandoned. We'll get in the car and go to a camping ground. We'll pitch our tent, hike around, do some fishing, and just kick back for a few days." Rand came and put an arm around Will. He turned him around and began to escort him back to the Subaru. "With a few days of R and R, you'll be ready for action again. Hey, I need it, too. What kind of fish do you think they have in the rivers up here? Perch? Maybe they stock trout? You know, fresh is the best way to eat fish." Rand laughed and slapped his head. "God damn, who am I to say that to you? You taught me that. It'll be like old times, bro. Remember how often we went camping, and we would fish up on Mount Lemmon? Those were some of the best times we had back in college. That and attending Dr. Sherry's philosophy classes. Do you remember those? We always left his lectures just loaded with new ideas. Talked all the way home." Rand kept talking as he led Will to the Subaru. No snooping police were there. They reloaded Will's possessions, got in, and drove. Will sat with his head propped against the door glass, his face turned away from Rand. Will's mouth hung from his head like a dead leaf on a branch. It was an hour later that Rand spied a sign that directed them to a campsite. A quarter of an hour more and Rand turned the car off. He expected Will to leap out and begin to rush about in excitement like a dog unleashed to sniff and pant and wag its tail in rapture at the freedom of its natural habitat. Will did not budge. Rand stared. Was Will an acute case? But an acute case of what?

"I'm going to pitch our tent." Rand got out of the car. After he shut the door and took a step, he bent over to see if Will had flinched. Will looked to be in the same spot. Rand went around back and popped the back hatch. He took out the tent, found a nice, level, patch of ground, and pitched the tent. It took him about ten minutes to erect the tent. Will was slumped in the front seat. Only when Rand came to the car to bring out the sleeping bags did he see that Will's eyes were shut. Asleep? That's what he needed. Sleep. He'll be fine tomorrow. Rand felt reassured.

Over the next several days, Will wandered about in the woods. He gazed at the height of the trees as if it was unusual that the firs should extend so high over him. He stripped and bathed in the freezing stream that ran not twenty five yards from their camp. To Rand that was insane. At night, Will sat mesmerized by the protean flames of their campfire. Rand observed from a distance all Will did. Was his friend suffering from Post-Traumatic Stress Disorder? When Rand had paid attention to the media that was what all the newspapers, books, and TV commentators had spoken of when they referred to vets from Iraq and Afghanistan. Why was Will suffering from it now? Was their own war bringing up old war memories, like that time with the three ragheads that Will shot during the firefight? That must be it. Maybe that memory was triggered by the firefight with the five gangbangers. Rand recalled that it was after that engagement that Will changed and became withdrawn, unfocused. Rand slept lightly, aware of Will's every move. Every night Will woke with a jerk and his arms waved in front of him. It would be after only four hours of sleep. After, Will rose and went to the campfire, which he stoked back to life with an additional log so that it rose like orange and red ghosts engaged in a fresh melee. To compensate for the loss of sleep at night, after lunches, Will laid in the grass under the shade of the firs and slept two hours.

The first two days there, Rand was okay. He busied himself with preventative maintenance on the Subaru. He changed the oil and oil filter. He pulled all the spark plugs to measure the gaps and ensure that none had oil, carbon scoring, or any other mark of decreased performance. He tested the tension on the belts and felt along each for any cracks that might lead to a break. There were none. Carefully, he pried open the battery to check the water level. Anything that he knew how to do, he did on the vehicle. The Subaru was solid. Comforted, he turned to their weapons. He stripped down his and Will's pistols and cleaned them both.

By the third day Rand was antsy. He was unable to sit for long. He paced around their camp. Will wandered and hiked. How long would this take? Rand wanted to get back into action. He put his feet into action, marched in as straight a line as he could. He scaled a ridge. At the crest, he stopped at the sight of a camp of five vehicles with more than twenty people. The campers were enticing targets as they bumbled about trying to show how they had fun in Nature, but how could you do that if you could not deal with what was serious? It seemed no one had heard of the Plato Warriors and their interrogations and judgments, their executions. What had been the purpose of their manifesto? Didn't people read the papers? Had it not been published? No, it must have been published. If it was published then it had to have been read. Was it comprehended? Was it debated? Did it inspire? Did it cause reactionary accusations of a lack of grounding in the basics of reason and logic? Apparently not. Here were two dozen people who seemed oblivious to the doings of great men. What if he descended the ridge to their camp, went to them and posed his questions? What would be the point? He sagged against an aspen's white trunk.

He shaped his fingers like a pistol and took aim. His pistol beckoned from his holster. Not here, he could not shoot them from here. The range, about a hundred yards, was too much. A thin, young blonde in a tank top and short shorts was his first target. He dropped his thumb-hammer, and he made a sound as similar to a shot as he could. In his mind she flew as if the giant hand of a god flicked her into the air and she flopped to the ground yards from where she had stood. He sniggered at the macabre film in his head. The campers worked to pitch tents, kindle fires, and unload camper trailers and pickups and SUVs. They were so small and insignificant, but it was people like them that determined so much about the world. They were the economy and government, the consumers and producers, the voters and PTA. He tracked individuals among them as they skittered one way and then another. He trained his "gun" on a man, the alpha male of the group, big and broad. He blew him away. Rand zealously picked off each camper. They were pathetic. A single splinter of fast travelling metal could stop them from moving, breathing, feeling, and thinking. How pathetic humans were. Back up a mile or two and they look smaller than ants at your feet. If he removed himself by just a hundred miles, humans might as well not exist. They were as valuable and potent as microbes. Except that microbes killed humans. And humans could wipe out the earth. Rand was down to just the children. He aimed his "gun" at them too, one by worthless one. If Rand was on the moon and searched for people, he would see absolutely nothing of them. And if humans destroyed all life, it would be without any importance. That was as far as you had to go, just to the moon, and all human endeavors failed to even show a sign of their passing. Rand's hands dropped to his lap. Was anything worth it? Was his war to educate and better the world, his war that had drawn blood for its cause, meaningless? When all you had to do was go to the moon to make all philosophy, history, art, and life absolutely trivial, then why should he carry on?

Rand crouched by the aspen as the breeze set the leaves to whisper like conspirators and judges, and the branches agitated each other like kindling worked by persistent hands. He observed the wordless antics of the players below on that stage of a camping ground. Why not kill them all? It was foolish of him to even think and believe that he could change humans for the better by debating with them, teaching them, and eliminating those who could not become better. Fool's gold! How idiotic he was. Youthful naiveté? You bet. He had been gung ho because he did not know better. He was green, and this led him on a fool's errand. It was time to make a course correction. If a rocket to the moon was all that was necessary to accomplish this goal, then that would be the next stage in the war?

As Rand headed back to camp, he got lost. He stopped and looked around at the forest. Rand missed the angles and lines, the grids and precision of cities, roads, and buildings. Damn it. Where was he? Where was Will? Rand thought of how Will slunk back into camp the night before, and he acted more like a feral dog who did not understand the flames from the fire that crackled and shook and twined around themselves. Will had regressed to an animal state.

That night, beside the campfire, where a can of beans warmed, a pan with rice boiled, a nice trout lay in the barbecue rack with Rand's foot keeping the handle positioned just right so that the contraption did not fall in the fire or in the dirt, Rand explained to Will that he would head to the nearest town for supplies in the morning. Will pined away at the fire. Rand detailed and listed what they were short on, like toilet paper. "I sure don't want to wipe my ass with leaves." Rand grinned at Will, but his friend's jaw was slack. Rand wanted to deck him into awareness.

In the morning Rand drove the Subaru to the nearest town and pulled up to the local store, a sort of mom and pop run operation with the log cabin exterior that made it seem old fashioned. Inside there were fluorescent tube lights spanning the ceiling and banks of reach-in refrigerators for both frozen food and chilled drinks, particularly beer, which thus ended the illusion of the good old western days. As he gathered their necessities into a hand basket he overheard the proprietor speaking to a woman who had a New York accent.

"I want nova and half a dozen fresh bagels, preferably multi grain," she said.

"We haven't fresh baked bagels, and I don't know what the other thing you want even is."

"Nova? You don't know what nova is?"

There was no verbal response from the man. Perhaps he shrugged or shook his head. An aggravated groan now erupted from the woman. "Is there a bagelry in this town?"

"No, ma'am."

"What? Are you kidding me? Don't you have anything in this town?"

Rand continued his shopping. The woman's voice was high pitched and nasal, a caricature of a person, unreal. What did she expect? Everything in Colorado had to be just like on Long Island or Manhattan? Yes, she did expect that. How inconsiderate of the world to be not like where she came from.

As he turned the corner and entered the next aisle, he found the woman and the poor, struggling proprietor—he looked the part of the man whose kingdom this was, with his gray hair, flannel shirt, jeans, and a short apron, pine colored with the name of the store stitched in white on the bottom right corner. The woman could only have been more alien to him and his ideals of customer/storekeeper relations if her head had split down the middle to reveal a miniature, mad scientist at the controls of his woman robot. She wore black high heel boots that shined brightly beneath the modern lights, black stretch pants, a leopard print coat, a black head band that shoved back a blast of black, curly hair, a purple top with a scoop neck that had her surgically lifted and amplified bust displayed in its middle aged, slack skinned glory, along with a Joker's mask of cosmetics and Botox. Rand guffawed.

Rand ambled to the counter where the single register was, set his basket there, and began to whistle "The End" by the Doors loud enough to cut into the woman's harangue. Both sets of eyes turned to Rand, who smiled as he whistled the words of Jim Morrison. This is the end, my only friend, the end. The store owner nodded and begged his pardon to the lady. He was bow legged, and he sawed his way behind the counter to the register. Rand winked at the woman. He wanted to freak her out. She blinked and whipped her head about. She stood there, though Rand could not figure out why. The proprietor tallied his items and announced the sum as he tapped it out on his register as if Rand might dispute the cost. Rand paid with cash. As he left the store with his two paper bags of groceries, the woman began to interrogate the man about sprouts, shallots, and beluga caviar. Could she really be that dense? None of those things would be in the regular diet of most people even in NYC, not to mention here in the Rocky Mountains.

Rand put the bags in the back of the Subaru. He would use his knife. He positioned himself at the front of her car, nonchalantly leaning against the wall of the store. When she came out, she stutter stepped with surprise at the sight of him. She was empty handed. He dared not look directly at her. His knife was in his right hand, the blade flat against his forearm. She beeped her car locks open and got in. Before she could begin to close the door he rushed the vehicle, blocked the door with his body, and slammed the knife in her throat and a second time in her chest just above those unmovable fake breasts.

September 6, 2008

Christopher and Sammy left her motel room. Like everything in this small town it was located on the state route, and Christopher had the sense that all he had to do was look left then right and he had seen all there was of the Colorado town. The antiseptic crispness of the pines was always in their noses. Sammy checked the pockets of her jeans and her coat. Christopher gave her a low pinch on her left butt cheek. She hopped, spun, and glared at him to implore him not to do that again, not in public anyway.

"What're you looking for?" he asked.

"I found it. Let's go."

It must've been the key she was looking for. They strode across the blacktop to a grocery store. It seemed that the proprietor knew who they were already. His eyes went to them and regarded their every move with hope, fear, and suspicion. The two agents pulled out notepads, pens, and a digital audio recorder. They interviewed the proprietor. Did he remember the deceased? Quite well, it turned out. And was there anyone here at the same time? Yes, a young man who paid for his groceries and left. He was quiet and kept to himself. Sammy held out the old artist's sketch. Yes, that looked somewhat like him. Did he and the lady talk? No. Did you notice if they spoke after she left? No, the proprietor didn't look outside. He was glad to be rid of her. She'd been something else. She kept asking for things he'd never heard of like "blue gel crab-R."

"What?" Christopher asked.

"Do you mean beluga caviar?" Sammy offered.

"Yes, that might have been it."

There was no scream, yell, or cussing to be heard. Three people in a single day even in a big city would be a lot of murders. Three people in this mountain town known only for hiking, motels, gas stations, and camping was like a holocaust. One lady in front of this general store, stabbed, and a couple shot while in their car, parked in their driveway, the engine on, their infant in the backseat. The eyes of the proprietor ducked around as if he feared the return of the killers any moment, every time the door opened. His teeth chattered off answers like long shivers brought on by the cold of death's proximity. Christopher did not sympathize. When you chase murderers for a living you forget that anyone can be frightened by something you consider habitual. The proprietor asked as many questions as he received. How much did the FBI know? How close were they to finding the killer? Why couldn't they catch him? Why had the killer chosen this mountain hamlet? How could anyone do this to a fellow human being? Who does the FBI suspect? It's not a local boy is it? No one here could do this, could they?

"What next?" Sammy asked as they stood on the torsional squares of the sidewalk beside a great, red barked fir tree. Christopher put his fists into the small of his back leaned his head to face the sky, and arched his spine. Crack, pop, crack went his vertebrae. She asked, "Was that your back?"

He exhaled. "Yes, it was."

A sheriff's cruiser came down the street. As soon as it was parallel to them, the brakes locked, there was a 'skirr' sound, and the vehicle careened over the curb and banged to a stop.

Through the passenger window, the local sheriff, Dean Buck, pointed his basketball head at them.

"Agents." Buck nodded.

"Sheriff." Both agents nodded in response.

"I'm taking a step that I feel is prudent and might yield results."

"And that is?" Christopher arched his eyebrows.

"We're going to throw up some revolving roadblocks around the county on all roads in and out."

"Roadblocks." Christopher twisted his mouth to one side in obvious doubt about the efficacy of such a step.

"That's right." To show that he didn't give a damn about Christopher's opinion of the idea, Sheriff Buck sat back in his seat and faced forward.

Christopher glanced at Sammy who gently nodded her head as if she was pragmatically approving such a course of action as the roadblocks. Christopher crossed the ten feet to the Sheriff's cruiser. "I'm not sure that's going to catch these guys. It's not their MO to lurk in one location. They kill and then they move on."

"Well, with all due respect I'd like to point out that five deaths in three days sounds like your boys changed their MO." Sheriff Buck fished out a box of toothpicks from his shirt pocket. He doled one out and clamped it securely between his middle teeth. "Assuming that you're correct about who the killers are."

"Five? When did it-"

"Ah, yes, you're not up to date. Well, you see, we just found victim numbers four and five. Two college students, a couple presumably, out in the woods. A hiker came across them. We've taken the bodies to the county seat where our ME's going to examine them. They'd been killed early this morning most likely. Riga hadn't quite taken charge of their bodies." The toothpick waggled about.

"Was there a note? If there was a note then that confirms that it was my guys."

Sammy was by Christopher's side.

"Of course, there was, though I didn't need a note to recognize a match on the two stab wounds to the boy's back, one to collapse each lung. The girl had managed to run a bit, but not far enough. Same kill stroke."

"What did the note read?" Christopher leaned an arm on the roof of the cruiser.

The toothpick came erect. "It read, 'They wouldn't join me, though they knew I was right.'"

"Notice the singular?" Sammy asked.

"Mm hm." Christopher drummed his fingers on the roof of the car and gazed at the red of the roof lights. Was she on his side or what? Of course, he noticed the singular pronoun. Had one of the men died? Had one of the killers quit? That murder at the gas station had been a few weeks ago. So much about Arlo Warren's death was different from so many of the preceding murders, from the use of a knife to the lack of a real philosophical question. The Plato Warriors had not used knives since their very first murder, the couple in the national park on July fourth. Why use knives now? To stay silent was the obvious answer, but that never seemed to be a concern before. The gun battle in the Portland, Oregon mall parking lot attested to their complete indifference to excessive noise. Why hadn't they cared before? Simply put, they wanted people to notice their actions. That was why it was out in the open and why they left their notecards. If you were nearby, you could also hear and witness the philosophical debates the Plato Warriors engaged in with their victims. So why the new found sense of secrecy? And then there was the plain fact that the notes left on the bodies were hastily scribbled statements about the poor behavior of the victims, as if the deceased were to blame for their demise on account of offenses they gave to their killer. Were the Plato Warriors out there anymore?

Christopher splayed his fingers across the warm roof of the cruiser and searched the narrow blacktop of the state route for clues. He said, "Do you have copies of the sketches to all your men in the field?" Christopher stepped back from the car and set his hands at his hips.

"They do."

"Maybe you're right."

"Say again?" The toothpick drooped and Sheriff Buck's face was soft with surprise.

"Either this is a copycat, or my killers have changed their MO, possibly because one of them is gone." Christopher shrugged.

"Are you staying on then?" Sheriff Buck's eyes narrowed their field to just Christopher's eyes. This was a hard man to please. Christopher doubted if he would ever hear praise from the Sheriff.

Christopher's eyes went to Sammy, who stood with her arms crossed. He'd like to wrap his arms around her while back in her motel room. "I'd like to accompany you to one of the roadblocks and help any way I can. I'm sure your force will be stretched thin by this all-out effort." He returned his gaze to Sheriff Buck.

Sheriff Buck's toothpick rose like a flagpole above his jutting chin. "Why don't you two get your vehicle and follow us out this way." He pointed the direction the cruiser ought to be pointed. "There's a T junction that I want to cover myself."

"Why?" Christopher dug his hands into his pockets for his keys.

"Just a hunch that if our killer's thought is to set up shop in this county, for whatever reason, that he might, if he's as smart as you two tell me, think to rove about between the various towns."

"And never strike the same place twice," Sammy said as she took the sunglasses that hung from the top button of her blouse and opened them.

"Precisely." Sheriff Buck jerked his thumb over his shoulder. The deputy in the driver's seat who had not uttered a peep throughout the exchange, pulled the steering column shifter to reverse and shot the cruiser into the street and the appropriate lane.

Before they went into drive, Christopher shouted, "What about the murders on the first day and how they all three happened here?"

Sheriff Buck raised a hand to halt the driver, who moved the shifter into drive anyway. "The two college kids were forty miles north of here."

"You think he's closest to this town though, don't you?"

Sheriff Buck touched the brim of his Sheriff's ball cap. "Come on out as soon as you can. It'll take you about ten minutes." He pointed forward, and the cruiser was gone.

Now aged forty nine, Sheriff Dean Buck became sheriff of this Colorado county when he was thirty one. In that span of time he was married and divorced twice. The second time, he liked to tell acquaintances, would forestall his ever stepping in the emotional quagmire of nuptials again. While he had been happy and settled in a conjugal bliss, neither of his wives were. Though Sherry and Rose could not be any different—the former was extroverted and relished any opportunity to hostess for sheriff department functions, while the latter was a willowy introvert who would rather knit and read a book— they both griped about his long hours, his silences that alternated with his sudden volubility when a case was solved or a lost hiker was found, and his desire to have his wife wait on him hand and foot in a chauvinistic throwback to the ideals, perhaps, of nineteenth century marriages. Dean would just assume return home at whatever time of day felt appropriate to the day's case load, have a good shot of schnapps—since he lived in the greatest mountain range of the Americas, he felt that his kin mountaineers of the Alps had invented and fermented the proper concoction to salve the soul of thin aired regions the world over long ago, and who was he to not imbibe of their spirit—and to reheat and eat some leftover victual from when he grilled meat on the weekends.

He had a child with each wife, and both girls now lived with their moms. Sherry was mother to Kimberly, and Rose was mother to Lily. Dean saw each girl twice a week, during the summers when they were out from school he made it three times. He felt proud of his abilities as a father. He always corrected improper behavior when he detected it, whether it was not saying "thank you" or "please" or slouching or when they mispronounced or misused a word. He was quite vigilant over his daughters. He spoiled them. Since he insisted that they earn A's and B's on their report cards, when they earned these marks—both girls excelled and received straight A's—he paid them money, took them out to dinner, and bought them something nice that they wanted, whether it was toys when they were younger or, now that one was a freshman in college and the other was in her last year of junior high, clothes. He frequently told them how proud he was of their accomplishments and how much he loved them. Dean kept in touch with both Sherry and Rose about his daughters. The divorces, though a shock to him, were amicable. Occasionally he was invited to dinner with one or the other ex and their daughter.

As Dean rode out to the state route junction, the site where he wanted to personally supervise a roadblock, he fretted over Kimberly as she was now at the University of Colorado in Boulder, beyond daily face to face contact. Was she okay? Was she eating properly? Was she partying like a rock star, as the kids liked to say now? Had she met boys? The right kind or the wrong? Was she lonely? Did she have friends? Were they good influences or bad? His tongue flicked the toothpick around in high pursuit of these worrisome questions. He and Sherry had raised her right hadn't they? He took the toothpick from his mouth. The end that had been in his mouth was soggy and split. He turned it in his hand, and worked at the intersections of his teeth.

"You all right, Sheriff?"

Dean turned to his deputy, Russell Claremont. "Do you think I'm wasting our time with this roadblock strategy?" He would not discuss his personal life with his men.

Russell scowled and shook his head. "No, sir. You've a real gift for knowing where to look for lost hikers, or stolen goods. And maybe we haven't had any murders that I recall, but I'm certain you have the instincts for that too."

Dean adjusted the bill of his cap to dry the sweat with the air from the open window. It was untrue that there had been no murders in the county. Four stuck out in Buck's memory. Two were what he thought of as dum-dum murders, husbands who killed their wives and were easily caught. Crimes of passion is what the papers called them, but really there was no passion to either man except rage and a sense that murder was the best way to resolve a dispute, and Sheriff Buck, who had divorced twice without resorting to strangling or stabbing either woman, had no sympathy for either man. The third was not much better, two business partners went hunting for deer and only one returned, who claimed that he had lost his partner. Maybe after he had put two thirty ought six slugs into his partner, he had lost track of where he had left the body. The fourth was an unsolved murder mystery that still bothered Buck. He inhaled the forest smells that were always purifying when he travelled fifty five miles an hour on the two lane blacktops of the county, but, which sometimes in the wrong places, could turn into a gut clenching stench from a pile of manure, garbage, or a decaying carcass. "Thanks for the compliment, but there was a couple murdered up here right after I was voted sheriff. Never did track that murderer down."

"Perhaps he wasn't from here?" Russell tapped the steering wheel, maybe to tick off the distance to that long sought murderer.

"I've suspected as much. It was just some drifter who took it in his head to kill them."

"Was the couple from here?"

Dean nodded. "Yep. The killer stole some electronics and jewelry, plus their wallets. Their murders always nag me when I think I'm feeling cozy about life. It's as if that one night when Michael and Angie Fleece lost their lives forever tainted my seeing the world as a good place."

Russell made no further comment either with words or by gesture. He braked as they came to the junction. A half hour later the roadblock was set. Dean had the two FBI agents on the straightaway of the T junction. He and Russell took the spur road. While three cars approached the FBI side of the roadblock, followed by two more, Russell and Dean stood and watched until a lone vehicle appeared and came down the road at about the speed limit.

"Here we go, Russ."

"Yes, sir. Glad to have something to do. Those Feds have been hogging all the fun for a bit now." He glanced over his shoulder at the continued presence of three cars, whose contents were being inspected.

"Mm hm." Dean squinted as the sun glinted on the windshield of the oncoming vehicle. What make was that? Could that be a Subaru? He though the emblem on the grill was the correct shape. If this was the guy, then they had the dumbest luck in all the world. "You do the talking, Russ. I want to hear that honey tongue of yours do a bit of work so you don't gripe anymore about this good peacefulness we've enjoyed while our Feds did all the grunt work." Dean nodded and stepped to the roadside where the lava rock crackled under his boots. He cast a look back to the line of vehicles that the two FBI agents were checking over. He snorted in amusement for the first time since their arrival. The FBI agents were doing something useful.

"Yes, sir." Russ positioned himself right on a yellow dash in the center of the road. He hooked his thumbs on either side of his belt buckle.

"Russ," Dean called.

"Sir?"

Dean's hand slipped along the side of his holster and came to rest on the pistol grips. Russ followed suit, his hand ran along his belt from the buckle to the pistol grip.

"You're locked and loaded, the safety off, right?"

For a moment, Russ's face went blank, then tightened. "Yes, sir."

"Good boy." Dean checked the distance to the vehicle and held up a hand to signal that the driver halt. Russ did likewise. "This might be our boy."

"It's a Subaru."

"Yes, it is."

"Oh, God."

"Keep your cool and don't take your eyes off that driver. I'll walk around and check inside the car. Hear?"

"I hear, Sheriff."

"Good."

"We can't be this lucky can we? Catch him after only an hour out here?"

"We just might be."

Rand applied the brakes at the hand signals from the two officers, one on the roadside and the other straddling one of the yellow dashes that divided the blacktop. A sheriff cruiser was diagonally blocking the route, its roof lights flashing. He slowed, the graphite brake pads dulling the momentum. Rand pulled his pistol from his holster, cocked it, and swiftly stashed it beneath his right thigh. He returned his hand to the two o'clock position on the steering wheel, his left hand still at the ten o'clock. What was going on? Was there an accident? Was this for him? If there were going to be roadblocks in this county, he would have to get the hell clear of this tightening noose of a jurisdiction. The officer moved to the opposite lane and waved for Rand to approach. With his first finger pointed, held at waist level, the officer indicated that Rand should roll his window down. Rand pressed the button on the arm rest. The glass whirred down. He halted so that the officer stood at his door. The second officer began to amble along the side of the car to search the interior. Could he see the pistol grip? Rand lay his hand flat over the grips.

"Afternoon, officer. What's going on?" Rand acted perfectly nonchalant. He was cool. He was just a guy out for a drive on a sunny, autumn day. Maybe he'd come back from sightseeing or hiking. Yeah, that was it. Hiking.

"Good afternoon, sir. We're searching for a suspect. Are you from Colorado?"

"Well, no." Rand could not recall what license plate he had on the back of the car so he said nothing more while he tried to recollect the color of the plate even. White?

"Where are you from then?"

"Uh," Rand struggled. "California."

"You're all the way from California, hunh?" The deputy whistled. And gave a slight glance to his companion who Rand saw was in the rearview mirror and must have nodded in confirmation. Rand guessed right, but his breath shuddered as he exhaled. "California's quite a drive. Are you camping up here or staying in a motel?"

"Camping."

"By yourself?"

"Yes."

"That takes a fairly experienced outdoors man to do it all solo."

Rand swallowed. His legs twitched, and he realized he had both feet on the brake pedal. The effort to stop had been great, he teased himself, though the humor hardly penetrated his mounting concern about all the questions from this cop. It was as if he wanted to chit chat out of boredom. Rand took a deep breath. "I like the solitude." He slipped his left foot to the floor, but the muscle spasmed and bounced. Had the cop noticed that? If he did, the officer said nothing.

"Which camping ground have you been at?"

Rand's body felt too big. He wished he could shrink and pass by unnoticed. He could not tell the truth. Rand pointed to the right, away from the truth, away from Will, feral and comatose Will. "It's just that way a bit. I'm sorry. I don't know the name."

"That way." The deputy pointed also, though he did not look. "Which one is it?" He said two names, presumably names of campsites, but what if it was a trick?

"Uh . . . The closer one." Rand knew that there was a camping ground down that direction. He had remarked its location when he went to a town and killed a couple who, while driving, had cut him off. He had followed them home and shot them. When he came out of their garage to jump back in his car there was a slaughter up in the sky as the sun died behind one of the peaks. He did not recall there being a second campsite though. This had to be a trick. "The closer one. I never saw a second that way."

"How long you been up here?"

"Two days."

"How many more days do you plan on being up here?"

Rand shook. This was too much. How many more questions was this guy going to ask? Why didn't he let him go already? Where was that other officer? Rand checked his rearview mirror with darting eyes. Where had he gone?

"Just a couple more days."

The deputy stared.

"I have a couple more days off from work before I need to be home."

"Uh hunh. It'll be a long drive back to California too."

"Yeah, uh, yes, sir."

"So you'll be up here about a week total then?"

Rand inhaled and adjusted his grip on the steering wheel. He started to lift his right hand, the one concealing his pistol grip, but dropped it back to the side of his quadriceps. He nodded.

"Are you okay, sir?"

Rand jerked. He gazed up at the officer. His name tag read Russell Claremont. Rand shook his head. "Yeah. Yes. I'm good." He nodded and his eyes longed for the road. And then Rand realized the trap that he had just set for himself. His stomach plummeted. He had just told this deputy that he camped at a site to the right, when the reverse was true. How in hell was he going to get back to his true site where Will was? Like a bullet, the idea that he could just abandon Will, shot by in his consciousness. No. He couldn't. Though he had no definite reason why he shouldn't, he knew that he couldn't. "Fine, but I don't know what all this is about." Rand locked his eyes on the deputy's. The deputy's head hung as he awaited clarification. Why couldn't this guy just be satisfied with that? "I mean, what's all this about, the roadblock, you know?"

"As I explained before, we're hunting a suspect."

"A suspect for what? I mean what did he . . . this person do?" Rand saw movement in the rearview mirror. It was another vehicle.

"How long have you had this car?"

Rand twisted. The second officer was behind where Rand sat, even with the backseat door, and his name tag began with the title "Sheriff."

"Uh, since it was new."

The sheriff bent at the waist and spied the dashboard. Rand followed his gaze. What was he searching for?

"That's a lot of mileage." The sheriff straightened, but then leaned back and surveyed the length of the Subaru. "What year is this? It doesn't hardly seem old enough to have—what was it? Ninety some thousand miles?"

Rand looked from sheriff to deputy to sheriff. "It's an 0-five."

The deputy whistled, impressed. "Where have you been driving?"

Why wouldn't they just let him proceed? "What's that have to do with your hunt for this suspect?"

The sheriff and his deputy exchanged looks. They each took a deep breath. Oh shit, Rand swore at his own impatience. Where was his cool? The sheriff said, "We're just talking here."

"Being friendly," the deputy added.

"We have to talk to everyone."

"We look them over too."

"We'll do the same to the next guy. Don't you worry about that."

"Different questions, mind you, but the same idea. You see?" The deputy held out a hand to maybe indicate that Rand should not feel special or neglected or offended. All Rand could consider, was not what that gesture signified, but how in hell was he going to go in the correct direction to get to the proper campsite where Will was? Rand opened his mouth to speak, and he turned his face to the deputy, but, as he did so, the deputy's head jerked up. The deputy looked intently at his partner, who had moved again, wraith-like, to the driver's side tail light. There was the hiss and mumble of the older officer's voice. Rand could not discern the words. What could it be? Was he telling this deputy to ask a certain question? Why? What was suspicious about Rand and the Subaru?

Rand twisted around to stare into his own car. What was suspicious? Why did they not just let him go? Rand stared into the backseat. There was nothing there.

"So, sir."

Rand snapped back around.

"You left all your gear back at your camp then?"

"Yes. I don't know why there's all these obvious questions. Why can't I go?" Rand whined. Once more, he nearly lifted his right hand to gesticulate, but he arrested the unconscious action. He was above reproach. And, anyway, Rand had the sticky thorn to get past as he tried to plan how he would make his way to Will at the real campsite. Ah, hell, worse came to worse he could sleep in the car, and Will could fend for himself just one night. Maybe he wouldn't notice that Rand wasn't there.

"Well, I'll tell you a few things." The deputy's right hand settled into the curve of the pistol's grip just above the top of the holster. "The murderer we're hunting for is from out of state. He drives a dark colored Subaru Forester just like this one. He's in his mid-twenties just like you."

Rand's body clenched as if dunked into Arctic waters. The deputy stared hard into his eyes. They both gulped.

"Sir." The deputy's voice was hoarse. He knew. How did they know so much? Had they not been careful? "May I see your license, registration, and proof of insurance? After that you'll be on your way."

Rand shivered from the ice in every inch of him.

Dean ducked and drew his pistol as the crash of metal, squeal of tires, and smash of glass exploded from down at the other side of the junction. His ball cap flopped off his head from when he ducked behind the corner of the Subaru and the bill of the cap wacked against the side panel of the car. Russell also ducked and drew his pistol, but he squatted there, exposed in the middle of the opposite lane. Further metal crunched and glass shattered. Then there was a third explosion, a sharp crack, totally different from the previous two. Russell pitched to the side and forward onto his elbows. Dean saw the brake light next to his head snap off. He tumbled forward to the blacktop. The Subaru's tires squealed. Another crack through the din set Dean's ears to ringing. Dean, in good shape for a man almost fifty, scrambled quickly to his feet. Russell. The Subaru. That was the killer. He whipped his pistol up into a solid two-hand hold and fired. His shot punched a hole into the rear window of the Subaru. He raced to Russell's side, slid to a stop, and fired again. The second shot was low and punctured the back hatch wall.

Russell lay on his left side. Both hands clawed at the stony surface of the blacktop. His mouth was as wide as possible. A strange sucking sound came from Russell.

"Russell. Russell, I'm here." Dean holstered his pistol. The Subaru screeched into a sliding arc of a turn to the left at the junction. Midway through the wild turn, the right window of the cargo area exploded from two shots, simultaneously. Two more shots burst the rear window. The Subaru sped up.

Dean put his hand on Russell's side where a hole was in his uniform shirt, the middle of his ribs. A red bubble of blood was welling there, and Dean pressed his hand into it. He blindly felt for the switch on his radio with his other hand. With his thumb he opened the channel. "This is Sheriff Buck. Officer down, officer down. Need immediate ambulance assistance at . . ."

Christopher hung up his cell as he finished his call to his deputy director about the Bureau's involvement in the incident at the junction: a triple car crash that precipitated a possible panic in the Plato Warrior who was being interrogated by the local sheriff. Any agent who discharged his weapon had to report it. There would be an inquiry, standard. Christopher pocketed his cell and set off along the hospital corridor. He passed a nurse's station, went past one door, and entered the next, a doctor's office. Christopher stopped in the doorway. Half a dozen people: a nurse in blue scrubs, a doctor in green scrubs with a white coat over that, another doctor in street clothes but with a plastic badge and a stethoscope around his neck and a vanilla, medical folder in one hand and three more people, presumably the family of the wounded deputy, were clustered around a desk. Just inside the door frame stood Sheriff Buck.

"How's your man?" Christopher asked.

"He's already in the trauma OR at St. Anthony's in Denver. Looks like he'll be fine." Sheriff Buck's voice was as deep as an empty grave.

Christopher nodded. In one hand the good sheriff had his cell phone, and in the other he had his radio. "There was another murder today. That son of a bitch had just killed someone else when he ran into our roadblock." The radio squelched to life as Christopher looked over the grim man in the shadows. Christopher and Sheriff Buck listened to the voice on the other end. "My search and rescue team in a helicopter." The sheriff raised the radio to his face. "They're flying over the campsite that the murderer was driving toward."

"Who's on board?"

"Pilot, copilot, and two deputies in the backseat each with a rifle and scope." Sheriff Buck's eyes rose from his concentration on the desk side scene and soared to meet Christopher's. "If they locate the suspect, they're to radio the location to a roadblock I have set up at the head of the trail leading into the canyon that holds the camping grounds and hiking trails. A SWAT team is ready to go in. If any of my men comes under fire, they have unrestricted shoot to kill authorization." The sheriff's voice dared Christopher to contradict that judgment. Christopher nodded and said nothing. So far this Sheriff had proven himself to be a sharp tactician in a deadly game of cat and mouse. Christopher was a guest in his jurisdiction even if the Plato Warriors were a Bureau priority.

"Sheriff, you there? Over."

"Go ahead." Sheriff Buck stepped past Christopher and marched into the bright corridor. Christopher tagged along.

"We got a car set ablaze out here."

"Can you tell what make?"

"Station wagon for sure. Can't be certain that it's our Subaru."

"Yeah, but what are the odds?"

"Roger that, sheriff. What do you want us to do?"

"How far are you from the state route?"

"We're at the farthest lot in the canyon. I'd say two miles back."

"Are the flames still bright?"

"Yes, sir."

Sheriff Buck said to Christopher, "The trees are pretty thick up there. It's unlikely their searchlight can shine through the top foliage." He took a deep breath. To the helicopter pilot he said, "Do you have your light on? Over."

"Yes, sir."

"I want you to start tracking back and forth toward the head of the canyon and our roadblock. Let's see if you can flush our boy to the SWAT. Understand?"

"Roger. The hound is on the hunt." The pilot sounded gleeful.

"Good boy. Over and out."

"Over and out."

Buck changed the radio frequency. "Darren, this is Dean. You still awake? Over."

"Yes, sir. We've got the midnight oil burning bright out here."

"The helicopter just found a car set ablaze at the back of the canyon. Be on the lookout for anyone trying to hoof it out of there. Who all is there now?" The sheriff listened to the list of assets in place. "All right. Here's what I want."

Christopher listened. The hospital was silent, and the sheriff's orders boomed and echoed in the clean corridor. This was a terrific lawman. Christopher didn't believe that there was one thing he could do differently or better. He kept his peace until Sheriff Buck signed off. "What can I do to help?"

"More eyes would be great." Buck sighed. He switched his gaze to the ICU door. "If you could get another helicopter up here that would be the best way to cover the acreage we've got to contend with.

I'm sure you know that this mountainous and forested terrain favors our killer."

"I'll do what I can. It shouldn't be a problem though."

Buck turned and motioned for Christopher to come along. This man was prepared to take Christopher in his confidence, he could sense it. They marched down the corridor, their heels striking the linoleum.

"Where's your other half?" Buck asked.

"What?"

"That other agent. What's her name again?"

"Samantha." Should he have said 'Sammy?' That was her prerogative, not Christopher's. "Why'd you call her that? My other half? She's not my wife." Christopher laughed and shook his head.

Buck didn't slacken his headlong march, even as they approached the electric, sliding doors that led to the parking lot. "Interesting." Buck looked away.

"I'm married. My wife's home in LA." Christopher smiled.

"My mistake." Both of them were in the crisp, mountain air, which caused Christopher to shiver. Buck veered toward his cruiser.

Buck thinks that he and Sammy are married? What gave him that idea? "Look, we're just-"

Buck interrupted. "If you can get that helo here before dawn to relieve my crew that would be helpful. I'm going out to the roadblock. I don't armchair quarterback. You're welcome to come and run patrol in your car with your, uh, fellow agent."

Christopher stared at the hard back of this backwoods county sheriff, who didn't pause to mark how his attitude and high handedness fell. The sheriff climbed in his cruiser, backed out and drove off without any drama or undue speed. Everything about that man was methodical, yet humane. Christopher scuffled to his sedan. He spun around and dropped butt first onto the hood. Should he end it with Sammy? Or should he end it with his wife? Are these the only options there are? He shook his head. Christ, what the hell is he thinking? He needs to focus on the task at hand, not behave like a ridiculous, love struck boy. He pulled out his cell phone and dialed the Denver office. He had to arrange for a helicopter and a team on the ground by morning. Capturing the Plato Warriors was a Bureau top priority. Or Plato Warrior? Which was it now? Seemingly, there was only one now. Which of the Plato Warriors was it?

The Denver office answered, and he made the arrangements with minimal fuss because that office was notified by the deputy director that anything which Christopher might requisition was to be relinquished immediately. When Christopher hung up, he thought back to the letter, the so-called manifesto that the Plato Warriors sent to the newspapers, seemingly in duplicate, that is until someone bothered to scrutinize the handwriting. Then it was obvious that there were two of them, and, after analysis by two experts, who agreed on most major points, that the writers of the different copies had quite dissimilar personalities. One was aggressive, intelligent, decisive and quick tempered, while the second was more pensive, slower paced, given to planning, and even tempered. Christopher didn't know which would be worse, the one who was unpredictable and, though easier to corner, wouldn't be taken alive and without certain loss of life, or the second who could methodically plan and implement complex actions. With that formulation of the situation, Christopher knew who was out here in the mountains, which of the Plato Warriors murdered all these people in the last few days. His actions this afternoon were all the evidence that was necessary. Would they take him alive? Would he fight his way out? How many would have to be hurt? And what happened to his comrade in arms, the even keeled, methodical Plato Warrior?

September 7, 2008

Rand slammed Will against the wall of the building. After a long night and morning of trooping through the forest down and up and back down ridges, they were at a small town by dawn.

"Listen, you son of a bitch," Rand said. "This is our asses, if you can't pull it together and do this."

Will's eyes were spheres with empty middles, empty like his head had been for nearly a month. Throughout their forced march, Will had stumbled along a good ten or more yards behind the unflagging step of Rand. Rand's muscles shook with violence. Will turned his head and gaped at the used car lot across the street. He felt like a worm, there was no strength to resist or overcome anything. Rand whipped his right hand back over his left shoulder and back-handed Will in the mouth. Will cried out.

"Pull yourself together. Now! Can't you get it? If you can't do this, we'll be caught by the police. This is our lives and our freedom I'm talking about. Do you hear me?"

Will put a hand to his mouth. When he pulled away his hand, there was blood. He blinked several times at Rand. "What happened?" It was as if he had just arisen from death. He shrugged to try and get Rand off him. When that did not work, he made a quick, upward sweep with his right and batted Rand's arm away. Rand had to take a step to keep his balance, but he was glad at the force of that movement by his friend. For the first time in a long few weeks, he saw a resolve, an understanding that a task must be performed, and an ability to plan for the execution of that plan that all indicated to Rand that his friend's old self was there again behind those brown eyes.

"There was a roadblock." Rand said. "I had to shoot a policeman to get away. A sheriff's deputy, actually, but whatever. I torched the Subaru. All we have is what's in our packs and our weapons." Rand reached behind his back and brought forth Will's pistol in its holster and the knife. "We have to get the hell away from here and right fucking now, like at an SR-71 kind of speed. Comprende?"

"Yeah." Will's eyes went back to the used car lot across the street. "How do we pay?"

"Use that credit card of yours. You still have that, right?"

Will patted his back jeans pocket. His eyes shot open. "My wallet!"

"It's in your backpack. I know I put it in there."

They squatted and searched the pockets of the backpack until they found the wallet.

"Go and get us something. Doesn't matter much what it is, just so long as you can pay for it-" Rand pointed at the Visa plastic that Will thumbed from its slip in the wallet. "With that. Got it? We'll figure out later how to deal with the bill, if we get out of this cluster fuck. Okay?"

"Yeah." Will strapped on his sheathed knife and clipped his holster to his belt. He tucked away his wallet in his butt pocket. With a deep breath, he regained more composure, more of his old self. "Okay. Be back."

Will hustled off at a vigorous stride. Rand exhaled and braced his suddenly limp self with an arm to the wall. All the Herculean adrenaline of the last day ebbed in a second. He twisted so that as he slid to the dusty pavement his shoulder and not his face bore his weight on the rough red brick of the building. He scraped and rasped down. Possibly, his flannel shirt ripped. Possibly, his skin bled. He panted and his heart sprinted. He closed his eyes and breathed with as much measure as he could demand of those sore organs.

In Rand's dream giants stood in a ring. They wielded long pikes with gold points on the end. They closed in on him. Rand spun, wild with fear, frantic to discover an advantage or a means to escape. The giants stepped closer, in unison, the right foot out. Rand reversed his direction and spun the other way. The legs of the giants were like concrete columns that left only a foot between them. He thought to charge between them, but the giants, again in unison, stepped forward with their left feet. Now only half a foot separated their column legs. If only Rand was a rat he could wiggle through. The pike points glinted closer. All their skewering terror was trained on his heart. There was no escape. There was no hope. He reached for his pistol, but his fingers fell into the empty holster on his hip. The giants raised their feet to step forward in agonizing slow motion. The giants relished their duty, Rand saw in their eyes a sense of ease with their task. Rand squeezed his arms in as tightly to his sides as he could. He inhaled and opened his mouth. "No!" The points sunk into his chest.

Will shook him awake.

"No!" Rand jerked and scrambled for his weapons.

"Sorry." Will jumped back. His hands rose to show no offense. "I got a car. Sorry, it took so long."

Will drove. As Rand laid in the back seat, concealed so that, in case they passed a cop, while driving at least, no one would see the man who had shot a deputy, he stared at the sky and marveled that so far they had escaped. Was the deputy dead? Maybe not. Most cops these days wear bullet proof vests, and Rand shot him in the chest. What if the cop had not lived? Well, what difference does that make? All humans are nothing, motes in the sun's rays. Even Rand was nothing. What did it matter if he did anything, everything, or nothing? It would add up to the same thing. If he killed people for no reason, it was the same as if he killed them for a reason. It meant nothing. Rand's action would fulfill no greater meaning because there was no greater meaning. Rand arched his back. It was late afternoon and the sky was changing to cobalt. It was pretty, but he recalled something that he learned in a freshman astronomy course, namely, the blue sky was an optical illusion caused by the sunlight in the earth's atmosphere. Despite that scientific knowledge, people constantly gawked and became eloquent about a phenomenon that was just an illusion. How foolish humans were. He didn't know if he should feel enraged, disheartened, superior, or amused. Maybe it didn't matter, and that was why he couldn't quite feel one way or another. He saw a lone buzzard with its great black wingspan like paired dark scythes effortlessly soar above him. What kill would it soon circle?

Will drove until midnight when they arrived in Boise, Idaho, once again. They checked into a Holiday Inn. Will guided his friend to the room. As they stumbled along, Will said, "Why don't we just disappear? Maybe leave the country? Shit. Every cop in the country is searching for you."

"Us." Rand's eyes tried to stretch from his head to the end of the corridor, to see beyond all that Will could envision.

"That wasn't me in Colorado."

Rand's head slowly swiveled like the turret of a battleship's main battery. "Only you and I know that. Do you think they'll believe your pleas of innocence? I wouldn't." His head cranked forward again. He grinned with malice. "You're in this until the end, my comrade in arms. And we will end it, end with our guns in our hands blazing away."

September 9, 2008

They sat in a bar. Neither of them cared what state or town they were in anymore. On the table in front of them sat a copy of *The Collected Dialogues of Plato*.

"I don't see the point in that anymore." Rand shoved it back across the table to Will. Will caught the paperback before it flew off the table. "It's nothing to me."

Will shifted on his chair. "You don't believe in questioning people anymore?"

"Everything is nothing to me anymore, so no I don't."

"Why not?"

"It's all a waste."

Will ran his hand over the book cover and its photograph of an ancient depiction of Plato discoursing to other Greeks. "So what now?"

"What?"

"Are we going our separate ways?"

Rand's eyes flared and he sat very tall. "How could I be sure that you won't go to the police?"

"To do what? Turn us both in?" Will shook his head. "Granted, I don't believe in our cause anymore, but that doesn't mean that I want to commit, what would be in essence, assisted suicide."

"Good." Rand slapped the tabletop and leaned forward. "I want you to never forget that. You just let self-preservation be your overriding instinct, and then you and I will never have a problem." Rand jabbed the air between them with a finger aimed at Will. "Don't forget that."

Why had Rand become like this? What sort of dangerous killer had he become? This man had been Will's best friend for four years, and now he'd morphed into this raging destroyer. Rand sat rigid with rage, and his eyes were sighted solely on Will's, perhaps to intimidate or to chase him off.

The bar door opened. Since they were close to the door, both men peered at the new arrival. He was dressed in jeans, a polo, a canvas windbreaker, and loafers. His face and walk seemed too delicate to enter a bar let alone order a beer or hard liquor. Will thought this newcomer ought to be at a yacht club in New England, fresh from scoring high marks during a semester at Yale, Princeton, or one of the other Ivy League schools, and he could discuss with exaggerated propriety to his chums about how his trust fund was doing while he sipped on a champagne spritzer. His name likely had numerals appended to it.

Rand snorted. Will turned to view a sneer on his features. "A joke walked into a bar dressed as a man."

Will rolled his eyes.

The man—Will wanted to demean him by calling him a boy, but pushed that back—gazed around at each occupant in the bar as if he was in search of a friend, though there was hardly anyone there on an early week day evening. Lastly, his eyes fell on Will and Rand. For an awkward moment he held their stares with one of his own. Will and Rand, seasoned to these games of dominance, did not blink or flinch. Finally, the man/boy got it in his head that two were stronger than one. He bowed his head and went to the bar. As he went, Will noted that he did not swing his left arm at all. That arm was glued to his side as if to sandwich something between it and his torso.

"So what's the joke?" Will asked Rand without turning from his study of the man/boy—he could not think of him without that description of immaturity. There remained something off about him as if he pretended to be what was not in his nature.

"He would be the perfect candidate for an interrogation. Wouldn't he?" Rand lifted his beer and took a drink. His eyes watched the man/boy the whole time the pint was at his lips.

"Only we're not in that business anymore. Are we?" Will turned to Rand, who paused as he set his pint down to flash his darkest glare at Will. "That's what we just decided. Right?"

"No, we're not. We're not working together anymore."

"The parting of the ways then?"

"It's time."

A chair scraped across the floor. At the table next to them, the man/boy sat down. From his windbreaker, he shook out a small paperback and set it on the table beside his pint of yellow beer. With his left arm still glued to his flank, he used his right to pull his windbreaker closed. He glanced over, not at Will and Rand, but at their tabletop. He grinned and pointed. "Good choice of book."

Will lifted his hand, looked from his copy of *The Collected Dialogues of Plato* to a similarly titled book, though of a different edition and publisher, on the man/boy's tabletop. Rand's eyes followed the same trajectory.

"What a coincidence, hunh?" said the man/boy with his grin like a Hollywood movie star, white and straight. Will's tongue ran along his crooked lower, front teeth. Neither man responded to this entrée to conversation.

"What's your favorite dialogue?" the youth pressed.

"Are you old enough to buy a beer?" Rand asked, which Will thought was ridiculous since Rand was maybe two or three years older than the man/boy.

"The bartender thought so." The kid jerked his thumb over his shoulder. "He even checked my license."

"How old do you think he is?" Rand turned to Will.

"Old enough to party, I guess."

"To party." Rand nodded.

The kid flashed that starry smile at Will. He hoisted his glass. "Cheers." He waited. Neither man made a move to oblige his call to drink. "Well, how about a proper toast?" He looked from Will to Rand's now smirking, slitted eyes. "To Plato, the philosopher who first showed us how to have a proper dialogue." He elevated his glass farther. The moment became uncomfortable. Will debated whether to toast him just to get this over with. "What's the matter with you two? Don't you like my toast? You're not very friendly. Has anyone ever told you that before?"

"No one that lived." Rand snarled.

That wasn't how Will expected Rand to reply. This was a situation that was rapidly heading south. Will took his glass, raised it to the kid, and said, "We're just being cautious. We wouldn't want to get into a debate with the Plato Warriors."

The kid blinked and gave a jerk. "No, I guess not," he said after he swallowed with difficulty.

Will and the kid clinked their glasses together and drank. A hint of bitterness passed over the kid's face after he took the glass from his lips. Rand remained motionless.

"Don't like your beer?" Will asked.

"It's fine," the kid said quickly.

"What did you get?"

"It's a Bud Lite."

"Tastes like cat piss, doesn't it?"

"Ha. I guess. I don't know about cats or their piss. You?"

"Only what I imagine."

"So then you don't know in the epistemological sense, then."

Will sat back and glanced at Rand, whose eyes were very narrow now. "Listen to this guy's vocab. Maybe he's older than he looks. Where'd you hear that word?"

"Ah, come on, you're just screwing with me now."

"Oh, of course, I am, but that doesn't mean I'm not curious about where you picked up that five dollar word. So?"

"I'm in college."

"Ah."

"Say, you mentioned the Plato Warriors."

Will nodded. Rand remained totally still.

"What do you think about them?"

"How do you mean?" Will asked.

"I mean, here's two guys that are out asking folks about their beliefs and thoughts on the world they live in, and they kill any of them when they give a poor answer. That's something, isn't it?"

"What? Do you admire them?" Will and the kid looked at Rand whose question caught them both off guard.

The kid's eyelids fluttered. "Well, now that you mention it, I do admire them."

"Why?" Rand leaned a hand on a knee.

"What's the root of evil in the world?" The kid gestured for an answer, a guess from the men.

"Humans." Rand now turned to his pint.

"Well, what about them?"

"I don't think you get it." Rand took a drink. He guzzled the glass dry and banged the pint down on the tabletop. "No." He glanced at Will. "He doesn't get it."

Will wondered what would come out of Rand's mouth next.

"Only humans can define human actions. 'Good' and 'evil,' or 'bad,' are just adjectives and nouns that humans created to label their actions to set limits, laws, and so on. So where does evil come from? Humans."

The kid was bobbing his head. "Yeah, yep. That's true but what about those actions that are labeled evil. What is the cause of them?"

"Don't tell me that you're of the opinion that it's God. You're not a naïf, are you?"

The kid chuckled, took a sip of his Bud Lite, and winced from the taste again. "No, no."

He was about to say more, but Rand interjected. "Or that there's some morality that is external to humans as it was suggested in the *Meno*? There can't be a Platonic form of evil because how would we *know* it? How would he have access to its law? We're only able *to know*, in your epistemological sense of the word, what is within us."

"Then it's all just relative? I don't believe that." The kid laid his hand on his book of Plato, scooted it across the table, and said, "Surely killing is wrong."

"Why? We do it all the time. We've done it for all time. We kill animals to eat them. We kill each other to gain territory or to protect it. We kill in jealousy, rage, insult, and defense. We are the baddest killing machines that Nature with a capitol N ever created.

Anyone who thinks we're made to be peaceful is a fool. Everything is permissible." Rand's hand slipped from his pint to the bulge beneath his shirt at his hip. The kid's eyes followed the motion of Rand's hand. For a long second, the length of a realization, the kid's eyes stayed on the position of Rand's hand, and then they widened and rose, once the moment of epiphany arrived. His right hand tried to slide off the table, across the air, and into his windbreaker where his pistol presumably was. Rand opted for no stealth but whipped his hand beneath his shirt and gripped the Browning's grips in plain view of the bar. The kid shivered into a frozen pose.

"Easy," Will said as he held both of his hands out, one toward Rand and the other toward the kid. "Easy. Both of you need to be cool. Let's not do this."

"Why not? What do you care if I grease this little snot nosed fuck? He's trying to be someone he's not. You hear me, kid? This isn't a game. You ventured into a situation that you haven't the proper thinking or training for. You get it?"

"Easy," Will repeated. He thought of moving his hand for his own pistol but figured that might provoke the other two to draw and shoot. Rand had this kid dead at any time he chose. The kid's hand was stuck in the empty space between his copy of Plato and the concealed pistol beneath his left arm. The bartender turned and looked their way, and his face gathered into a storm of consternation at the sight of these three men. Will spoke through his teeth, making an effort to not be audible to anyone but Rand and the kid. "Stand down." Will placed his hands flat on his knees. "Let's all three set our hands down. We're attracting some unwanted attention. All right? Come on, kid," he said to the kid. "Just put your hand on the table."

The kid's eyes batted back and forth between Will and Rand's hand on his pistol.

Will continued. "Don't worry. He's not going to pull and shoot you because then there'd be the likelihood of his being shot by the bartender."

At the mention of the bartender, Rand's eyes finally broke away from the kid. He took in the sight of the bartender staring at them with his hands on hips. Rand checked the aspect of the kid whose hand gently came to rest on his Plato. The kid's eyes were blasted wide with fear. Rand's shoulders relaxed and his hand came away from the Browning in its holster.

"Not one of us wants to die right here and now, so not one of is going to. Got it?" Will said. "I suggest that we three finish our drinks as quickly as we can. Then, kid, you're going to leave after we do. Don't follow us. I don't care if you do have to go in the same direction as us. You can drive around in the other direction for a while and contemplate about how you're not really cut out for this kind of thing. Okay?"

Rand glared at the kid. Will had only a third of his pint remaining. It required two long gulps before it was drunk. The kid sat still, his Bud Lite untouched. "You sit there and drink that like a good little boy should," Rand growled. "If we go out there, get in our car, and start down the road only to see you tear out of here to chase after us, we'll make you pay for your ticket to Hell."

The kid quaked. His jaw trembled. He was scared like he had probably never been in his life. Rand and Will stood. The bartender crossed his arms and continued to stare their way. They exited, hopped in their car, and Will drove them out of town. Rand sat in the seat facing backward, his gun drawn and held just below the top of the seat back. Finally, satisfied that they were not pursued, he said, "And we once thought we'd had no effect. Now we have that dumb kid who wants to be our copycat."

Will nodded thoughtfully. "Yeah. Great."

September 11, 2008

Another bar, somewhere in the United States, it did not matter anymore where. Rand sat at a small table, while Will sat at the bar. Neither looked at the other. Rand looked at the fellow who sat at the table beside him. It was now. This was the time. Rand's face pinched into his old smirk. "Hey. Hey!" The fellow's eyes switched to him. "Do you think there is meaning in the world?"

"Excuse me."

"You heard me. Don't play shy. The world is already speeding to its end, ever since it was created." Rand smiled and his eyes filled with a delirious joy. He giggled. Will shivered at the sound from where he hunkered over his beer. Rand's interlocutor leaned far back into his cane back chair and narrowed his eyes.

"Yes, sir, I believe that everything has meaning."

"And I say nothing does. Nothing, you hear."

"I hear. Is that some sort of atheism?" The fellow took his cell out. "I hope you don't mind." He dangled a finger above the cell phone. "I just need to text my old lady to tell her I stopped off for a beer after work." He typed the tiny keys with his thumb.

What was Rand doing? He was acting crazy. Everything in Will's gut turned cold and nauseated. Will nodded to the bartender, who was at the other end. What was Rand about to do? Was he going to shoot that man while inside this bar and with everyone watching? He wouldn't. That was stupid. That was insane. He would never, would he? Behind Will's back, Rand and the fellow verbally sparred.

A new voice piped up. "What's he asking you, Paul? We've been listenin' and we find it all suspicious. Maybe he's the Plato Warrior."

Will's whole being became a tuning fork. He shivered and rang as if he was struck against metal. Plato Warrior? Every muscle strained in sickened anticipation of combat. Will did not hear what else was spoken. He thought he heard Rand's voice, but now there was a Babel of tongues wagging. The bartender served Will another beer, but did not leave. He listened to the melee that surrounded Rand. The bartender planted his hands on the bar, elbows locked, and his eyes fixed on the gathering battle royal. Without looking away, the bartender side stepped to his right and reached beneath the bar for something. Will, without taking his eyes off the bartender, smoothly and quickly drew his pistol from under his sweater. He held it between his knees where no one would likely look and flicked the safety off. Should he turn? Everyone in the bar had their attention fixed on the raised voices, the shouts and commands. Will pivoted the stool to see Rand up on his feet, hand inching toward his hip, and the fellow he had started speaking to on his feet too with one hand holding out a gold star badge and the other hand on his hip where he had a sidearm in a hip holster. Oh, no.

Rand shouted, "Nothing." He drew.

"No!" the cop shouted as he drew.

In Will's peripheral vision he saw the bartender step back and haul up a shotgun. Bang, bang, bang. The shots came almost all at once. The bartender was down. Will dropped from his stool behind the bar. A group of men in camouflage and hunting vests all pulled handguns. The noise was as loud as any combat he had heard in Afghanistan. The smell of cordite was on his tongue. Will opened fire.

He moved in a crouch. He had to get to the door. He had to get out of here. Will aimed at the chests of all those hunters. Two of them dropped a second apart. The last two turned and tried to duck, but he shot them both. Will looked ahead as he scrambled down the aisle between the tables and chairs on one side and the stools and bar on the other. When he came to the end, he spun and aimed at the small area at the front beneath the window where there was a table and more stools along the bar. A shot whined over Will's head. He shot down three more people as he raced for the door.

Out the door, Will staggered into a slashing rainstorm. His pistol smoked. Rain sizzled on the barrel. The rattle, splatter, and roiling of the rain on the parked cars and the gravel lot deafened him. What had just happened? Should he go back in for Rand? No, he was gone. Will's mind reeled. Rand was gone! What now? What should Will do? Focus. Get out of here. The police will be on the way. His left foot slipped in a puddle that hid a pothole. He crashed to his knees and hands. His pistol flew. "Oh, shit." Find it. Retrieve your weapon. He scrambled over the points and sharp edges of the gravel lot that tore at his hands and knees. Blindly, he groped for his pistol. He had to have it back. The police had to be on their way. He ran his hands first one way and then the other. The rain and sleet soaked him, and the cold gripped his body. He blinked to get rid of the water in his eyes. He squinted at the murk. His hands ached from the numerous gouges and scrapes they suffered as he searched the ground for that pistol. Now, somewhere out there in the cold, wet night, he heard the wail of a siren. He knew that a few people had bolted when the guns were drawn. Their calls had summoned the police. The siren wavered, drew near, and receded. Damn it! Where was that pistol? And then his fingers contacted the still hot metal. With both hands, he scooped up the pistol and clutched it against his gut. He jumped to his feet and ran in a crouch to the Oldsmobile. The sirens cried out closer now. He tugged at the door handle. The keys. He took one hand from where he clutched the pistol to his gut. Did he have his keys? He had driven all the time lately, not Rand, so he had them somewhere. In his front right jeans pocket was his set of keys. He dug, he retrieved, he pressed the button on the fob, and he looked to the state route. The red and blue and white lights fractured in the tumult of the wind, sleet, and rain. How far? It was too close no matter how far away. He threw the door open and it banged against the side of the pickup parked alongside. He leaped inside. As he shut the door, he rammed the key into the ignition and turned it. The Oldsmobile started. He threw it into reverse and mashed the pedal. The Oldsmobile shot out. Only as it passed the ends of the other parked vehicles, did he simultaneously slam his foot on the brake and spin the wheel so that the Oldsmobile grated and scraped over the gravel and stopped. He faced the state route. He dropped the gear shift into drive, and gunned the engine. The gravel erupted under the tires and beat the wheel wells like machinegun fire. Will ground his teeth. He cranked the wheel and angled the car to veer away from the speeding police car, which was nothing but piercing, straining lights and the awful cry of the siren now. He roared off the gravel lot, hit the soft embankment, but, despite a terrific crunch to the front bumper, the car's momentum bounced the Oldsmobile onto the state route. He fishtailed, nearly went off the opposite side of the road but recovered. He leaned as far over the steering wheel as he could. He raced into the nothing-night without his lights on. He hoped against his own stupidity that the police had not spotted him. He prayed that the road stayed straight for just a little while. He jerked his foot from the gas and tried to look in the rearview mirror and through the windshield at the same time. The red and blue and white lights closed on him. Did they see him? The cacophony of the rain on the car was terrible. How could he tell if he was being shot at? Was this it for him? They'll catch him for sure. Should he try to shoot it out with them? It could either be suicide or escape.

The red and blue and white lights turned. They had gone into the lot. He had to risk it. He flipped on his lights and floored the accelerator. Immediately, he wrenched the wheel to keep from going off the road, but within a minute he was among trees. For a long time, nearly an hour, he kept looking in the rearview, but he was not followed.

September 12, 2008

Christopher had been home four days, but it was time now to pack for his departure. He packed fresh socks, underwear, polo shirts, jeans, a box of nine millimeter rounds that always accompanied him but which was quite smashed at the corners because he had toted it around for a year or more without any need for it, and his toiletries in a black kit bag. This ten minute process, in which he criss-crossed the room several times to the dresser, the closet, and the bathroom, transpired under the sharp surveillance of Mrs. Delilah England, whose eyes were cracked bloody, wrathful, and doleful. He did not want to utter a syllable.

"I can't take this anymore. I can't," she blurted. He'd heard those exact words ten minutes ago when he declared that he ought to pack for his morning flight. He still had nothing to respond with to her plea. He went to his night stand, opened the drawer, and removed his holstered pistol.

"Say something goddammit!"

He rose to his full height and held his weapon, one hand on the grips and the other over the barrel so that the pistol disappeared. He stayed put, but he refused to look at her because he really had nothing to say. Didn't she understand that? What could he say anyway? Oh, honey, maybe he could say, oh, honey, I'll give up my career, my livelihood, and the thing that makes my blood pump, my brain work, that makes me have a purpose and fills me with a sense of duty because I've helped the world by ridding it of some very nasty, demonic sons of bitches like that serial rapist down in Arizona, or that pair of snipers on the East Coast, or some of the dozens of others who destroyed families, slaughtered innocents, and caused anxiety in the minds of so many thousands as the news of their deeds travelled via the evening broadcasts, the morning papers, and the eternal internet. Was that what she wanted to hear? How could she ask that of him? Give up everything! That, in effect, was what she was shouting at him. Why didn't she just ask him to not live, breath, and be anymore? That would be easier. He stood and was silent.

"Goddamn you!" She leaped from the bed, stood, and trembled with rage like he had never seen before.

"What do you want from me?" He did not intend that to be a question, but his voice did rise at the end of the statement.

"Wha-" She tried to lob her eyes at him like a pair of hand grenades. She slapped the bed with both hands since her eyes wouldn't fly and explode. For a moment she remained bent over then she smacked the bed again as if it was what offended her, and maybe the bed had, since she had made love to him five times since his return.

"I want you to be here for me. Be here for me in the way that I'm here for you. Whenever you come into town when you breeze into our home and toss your bags on the floor, I know you expect me to be ready with open arms to hug you, with open mouth to kiss you, and open legs to . . . to have sex with you. You expect me to cook and clean for you and smile at you and be a pretty and perky little housewife for you. You know what though? I'm a person too. I've got expectations also. And I need you to be here for me. I didn't marry you so that I could be alone. If I wanted to be alone all the time I'd have stayed single and become an old spinster maid. I married you to hear you talk to me, to have you hold me on both my good days and my bad, and to have you listen to me when I have stories to tell or gripes to share. Do you understand that? Can't that get through to that brain of yours that spends all its energies in pursuit of understanding the motivations of criminals? Can't my motives get through to you?"

His cell rang. Her eyes looked ready to fire from the barrels in her skull and obliterate him. "Don't you dare pick up that phone." Second ring. She pointed at him as if her finger was a pistol aimed to gut shoot him. Or maybe it was his heart that she would shoot. No, she probably thought he did not have a heart. He did not give a damn. Third ring. He snatched up the phone. His marriage was dead anyway. "Chris," she blubbered and tears assaulted her smooth cheeks.

Fourth ring. He turned it on. "This is Special Agent England."

"Christopher, it's Dick." His boss, the deputy director.

"Yes, sir?"

"It's your Plato Warriors case."

"What? Did we catch a good lead?"

"Listen closely. There was a shootout in a bar in Montana. We think one of the dead was one of your Plato Warriors."

Christopher turned from the smoldering face of his wife and stepped over to the windows that looked out on his backyard. It was southern California autumn, everything still green, from the grass to the leaves on the shrubs, nothing was different. "How many died?"

"Not counting the perpetrator, eleven, including a local sheriff's deputy. Witnesses report that the Plato Warrior tried to strike up a conversation, a philosophical debate, I guess, but when some of the other patrons, a group of hunters in fact, overheard, they knew exactly what was going on. That's when the shooting started."

"Jesus Christ."

"Yep. Worse than the OK Corral as far as the body count goes."

"What do you need me to do?"

"Right now we've got a few people out on site. I want you to stay put and coordinate the field units and the sudden surge of evidence I expect to pour in as a result of this."

"Yes, sir."

"We have to track down that second Plato Warrior, and to do it I think it best if my point man takes a step back to really see the big picture. Understand?" So, the second Plato Warrior was at large. Christopher had wondered for weeks about whether he had died prior to the Colorado killings.

"Yes, sir."

"I'm not sidelining you, Christopher. All right?"

"Yes, sir."

His boss sighed. "I want this son of a bitch caught and I know there will need to be someone who can coordinate people around the country involved in the multiple tasks necessary. That someone is you."

Christopher nodded. Now he had to stay. His boss spoke for several more minutes, but Christopher did not listen too closely. He knew there was nothing in what the deputy director said that he did not already know. Track down friends, relatives, coworkers, fellow students, teachers, preachers, enemies, etcetera, and interview them for a thorough psych evaluation. Pull and collate all records from schools, doctors, police, and other institutions that had a relationship with him. All of this not only in an effort to find what happened to this young man and why, but also to locate and bring to justice his accomplice.

"Everything will be routed through you. Got it?"

"Yes, sir," he said automatically. The sky was purple as night worked to shade the world.

"Head to the office and begin to sort through this morass of data. With any luck, we'll nab our man by the day's end, at week's end at the latest. I want a fire under this, right?"

"Yes, sir." It was all he could say because he would rather not say anything at all. The conversation ended and Christopher hung up. He turned in place and pitched the phone to the bed. She was not there. Her sobbing burbled in the bathroom. "I'm not going anywhere." He told her why. When she appeared in the bathroom doorway, he was removing every article from his bag. He said, "I don't know what we're going to do. I don't think I can tell you anything that will please you because I'm not going to quit my job. It's what I live for. It's what

I do. And, frankly, it's what pays the bills. But that's what you want from me, isn't it?" He looked her dead in the eye. She blinked, and there were still tears that dribbled down her cheeks. Her face was livid pink. The sight of her bothered him. It was never easy to cause someone pain and make them cry. He had told parents their children were dead. He had told small kids that their parents would never come home again. He had told spouses how the love of their life was killed for kicks. That was hard, but this was alien. What he really needed to tell her was that he had met someone else. Her name was Sammy and she was in the FBI. Sammy understood him. He felt sorry for his wife, but he knew that she would never be happy with him. They should really divorce.

"I won't do this anymore." She clawed at her tears.

He merely nodded. There it was. They were at the end.

Will (Anderson) and Jerusha

Cold. Snow. Cold snow. Cold and snow. He soldiered into it. What was his duty? Was he alone? Where was his unit? Where was his friend? The trees were frozen. How long was it since he saw a face, any face? Or how about the last time he heard a voice? When had he spoke last? Everything was white like snow. The air, the ground, the tree tops, and his breath were all white. Why was everything white? Where was the car? Gone. Something happened to the car. What was it that happened? He thumped his forehead with his gloved hands. Why couldn't he remember? What did he know? His name was William Anderson Cooper. He was hiding, on the run. What had he done? He saw a round woman's face, eyes wide dead, and a hole blasted in the forehead with blood flowing. He knew he killed her. That was why he was on the run. Why had he killed her? He could not remember. And there were others too. Oh, the cold. His toes hurt. He crashed shoulder first into a pine. There was the sound of the frost rasping against his coat. When was the last time he ate? The umbrella canopies cast the white into shadow. He was famished. He scooped a handful of sugary snow, but found the taste of emptiness when he put it on his tongue. The pine trunks looked like dried figs, edible to his eyes only. He lurched and staggered through the snow. He needed food. The only other sounds in the muffling snow were from him as his breath pulsed frozen in the air and the clicking of his teeth. He wanted to drop to the snow and lay still. His shoulders ached and the small of his back too. No, he had to troop on, a voice distant though quite stern said. He hesitated. He heaved on the sharp air. It was so hard to pull in and out, that air. Get a move on, soldier. Step right, step left. Your left, right, left. Company, march. Keep moving. Left, right, left. Step, step, stumble, reach out hands, and crash into the snow. Don't just lay there. Get your lazy ass up. Come on, look alive. Push and struggle up. March. Sir, yes, sir. His shoulders burned where the pack's straps cut in, pressed through his coat, sweater, flannel shirt, and thermal undershirt. His feet weren't there. They should be at the ends of his legs, but he felt nothing. He was in bad shape. He staggered through the trees and raised his face to find a busy four lane interstate in front of him. Which way should he go?

The first night Jerusha saw him at the diner was a Friday. The dinner rush would start in a few minutes, at six, but he beat it in. His hair and beard ranged wildly from his head, his clothes were smudged with mud and there were pine needles and leaves caught in the fibers of small tears. Collectively, the patrons and staff of the small diner in Flagstaff, Arizona turned on him and appraised him with eyes either critically narrowed or shocked wide. He blinked beneath the unaccustomed glare of their eyes and the fluorescent bulbs. Jerusha refused to conform to the critical and shocked reception this wild man suffered. She put on her brightest smile. Go to the places that scare you, she told herself. Everyday experience is the greatest teacher. She repeated these two sentences as she went around the bar counter to serve him with a pot of regular in one hand. He had sat in a booth. Crouched over, he reminded her of a wolf without its pack, lost and cautious, terrified for its survival. He kept on his coat, gloves, and hat. She asked if he wanted coffee. Perhaps he meant to bolt at any moment. He tugged the cup and its saucer over in front of him. She poured the coffee. He centered the cup to his torso, which she thought was unusually fastidious for a man in his state. She left, then returned with a saucer of creamers, and presented a menu to him. His gloved hands on his thighs, he drew back from the laminated eight and a half by fourteen page.

"We have some very good soups that might warm you up more than the coffee." She tapped with her free hand the list of soups at the top of the menu, but his eyes stayed on her, alert to her every movement and intention. She listed them verbally. As if he did not comprehend the term soup, he stayed mute. "I like the lentil." She gave her broadest smile, while the blank page of his face failed to reveal any written expression. "How about I bring you a bowl?" She nodded, retracted her arm with the menu in hand, and left him.

Behind the counter, Lisa, Jerusha's fellow waitress, who witnessed the exchange, raised her eyebrows when Jerusha came to the order window. She said, "Wow. Do you think maybe he doesn't understand English?"

Jerusha slapped the ticket on the window ledge. "Lentil soup on the fly." To Lisa, she whispered, "Dunno, hon."

"Up." Bob, the cook, clacked the soup onto a liner plate.

Jerusha set a spoon on the side of the liner plate then took the bowl to the man. "Here you go, stranger." She set the bowl down and paused. The man was frozen in the pose he had when she tried to hand him the menu. "You enjoy, okay?" She waited for just a second or two to see if he would not come away from his fearful surveillance of her motives. What had happened to this fellow? She left him and checked on the booths to either side. He scrutinized every customer around him as his body bent by inches. He inhaled deeply, and his back broadened noticeably. He took up the spoon and began to lift bite after bite of hot lentil soup into his mouth without slackening his pace. She saw the steam play in the air over the bowl—though he showed no sign that it pained him. He ate with a relentless absorption that awed Jerusha. The diner's customers all seemed contented at that moment so she leaned a hip on the bar and studied this man. There was something about his muteness, his clothes (dirty but nice and warm) his build (a bit thin but barrel chested with noticeably thick legs and neck), and his complete lack of facial expression that intrigued her. Whenever she had volunteered at soup kitchens—something that she did from high school through her undergrad days—and met the transients and homeless and jobless, they were eager to talk and show their gratitude. They obeyed rules of common courtesy. They were grateful that anyone treated them with humanity. Yet this man seemed to not have even the slightest connection to those sensibilities. She kept thinking of him as an animal, a description that she abhorred though it seemed entirely appropriate. Was he from a mental institution? A recent release? She mused on that, conjured scenes in her mind where he sat among patients in pajamas, robes, maybe non-descript cotton clothing—do they still issue mental patients uniforms these days, badges of their status as the insane, she wondered—while nurses, doctors, and counselors tried to coax, medicate, and engage his lost mind. A regular who sat at the bar thumbed his plate back from his middle aged, man gut. Jerusha crossed over and took it to the dish room. That mental institute scenario seemed unlikely. This man was utterly untreated by professional Western medicine and psychological practices.

When she returned from the dish room, she paused after the swing door and saw that he had finished the soup. The bowl, with the spoon sticking out, sat drained before him. His gloves were off now, both rested on the table, one to either side as if he needed to separate them so as to remember which glove went with which hand. With his elbows on the table top, he held the coffee in both hands and drank slowly, without pause, his chest swelling by the second. After almost half a minute, his hands righted the mug, his lips closed, opened, closed as if he was only just testing the coffee, but then he tilted the cup to his mouth and proceeded to drink again. When he took the mug away again, it was empty. He set it on the saucer.

Jerusha approached. "Would you care for more coffee? Or is it a dessert that you'd like now?"

For the first time, there was a hint on his brow of some expression that wanted to alter the blankness of his face. The struggle went for a moment until he shook his head, maybe only a fraction of an inch to either side, but it was something and she registered it.

"Just the check then?" She did not budge. He would have to respond to make her leave him alone. The struggle at his brow began again. His eyes were terribly empty of anything and this forced her to be brave enough to continue to return that stare with a smile that was warm and humane, not frozen and scared. What was wrong with this man? His head drooped and rose again. That was a nod, all that he could summon past the no man's land that partitioned him from the rest of humanity. Had he gone on a journey into his mind, a valiant genius, only to become stranded far from the quotidian territory where humans interact? She wanted to know.

She went and tabulated his check behind the bar with a small calculator. Lisa came up. "Do you think he'll bail without paying?"

"If he does, I'll gladly cover the tab. He seems to have enough troubles in his head that he doesn't need to be busted by the cops for skipping out on a four dollar tab."

"It's your money." Lisa rolled her eyes.

"That it is. And I'd rather it went to help someone than to taxes for the government."

Lisa blew air through her nose, perhaps in disagreement.

Jerusha returned to the stranger's table. As she set the ticket down, she took from a waist pocket a red and white mint which she laid atop the green and white ticket. "Either you can take that up to the register or I'll take it for you now." She stood her ground to await a response. He blinked, swallowed, and his body arched while his right hand dug into his front pocket. The neatly folded bit of cash he fished out, caused her eyebrows to rise. She controlled her reaction, recomposed her face into attendance, and put a hand to the tabletop. Outermost on that folded pack of dollars were a few twenties, some fives, and then ones. He pulled out a five, leaned, checked the bill, stared at it for several seconds as if he had to translate what was written, and pulled an extra two ones. He laid the three bills on the check. Where had he come up with that cash? Jerusha reached halfway and asked, "Do you need change?"

He had already stashed the cash into his front pocket again, and now he began to tug on his gloves. He did not pause, but he made the same fractured head shake and his mouth came unstuck for a second as if the word 'no' was said, though it was inaudible.

"Thank you very much, stranger." Jerusha stepped back so that he could escape from the booth. She had left the check and cash untouched, in case of what though, she didn't know. "Have a good night." She smiled and looked right into brown eyes that seemed to expect a violent and sudden attack any second. He stood, did not make eye contact, turned, and stalked to the door and was gone. Jerusha took the ticket and cash, spun, saw Lisa's eyes on her, and held aloft the seven dollars to say, see, he was all right, I was right, and you, Lisa, were wrong. Would she ever see him again? What if he became some sort of odd regular? No, probably not. He was a transient, and she'd never learn what was so seriously damaged about him. At least she'd done the right thing and shown him compassion, an enlightened way of behaving towards others. Maybe it would help him.

Will couldn't recall days of the week and his only knowledge of time was when the sun was up and when it was down, which equaled day and night, respectively. He wandered into Flagstaff and stood on street corners and witnessed the traffic of cars with their dirt spotted paint and clumps of clinging white snow on rooftops or trunks and brown chunks of gunk glued to wheel wells. All the traffic seemed as loud as cannon fire, like warfare against his senses.

He dared not to enter the intimidating buildings that squatted all around him in obscure, riddling designs. Once inside one of those brick, geometric edifices, would he ever be able to escape, to see daylight once more? In the January weather of Flagstaff, there were not too many pedestrians. The few passersby he encountered, he distrusted and retreated from the sidewalk as they passed. He neither turned his back nor shifted his eyes from them. He had to gauge their intentions. If only he was a dog and could smell their fear, the pheromones of their desires, he wouldn't have to stare at them. What if they pounced on him and shredded his body? Everyone was seeking him. Weren't they? Yes, he recalled that now. He was a fugitive. He was a murderer. He had killed many people, but, at least when it was day, those events and the faces of his victims seemed like influenza dreams. At night, it was a different story.

He had a backpack with his rolled sleeping bag. When he stood on the street corners, uncertain about what path to take, he shucked the pack from his aching shoulders and set it atop his boots, and he grasped the top to keep it balanced and dry from the slush on the pavement. When he turned his eyes down to the pack, it reminded him of his car, which had failed to start the morning after he pulled into a campground to sleep for the night. It snowed during that night and the doors froze shut. Will panicked, and, holding the handle open, he kicked with both feet until the door cracked open and crisp, cold, shocking air blasted into the car to slap his sweaty brow. He inhaled deeply for several minutes. He should leave, but when he turned the key in the ignition, there was no sound at all. No electric current and no motor turning. There was nothing. The battery was most likely dead. Will's stomach and scrotum contracted and his mouth filled with a cold, metal taste. What should he do?

He'd been in Flagstaff at least two days, maybe three. He ate somewhere and there was a girl who smiled. He began to remember more as he witnessed the speedy workings of the small city, as if the quick movements of cars and traffic lights caused his synapses to quicken also. Memories came like bursts of machine gun fire in the night, sudden, disorienting, terrifying, and with the grit of death. Rand was there. Will talked to him on the streets of Flagstaff. Where are you? Will asked Rand. Why am I alone? Why did we do the things that we did? We killed people! Will shouted at Rand. How many? And for what? We set out to change the world. I wanted to make the world better. We wanted to teach people to be better, to live more conscientiously, more fully aware. But it didn't work. Look around! It's all the same as it was before we began our war. We meant to elevate everyone's lives. We meant to enlighten people. Instead, we took lives and wasted them. Will shook his finger at Rand. You, you began to kill for no reason. What happened to you? You went crazy, didn't you? And now where are you?

"Sir, are you okay?"

Will's body trembled. He turned. Two police officers, dressed in navy uniforms with black Glock pistols in black nylon holsters stood between him and a police cruiser with its hood lights flickering.

The officers, one husky with a mustache and goatee, the other muscular and quite dark skinned, maybe a Navajo or Hopi, looked him up and down, settled their eyes on the pack and sleeping bag balanced atop his boots to stay dry. The husky cop asked, "Do you need help?"

Will shook his head.

So this was it? It was over. They'd caught him in mid-confession. To show his surrender, he shot his arms high into the sky. His backpack dropped like a dead man onto the wet sidewalk. Will, relieved, said, "You got me."

"Uh, sir?" the darker cop said. He reached and picked up the backpack. His eyes began to examine the visible aspects of it.

The husky cop pulled at his goatee. "Do you have somewhere to stay? Are you from Flagstaff?"

"No." Will shook his head and kept his arms up. When would they slap the cuffs on him? "My car broke down." He didn't know why he told them that. It just slipped out.

"You have a car?"

"You can lower your hands, sir. You're not in any trouble."

"Yes, I have a car, but it broke down." Will's brow furrowed. When was that again? "It was a few days ago." Where was the car? Could he ever make it to where it was? Could he remember?

"Is your car here in Flagstaff?"

"No. No, it's in a camping ground. I walked here. I think it's the battery."

"Sir, you're not in any trouble. You can put your hands down."

Will looked up at his hands. He'd forgotten them. Slowly, he lowered them. "I'm not in trouble." He dully repeated the officer's words. Didn't they know who he was?

"You haven't been drinking, have you, sir?" It was the darker officer who asked this. His eyes narrowed until all he saw was the black of his pupils.

"No."

The officer, who asked this, stepped closer until he was a foot away. A few inches taller than Will, he leaned over and took a long inhalation of the air around Will's head. Will's eyes widened. He felt oddly violated by the officer's action. He wanted to protest. He took a step back, and his upper lip pulled up in one corner in repugnance at this encroachment of his personal space.

"No, he doesn't smell of alcohol," said the darker cop.

Will crossed his arms, and pulled his other foot back beside the one that had retreated.

"We have to ask. You do know why we stopped to talk to you, don't you?"

"I may have been talking to myself." Will rubbed the back of his neck.

The cops exchanged looks with raised eyebrows. The husky one said, "Well, actually, you were shouting at the traffic."

"Oh. Shouting. Oh." Will's head drooped and his shoulders rolled forward. "That's . . . embarrassing."

The cops nodded, perhaps they were mollified by that answer. "Are you okay now?" the husky one asked.

Will's eyes darted to their faces, first one, then the other. "I'm sorry. I'm not crazy. Really."

"When we got out you were asking if somebody was crazy. Who was it?" The husky one continued in his role as the inquisitor, while the Navajo officer looked down his nose at him with suspicion. "Who was the somebody?"

"It was a friend of mine. He . . . killed himself. I saw it happen. Sometimes I forget that I can't really talk to him. He was my roommate for four years." Will nodded and scratched his scraggly beard. "That's a long time, you know."

"Uh hunh," the Navajo cop said.

"Do you need some kind of assistance? I mean," said the husky cop. "Do you have a place to stay?"

"No. No, I'm fine. I'll get a room at a hotel." Will waved his hands. If they weren't going to arrest him, if they didn't know who he was, he wanted to get away from them as fast as possible.

"You have money?" The husky one cocked his head at him as if he didn't believe that.

"Oh, yeah. Yeah, I do. I'm okay. Really." Will patted his back pocket where his wallet was.

"Uh hunh." The Navajo cop raised his chin to stonily eye Will.

"All right. I would suggest, sir, that you go check into a hotel, get yourself a hot shower and warm up. There's no need to stay out in this weather. There's another storm on the way." The husky cop shivered and rubbed his hands together.

"Okay. Yes, sir, I'll do that. Thank you." Will shivered to show them that, yes, it was cold. "May I have my pack?" He tentatively put his hands forward.

The Navajo cop thrust it into Will's chest. The cops turned and went to the warmth of their idling cruiser.

He checked into a room at the Econo Lodge. When he entered the room, he began to strip his clothing and cast it onto the floor. It was stuffy in the room. All the familiar smells of the woods and of campfires were absent here. He couldn't identify what the smells were in this place. He ran a hot bath and lay in it until the water was cool. He marveled at the feel of his body immersed in water. How long had it been since he took a bath, let alone showered? His leg hairs wafted in the currents. He lathered his body with a bar of soap, the wrapper of which he tossed onto the gray tile. When he finished, he saw a washcloth, soaped it, and scrubbed his body a second time. The water was gray. He drained the tub, stood, turned on the shower, and used a finger sized vial of shampoo to wash his hair. Though he felt clean, he spied a matching vial of conditioner, emptied it over his head, and scratched it into his scalp as well. When he stepped out, his thighs squeaked together as he took a towel and dried off. From his pack, he drew out a frayed toothbrush and a smashed tube of Colgate. He brushed his teeth. The hotel had provided mouthwash, which he gargled. He stared in the mirror. He didn't think he could clean himself any more. He found his comb in his shaving kit which he'd brought out for the toothbrush and Colgate. There were numerous knots in his hair, and he snatched a few clumps straight out, which made him wince. That was that. Well, maybe he could track down a razor tomorrow and shave off his beard.

He went to the double sized bed, climbed in naked, and lay on his back. It seemed like a long time that he lay there. His muscles had difficulties relaxing into such expanse as that mattress. This wasn't the Oldsmobile's front seat or the tightness of his sleeping bag. What should he do tomorrow? Where should he go? He couldn't afford to stay at the Econo Lodge long. Cheap as it was, he would still be broke in a few days. He should find a laundry. Did they have machines here in the hotel that he could use? And he needed a few supplies. He drifted to sleep as he contemplated what his next move should be.

The next day he spent time in the city. After the heartening experience of the hotel, he dared to enter the Target. He half expected wanted posters with his face and name on them to be taped in the front glass. He slunk in and mingled with the shoppers, gazed at the merchandise, aisle by aisle, until he covered the whole store. It was hard to remember what all those buyable products were meant to do. As he passed a security guard, an African American woman as tall as him, he avoided eye contact, pretended to peruse the shelves for a sought after item. He listened to shoppers talk. Ninety percent were women and children too young for school, presumably the men were at work. The manner in which the women dressed was intriguing. Some wore exercise clothes over bodies as fit as could be after the most recent birth, but they wore makeup that demonstrated how they had not dashed to the Target after the gym. Other women dressed in comfortable jeans and blouses with accommodating shoes and their figures were as broken in by bearing children as by eating heftily on a diet of processed, unhealthy products. Babies were in cart seats with variegated, plastic pacifiers clamped in their mouths to keep them mollified and silent. Mothers nagged, instructed, scolded, and pleaded with the toddlers, and tried to include them in the choices of the purchases.

"Don't touch."

"If you don't stop, you can't watch a movie when we get home."

"Where's the Tide? Which do you think I should buy? The biggest or the next biggest?"

"What do you think daddy wants?"

"Leave your sister alone."

"Stay right by my side. Don't wander off. Someone might steal you."

"You need to choose, sweetie, you can't have both. If you don't choose, you can't have either."

Will felt besieged by the information, the onslaught of meaningless verbiage, all constructed to consume the products neatly rowed and lined, displayed in perfection to entice.

"Where did mommy put her coupons? We need those to save money."

"Fine. We'll get those today, but this is a special treat. We're not having Oreos every time we come."

As Will methodically trooped down the aisles, he speculated on the quantities of products. How many beds could this store's supply of sheets cover? How many cold passersby in the winter would be warmed by those coats on the racks? How many people could have a glass of milk from all those gallons of milk in the glass-fronted coolers? Hundreds? None of this was free though. Money, money, money. How do we come by the money? Work, work, work. Steal, steal, steal. Work, work, work. Employ, employ, employ. Stocks and bonds, stocks and bonds, stocks and bonds. Inherit, inherit, inherit. Work, work, work. Will wanted no part of any of that, but his money was running low.

Will wandered up Milton Avenue. Often he stood and shivered in the cold while he marveled at the items for sale. There, placed at attention in battalions and regiments, were cups, glasses, tumblers, goblets, flutes, and mugs. Over there were platoons and companies of saucers, plates, and chargers. Everything was for sale. Everything was for people to stare at, display, serve on, dine on, to talk over, and to talk about. So many colors, styles, uses, and decorative options. He wanted to puke, or to drop a nuke on it all, to disintegrate it in a millisecond with a hydrogen bomb. Or maybe it was the idea represented by all those objects—objects that were just atoms in different arrangements, as was the air between him and them, and, for that matter, so was he—that he wanted to make vanish, and the best way to do that, maybe the only way, was to obliterate that idea. How do you do that though? Ideas are hard to stop, they move like influenza through the air between potential hosts, and they enter their victims to quickly spread and reproduce throughout the mind.

There was something infinitely more humane and congenial about the smaller shops along the tight streets of downtown just north of Route 66. Often, the shop was devoted to a niche, a particular need or product, like a sweets shop, a jewelry shop, a Western wear shop, ski equipment, and so on. The proprietors of these small shops, which occupied not much more than a large living room of a house, had an affinity, perhaps a passion, for these objects for sale, and that was why the person opened the shop, to cater to those who were like minded. The smiling face behind the counter was often middle aged and their eyes gleamed with a fervent desire to meet and to realize that you, the prospective customer, were a person of similar temperament.

On Tuesday he went to the Cineplex. He paid for the film that started first. Movies explained and displayed the culture of its society of origin. He figured that he would sit and watch every film that was on view. Maybe he would learn something, maybe he would remember something, perhaps that he once liked being a part of American society. Well, that wasn't quite true. It wasn't that he loved American society, or liked it even, but it never bothered him. He hadn't previously disliked it or abhorred it, but when he went to the Target on Monday and then strolled along Milton before he wandered through the downtown shops of local entrepreneurs away from the corporate dominated big stores, he had felt a revulsion not just for the signs of greed, money, and consumerism but also for himself. After all, he had fought to both preserve the American way and to project it farther beyond its borders. He could not despise the society without despising himself. Hypocrites were pathetic.

He endured movie after movie: a kids' movies, a comedy, two romantic comedies, two action flicks, and a horror, seven movies in all, from ten in the morning until half past midnight. He had a headache by seven in the evening. On screen he witnessed how people kissed and made love, how they fought huge gun battles with ballet like moves, how heroes and cowards and villains died or triumphed, how people fell in and out of love, how they created mental obstacles to their own happiness, how children were taught life lessons by talking, humanized cartoon animals, how Ford invested in one movie and Pepsi another, how rare a well-made movie really was, how the attractive people were always in the lead roles while the short and ugly and fat and old had all the small parts, how music had to always accompany the important moments of the movie and consequently of our lives, how the soundtrack was available for purchase, how every person involved had to have his or her name listed at the dead end of the film, how the world only mattered if there was a human to act in it, how there was no one who was really and truly impoverished, how there was someone who always had hope, how happy endings were the only ending, and many more lessons, some big, some small, but they accumulated like a clot in an artery ready to stop Will's heart.

It seemed like ages since he ate a meal that someone else cooked for him in a proper kitchen. He was disgusted with the idea of the foods he had eaten for the last few months while he lived in the wilderness. He entered a diner that looked familiar.

She stood in her old style, sky blue and white, waitress uniform, one hand brandished a brown plastic collared glass coffee pot half full, poised between two mugs, and she smiled broadly and said,

"Welcome back, stranger. Care to sit at the bar? Need a cup of hot joe? It's not gourmet, but it'll keep you up for hours with heartburn." He realized from her voice, from her buzzed hair, and the way she spoke to him as an old associate, that this was the diner he'd come to a few nights before. Wasn't that his first night in town? Probably. He still couldn't make out the timeline of his first few days in town, it was like trying to decipher a news article after someone had run the paper through a shredder.

A young, uniformed police officer, whose cup the waitress just filled, and beside him a man who could have been a lumberjack with his green and black plaid, flannel coat, his black wool cap, and the leather tool belt on the stool next to him, whose cup the waitress now held the coffee pot over, both nodded their heads in greeting. Will brought his hands together, rubbed some feeling into them, and nodded at the offer of the waitress whose most obvious physical trait was her buzzed hair. She looked ready for boot camp. Knowing that he cut a pathetic figure with his dirty, worn clothes, Will pulled his shoulders back and strode to a bar stool two down from where the lumberjack, his tool belt, and the cop sat. Why did there have to be a cop? Will sawed a leg over the top of the stool. His leg halfway over, he thought how ridiculous he must look as he tried to be macho, or whatever this charade of his was.

The waitress topped off the lumberjack's mug from the pot. To Will, she asked, "Would you like regular?" She seemed too cordial.

Will nodded. The cop, who was farther down the bar, had to lean forward so that he too could stare at Will just like the lumberjack. Will directed a slow nod to them. In response, the lumberjack jerked his chin up, and the cop said, "Good evening, sir." That politeness was trained, not genuine.

Will had to speak now, it was his turn. "Hello."

In front of him the waitress set a saucer and a mug which she filled. "Do you need room for cream?"

"No, thank you." As the brown liquid fell and steamed into the mug, Will examined her. She had green eyes, was in her early twenties, maybe five feet five, and very slender, though at first, it was hard to tell if that was because she starved herself or if she was athletic. The short sleeves of her uniform ended at the tops of arms. Visible muscles worked easily to stop the flow of coffee to his mug and set the pot on its burner. So, she was athletic.

"Soup again?"

At the mention of food, Will's lips unconsciously moved to the thought of steak on a fork to be chewed. "So you remember me?"

"Of course. It's not often that I wait on a mute. But lookee here, you speak just fine." She laughed at him.

Will nodded. He returned to the question of food. His stomach was in an awful state. He hadn't eaten all day. "Do you have steak and potatoes?"

The waitress's head jerked back in surprise. "Of course, stranger. How do you like the potatoes? Baked, fried, mashed . . . ?"

"Mashed."

"We've got gravy to cover them."

"Okay."

"You need a vegetable too. Would you like green beans, carrots, or broccoli?"

"Carrots."

"Good choice. They help your eye sight."

Will liked this girl. She didn't have to talk so nicely to him. It was as if she bucked the suspicion and hostility of the cop and lumberjack out of some deep principle about how to treat all humans.

"You also get a choice of either a roll or a biscuit."

"Biscuit, please." Will's manners were awake now.

"I bet you might like butter and honey on that biscuit." She smiled slyly as if she had insight into his taste buds.

"Yes, thank you."

"And just one last detail. How do you take your steak?"

"Medium's fine."

"All right." Finally, she pulled out a pad of tickets and a pen from the pocket of the uniform and wrote out his order. At the end of it she popped the pad with the point of her pen, like the final period to end a long novel, her own *War and Peace*. She spun one eighty and, with a quick rip, tore the ticket from the pad and plunked it on the ledge of the order window where the cannonball shaped head of the cook was framed. The cook's mouth broke open and Will heard his growl and the words money, pay, and sure. The waitress waved a hand and said clearly, "If he can't, then I got it."

Will leaned back and dug a hand into his front pocket. Interrupted conversations had resumed behind him in the diner, though the cop and lumberjack quietly drank their coffee with their eyes forward to allow their peripheral visions to continue their observations of Will. He produced several crumpled, heavily creased bills of various denominations. They were a sorry looking lot, but there was about twenty five dollars there. He snuck a glance at the immobile cop and lumberjack. Will set about the process of smoothing and ordering his cash on his thigh. When he finished, he folded the money in half and stuck it in his shirt breast pocket. He was in need of cash. He'd blown through a lot in the past week with the hostel he was now staying in, his food, that day at the movies, and so on. Could he get a job? Could he keep a job?

The waitress was leaning against the counter with a compassionate smile on her lips and eyes.

"May I also have a glass of milk with my supper?"

"Of course." She took a glass, filled it, and set it before him. She leaned her elbows on the bar and folded her arms so that her face was only a foot from his. "You didn't have to do that."

"What?"

"Prove that you could pay."

"I didn't want anyone to think I was a bum."

She turned to look at the cop and lumberjack. "Anyone? You mean like them?" She turned her head further to gaze at the cannonball headed cook. "Or him?"

"Yeah."

"Be yourself. Why care what they think? They're no one to you." Her eyes came around, and he swore the green irises were like worlds of wide open meadows. "What's your name, stranger?"

His name. He couldn't use his real name. There was a cop not five feet away. His body felt as if he had dove into the Arctic Ocean. A name, now, he ordered. He blurted, "Anderson."

"Is that your first or last name?"

"First. Anderson Williams is my whole name." He sipped his coffee. "And yours?"

"Jerusha Liebgott." She tapped a white plastic nametag with her name stenciled in black.

Will blinked. "Jerusha? Does it mean something?"

"All names mean something. Jerusha means me. Anderson means you. But why not go by Andy?"

"Andy sounds like the name of a kid."

"Fair enough, but a rose by any other name would smell just as sweet, so the Bard said."

"Maybe the physical properties would be unchanged, but the perception of them would be altered."

"If a word is all it takes to create new inferences then how difficult is it to name something a second time?"

Will drank his coffee. After he set it down, he swiveled on the stool and studied the other customers. Everyone was dressed warmly. Heavy jackets lay in the booths beside them like slain bodies. The last two that he looked at were the cop and lumberjack. Their eyes were on him. Will nodded at Jerusha, and to the men he said, "I might get involved in a philosophical exchange with her if I keep this up."

Both men gave a jerk of a chuckle. The lumberjack said, "Yeah, maybe Jerusha here is one of them Plato killers, they've been huntin'. Hey, Henry." He nudged the cop in the arm. "Maybe you should question her. Run her downtown and get the Feds on her case. What about it?"

"The wanna-be Buddhist from LA, a serial killer?" Henry the cop took a deep breath and rattled his head back and forth. "I doubt it. But maybe I'll get my hand cuffs out anyway." He wiggled his eyebrows at her.

Jerusha rolled her eyes. "It's important to engage in dialogue about the more esoteric questions of our existences." She jerked her head haughtily.

"Uh oh," the lumberjack said. "Here comes the graduate student in, uh, what is it you're studying?"

"Literature."

With raised eyebrows, Will said to Jerusha, "A wanna-be Buddhist from LA who studies literature at the post graduate level? That's an intriguing mix."

"Want some more coffee?" she asked the three men at the bar.

Will held his mug out toward her. "Please."

She refilled it. "Yes, I'm from the smog capital of the great US of A. Where are you from?"

"Oh, all over."

"Like?"

"I last lived in Tucson."

"Where do you live now?"

Jerusha's question prompted the eyes of the lumberjack and Henry the cop to focus on him again, Will sensed it. "I guess you could say that I dropped off the grid. You know, like a protest against capitalism." Will wanted to stop right there but felt compelled to continue so that he could cut off further questions. "I had some money saved. I bought some supplies. I went into the wild." He smirked. "I went to the woods because I wanted to live deliberately." He hoped that Jerusha would catch the quote.

The smile that lifted her face told him that she knew that literary allusion. She said, "I love Thoreau."

"I recently reread him for the first time since I was a junior in high school," he said. They nodded at each other as if they were members of a club. "Anyway, I've been living out there." He jerked his thumb to indicate a place beyond the city's pale.

"During this winter?" the lumberjack asked.

"Yeah. If you have the right gear, you'll be fine."

"What did you live in?" the lumberjack persisted.

"My car mostly." Will wanted to shift the conversation. He did not like to discuss his own story, especially not with a cop a few seats away. He would not be able to keep track of unrehearsed lies and so it was better not to tell any. It was best to not talk at all. He really just wanted a private conversation with Jerusha, this kind waitress. He could just change the topic, ignore the two men, and focus on her. "So what's the Buddhism about?"

"Can't you tell?" The lumberjack heckled. "It's about getting your hair buzzed, even if you're a girl."

Jerusha planted her fists on her hips and set her jaw as she glared at the lumberjack and Henry the cop while they guffawed and slapped the counter.

Will felt the need to rise to her defense just as she had his. "Hair grows back, it goes gray, and sometimes it falls out." He had their attention. He locked eyes with Jerusha, whose shoulders fell from their defensive positions as she took a long breath. The cannonball shaped head of the cook appeared in his window along with a plate of steaming food. Will hoped that plate was for him. Jerusha grabbed the plate before the cook could say whatever he was going to say. She pulled from a plastic cylinder a napkin rolled around a knife, fork, and spoon. All this was placed before Will, and her smile stood above it all, just for him. "I can see that you're pretty even without the hair," he said.

Jerusha smiled but looked away, and he had the impression that this was not the correct thing to say to her though it had put the two jokers farther down the bar off in shut-up-land.

"So Buddhism is all about meditation, right?" Will filled his mouth with the slightly lumpy mashed potatoes and the rich gravy with its pools of glinting grease, good to taste but probably not that healthy.

"No. Meditation plays a key part in it, but it's used to gain enlightenment, which is the goal. Not that you can ever achieve total enlightenment. There is no final point of total knowledge, whether of the self or of the world. What you have is a path, and that path is the goal, rather than some far off moment of mystical communion with power and glory and the divine. You get it?"

Will tilted his head as he attempted to absorb that vague description. He was out of practice for this kind of discussion. "Um."

"Have you ever heard of the *Dhammapada*?" she asked. Will shook his head. Jerusha reached into that small pocket at the front of her out dated waitress uniform. Her slender fingers fished out first the ticket pad and then a tiny paperback book, the object of her quest. She offered the book to him. He accepted the book which was smaller than his palm. He randomly opened it. She said, "*Dhamma* means law, justice, truth, while *pada* means path, foot. These are the sayings of the Buddha. It is his path to truth, that we can read, learn, and pursue over two thousand years after he lived." Under the title "*Violence,*" Will read, *Believe, meditate, see. Be harmless, be blameless. Awake to the law. And from all sorrow free yourself.* She reached and took the top of the book though she did not pull it from his grasp. She allowed him to relinquish the book. "Let me read to you the opening." She took note of the page he was on, glanced at him, flipped to the front, went forward a few pages, and located the passage that she wanted to read. "We are what we think. All that we are arises with our thoughts. With our thoughts we make the world." She paused, and he expected her to continue, but maybe all she did was reread the same lines. Finally, she closed the palm-sized book. "Isn't that amazing? How about the emphasis on thought as the means that we humans use to create our perceptual frameworks?"

Will nodded. Through the swinging door, came the rotund cook who held a metal spatula as if it was a sword, both ceremonial to indicate his position in the world and as a weapon to fend off those dangers likely to happen in a diner.

"Blah, blah," the cook said. "No one talks like that 'cept in a college class. It ain't real. It ain't solvin' any problems that anyone in this world has."

"I don't really know what she's talking about, but I find it interesting, and I don't mean that in a condescending way either." Will spoke to the men but his eyes were on her.

The cop, the lumberjack, and the cook exchanged glances and shook their heads.

"What? You think she's wrong to be interested in Buddhism because it's so alien to everything you know? Well, that's you not her. I'd like to hear more."

Jerusha checked the clock on the wall. "Not tonight. It's almost closing time. Gentlemen." She motioned to the door as if to shoo them all out. "I need to go home and get my beauty sleep."

He could not let her get out of it so easily. He had neglected his dinner during this conversation and now he set to it with relish. That cook might be closed minded but he made good chow. Will took a bite from one item then the next in a cycle. He said no more and ate without cease until the plate shined with a moist swirl of residue. To top the meal, he drank his milk, slowly. It was whole milk and it felt like a cream blanket laid over all his insides. It was a few minutes to ten when he drank the last of the milk.

"Anything else tonight? Last call, I'm afraid." She was scrubbing the counter with a wet towel.

"No thanks."

"It's nice to hear you talk."

"Sorry, I hadn't spoken to anyone in a few months."

The lumberjack and cop rose from their stools, waved, and called out their farewells.

"Do you work tomorrow night?" Will asked her.

"Yes, I work Thursday through Sunday."

"I'll see you tomorrow then."

"Okay," she said as if she didn't believe him.

He rose and left the twenty on the counter to cover the bill and her tip. He buttoned up. "Thanks."

"You're welcome."

"I don't mean for serving me."

She looked away and gave a single nod. "It was no trouble."

He crossed to the door, and she came around the counter and met him at the door. He said, "But thanks. No one else would've done the same, you know, treating me so kindly. No one was as nice to me as you were." He went out the door and turned to take a final look at her, all thin and shaved headed in her small, sky blue uniform.

"It's the right thing to do." She shrugged to dismiss the deed as irrelevant.

"Most people don't do the right thing though." He took from his coat pocket a thick pair of ski gloves and tugged them on.

"You're very pessimistic about people." She shivered and wrapped her free arm around her.

"You're not?"

"No."

"I should leave so you can shut the door. You're freezing. I can see the goose bumps." He also saw the hard points of her nipples through the thin synthetic fabric of that uniform. "Go in. I'll see you tomorrow."

She glanced at her arm that held the door and nodded with a grin.

"Go in, now. Bye." He turned and strode away though he looked over his shoulder. Inspired by some silly notion, he called out, "I'll bring my copy of *Walden*."

"Okay." She wagged her head slowly and slightly as if she thought he was crazy, or maybe lying. "See you then. Bye."

The following morning, at a café by NAU, he bought a large coffee and a local newspaper. To have a job required an address. That's what he'd always heard. An odd fact, since homeless people need jobs too. The hostel was cheap, but he couldn't stay there long, too many people, not enough privacy. If he wanted to live in an apartment, there were several considerations. First, he had no job. Second, he would need to find a small place, a cheap place, a place that was quiet where he could live inconspicuously. That last requirement would probably be the most challenging to meet since Flagstaff was a small city built around tourism and Northern Arizona University, and college students primarily rented apartments where they partied, which meant public disturbance and noise nuisance calls by police conducted in the early morning hours. He checked the paper for job and apartment listings. There were a number of the latter but few of the former. The dearth of employment opportunities was explained by articles throughout the front of the newspaper about the calamitous economic events melting into unrecognizable shapes all over the world. No nation was immune, no community escaped the tendrils of deprivation and foreclosure. He read the articles with a mixture of awe and outrage at the pervasiveness of the new misery and because of the origin of this turmoil, the rapaciousness of humans. Maybe he should go back on the road? Maybe he should lock and load, take aim, and execute the true criminals of the world? He could be the avenging angel against the scourge of the amoral agents of bad banking deals, uncontrolled real estate transactions, and dishonest board members that bilked the accounts of average people who wanted nothing but to survive comfortably. Slaughtering these petty financial tyrants would make him a hero to millions, maybe billions. He would gladly sacrifice his future for the sake of mopping up the world of these vile, unconscientious bastards. A bullet spent would right the evils of so much wrong.

How could he start? He watched coeds file in to get lattes, espressos, and mochas while snow flopped to the pavement outside. Where could he start? Who were those responsible? He had only a vague idea. Go to the ritzy neighborhoods and just start there. But would he kill the wives and children of these criminals too? They profited heavily from the moral indifference of their husbands and fathers. The wives and children had little care for the welfare of those that suffered to line their lives with wealth and splendor.

How many could he kill? The rich have the leashes of the police, after all, because the rich include judges and attorneys. The police would be hot on his trail from the first kill. He would have to work quickly then, inflicting maximum carnage in very little time. Bombs would work best. A fifty gallon drum filled with the proper combination of chemicals would demolish a fairly large structure, but this would lead to the deaths of anyone who was home, regardless of their culpability.

He fantasized about sighting the crosshairs on some soft bit of a banker in his tailored suit and blasting a hole in his face. That's righteous retribution! That's a worthy and appropriate moral response!

People, the average citizens who toil for wages or salaries, who want a house with a thirty year mortgage, who want to raise kids, relax at night with the TV on, enjoy the shopping and social networking pleasures of the internet, who send their kids to clean, safe schools, who dress their kids in the nice clothes from the Gap or maybe just from Wal-mart, it was these people who allowed themselves to be victimized. They expected the government, staffed with the rich or the aspirant rich, to guarantee the safety of the poor when the status of the wealthy depended on the constant spending of all those millions of citizens. The remedy to the inequality was so simple: execute the offenders. And when more aspirants appeared to succeed those dead, rich fuckers, then the same bloodletting had to be applied. Learn or die, you malevolent bastards, that would be his credo.

Will held his newspaper in one hand, his coffee in the other and giggled like a girl. All so easy. All so obvious. In the shooting gallery of his mind he gunned them down one after another. His mind sped up the motion picture of his fantasy until it was a collage of blood and gore. The bullets he fired ejected brain and bone from the exit wounds. Over and over. As he saw this collage of unfettered violence by his hand, his shoulders hunched. He dropped the newspaper. He spilled his coffee on the gray and black pages when his arm gave and the mug thudded to the tabletop. More bodies and more bodies. They flopped and flew, stacked and piled. His jaw tightened and ached his molars. His head drooped and his back bent. The now familiar ennui resumed. He had to stop the death. With both hands knotted into fists he pressed his eyeballs into his skull until he saw red and green fireworks, and he felt that in the next instant his brain might pop and leak its contents. That would be his end. He could not take anymore.

He returned that night to the diner. He brought with him a copy of *Walden.* He took *The Stranger* by Camus on Saturday. Henry the cop and one of his cop brothers came into the diner while he was in the middle of telling Jerusha about *The Stranger*. She asked, "What's wrong?"

Will said, "I don't like him."

"He's all right."

"I don't like how he and his buddy, that lumberjack from the other night, talked to you."

"Pete."

"Yeah, whatever. I can't believe you let them run you down like that. They're so ignorant. It's repugnant that they think they're smarter than you."

"Actually, I doubt either of them thinks he's smarter than me. If anything they know I'm smarter and they're intimidated by that."

"That doesn't mitigate their prejudicial stupidity."

"I feel sympathetic toward them," she said.

"Why?" Will finally broke off his observation of the two pigs at the mention of her sympathy for them. "They're just dumb bozos."

"I'm sure there are things they know that both of us are ignorant of."

"I doubt that."

"How can you be so sure, so arrogant? Do you believe they have nothing to teach you? Are you all knowing?"

"Well, no, of course not."

"But you still think they're not just dumber than you but flat out dumb?"

Will tapped his book on the bar top. "Yes."

"I see." She nodded. "You know all the features and maintenance for a chain saw then?"

Will stared at her. She had him. He would neither contradict her nor debate her further on this. She nodded slowly. "Hm. That's strange."

"It's not important for me to know that kind of technical knowledge."

"Maybe it's not important for them to know the book learning that you know."

"But we're talking about life. This is the kind of wisdom that we all need. If you can't explain to people the difference between good and evil, or what's the meaning of life, or why you hold certain beliefs and not others, then how are you any better than an animal, which can't think of such things? No dog can follow Buddha can it?"

She whistled. "A few nights ago Henry and Pete teased me that I was the Plato Killer, but maybe it's you."

Will's body went rigid, and he felt as if all the ninety eight point six degree blood had vanished from his body. All that remained in him were his cold bones. He fought every urge he had to fly out of that diner and never come back. He shivered.

"You okay?"

"I don't think that's a very funny joke." He knew he had to excuse his sudden change in character somehow.

"Oh." She blinked a few times.

"You know, those guys killed a lot of people. What would you think if I'd made a smart ass joke like that and it was one of your friends or relatives who was murdered?"

"I'd be quite upset. Why does it bother you so much?"

"It just does."

She studied him in the eye, but he turned *The Stranger* over in his hand and read the synopsis on the back cover. He had sat and reread *The Stranger* during the day. How much was he like Mersault? No, he was nothing like Mersault. He had killed not because of the sun and the heat, without any thought or malice. He, William Anderson Cooper, killed out of arrogance and a skewed belief in justice.

"I wouldn't have thought you were so sensitive." She moved to the pots of coffee on their warmers, took one in each hand, and set off to make a round of the diner's customers. Damn, he swore at his own guilt. If he behaved like this, he would be captured before he knew it. He drank some coffee. What could he do to mitigate the incident? Did she suspect him? Why would she? It was not as if he had confessed or let slip that his friend was Rand, or that he once drove a Subaru, or was in Colorado in the fall or had a 9mm Browning, or even divulged his true name. He had done none of that, nor revealed any of a million other details that an astute cop would have compared to the facts that he knew of the case and then make the one connection that this man who claimed to be Anderson Williams was indeed the second, un-killed Plato Warrior, William Anderson Cooper.

Jerusha returned and replaced the coffee pots, a little lighter now, on the warmers.

"I think," Will said as he looked from his coffee to the book. "What bothers me so much about those Plato Warriors is that I believe we should seriously consider questions like those I mentioned, but what they did was awful. They murdered. I wish I could take back what they did." Will gripped his book so hard it folded in half. "They perverted the ideas I think they set out to espouse. 'Be thoughtful and intelligent' became 'kill those who are dissimilar to you.' Do you see?"

She nodded with a slow beat. Did she find that explanation plausible?

On Sunday, the last night of her work week, he took Eric Hoffer's *The True Believer*, which he admitted to her had been like reading about himself, a self that he felt embarrassed by as he read. He sat at the bar, as before, and, when she had the opportunity, she stayed near him while she brewed fresh coffee, rang up departing patrons, and stocked dishes still dripping from the dishwashing machine. Their discussions were pleasant and he thanked whatever or whoever there was to thank that neither Henry the cop nor any of his brothers in arms came for a supper or shot of caffeine that night. Jerusha did not raise the spectral topic of the Plato Warriors or what he had said about them the night before. After a majority of the clientele emptied for home, and there were few people near to hear, he read underlined passages from pages he had dog-eared. They discussed the texts. In turn, she plucked from the pocket of her sky blue waitress uniform the palm sized copy of the *Dhammapada*. At closing time, she said, "It's time to kick you out."

"I know. I'm looking at apartments tomorrow."

"Coming back to society? Are you sure you want to?"

He looked her up and down, then shuddered and sighed, and his back elongated so that his head moved over the counter toward her. His eyes closed. He wanted to ask her on a date. When was the last time he had asked a girl out? What should he say? He reopened his eyes. She had turned and was sorting silverware into plastic cylinders. Go for it. Be fearless. Be a man. Get that girl. Guys ask girls out all the time. That's the way it's supposed to be. Do it. "Jerusha?"

A few days later he met her for lunch at the same café by NAU that he'd gone to read the ads. As they stood in the queue for ordering, he told her about the apartment he'd found. One bed, one bath, on the second floor with a balcony. She nodded and told him about the house she rented with a friend. They purchased their drinks. He had black coffee, and she had green tea.

"Where's it at?" She asked.

Will spotted three tables open. He steered her toward one that was in the back corner, and he sat with his back to the wall. As she hung her book bag over the chair back and sat across from him, he studied the crowd, searching for anyone who watched him closely or appeared out of place in the crowd of casually dressed college students. Anyone who was over thirty or dressed in a suit could be a police or FBI agent. No one seemed to be in this category. His eyes came around to find Jerusha watching him with her eyebrows raised.

"Why don't you like to be around people?" Jerusha asked.

"What makes you think I don't want to be around people?" He concentrated on his coffee and not the crowd.

"You're nervous, agitated, and, if you had a home, I don't think you'd leave it."

"Most people aren't very . . ." He drummed his thumb and first finger on his thigh in a rapid rhythm. Lips compressed, he shook his head, barely.

"Enlightened?"

His head snapped up, eyes caught by that word. "I would've said intelligent."

"Hm." With a nod, she sipped from her mug and avoided his eyes. "That's very judgmental, that word."

"Do you think I'm wrong? Besides, is your word so much better?"

Her mug clicked on the table top as she set it down and looked out the café window. Lips pulled in, she twisted in her seat to meditate on the crowd. "Yes. Judging is wrong. They're unenlightened not unintelligent. If they'd come across the same books or teachers or grown up in the same way you had, then they wouldn't be as they are. Besides," she looked him square in the eye, "How enlightened are you? Do you pretend to think that your shit doesn't stink too?"

"No. No, I don't." With that pause, his foot took to a manic rhythm on the table base. She watched the table jiggle and she laid a hand on it to detect that pulse. He stopped, put his foot on the floor, and drank his black coffee. As he lowered the mug, he watched the coffee's surface tilt and right itself as he angled it down for a landing. "Anyway, I think we're using different words to say the same thing."

"The connotation for ignorant is harsher, more judgmental, than the one for unenlightened. Word choice matters. Tone matters too, and you're downright sanctimonious."

"I'm not your student. You sound like you're lecturing. Is that the voice you use on your freshmen comp students?" They eyed each other.

She grinned. "Yeah. Sorry. That's what happens when you meet me right after class."

"Maybe I should meet you after one of your classes when you're the student instead of the teacher."

"Maybe." She shrugged, resettled on her chair, and glanced at him sideways, a playful glint in her eyes. "But those classes aren't lectures, they're discussions. How far did you go?"

"Where?"

"In school?"

"Just my bachelor's. That was enough."

"You think so?"

"What would I learn except how to imitate the thoughts of my professors? Isn't that what you're basically doing?"

"No." She sat straight against the back of her chair. "We all read the texts differently. When we discuss in class, different people engage the text differently."

"You sound like a book."

"Don't we both? Don't you find yourself imitating models of one sort or another, whether it's books or movies or people you've known? How original are any of us?"

"So we have no authentic self? We're merely a hodgepodge of everyone we've seen and heard before? If that's true, we might as well kill ourselves." He pinched a smirk at her.

"It's the combinations that are infinite." She laid her face in the cup of her hand. "What were you like as a child?"

He braced back in his chair and glared down his nose at her. "Why?"

Her eyes dropped then rose. Inhaling, she leaned forward, stretched her arms, and covered the table until her hands clasped an inch from his still steaming mug. Did she approach him in attack or in ardor? Hands set on his thighs, he waited. "I want to know," she said.

Neither looked away, unyielding, adamant.

She said, "You talk a lot, but never about yourself. Give up. Right here." Her voice demanded that he acquiesce.

With a tremor and an enlargement of his eyes, he inhaled to shore up his courage. What seemed at first to be a further tremor transformed into a head shake. "It's not good."

"What can be so bad?"

He took the warm mug in both hands and hunkered over it as if it was the final heat in a cold, dying world. He told her about being orphaned at age five and of how he moved between relatives, some one or all of them, having decided that it was best to shuttle him about so that they could share the burden of raising the extra child. He then perfunctorily added, "Then I joined the army right out of high school. I was in the war in Afghanistan."

"So that's the problem with you?"

"What?" He gave a snort. "I don't have a problem."

"You're a terrible liar, and, even if you were a better liar, I still wouldn't believe you."

"What? Why not? How do you know me well enough to say something like that?"

"I've known you almost two weeks. When I first saw you at the diner I thought maybe you were a mental patient, but I didn't think they would let you out in the condition that you were in."

"A mental patient?" Will's jaw unlatched.

"Then I thought that you suffered some kind of terrific trauma. I guess it was the loss of your parents and the war."

"You thought I was crazy? The war wasn't that bad." He put his hand on his chest and felt his heart banging there like an alarm. She analyzed his every motion. Her eyes were those of a doctor or therapist. He couldn't tell her the truth. Could he? No. Who would want to have anything to do with someone like him?

"Yes, and I still do. Your behavior isn't normal, at least not within the norms of our society."

"I don't believe this." He shoved his coffee away. He had to escape. The door was five yards away. If he sprinted, he would be gone before she got to her feet.

"What was it?" She took his arm. That small hand, steady and purposeful, on his arm, anchored him. His eyes finally meandered from the door back to her. "What was it? An accident? Death? Tell me, and I promise not to judge you."

He blinked. Her voice soothed and cooed to him. She might have just sung a lullaby. He breathed rapidly and perspired. Could he divulge the truth? While a side of him wanted to tell her, to finally unload the truth, to make it not just his but perhaps communal property, he knew that there was not a person in the world who could not help but judge him, and he knew this because, if the situation was reversed, he would not only judge but condemn a man who did what he had done. "I, uh . . ."

"It's okay. I want to help you. When did it happen?"

There was that compulsion to help again. Why did she care? He relented, but in a guarded way because he couldn't reveal everything. Could he? No, never. "This past September."

"Were you with someone?"

"Yes, my best friend."

"What's his name?"

"It was Rand."

She nodded because of her comprehension about the conjugation of the verb tense. How much could he admit?

"Why do you want to help me?" he asked.

For a moment she looked away, her eyes searched their surroundings, and her mouth slipped open. She smiled and said, "It's the right thing to do."

"Be your brother's keeper?"

"Keeper implies possession. That's a form of control. Right? That's not what I want to do. I don't want to control you or possess you."

He thought about what it would be like to be sexually possessed by her. Her hands would be on his shoulders or his chest. Her thighs would grip his waist. He had to stop. It had been so long since he was with a girl, but that was not what she said.

"And how did it happen?" she asked.

He twisted in his chair and faced the wall. His face hurt with the effort to hold back. "He was shot."

Closing his eyes, he did not want to look at her, but, over the chatter of the other patrons, he heard her breath, rhythmic and empowered, the faintest breeze, white and cool, fresh and light. He knew that she was close, she had to be leaning with her elbows on the table, her face inches away.

"And you blame yourself?"

He locked his eyes against her view. "I tried to stop him. I wanted to, but he went ahead. Even though he had to see the danger he was in, he went ahead. He was crazy, nuts. I don't know when it happened to him, but I saw it then and there that he was gone."

"Gone?" She did not understand what that meant.

He repeated, "Gone. He wanted to kill anyone and everyone, and he wanted to die. Have you ever seen someone like that? You can't imagine the look on their faces until you've seen someone like that. It's awful. You can't get it out of your mind. That crazy, fucking look in his eyes just won't go away." He jammed his fists into eyes and the explosions in his head were a relief, at least for a moment. "That's what it's like to look at evil."

"You couldn't have stopped him."

"Maybe not, but I should've tried. I could've . . . I don't know . . . leapt on him, but I sat still."

"He did what he did of his own will. It was not in your hands to stop him. He would've taken you with him."

"He did though. He took me with him. I feel dead. Every moment is a nightmare since then. I have no future. I have no dreams or aspirations. I'm dead." How had she guessed that Rand wanted him to die, too?

"You're alive. You survived."

"No, I didn't."

"Yes, you did." Her breath, which for a long moment had been un-sensed by him, suddenly, pushed through his black, heated despair and caressed his eyes. He opened his eyes and found her smile near. She had scooted her chair to the side of the table, while he had his eyes shut.

"Why won't my body just fall into the earth?" He groaned. His fists pounded the tabletop and rattled their cups.

"That's not yours to will." Her hands went into his fists and cracked them open like new shoots of grass that bore through seemingly permanent concrete. "You're alive. You survived. Take the power of life and go on. That moment of trauma, you can't forget it, undo it, or deny it. It will never be gone from your memory, but it is not where you are now, and it will not be where you will go. You must face it and learn from it. Your pain is due to your attempts to act as if it didn't happen. You can't do that."

Is that what was wrong with him? He twisted to sit forward. She was so beautiful, and she held his hands. Strangely, he felt a little better having told her about Rand. At least that little bit was out.

The following day, a Friday, he went into an Ace Hardware off Route 66 for a job.

"Hello," the manager of the Ace Hardware said. "My name is Paul Dolphy. I'm the general manager."

Will nodded and shook hands with Paul. "Hi." They both had strong grips, but this manager had fairly rough hands. In Dolphy's opposite hand Will saw the application he'd just filled out. Will said, "Anderson Williams. I'm here to interview." He lifted a copy of the wanted ads from that morning's paper.

"Very glad to meet you. You're our first applicant. That ad just started running today. Come on back to my office."

"Thanks."

Once inside, Paul waved his dark hand over the seat beside his desk which was positioned along the wall. There were no windows and the office was only nine by six feet. Will felt imprisoned. Paul picked up the application in both hands, skimmed it, and then let it flop to the desktop. "Well, I see you don't have any actual experience in a hardware store or in a relevant business like construction." He leaned into his chair.

Will pursed his lips. This would be impossible if he had to prove his fitness in this kind of job to say nothing of a background check of his new, bogus name. "No, but I know a lot from when I was a kid. You know, I had relatives who showed me a lot. I just-"

"Oh, don't feel defensive about it. I only felt the need to push the obvious shortcoming out of the way first."

"Oh." Will scratched his shoes across the floor.

"I saw you were in the army, Tenth Mountain." Why had he written the truth? For the simple reason that he did not know what else to put there.

"Yes, sir."

"I was in the Second Armored."

"Really." Will wasn't sure if he was supposed to be impressed or feel an instant camaraderie or what. He nodded only to show some reaction.

"That was back during the first Persian Gulf War, back when we booted that bunch of camel jockeys out of Kuwait. I'll bet by the years you were on active duty that you saw some of that part of the world."

"Yes, sir. Afghanistan."

"Chasin' after Osama, eh?"

"Yes, sir."

"I thought they would have stop lossed you to retain you."

"I had a medical discharge."

"Were you a Purple Heart recipient?"

"Yes, sir."

Paul nodded and his deep brown eyes inspected Will's full frame to detect where the wound was. "Any other medals?"

"No, sir."

"Okay. Are you fit to help our customers lift and tote items from the shelves to their cars?"

"Yes, sir. I keep in shape. You know, work out daily." Will almost said more but stanched the flow of information. There was no need to detail his recent calisthenics routine for the man, who wouldn't be interested anyway. Will gnawed the inside of his lip.

"What was your specialty?"

"Infantry assault."

"You ever get to ski?" Paul grinned.

Will had heard this line of inquiry before. Likely, there would be a joke at the end.

"Only in training, never for combat."

"Skiing on the job. That must be nice." Paul's teeth were out and dull with yellow stains.

"Sure." Will decided to screw with him a bit. "Those snow bunnies were great target practice."

Paul chuckled. "You get a lot of action against those snow bunnies?"

Will smirked. "Sure, that's why I joined the Tenth Mountain. Skiing, rappelling, rifle training, and snow bunny targets. It was the best gig around. You know all women love guys in uniform."

Paul laughed with his whole body. "And I thought I was cool to be in the motor pool of the armored division so I wouldn't have to see actual combat."

Will shrugged. "Never used all that skiing, rappelling, and other stuff they trained me to do. Not in Afghanistan."

Paul smiled. "Well, they want us to be boy scouts. Always prepared, isn't that the boy scout motto?"

"I don't know. I was never a boy scout, but that sounds right."

Paul tilted back in his seat and laced his hands behind his head. He studied Will, and he took his time about it. "You went to college on the GI Bill?"

"Yes, sir."

"Right after you got out of the service?"

"Well, there was about a five month lag, you know, before the fall semester started."

"Uh hunh. What did you do with yourself then?"

It was a time in Will's life that he had forgotten. He hadn't even spoken to Rand about it. "Well." Will sat up though he was already arching his lower back with how tall he sat. He took a long inhalation. "I used a lot of that mountain training."

Paul blinked. His hands came from behind his head and settled on his gut, which was only just showing a bit of excess. Will figured he was in his forties. "Things just didn't seem right after you came back, did they?"

Will's eyes shifted to the door where a large calendar hung on a hook. "Not things exactly."

"You?"

Will shrugged a shoulder.

"Sorry, I know that question is a stinker."

Will sucked at a corner of his mouth. "Maybe you have a right to ask." The statement almost emerged as a question.

"I don't know. I don't think so. People that weren't there can't know. My marriage ended after I rotated." Paul's eyes shifted to something other than Will, so he followed the other man's gaze. At the far corner of the desk was a framed 5X7 photo of a woman holding a small child, presumably Paul's ex-spouse and their offspring. Will nearly asked where the boy in the photo was, but he ground his teeth instead. Paul realigned his body, which had slowly twisted to face the photo. He put his hands to the arms of the seat, pushed up, and lowered his body down to square up with Will. He said, "Well, let's see. What was your degree in?"

"A double major in philosophy and history."

Paul's eyebrows rose. "Hm. Well, I'd bet, if your abundant military training and college education are any indication, you can learn to do anything." Paul took a few minutes to outline the nature of the job: stocking products, customer service, and register duty. "Try to keep a positive demeanor and a smile no matter how mentally lost some of these wanna-be do-it-yourself types will be. All right? Do you think you can hack it, soldier?"

Will smiled. That was the kind of thing a good non-com would ask, point blank and with no effort to spare his feelings. Just a simple yes or no answer. "Yes, sir."

"Fine." Paul reached, snatched Will's application off the desktop, jerked the center drawer of his desk open, and, with a flick of his wrist, sent the sheet of paper in to where it was to be filed. "Can you start Monday?"

"Absolutely."

"Outstanding."

They rose, shook hands, and Paul led him out. Will had done it. With one application and one interview, Will had a job. It seemed too easy, except that he now had to endure the actual routine of a job for the first time in nine months. Could he really hack it?

He did not need much. The one bedroom apartment, unfurnished, was five hundred a month, utilities included. Located on the second floor, he had to hump everything upstairs by himself. He went to the Goodwill Store the morning he signed the lease and received his keys. There among the donated goods he found a small bookcase, a round kitchen table, two mismatched chairs in good shape—he sat in them and rocked about to test the stability of the nails and glue holding the wood together—and a shoulder high dresser. There were beds there, but he didn't trust second hand beds, what with bed bugs, lice, and who knew what other kinds of creepy crawlies that could inhabit a mattress. For the time being he would sack out on the floor in his sleeping bag.

Through the door of the café, a large group of college coeds, mid-twenties, so probably graduate students—that was Will's guess—stomped the snow from their boots and ruffled their coats to sift more snow onto the floor already wet from previous others. Jerusha's words—she had been speaking of the evidence for a massive volcanic eruption which caused an equally cataclysmic tsunami to devastate the once monumental Minoan culture of antiquity—ceased, her jaw still ajar after her final syllable. She followed the commotion of this gaggle of apparent couples. There they stood in ranks of couples, up first a duo of lesbians, broad and squat like dwarves from Tolkien's bestiary, and Will blinked at the stereotypes since one had a mustache while the other had a single, heavy eyebrow that demarcated her face like an axe blow. Second, were a set of gays. One of the guys managed to create a twitch in his body with each step, like a flirtatious femme fatale of the forties or fifties though he had no appropriate curves. His partner was the masculine one, complete with a goatee and sharp eyes that criticized his partner's moves. Third, there was an average heterosexual couple. He was Indian with a professorial beard and wire rimmed specs—Will imagined that he wore a tweed coat with elbow patches when he stood before freshmen in whatever introductory course that he taught, probably humanities or English—while his female counterpart could have been a hippie, with her knit, wool hat maybe woven by the indigenous people of Nepal or Tibet and her beige coat of thick lamb skin, lined with fleece and brought together in the front with huge plastic, brown buttons that she must have purchased second hand. And, lastly, bringing up the rear, came a single man, six plus feet tall with an accommodating smile and a lazy gait, who caught sight of Jerusha and ejaculated his pleasure with an: "Oh, look, it's Jerusha."

The three couples wheeled about and fell in line behind Mr. Orgasm, who advanced toward Will and Jerusha's table. Jerusha waved and smiled with all her teeth.

"Hi."

"Hey."

"Howdy."

"How's it going?"

Etcetera. Will didn't listen to this flaccid conversation of salutations and indifferent interest to a person's state of being. Introductions were then directed at Will, or Anderson as he was now known. He said hello to all of them. He missed all the names until Jerusha gestured to Mr. Orgasm. She said, "This is Davis Patterson."

Will cocked an eyebrow at the high brow name. He half expected there to be an appendage of numerals, but Jerusha said nothing more. Will reached, gripped, and pumped Davis's hand, pliable as putty.

"Aw." Davis bent at the pressure of Will's handshake. Will released the limp end of Davis's arm. Davis gingerly retracted his red hand.

"Sorry," Will said. "I was taught to always give a strong shake to another man." This was true. When he pumped the Indian professor's hand, he was glad to receive much the same pressure.

"That's okay. I just wasn't prepared for it." Davis shook his head and shrugged away that display of pain and effeminacy. He chuckled, but to Will it was more like a giggle.

"Well, sorry anyhow." Will was not sorry in the least. He sat again to show that he was with Jerusha, they were having coffee together, talking together, and that these interlopers could hasten on with their separate engagement.

"So where was it you were off to?" Jerusha asked as she lifted her tea to her full lips. Will yearned for a kiss. That would never happen with these people around.

"Ah, I suggested that we go for a hike," said Nitin, the Indian professor.

"A hike?" Jerusha jerked from her cup and wiped a stray drop of tea caused by her surprise. "And you all went along with this?"

"Uh."

"Well."

"Now that there's a blizzard. . ."

"You know, it was nicer earlier. . ."

"Maybe not."

Nitin broke through the half-hearted protestations. "Ah, but the culmination of the proposed trek, that was the major point in bringing out their agreements."

"Okay." Jerusha set her cup down on the saucer. The others had retaken their places as the Greek chorus, silent at the moment. "So what brilliant, culminating event to a possibly dangerous romp in a blizzard had you plied them with?"

Nitin smiled whitely through his wild, black beard. "At the summit of Mt. Elden, I meant for us to stop, drink, and read passages from our favorite books. Oh, I know," he added in a rush to defend himself to Will of all people. "It sounds ludicrous and not the least bit fun, but I wanted to invoke a spirit of sublimity." He spread his arms.

Will cocked an eyebrow. Who were these nuts, these friends of Jerusha's? Will knew that the hastily worded addendum was primarily meant for him because he had leaned forward and let his jaw unlatch. He sat back, composed his expression into a guarded interest, and picked up his coffee to have a prop for his neutrality on what was patently a stupid idea for a trek. Perhaps if it was not twenty degrees outside and if there was no blizzard, then it could be a tempting notion. Will could just imagine the florid poetry about beauty and amour that this dull lot would choose to recite. If only he and Rand could read some of their favorites. That would be a blizzard of discomfiture for these flaccid intellectuals. Hell, they were going to Northern Arizona University not Harvard or Oxford. Their pretensions in that light were risible.

As Jerusha talked—her tone suggested that she approved of the broad outline made by Nitin—and the others once again made timorous excuses about the weather being too much of an impediment, Will remembered Rand, his old comrade, roommate, best friend, and, for the first time he could admit the truth, his leader. It was that final time that he saw him that came back to Will. The mad, cocky smirk on his cheek, the way his eyes tried to skewer the man that he was engaged with in dialogue while in that small Montana bar lit in neon reds and oranges as if natural lights were improper for an establishment of this function, and the tactile sense of doom which emanated like sonar waves from Rand. He turned his face from the company of Jerusha's circle and brought his hand up to shield his face from their frivolous and vain glances. If Rand was here now, he would wink or nudge Will to notify him of the intention to confront this bunch of randy intellectuals, who must surely be intoxicated by their education in graduate courses that engorged them on knowledge gleaned by someone else's writing and reasoning and not their own. Rand would taunt them. Will should too.

Will cut impulsively through their talk, "You know, I'm an experienced outdoors man, and I gotta say that it would be very unwise for you to venture into that mess. I'd hate to ponder the scene. At the least there might be a twisted ankle or a broken leg. Frostbite would be likely, too." Will paused to scrutinize their inadequate shoes and boots, which forced all of them to do the same. "Beyond that, I better not scare you with. Maybe you can sit by a fireplace somewhere and do you poetry reading there?"

Jerusha's eyes were on him, and he detected disapproval. Oh well, he couldn't retract his opinion, and it was the right one anyway. He was helping them. The group all looked at Nitin, who tugged his beard in rumination. What could there be to consider? Was his heart and mind that set on his epic foolishness?

Nitin bounced his head from side to side as he conceded to Will's argument. The hippie girl, Sunshine, swayed the group to decide to go to her house. "What do you say, roomie?" She asked.

Who was Sunshine's roomie? Will wondered, as his eyes roved over the assembled faces.

Jerusha said, "Okay."

Will's head jerked about. "Heh?"

"She's my roommate. Besides, you love books. You'll fit right in with this passionately literate crowd. I think you should jump at the chance to show off your stuff with a group of peers." To the crowd, she said, "Anderson and I have talked about Thoreau, Camus, and the *Dhammapada*."

A few heads nodded and there were approving, respectful glances directed toward Will. On Jerusha's word they now would think of him as on their level.

"Come on," Davis said. He taunted Will with twinkling eyes.

Will glared at that broad grin. What he wouldn't give to snag him into a blind alley and beat his head against a brick wall. He couldn't help but charge into the gauntlet of these jesters and prove that he was better than them. "All right." Will smirked.

The morning at Jerusha's crossed into the afternoon. Alcohol was brought out. Friends were phoned. Alcohol was brought in. Food was ordered. The afternoon, never light anyway, burned into the darkness of the winter night. He and Davis both stayed near Jerusha. They vied to get her fresh drinks. Will hated how these people simpered. The pseudo-intellectuals traded in gossip about who slept with whom, and who snubbed the other, who published and who failed. They were as catty and vapid as the stereotypical high school cheerleader. He forced himself to speak. He damn well did not want to be outshined by this Davis doofus. It was still a struggle. His wine glass was a prop, not meant to be drunk, so that he remained warily sober of what he might divulge. Somehow they got on the topic of Plato and love. Davis, dull and arrogant, tried to quote *The Symposium*, but he fouled it up. Will, who knew Plato's work as well as a professor, sneered as he correctly attributed the quote—it was not by Socrates but Aristophanes—and recited it verbatim.

"Oh, well, that's not important." Davis blew him off with a wave of his hand. "What's important is-"

"What the fuck do you mean it's not important?" Will exploded. "If you can't say it right and know where it came from then how can you pretend to know anything about it? All you're doing is showing how stupid you are." Davis couldn't dismiss him with a wave of his hand after that.

"He does have a point," Jerusha said. Will caught her eye and nodded his thanks for her agreement. She was on his side. She had to like him then. Right?

Davis shrugged and pushed air at Will with a limp, drunk hand. "Not important."

What Davis meant was that Will was not important. Davis's causal indifference to him meant that he did not see Will as a serious rival. The son of a bitch. To Davis, Will was nothing at all. Will would show the stupid bastard. Will stepped into the middle of the huddle of people he stood with. He squared his shoulders to Davis. Will punched Davis in the nose.

Everyone bounded back and all the inane gibberish in the room ceased. Davis buckled and stumbled away. Will advanced. He grabbed Davis by the shirt front, jerked him up and slammed his fist into his mouth. Will felt and heard the satisfying crunch and give as Davis's teeth broke. Davis bent at every joint until he hit the floor like an accordion, all closed up. Will grinned at the lump of sub human shit in front of him. He realized that he stood in the midst of stillness and silence. All around him, as if sucked into the wall were sets of eyes almost completely white with fear.

Will spun around in the center of that jury. "Well? Who's next? Come on. Who's up for a shot at me?" He extended his arms. His fists were medieval maces prepared to club any attacker. He would give them a fight. He wanted to be beaten, pummeled, and crushed, but they would earn their judgment against him with their own blood and pain. No one moved. "What? No one? You all stand there and judge me and condemn me, but you don't have what it takes to enact justice. Do you? Come on, you cowards, beat me down, stomp me into the floor." They just stood there and leaned into the walls. Their eyes were doughnuts, their bodies were stiff with weakness. He dropped his eyes and fists and eyed Davis, curled and bloody on the carpet. "How about I give you more provocation, more reason, and a greater feeling of righteousness?" He kicked Davis in the gut. The little wuss crashed onto his side and quivered as he tried to tighten into an impregnable ball. Not a single one of them stepped forward to challenge him. If anything, they cowered deeper into the paint on the walls.

"What? Nothing. No one has the balls to take me down? What a bunch of fucking cowards. Phony, intellectual cowards, that's what you are. I can't stand the sight of any of you bullshit academics. All talk and no walk. You're nothing, nothing at all. Why don't you call the cops and get them to come out and do what you lack the balls to do."

He stepped over Davis and marched for the door. The spectators fell over each other to clear a path. He snatched the door and flung it open.

He didn't halt until he stepped from the curb into the street. The full moon, winter silver, illuminated the world with a spectral glow. Everything, the homes, cars, sidewalks, small picket fences, the residential road, the oaks and aspens, the evergreen shrubs, and the drifts of smudged snow, all were recognizable as what they were, and yet they were totally alien because of the blackness that sat between separate objects like the effluvium of a deeper world risen into view for those, like Will, who wandered unprepared into this moment and place. He tilted, and his face felt ready to explode, his eyes first. When his knees buckled, he flopped like a dead thing to the curb where he hit backside first and then sprawled into the cold of the snow. Above him the hemisphere of pitch seemed to leer and descend, prepared to give him the press, mass upon mass laid on his chest until his last exhalation shuddered out and all his infamy was damned. He wanted to howl with all his being at the down-rushing terror, to declaim that he was the monster that deserved all the loathing possible from all of existence. He was a murderer. "Destroy me," he whispered.

Her presence and her footfalls were swift on the sidewalk. Above, the obstinate universe hung above him, a sword yet to fall. She scraped to a halt a foot away. He waited for the welcomed scorn. Any moment now. He would not look at her until she vilified him. He detected no inhalation from her, the necessary preparation for a harangue. Instead, she melted into the night. Was this one of her Buddhist tricks? Was this some form of self-abnegation? He could not turn to her, not before the needed condemnation. When would she say something? His neck twitched, and he had to suppress a reflex to turn to her. The snow was melting coldly. Had she stealthily gone into the night to leave him, un-demolished and whole? How could she? He had done more violence in the world than what he had done tonight. Now she and all her friends knew what he was. He was the monster! Damn her for abandoning him to his life and his misery. How could she leave him here? Where's her sense of morality? She should have stepped on his face and crushed his skull with her heel. He flopped over onto his belly to search for her. Her hiking boots were inches from him. He jerked back, rolled onto his side and looked up. She loomed into the black universe. Her face was swathed in the silver light of the moon, but he couldn't discern what her attitude was.

"Well?" he asked.

Nothing. She was a stalagmite, raised in potent rejection of him.

"So what? What're you gonna say?" He scrambled up. If she was going to strike him, kick him, then he wanted to take it like a man, he wanted to show he wasn't afraid of whatever punishment she chose to mete out upon him. He stood at attention, eyes level, shoulders squared, and arms right at his side. "Go on." No punch came. "Is this better?" he growled through his teeth.

He flinched. So instinctual. Her fist was there, maybe an inch from his left cheek. He never saw her move. His whole body tensed from his heart to his throat to his sphincter.

"I just showed you the gates of Hell." Her voice was lower, stronger, and deeper than he had ever heard it. He cringed. His head bowed, and all the bravado dropped from him as if to depart to the very place she just showed him.

Her fist vanished into the night just as suddenly as it had appeared. He searched for it—though he did not raise his head, only his eyes—and there it was back at her side. She stood with no coat in the cold night, and, though she might be freezing, she never shivered, never gave the least sign of discomfort. She had her resolution as insulation from the cold world. Will felt weak, pitiful, and as low as a man could get in the presence of her magnificent strength. This tiny woman was more powerful than he could ever aspire to be.

He sagged into a crouch. "I'm guilty."

"You're absolved. You're innocent now."

"No, that's not true. It can never be true. I know what I've done. And it's the worst kind of evil you'll ever know. You should be happy you don't know what I've done. I know what I've done, and you have no clue."

She shook her head sharply to the right, sharply to the left. "What you've done is not what you have yet to do. That isn't decided. You haven't decided."

He wagged his head. "It's in my head, the things I did, things I still would do, but I don't."

"Why not?"

"I want to be a better person."

"You already are then."

"No, I see me, in my mind. I hit people. They've done nothing to me, but I want to murder them. With my hands I want to choke them and break their fragile bodies. Unsuspecting, they'd be like babies, utterly defenseless. I'd snap them, their larynxes, ribs, arms, spines, knees, skulls are all so easy to smash because I know how to do that, I was trained, I was schooled by the best in the world. I honed my killer instinct. My grips, punches, kicks will lay them out, lay you out, put you on the fucking slab, 'cause that's what I am. That's what I've done. I'm a killer."

Her hand came to the peak of his head and it did not force him down farther. If anything, he felt imbued with the courage to raise his eyes, raise his head, and raise his body. Kneeling still, he gazed at her angelic being, illuminated in the sable night, as if emanated from an alternative existence, and a small voice in him conceded in a tiny whisper that maybe he was not a monster. A few tears came onto his raw cheeks. He shuddered from the freezing night.

"I don't know how to go on," he said.

"I've shown you now the gates of Heaven. Do you see them?"

He was mesmerized by her eyes, but the colors and the contours he thought he knew from the past few weeks were gone. She might no longer be human. He nodded. He said, "I see."

"You were a terrible person. What you just did was inexcusable. What can you learn from what you did? Can you learn anything from what you did?"

"Yeah."

"You want me."

His head jerked up. How could she just blurt it out? How could he answer? Of course, he wanted her.

"But I could never like you as you are," she said. "The compassion I have for you is only what I have for any human being, for all human beings. You want to have passion with me, but I don't think I could ever be passionate with you as you are."

He dropped his head as if the guillotine had severed it. She turned and strode away. She went inside her house without looking back even once. After a few minutes he began the long walk home.

The Friday after Will beat Davis, Jerusha said, "Let's go."

She handed him a sheet of notebook paper with her fine, bent handwriting. He had only just trudged through the door of their usual café, but before he could sit opposite her, she hopped up, slung her bag onto her shoulder, pressed the sheet of paper against his chest, did not wait to see if he caught it, and glided through the irregular placement of tables and chairs on her way to the door. He shambled after her. His boots kicked chair legs and his thigh whacked into a tabletop. He tried to read the page. Was this for real?

"Hey, what is this?" he shouted at her back as she barged through the exit. He hustled. She never turned her head to see if he followed. "Dammit! Where are you going? What's this all about?" He waved the page around in the air. She charged ahead without the least indication that she gave a damn for what he said. Finally, he broke into a jog and pulled alongside her as she passed the last shop in this corner lot, business strip. "Where are you off to in such a hurry?"

"Did you read that?" She kept her eyes forward, but she jerked her head to the side to indicate the sheet of notebook paper.

"Yeah, but what the hell?"

"Well, the way I see it you owe everyone who was at my house last Sunday an apology. Every one of them. And to make sure you do it correctly—since I don't trust you yet—I'm going to come with you. I also decided that you need to do it the same way every time. That's why I wrote out what you're going to tell each and every one of my friends."

"You really expect me to-"

"I do, and either you will or you better not come with me. If you can't do this and do it with the utmost spirit of humility, then I don't want to have anything to do with you."

"You're serious?"

"I meditated all week on what I should do with you. My first reaction was to force you out of my life, to shun you like the criminal you are, but I knew that was absolutely the wrong thing to do, morally and spiritually, and not just to you, but to me also."

They were on campus now, passing two of the southern end dormitories. He halted. He stared after her figure as she kept on at that grueling pace. She was in khakis and had a jacket on. Really, he could not see much of her body, but he yearned to run his hands all over her. And she was smart. She was smarter than possibly anyone he had ever met, definitely smarter than he was. He sprinted after her. "Look, I don't know anything about 'spiritually,' but I know I deserve whatever punishment you offer. I know I do. I want to be destroyed. I-"

"You're really the masochist, aren't you? Oh, I'm sure you would like that, but that's precisely why I knew that my first reaction, the one I was taught by our culture to embrace and enact, was the incorrect one, the one non-solution that was one hundred and eighty degrees in the wrong direction. The only way that I can help you is if you agree to do what I say. The first part of that is to do what we're going to do right now. I can't force you to do this. It's your choice. If you choose to perform this act of . . . contrition, then I'll know that you can be someone other than the person I saw last Sunday night. And my friends will know it too."

She led him into the Liberal Arts building and they journeyed to offices and class rooms. She had him kneel before each of her friends who'd been at the party. He bowed his head, submissive and penitent, and he made his apologies. Feeling ridiculous, uncomfortable and embarrassed on both knees with his hands clasped behind his back per her instructions, he said, "I'm very sorry for the fear I caused in you. I apologize for the violence to which I made you a witness. Please, accept my sincerity as the truth."

These were Jerusha's words, and they were as bizarre as if he was in a Shakespearean play. As he said this tiny speech, she stood directly behind him with her arms crossed, and her eyes bore into the back of his skull like the press of a rifle barrel. While he primarily was aware of her presence, he was not insensitive to the effect he had on each of Jerusha's friends or passersby who witnessed this. Every one of them was dismayed and flustered by this act of contrition that ought to belong to another century. Her friends leaned into what support was near, whether it was a fellow human being, a dry erase board, a chair, or a wall. Will lost track of how many times he delivered this little speech.

"You're doing fabulous," she said with a caustic tone. "We're almost finished." They entered a larger room where desks, not student desks but real desks, complete with drawers down the sides and one across the middle where the chair sat, were placed within cubicles. Late afternoon sunshine slipped through the blinds and gave the desks, chairs and walls a putrid, greenish gray color. Only a few heads peeked above the many cubicle wall tops. Jerusha marched Will to the far corner. There they found Davis Jefferson.

"Davis."

At the sound of his name and Jerusha's voice, he swiveled in his chair to greet her with a beaming smile despite his mashed up features. When he saw Will though, he shuddered, the smile cracked and crumbled so that his missing tooth was visible. The poor bastard. Will had really beaten the crap out of him. Unconsciously, Will stepped back, but Jerusha's bony hand jabbed him in the ribs so that he hopped forward, closer than he had been to Davis. Assume the position, Will commanded. He went to his knees and bowed his head. Even the floor had the same brightly lit, greenish gray hue of a dead thing that the furniture and walls had. Will intoned the words that he now had memorized, he had said them so many times. At the end he bowed his head farther, placed his chin on his chest.

There was a strange gurgle and a moan from Davis. Then he kicked Will in the stomach. Will keeled over onto his side and curled up reflexively. His arms wrapped around his gut. Davis stepped back then drove his foot into Will's chest. Davis reared back and kicked again though this time Will got one arm out to deflect most of the power of the blow. Will expected more. Jerusha, the bitch, stood by impassively. Davis suddenly cried out. "You think this makes up for what you did? I wanted to call the police. I wanted you locked up. You belong in jail, you, you, you fuck!"

"Kick him again and see if that makes it all better." Jerusha nodded nonchalantly.

Was she telling him to kick Will again? She was really enjoying this. Damn her.

Davis spluttered and spit seeped from his cut and bruised mouth onto his chin. He shook his finger at her. "Why did you bring him here? You talked me out of calling the police. Why? What's wrong with you that you just stand there all nonplussed?"

Tears drooped onto his cheeks. Will lay on the floor, still on his side, as he tried to regain his breath with his mouth agape.

"What?" Davis's arms shook with violence. "Are you sleeping with him?"

"Are you going to kick him again? Go on. Lower yourself to his level. Glory in that sense of justified hate. Go on. You can be just like him." She gestured at the two of them.

Davis gawked at her. Will rolled onto his elbows and knees. He would rather take another kick while he was upright. He walked his hands back onto his knees and then the tops of his thighs. He stopped and panted. Davis watched him heave on the air. His face was a terrible mask of hate and pain, but now Will thought confusion swirled into his features too. Unresolved, Davis's eyes rolled. Either do it or sit down, Will wanted to say. If Davis was not going to kick him again, Will was going to get up and tell both these grad student bitches where to go.

"Just take him and get out of here," Davis said, before Will could start to move.

"He apologized and you had your chance to hit him back." Jerusha came around so that she was in front of Will, and she offered her hands to help him stand. "Don't you feel better? All week I had to listen to you say you wanted a chance to get revenge. Are you avenged now? Are your mind and your mouth going to be at peace?"

Will ignored her hands. It was on account of her that he just got popped by that weenie Davis. He got to his feet.

"And I'm sure," Jerusha went on, "that you feel free of any remorse."

"Remorse?" Davis's jaw dropped.

"He punched and kicked you without provocation, and, to make it even, you kicked him a few times. Of course, you did get an apology. Maybe everything's even steven now."

"I'm not going to apologize."

"So the animosity will continue? The cycle of violence will wheel itself around so that now he," she indicated Will, "will feel like the aggrieved one. He may wish to redress the imbalance that he feels exists in your favor."

"You're impossible. No, you're ridiculous. How can you even buy into this mindset? He knocked one of my teeth out." Davis opened his mouth and pointed to the missing upper bicuspid. "To get even I'd need to knock out one of his."

"Ah, you're still working at being the victim, still hoping to have all righteousness on your side. Don't you see how you cling to something so petty, so infinitesimal as your lost tooth?"

"I didn't lose it."

Will became re-aware, as the confrontation now revolved around Davis and Jerusha, that the room was not devoid of witnesses. From the tops of the cubicle walls were shoulders and heads of another half dozen grad students. Had any of this audience been ringside, at the last fight? Had they enjoyed Will's beating? Were they rooting for Davis? Were they simply confused individuals who had no inkling what had transpired in the midst of their placid office?

"Regardless," Jerusha said. "You can't admit your part in an event that grows larger all the time." Suddenly, she snatched Will's arm and spun him at the same time that she turned to depart. "You'd rather be right, you'd rather have power, than be just and equal." She went into motion and towed Will along with her. He marveled at her grip. She was unnaturally strong.

"Oh, you're such a pedantic bitch," Davis shouted.

"Cussing is the recourse of the feeble minded." She fired back over her shoulder at Davis.

"I don't want to see you again, and, if I see him again, I'll call the police."

Jerusha and Will burst through the door. She continued at a savage pace until she shoved him through the exterior door of the building and it banged open like the report of a rifle. Her hand released him to his own recognizance, but she halted as if mired in something unexpected. Was it the freezing temperature? The low, iron sky looked about ready to bury them beneath a new deposition of snow. Jerusha stood a few paces ahead of him, her back to him, and her hands clenched her waist. Her bundled torso swelled and relaxed, swelled and relaxed. That title bout with Davis had keyed her up. Will's hands became cold and he pocketed them. Was that it? Were they done? His chest ached some, but Davis hit like a puss, just like he took a punch, he could hardly dish one out. Will said, "So, that's it?" A cloud of his frozen breath hung between them. She spun about. "No. You have one more person to apologize to, and she's right in front of you."

Her cheeks and nose were red from the cold. She crossed her arms and waited. He could hardly believe it. With a vague gesture to say "okay," he lowered himself to his knees. He began the apology.

"No. No, you need to say something else to me. I don't want to hear my words. I deserve to hear your words. You need to say what needs to be said to me, in your own way, and whatever you say has to address all that I've done for you."

He gawked at her. What did all that mean? What all did he owe her? He raised his hands, began to shrug, and his mouth unclamped to utter, "I don't know what you want from me-"

"I want my apology."

"For what?"

"I want your apology to me for talking everyone out of calling the police to incarcerate you. I want your apology to me for helping you to acknowledge your evil. I want an apology for all the effort I put out to make you not feel like a vile insect, and instead how I made you attempt to make up for what you did."

Slowly, he nodded. Yes, he owed her that. Undoubtedly, she had done all she said. He bowed his head and closed his eyes. His hands clasped behind his back. "This is as vulnerable as I can be. This is as defenseless as I can be. You've done all that you just said and more for me. You've been a friend when I had no one. You were a kind smile to a stranger. The last few weeks mean so much to me that you can't really understand. I'm sorry. I apologize. If you don't want to see me ever again, I'd understand. That's what I'd probably do."

He did not feel that there was more he could add, though that was because he lacked something and not that there was nothing more possible to say. He awaited her response while trapped within the darkness of his closed eyes. Would she kick or punch him too? Would she say that she never wanted to see his disgusting being again? How long would he have to wait?

There was the sound of the door opening behind him.

"Uh, excuse me."

Will opened his eyes. In front of him there was no one. Behind him stood a girl with an armload of books and an eyebrow cocked in plain, befuddled irritation, who must have been the one to speak just now at the sight of him blocking her exit from the building. Will jumped up and out of the way while he whipped his head about to track down Jerusha, but she was gone.

Will halted in front of the house. He dismounted from his bike, let it fall on the sidewalk, and marched into the front yard. Should he just call her out by shouting? That was ridiculous. He did not want to go inside her house though. For some reason, his security lay in being in the open. She might not invite him inside anyway. Maybe she would not answer the door. What if she saw his arrival and was at the back of the house in fear while she dialed 911 to summon the police? They could arrest him for one thing then discover the hideous trail of murders that lay behind him like a noose around his neck. So should he go to the door and knock? He absolutely could not remain in

Jerusha's front yard all day. Neighbors would talk, grow suspicious, and phone the police. He had to act. He had come to do this, and now he must get it done. Don't pussy around, the drill instructor in him ordered. Get cracking!

The front door opened. Jerusha and her housemate Sunshine strolled out, their backpacks and purses slung on their shoulders. At first they did not see him. He froze. Was this serendipity? Why did they come out just now? She was so pretty. Her nose, lips, chin, eyes, every part of her face made his eyes want to dwell there. This was the girl he liked. Did she have any interest in him? Sunshine halted, she saw him. Jerusha nearly fell over her.

"What are you doing here?" Sunshine rummaged in her purse.

"What do you want?" Jerusha asked.

"I want to talk to you." Will remained where he was.

"Stay back!" Sunshine whipped out a canister of pepper spray and aimed it at Will who, since he was well out of range, made no defensive movement.

"Is she serious?" He gestured to Sunshine.

"This will burn your eyes out." Sunshine shook the sprayer at him.

"She seems serious enough." Jerusha seemed bored by this.

"She couldn't hit me from there even if she emptied that whole thing. The range is too great."

"Then you'll be fine where you are. What did you want to talk about?" Jerusha folded her arms.

Well, he was having his way about not being invited in the house, though, on the other hand, this hardly seemed the ideal way to say what he wanted either. "I've apologized to you and every one of your friends. That took a lot of guts. Wouldn't you say so?"

"Yes."

"I doubt that anyone who ever made a mistake would do all that I did. They wouldn't let Davis beat them up. Would they?"

"No."

"Haven't you ever made a mistake?"

Jerusha nodded.

"Wouldn't you want a second chance, a chance to prove that you were better than the person people saw you as?" Were there second chances for people like him? Did he deserve it?

Jerusha posed her hands on her hips as if to assume the authority of a judge.

"Please," he said.

Sunshine hissed some negative response, but Jerusha's face pinched in annoyance at that suggestion. She said, "All right. Everyone deserves a second chance. In Buddhism, compassion is one of the three chief virtues. If I'm going to have compassion for you then you need to have compassion for yourself."

Will's hands rose. What the hell did that mean? Have compassion for himself? "Okay," he said because he had to say something that would indicate his agreement with this term of hers.

Despite complaints and protests, she dragged him to yoga classes at the university recreation center. University rules allowed her to bring a guest. Will figured she abused this rule though because she brought him every day.

"I don't need to get into shape, you know." Will crossed his arms as he watched the participants, all women, enter.

"That's not the point. There is a point to this, but that's not it." She laid her rolled yoga mat at her feet.

"So what is the point?" He would much rather go and lift weights.

She kicked the rolled mat flat. "I can't spoon feed you. You need to learn on your own. There are extra mats in that closet over there."

Her retort humbled him somewhat, enough, anyway, that he engaged in the classes. His muscles were solid, but they were tight and many of the yoga poses were excruciating. Still, he followed the details as explained by the instructors, who spoke in monotonous voices probably meant to calm the mind. Will's mind behaved more like a sniper as it darted from concealment to concealment, shot doubt at the encroaching words of these unstressed instructors to their zombie-like students. Here, in the room of yoga, motion only ended in stillness with a call for even breathing. After a few weeks, when he lay on his mat in relaxation pose to finish the class, he was shocked when his arms twitched and spasmed. They felt like they were beyond his control. His arms wanted to do something he was unfamiliar with, they wanted to melt and fall back to the floor. It was a struggle. He did not know if he should force them back, or reach and press, or tighten back up. He was entirely uncomfortable.

Jerusha taught him to meditate, usually right after the yoga class finished. "Why?" he moaned.

"You were in the army."

He gulped at his dry tongue.

"They trained you to do what you did, right?" she asked.

"Yeah."

"It all started simply, didn't it?"

He cocked his head and scowled with uncertainty. "What started simply?"

"Training you to hurt, to kill. First, they taught you how to hold a rifle. How to clean a rifle. Then it was how to march with a rifle on your shoulder. After a few weeks they taught you how to load a rifle and shoot at targets a long way away. Finally, they taught you how to fix a bayonet on the end of the rifle and stab a suspended sandbag. The whole system took weeks, and through that system you went from just holding a weapon to doing the worst deed that you could with a weapon, taking a fellow human's life. And it all seemed natural. Didn't it?"

He blinked. He had never contemplated basic training at Fort Dix at all. How did she know all that? She never enlisted, he was one hundred percent damn certain of that. Yet she had it right. He nodded.

"So, why am I teaching you meditation and towing you into yoga classes? I'm training you to be something else."

"What? Some tree hugging hippie? A guru?" He brought his hands together and shimmied about as if he heard sitars and tablas and Hindi chants.

"Sarcasm is not a path to enlightenment, nor is it the path to the carrot that you, Mr. Donkey, hope for."

"I doubt there's a carrot coming from you anyway."

"Then go." She pointed out the yoga room door. "You've been so happy up 'til now, why don't you go that way again? You did so well." She smiled, and, while he tried to characterize her attitude as icy or sarcastic, her eyes shone with a good will that in light of what she said to him was perverse.

He wanted to defy her and march out, but it would not be her hopes that he would hinder. He grumbled, "Fine."

She sat in the lotus position while he managed to cross his legs, barely. "Just breathe. Let your body do what is natural. Your mind must let go of its learned need to control." Her voice was like a whisper that had no relation to her as an individual, neither young nor old, not American but clearly not from anywhere else, still feminine but only just. "As you exhale say to yourself 'breathing.' That's all. Just that one word. If your mind tries to wander, if you catch yourself planning what you will do later or remembering what you forgot to do yesterday or if you try to analyze what I am saying and want to criticize that, I want you to label it 'thinking.' You must say that word not as a reprimand but only as an identifying tag, like you might say of a clear sky 'blue' or a stormy sky 'gray.' You are not harsh with yourself. Be friendly to yourself. After you label your thought as 'thinking,' you resume labeling your out breath as 'breathing.'"

She fell silent, and he thought how ridiculous and easy this whole thing was. Breathe in. Breathe out. Breathing. Breathe in. Breathe out. Breathing. Anyone could do this. Breathe in. What was so difficult? Breathe out. Breathing. Wait. Breathe in. Aren't those thoughts? Breathe out. Thinking. All right, no biggie, start again. Inhale. Exhale. Breathing. Inhale. Exhale. Breathing. There, got it. Inhale. No, dammit that was thinking. Exhale. Okay, clear the mind, clear the mind. In. Out. Breathing. In. Out. Breathing. In. Out. Breathing. Nice. In. Out. Breathing. Wait, saying 'nice' is thinking too. All right, this is pointless. He could not turn off his mind. What was with these meditators?

"I give up," he cried in exasperation.

"Congratulations, you almost made it a minute." She didn't open her eyes or shift her body.

"Hardy-fucking-har."

"I'm actually serious. I didn't really think you would make it half a minute on your first time." She grinned.

Once a day she worked with him. Sometimes she said merely, "Okay, meditate." She began her meditation and abandoned him to his own methods. Those were frustrating times. Every effort lasted only a few minutes before he surrendered to the inevitable obstruction of his thoughts. He yearned to abscond from the trenches, foxholes, and enfilades of his combat rattled mind. Often, during meditation, he recalled men whose faces and names he thought he no longer knew even though he once thought of them as his family. PFC Erik Hankton,

Staff Sargent Danny Robbins, Second Lieutenant Warner Paul, and others from his platoon visited him. Where were all those men? How many were still in the service? How many had shipped out to Afghanistan or Iraq on another combat tour? Who was fucked up? Who died? Natural, combat, or other? He always saw them in their BDUs and never in their civies, though he knew all but the officers from parties on or off base before they shipped out. These men haunted his mind, and his thoughts conjured their continued existence in the mountainous and dusty battlefields of his Afghanistan mind.

There were better attempts at meditation, such as when Jerusha guided him, her whisper crept into his mind and with gentle authority commanded that he do her will. She asked him to do different methods of meditation. She had him say 'breathing' on the inhale one time and on the exhale another time. A few times she created visions for him to experience. A favorite vision for him was to see himself in a room where he sat in its center. By the power of his breath he caused the walls to dissolve. Yet there were always titanic chunks of wall, jagged with crumbled bricks, that clung to his room. She explained that these were symbols of mental blockades that he must explore and come to terms with so that he could be enlightened. He struggled to defeat, to obliterate those walls that desired to be impregnable. To penetrate those constructions, Will faced his orphaned childhood, the war, and Rand, especially Rand.

One day he asked her, "How come you don't go to a Buddhist monastery or have a teacher or something like that?"

"That's who I am." She played her slender fingers through her cropped, brown hair that popped up with each pass of her fingers. "I always want to do things on my own. I want to pay my own way through school. I want to teach myself. I want to learn the truth on my own. I think, rightly or wrongly, that the best way for me is to go my own way. Sink or swim. There'll be no one to blame but me."

They went to a large used bookstore called Bookman's located just off campus. As they went through the electric, sliding doors, Jerusha said, "Why don't you just borrow my books? I said you could."

"I don't like to borrow books. If they're really important to me, then I'm going to want to keep them and read them over."

"Well, I hope you want to keep these."

They traversed the entryway past a display table and a line of customers waiting at the register. She pointed toward a back corner of the store, and she led him along the aisles between the tall, full shelves. She was in jeans and a flecked maroon sweater, and he marveled at how tiny she seemed.

"So are you just going to load me up with every book on their shelves that has to do with Buddhism?"

"I don't know."

"Will this be the heaviest reading list ever? Bigger than the toughest professor I had in college once gave me?"

She smiled, but her expression seemed more beleaguered than mirthful. "How much are you willing to spend?"

As she slowed, her eyes went to a spot on the numerous shelves that she probably knew well. "Here we are."

He halted beside her. He had his second check from the Ace in the new account he'd set up at a nation-wide bank branch in town. That money was mostly earmarked to pay his rent again.

"It's all for nothing if you don't read them." She squatted and put her hand on a shelf that had a plastic divider that read Buddhism.

"I'll read them." He dug in his front pocket and dislodged a small rectangle of dollar bills pressed into an unruly packet. He pried and pulled the bills apart. Jerusha tilted her head and watched. When he had them sorted, he counted through the small stack twice to insure accuracy. "Well, if we skip our weekly trips at the café then I have twenty seven."

"We don't have to spend it all."

"I know."

"We're not aiming to throw you into poverty."

He snorted. "Understood. I just want to throw myself into my new studies."

"Balance is a necessity along the way," she said. He blinked and realized that, when she said "the way," it meant his pursuit of Buddhist enlightenment. "Balance," she repeated.

"Yep." He gave her the okay sign with his hand. "So? What's required reading?"

She pulled out a copy of the *Dhammapada*. "This one. Are we blowing your whole wad?"

Though he knew she meant his money, he said, "Yeah, I like to blow my whole wad. No half measures for me." He grinned from ear to ear and folded his cash into a neat square.

All the air came out of her and she closed her eyes. When she opened her eyes again, she turned to him. "Really?"

"Hey, relax. It's a joke." He threw his free hand up and with the other he buried his cash in his front pocket.

"Okay." Her eyes were hard on him.

He inhaled deeply. "What?"

"I want you to be serious about this."

"I am, but that was a joke about the ambiguity of your word choice. Was what you said about money or about sex?"

"I want you to be serious about this."

"I am."

"You have to be aware about your every thought, word, and action."

His head bobbed. "Okay."

"Be conscientious."

There was nothing left of his humor after this harangue. He stood like a scolded child. They left with five books and about twenty dollars less in Will's pocket. They walked to the café, and she insisted on buying his drink so he ordered an inexpensive, hot tea like her, and drank it with a bitter face. He began the *Dhammapada*, which was the teaching of the Buddha. She studied, he studied. The simplicity of the language concealed far reaching concepts that he turned his mind to with his usual inquisitiveness.

He worked weekdays, eight to five. He wore the red vest and plastic name tag of an Ace employee. Paul was a good boss. He expected precision and cleanliness from his staff. Registers had to be spot on at the end of the day, off by no more than a few cents. The aisles were to be dust mopped at opening, midday, and at close. There was a restroom that was available to customers and this had to be checked hourly to insure that there was no garbage on the floor, that the trash can was not overflowing, that the toilet was not clogged or pissed or shit on, and that there were plenty of toilet paper, soap and paper towels. Each employee had an hour for lunch, but Will always brought a brown bag with his lunch of a sandwich or a bagel with a piece of fruit and some sort of vegetable that he sliced. When his coworkers saw the contents of his lunch, they teased him about having his mom put that together. He sat in the stockroom to eat. The first time Paul and a coworker had seen that, the latter asked if Will was anti-social. "No," Will said.

Paul said, "He's just a quiet guy. Maybe you could learn something from him." They carted out what they needed. Will wondered if he should go to lunch with the others. Should he be more social? He could not force himself into that though. He 'craved the solitude' and 'the company of his thoughts,' but he knew that those phrases were not his, those clichés were from others. He knew that what he feared cornered him into solitude. Could he be recognized from an old sketch? True, he had changed his name, but he did not think that was enough. There was only so much he could alter about his appearance. He had not had a haircut since he did not know when, so that made him look different from that sketch after the killing in Seattle. And he no longer had the beard. He would never be able to have a beard like that until he was old and wrinkled or fat and distended.

Four weeks into his employment, Paul's invitation for a beer after work perplexed Will, but he decided to go along because he did not want to return to the sarcophagus silence of his new apartment. Company seemed preferable for once. When the snow had thawed, Will had bought a used mountain bike. Paul and he loaded the bike into the back of Paul's 4X4 SUV. They sat at the bar, and Paul flagged down one of the two bartenders on duty. It was Friday night and the place filled with people just off from their week at work and thirsting for happy hour. Most customers wore shirts with the logos of their company's name on the left breast. At one table, Will saw three men and two women, four of whom had the six pointed stars of the Sheriff's department pinned or clipped to their shirts or belts. Those four with their badges also wore pistols on their hips. Why did they have to be here?

"What do you like?" the bartender, a man in his twenties, asked.

Paul ordered his beer, and Will asked for the same. The bartender pulled from a cooler the two brown bottles, popped the caps, and set them before the two men. Paul took up his bottle and held it in the air between Will and him. "To your first month at a new job." Paul smiled.

Will clicked the neck of his bottle against Paul's. "Thanks."

They drank them down with zest. Will glanced at the label. "This is good stuff." Casually, he twisted to spy on the sheriff department table, who were absorbed in their own conversation.

"Yep." Paul drank again. When he set the bottle down, it was half empty. "So, it wasn't too difficult, was it?"

"Nope." Will set his hands to either side of the bottle and began to rotate it by pushing one hand forward and the other backward. Will watched the glass catch the light in different ways, bend and stretch the reflections.

"Boss wasn't too hard was he?" Paul grinned.

Will smiled and shook his head for definite emphasis. "Not at all. A very good guy."

"Good, good. So you'll stay with us for a bit?" Paul drank again, stared down his bottle at Will as he did so.

Will lifted his bottle to his lips, but, before he drank, he said, "That's the plan."

"Fine, fine." Paul drank again. He leaned his head back, his Adam's apple pumping as he drained the bottle. "Ah!" He lowered the bottle, rapped the bar top twice as a summons, and, as the bartender arrived, handed him the empty. "Another, please." Paul twisted and eyed Will's beer. "Don't you like it?"

"I do."

"You not much of a drinker?"

Will shrugged and pinched his face to one side. "I guess I'm just not in a hurry."

"Not in a hurry to what?" Paul's fresh beer came, and he lifted and guzzled a fair amount. Will's eyes followed the trajectory of the bottle.

"To feel my beer as opposed to just tasting it," Will said.

"Ah . . ."

"So, I guess, I did okay this month?"

"If you hadn't, you would've felt my foot up your ass so I could wear you like a shoe."

"Fair enough." Will craned his head to look in a mirror hung behind the bar at the sheriffs. Half expecting them to be staring at his back, he found them laughing and pounding shots.

"You didn't have plans tonight?"

"No." Will had thought of eating dinner at the diner so he could be around Jerusha, but they were supposed to have coffee the next day. Besides, it might be nice to have her ask where he had been tonight if he had not been with her. Would she ask? Man, he wanted her to ask.

Paul and Will chatted for a bit, some about work, some about where they came from. Paul blinked and leaned back when Will mentioned that he had been orphaned and spent much of his childhood bounced from one relative to another until he went the rounds and then the cycle repeated.

"So you had nothing permanent growing up?" Paul drained his fourth beer. Will sipped at his second. "Shit, kid, I thought I had it rough. I had my ma, my grandparents, and my sisters though. Didn't no one want to take you in permanent?"

"No. I prayed to God that someone would, but, when I was about fifteen, I gave up on that. I just wanted to be grown so I could go out on my own. Then I wouldn't have to move from house to house, relative to relative."

"Wasn't any of them lovin' enough to you?" Paul waved the bartender over to receive his fifth.

"Uh, yeah. No one was ever mean to me. They fed me, clothed me, helped with homework, entered me in sports if I asked it, put a roof over my head and all that spiel, but I always knew that they did it because I was family and not that I was their kid. They loved me in a distant way, not in the close, hold on for dear life, kill for you, lay down their life for you, all-encompassing way that you have for someone who you really love. I always felt like a burden, though no one ever explicitly said so."

"Shit, kid." Paul shook his head. "Should I adopt you?"

Will stared at his bottle and his scarred, callused hands. "No. I think I'm going to try for a girl."

"Now that's the spirit." Paul clapped him on the back so hard that Will nearly lost the grip on his beer. "Go find some great girl, marry her, and make your own family." Paul rambled on with plans that Will ought to have. Will wondered if he could ever get a girl to love him. Could Jerusha ever love him, the former soldier, ex-Plato Killer? He must be everything she despised and thought was wrong in the world. He spied on the sheriff's table once more. The lot of them rose and left. Will's chest suddenly released a big blow of tension.

He collapsed on his mat as the room emptied. Four weeks of yoga classes and his body ached in ways he had never known. How was that possible? He had survived combat in some of the most difficult mountainous terrain that there was in the world. He had lugged a hundred pounds of gear and weapons up and down Afghanistan. Yes, that had been painful. This yoga crap was something else. He stared at the ceiling and panted. All the ladies had left. He no longer heard the slithering of their exercise shorts and pants as they moved about. Again, he was the only man in the room. Maybe he was uncomfortable physically, and maybe he was anxious about being singled out by the instructor because his form was wrong, but his chief problem was the level of arousal he felt. How long had it been since he had sex? How long since he had touched a girl? Now, he was in a room and no matter where he looked he seemed to be unbearably near to a woman's breasts, hips, ass, thighs, calves, neck, face, hell even their fingers drove him nuts now. All those stretched, twisted and sweaty bodies made him weak with lust. There was no better word for it.

As he lay supine on his yoga mat, all his mind wanted to do was ogle their bodies on his mental replay.

"Well, are you going to get up?" Jerusha was close.

"Yeah." He groaned and turned his head. Like all the other ladies, she was in form fitting pants, hers dark gray, and a tank top with a sports bra. She patted her face with a hand towel that she always brought.

"Any time now." She waved the towel in the air then sipped from her water bottle.

She was so lean. How would it feel to lay his hand on her flat belly? "You know what?" He brought his knees to his gut, kicked his legs out, and rolled into a seated position. "This isn't easy."

"Are you going to quit? We've got meditation to practice now."

He turned his eyes to her. She now had a hand on her hip. The towel dangled like a sash. Her weight was on that hip where her hand posed, while the other leg stretched to the other side. That was the pose that all women had when they wanted to show a man their impatience, their haughtiness. He smirked. "Kiss my dick."

Her eyebrows shot up and her jaw plunged. "Excuse me?" She blinked rapidly.

She could act pissed all she wanted. "Yeah. You know what?" He rolled onto his toes and fingers and sprang up. He reached his arms out. His legs felt like goo. His muscles trembled. "You're used to this. I'm not. This isn't easy. This is god damn painful to be honest. Yeah, that's right. And I'll tell you something else. You know what? I think you're enjoying how this is so obviously painful to me. I bet you're just laughing your ass off. Aren't you?"

She brought her extended foot in and evened her weight between both feet. Her arms crossed as she held her water bottle and towel still. Jaw set, she said nothing.

"Well." He leaned and snatched the mat from the floor with his right, while his left stretched behind him for balance. As the mat swung, he caught it with both hands and rolled it up at a furious pace. Finished, he continued, "You're not denying it. Thanks. 'Cause, you know, originally you had all that stuff about making me a better person. Now I know it's all bullshit."

He marched to the closet and rammed the mat onto a shelf. As he slammed the door, he hoped that it made her jump. He tottered to the door and paused. "You know I think I got a date with my bed tonight. Meditation? Not tonight. I don't think I can handle you're oh-so arrogant happiness as I try to focus and relax my mind to no point. Okay?"

She stepped over to her mat, squatted, set aside her water bottle and towel, rolled the mat, and stood again with all her possessions. "Well, then I guess you can just have a good night, quitter." She crossed the room and came within inches of him.

He jammed an arm across the doorframe. He could see the overhead lights glisten in the slick sweat at the hairline of her neck. How soft was her skin? Could he smell her? He inhaled deeply. His nostrils extended as he sucked at the pheromones in the air. Her smell was only a light musk, very nearly sweet. He spied the contours, the seams in her pink lips. If he kissed her, would she like it? Did she like him at all?

"Are you going to go, quitter, or are you just going to keep us both here?"

To hell with her. He lunged, latched his lips to hers, and gripped her shoulders. He had his eyes closed, but he knew it was not going well. She was rigid with anger. This was awful. He pulled away. When he opened his eyes, hers glared at him. A tremor shot from her body into his hands where he gripped her arms, and his grasp jumped away. That had been a mistake. He had probably just blown it with her. She would never want to see him again. Maybe she would deck him in the chin. He recalled how fast her fist flew at his face that night he had beat the shit out of that dickweed Davis. With a swing like that, she could knock him flat on his ass. Any second, any second. She stood. He wilted.

"Feel better?" she asked. Though he could not bring his eyes up, he heard that tone in her voice that conveyed her will to power, her need to belittle him.

He shook his head. "No." He let his arm drop and smack his side. Without looking at her, he shoved at the door and bolted. He did not pay attention to whether or not she followed. He felt like shit. Any more of her hard attitude, her sanctimonious bull would just be nails in the coffin for his ego.

The next day, seated on his bed, he held, one in each hand, the murderous instruments of his past life. His heart thudded at the cool sensation of the steel in his hands. What should he do with these weapons? He never wanted to wield them again. He was a new man. Was he a new man? Well, he wished to be a new man. Through Jerusha's teaching and prodding, he strove to be a new man. Could he accomplish that goal? Would he be allowed to change into a new man? If the police, FBI, or some other law enforcement agency ever caught up with him, then, no, he would never be allowed to change into a new man. He would forever be that old man, William Anderson Cooper, one of the two Plato Warriors, along with Randall Krieger, who together murdered a few dozen people in the autumn months of 2008 for the sake of an idea that seemed ludicrous, that people could be interrogated, found wanting of philosophical ideas and guidance, and be executed for that lack. To him it seemed a horrifying campaign of terror committed by strangers, men as remote from his comprehension as that of the men who, on September 11, 2001, took control of four airliners and then flew them into three buildings, killing thousands. Somewhere, in a shadow that he refused to cast a searchlight into, lurked one of the men who had committed those atrocities of 2008. Would he return? Was he frightened of being captured and executed or sent to jail? Did he yearn to carry on with his war, gun and knife in hand? Did he feel betrayed by the new man who called himself Anderson Williams?

Will returned the pistol to its case and its resting place on the shelf at the top of his closet, then stood in the middle of his room with the knife. In itself, there was nothing menacing about this knife. It was an ordinary survival knife, nothing more. No, it was a lethal remembrance. Will had used this knife to kill a couple in a national park in Colorado. Their murders were the first by the Plato Warriors. Will had since cleansed the knife of all blood by tossing it into a sink filled with bleach, but he knew it was still tainted. He could recall the effort he used to stab that man and woman in the heart, and he trembled just as they shuddered while every nerve in their bodies protested at the sudden arrival of their deaths. He went to the kitchen and tossed the knife and its scabbard in the garbage. It only felt a little better to have done that. There was still the pistol. There were still the memories of all those deaths. Maybe those were what was left of William Anderson Cooper? As Anderson Williams, he consulted his watch. It was time to meet Jerusha. He was going to be late.

She sat outside the Rec Center, same time, same place. Yoga would start in ten minutes. Was Anderson going to come? Did he have the will power to come and face her after last night? It took all her will power to return. How resilient was his will? When he rushed away last night, he hadn't even lifted his head to look where he went, and several people had to dodge him as he bolted. What had his kiss meant? Did he really like her romantically or was he trying to dominate her by sexual force? He seemed genuinely ashamed after he pulled away. Why hadn't she kissed back? Sheer shock had a lot to do with it. She hadn't expected him to kiss her. Actually, she thought he would insult her again. That "kiss my dick" comment was pretty crappy on his part for sure, and she had anticipated an even nastier retort after it, not a kiss. His words had struck her in some tender spots, places she didn't know she was vulnerable. How did she feel about Anderson? Until now she had thought of Anderson as a new project, a test of her discipline in regards to Buddhism. The sensation of his lips pressed to hers had hung on her until past one in the morning when she finally fell asleep. Why should a kiss bother her? Strangely, she did not hate him for it. Did he like her? Why insult her and then turn around and kiss her? She checked her watch. He wasn't coming. That was a shame. She wanted to help him. Maybe she pushed him hard, but it was because she believed that what she knew, what she had to teach him would make him a better person. What was so wrong about pushing him? If she left him alone, would he be a better person for it? Definitely not. She pushed because she cared. She cared about him. He was an orphan. He'd been a soldier who went to war. He'd gone to college and graduated with a degree in Philosophy and History. He was a sympathetic person for all those things. He was deeply broken. His friend killing himself only months ago, right in front of him, was an event that probably triggered all the other traumas and losses in his life to resurface. When they had their drinks at the café on the weekends, she enjoyed the sound of his spirit. The husk of his voice and the pain of those memories were genuine. Most of the time, he carried himself with a macho determination because he would otherwise crumble. Who could not be moved by that? Who would not care for him when he showed those tender parts of himself? Yes, she liked him. She snapped her wrist up to see the time. Only a minute until class, and she needed to pop her bag in a locker first. She rose. As she did, she gave a final glance up and down the street.

There he was. He shuffled along with his sweats on. His gray sweatshirt had black letters that spelled out "ARMY." It was not until he took the first stair to the Rec Center that his eyes rose from his pursuit of the gray concrete he travelled. He halted.

She forced a smile. "Come on. We're late, I think." She whirled a hand in the air to reel him in. He covered the distance and took her side. Out of her bravery or her compassion, in a gesture that surprised herself, she slipped her arm around his. "Come on." She tugged him, and she never once slackened her urgent stride while she was underway as they shot through the doors, past the desk, into the turnstile, and along the corridor to the yoga class. They were late, but they were there. She had him where he needed to be.

After yoga class and their meditation session, they sat in the snack bar area and ate the dinners they packed. She raised a celery stick, bit it through, but a string clung to the piece in her mouth and to the remaining stick in her hand. She reset her teeth and snapped off the stubborn celery string. There was something on his mind. She could see it in his face. What was he mulling over? She would not pry. It was better if he opened his mouth on his own without her. If he broached the topic, then she could prompt him with further questions, and if he was forthcoming, well, so much the better. "Do you think it's possible to gain redemption for several really terrible acts?" he asked.

She paused in her chewing and eyed him. When she had the food in her mouth to one side, she lifted a hand to politely conceal the contents of her mouth. "What? Like forcing yourself on a woman?" She grinned to show that she was really only joking. Would he take it that way? She was not upset about it now.

"Well, no. And I'm sorry about that." He set his sandwich on the Ziploc bag that he had brought it in. "I was thinking of something more sinister. Let's say Hitler wanted to atone for his sins. Could he?"

"Hitler?"

"Yeah, well, I guess I want to give you an example of someone who is truly heinous and see if you think it's possible for that kind of man to make up for what he did."

"But Hitler never would've wanted to atone for the Holocaust."

"What if he did want to? Could he? Do you think if he did a whole slew of decent and kind acts that he would then make up for it?"

"We're talking about Hitler."

"Okay, not Hitler but someone else. Let's say there's a guy who kills a dozen people, maybe two dozen. Could he ever make up for it by doing good things?"

"Without jail and without being executed?"

"Yes."

Jerusha dug her fork into her salad a few times, more than enough times to spear several pieces of lettuce. "What kind of acts of goodness?"

"I don't know." He shrugged and switched his gaze to the university students as they passed along the sidewalks and over the grass and into and out of the campus buildings. The melted snow meant spring was here. "Perhaps he volunteered at soup kitchens. Maybe he went to nursing school and helped to save lives and heal people. I don't know exactly how, but this guy does his best to make people happy, healthy, and stronger because he knows he messed up by killing all those people and it eats him up inside so he knows that he has to make up for it. Could he ever redeem himself? Is there a way?"

"Yes and no." She had scrutinized him as he spoke, and now that he was finished she blinked at the Tupperware of salad she held in one hand. "Every religion and law has its way of redeeming the evil acts that people do."

"You think that the Buddhist path is the correct one?"

"Well, yeah. For several reasons."

"There's no god though to say, 'You're redeemed.'"

"No, of course not. The thing is that there's not a separate course for criminals that's any different than what any of us would take."

"Why not?"

"The path to enlightenment is the path to enlightenment, the path is the path, and there's no differentiation between people. You still have to practice meditation. You still have to study the *Dhammapada* and the other texts. You still have to submit to an instructor. You still have to relinquish your desires. Who you are and what you did before are irrelevant, all that matters is the present and your practice of the teachings."

Will's brow pulled together. "But then… Well, you might say that the evil that this man did might as well not even be taken into consideration. A person's history, anything and everything that he did, doesn't matter as long as what he does in the present is good and right."

She nodded. "There is only the present."

He picked up his sandwich. After a moment where he just stared at it, he bit. He did not finish chewing before he asked, "Do you believe all this yoga and meditation can change me?"

"What's the *Dhammapada* say? Remember?"

"Yeah, yeah, I know. 'We are what we think.'"

"You don't believe. You don't know it. You aren't fully accepting it. In order to make that change, the kind that you speak of, you have to let the teaching inhabit you, let it fill you."

"I need someone. I need you. I want to be with you. You know what I mean? I need someone to help me. I think you're the best person to help me." He closed his eyes.

Sunshine asked, "Why are you with him?" She scraped at her scrambled tofu, broccoli, onion, and spice concoction as it cooked in the pan.

Sharp aromas of onion and cayenne filled Jerusha's nostrils. She crinkled her nose. "What *are* you cooking?" Jerusha snorted the aromas from her nose, but the vapors dug farther into her olfactory senses. "My God, girl, how much onion did you use?"

"Enough. Hey, leave me alone. I don't whine when you cook dead animal flesh."

"We have canines and incisors for a reason, and that reason is not to munch on soy products."

"You like some of my vegetarian recipes. Just last week you said that my tofu casserole was delicious."

"I did not." Jerusha sipped her green tea with diced ginger and lemon wedge. She glanced at the bowl of granola. She took her spoon and stirred the granola in its skim milk. There was some give to the chunks of baked oats, honey, and nuts that indicated the milk had soaked in enough to not break her teeth when she took a bite.

"You liar." Sunshine scooted her latest tofu meal onto a plate. She dropped the pan into the sink.

"Watch out for the metal pans. They'll scratch that sink, and we won't get our deposit back." Jerusha spooned her first bite into her mouth. It was cool and sweet after the tang and bitterness of her tea. For a moment, as she gnawed at the still hard center of a granola cluster, she imagined a field where oats wagged in the breeze and she wondered how much labor went into creating her breakfast cereal. Who grew those oats? Was it a family? She preferred that to an impersonal, corporate-run agri-business. If someone's life depended on her buying a product that was okay, but not if someone's profit margin was in danger of dipping below the level where a wealthy family couldn't go to the Bermudas that summer. Jerusha finished her bite as Sunshine sat down in the nook opposite her. Jerusha said, "Maybe. Okay, yes, I liked the casserole, but tofu is not a replacement for meat. It's an alternative for something different and not a replacement. Not for me, and it shouldn't be for you."

"Well, I disagree." Sunshine forked up a bite to her lips. After a few trips of the fork to her eager mouth, she said, "So why do you like him?"

"What?"

"You're not going to throw me off of my question again no matter how many times you change the topic. Now, answer."

"Why do I need to answer at all?"

"Why? He's dangerous. Look what he did to poor Davis." Sunshine gestured to the front room as if the evidence still lay on the carpet there, bloody and sore, about to moan any second.

Jerusha's eyes went wide, but she took a mouthful of granola and stared at the bluish surface of the milk in her bowl. What would Sunshine say if she knew everything that Jerusha now knew?

"That was awful, disgusting." Sunshine shivered and scooped up more of her breakfast, but set her fork down with a clank. "Jerusha, honey, look at me."

"Hm?" Jerusha's spoon stopped in mid dive for the bowl. Sunshine was such a sensitive soul. Jerusha tensed her arms as she watched her friend, and she thought of how much tougher she was. That's pride talking, Jerusha prodded her conscience.

"A man like that is dangerous."

Jerusha bit her lower lip. She took a long breath. "Yeah, I know." Even to her own ears, she sounded defeated.

"Then why are you going out to have coffee with him all the time? And this business of taking him to yoga classes? What's up with that? Do you want to be the next to get beaten?"

"He wouldn't ever beat me, and you're being very dramatic." Jerusha shook her head.

"Oh, really? Tell me, how do you know? Hm? See? You don't know that for sure."

"I do. He just . . . he would never hit me."

"No, you don't know."

Jerusha rolled her eyes.

"What else has he done? Do you believe he tells you the truth?"

"He likes me. That's why he would never hit me. Okay? Besides, you didn't see him the first time he came into that diner. He looked . . . shell shocked, like in an old war movie. I guess they call it Post Traumatic Stress Disorder now, PTSD."

"Whatever! You have no idea. You're sounding like some little girl who hooked up with an abuser. No idea, none at all, do you? What if he raped someone? He might go for you. But, oh no, he likes you. He likes you?" Her now shrill voice hurt Jerusha's ears. Sunshine nodded with angry jerks of her head. Was she going to hurt herself? "So if he likes you, then everything will be all right. That's what you think? My Lord, you're not that naïve are you? And what if he decides that he wants to have sex with you? Imagine if you say no. Do you think that will stop him? What then? He'll rape you just like he raped that other girl."

"What other girl? You're acting like you know he did that. You know nothing about him. I do, and I'm not at all worried about that."

"What?" Sunshine shrieked.

"Stop screaming." Jerusha covered her ears this time.

"You need to listen to me." Sunshine leaned all five feet and two inches of herself across the table and pulled one of Jerusha's hands down, but it took both of her hands to overcome her friend's greater strength. Once she had tugged Jerusha's now free hand to the table, Sunshine encapsulated that hand in both of hers. "I worry about you. I love you. I'm your roomie and your best friend. Okay? I absolutely, positively do not want you to get hurt or raped or, even scarier, killed. And I see the capacity for all that in him."

Jerusha tilted her head. She looked at her granola, probably quite soft now, and wondered if Sunshine was right. She suddenly felt meek. Could Anderson kill her? Of course, he could. He was a man, and, in Jerusha's opinion, all men were capable of killing. Though she wasn't one hundred percent sure, she believed that warfare might just be in the genetic makeup of humans, males particularly. Yet the world had seen the Buddha, Socrates, Jesus Christ, Ghandi, Martin Luther King Jr. and countless, anonymous others that had taught the efficacy of peacefulness in action and words. All of them were men, too. If it was in the nature, in the genetics of humankind from their evolution into a separate species from gorillas and chimpanzees, to engage in combat to conquer and control territory in the ancestral ecological niche they came into, then those men, like Buddha, demonstrated a cultural and philosophical evolution that could master that innate part of themselves. Jerusha shook her head. "No, I tell you what. I know you love me and worry about me, but I need to believe that a man that is capable of what Anderson did to Davis can be changed. Can't you see?" She now grasped Sunshine's hands between both of hers, and because she was stronger her roomie could not withdraw from her grip. "That is the kind of man who most needs help. If you let him loose, if you throw him out into the world where he will do what is his natural inclination, we are culpable of the failure to help. We fail to live up to our own beliefs that the world can be better than what it always has been. If we can't change this one man, then we can't change any man. Our beliefs, our dreams of a better, more peaceful future is null and void. I do know what he's capable of. He was in the army, and he fought over there." She nodded to the west, what she believed to be the closest distance to the Middle East.

Sunshine's eyes nearly dangled from their sockets. She blinked long and with pain to recover from the shock.

Jerusha said, "I want to help him, and, though you might not believe it, he wants to change. He's trying to change. I take him to yoga. I teach him meditation so that he can be retrained to do what is peaceful. Don't you see?"

Sunshine's head bowed, and Jerusha hoped that the movement of her roomie's body was to indicate her agreement.

"Please," Jerusha went on. "Help him. I need to help him both for his sake and mine."

Sunshine took a deep breath, sighed heavily, and rolled her eyes. She was relenting. "What do you want me to do? I'm not going to hug him or share a bowl with him though. No fucking way."

Jerusha grinned. "I wouldn't expect that much of you. I only want you to engage your hippie self and be nonjudgmental." Sunshine compressed her lips. Jerusha cocked an eyebrow. "It's for world peace."

Sunshine rolled her eyes again. "Oh, please."

"I thought we could have him over for dinner."

After she ate, Jerusha went to her room and packed her backpack for school. She reflected on the situation with Anderson. Sometimes, Jerusha felt burdened with what felt like a job. Why had she thought that she could do whatever it was that she was doing with Anderson? Was she his counselor? Was she his teacher? Was she his guard and police? His master not in the slavery way, but in the Buddhist way? Was her goal attainable? Did she really know what her goal was? To start Anderson on the path of enlightenment was her ideal, her plan. Was a goal something that contradicted Buddhism though? She assailed herself with these questions, they swooped and harassed her mind all the time. She had her own graduate studies, the papers of her undergrad students to grade, she had her own being, her own path of enlightenment to pursue, so why did she think she could aid this wreck of a man? That was selfish to think exclusively of her own worries. He needed someone, and she was involved now so it had to be her. Yes, she could teach him, and he was an experience that she could learn from to move herself along her path of enlightenment. She wanted to heal him, to redeem him from what he believed was an evil life, but was this attainable?

He scrubbed his hands after he flushed the toilet. He always obeyed the sign over the Ace toilet that read: "All employees must wash their hands before returning to work." It was printed in red lettering on a white background. Was it really a reminder for the staff or a reassurance to customers? Will dried his hands and glanced in the mirror over the sink. There was his face. It was the face of a man wanted by the 'long arm of the law,' as they said. His chest clenched. When would the day come when a police officer would recognize him? If only he could have plastic surgery. Poor criminals cannot afford such safeguard luxuries. We are cursed to be caught eventually, Will decided. When would the police catch him? That question agonized him. He tossed the wadded, damp paper towels into the waste basket. As he turned to the door, he imagined a pair of cops on the other side of the door, pistols drawn, and the rest of the staff at the entrance into the store peering with eyes goggling at the arrest of America's number one most wanted. Fear is measured by how much your body contracts upon itself to avoid harm. His testicles climbed into his body. His tongue clung to the top of his mouth. All this fear caused from the fantasy of two police on the other side of this door. Was it today? He could not stay in here forever. Go, he ordered his hand, turn the handle. Fuck it. At least the awful wait, the unceasing paranoia would cease. He slung the door wide and ventured into the stock room where the restroom was located. To the left, there was no one between him and the doorway to the store's floor. To the right, between him and the loading dock door, no one crouched with a pistol aimed at his heart. Not today. He shivered and felt on the verge of collapse. How long until this nightmare came true?

As he returned to the Ace floor, Paul met him en route to his office. "Ready to face humanity again?"

Will hesitated in his stride. "I guess."

"You can't hang out in the bathroom forever. Or the stockroom, for that matter."

"I know." Will inhaled with a shudder. Paul entered his office, unaware of the effect that his words had made. He clenched his jaw and stepped into the view of the shoppers.

Sunshine returned from her room with a Ziploc of green weed and a Bic lighter in one hand and a tall, jade colored, feminine bong in the other hand. Was she going to just light up? "Who wants a bowl?" Sunshine asked. Yep, she was going to get high, Will realized. Wasn't she past this sort of hippie, doofus stuff since she was a grad student? Will was glad to see that Jerusha did not pipe up with an exclamation of, yes, please.

"Do you want me to pack it?" Nitin reached for the paraphernalia. Sunshine nodded.

"He's such a gentleman. He packs his lady's bowl for her." Sunshine clasped her hands in front of her and began to moon at him.

"It's love," Jerusha said as she took her wine. She sipped then set it on the same spot on her placemat. "Will he start it for you too?"

"What man wouldn't?" Nitin said as he packed the bowl with some of the redolent, green weed. Man, the stuff was powerful. Will blew some of the scent from his nose into his shirt sleeve. Was this the norm for these people? Satisfied with the fill, Nitin put the bong to his lips, angled the lighter and clicked the ignition. The flame whiffed to life and within a few seconds the weed caught and glowed. Nitin inhaled. "Mm. Good shit. Where did this come from?"

Sunshine explained the origins of the weed and who the seller was. Apparently the Pacific Northwest had good marijuana these days, Will learned. Sunshine toked next. She held her breath then exhaled a cloud of smoke that shrouded her head. "Anderson, I told Jerusha I wouldn't offer you any," Here she snuck a sidelong glance at Jerusha. "But I'd like to be a good hostess." She extended the bong across the table toward him.

"Uh…" Will checked Jerusha's attitude toward such an action. She sat with her spine quite prim and proud. "Are you having any?" he asked her.

"Not my thing."

"Truth is, I never smoked before."

"Never?" Sunshine stared, aghast. "Jerusha has. It was hard to get her to do it, you know, a lot of arm twisting. Oh, and we had to extract the rod from her tight ass." Sunshine giggled. She brought the bong back to her and took another pull from it.

"The rod?" Jerusha wiggled about on her chair and sat straighter than ever. "In my ass? I've got such a great friend, don't I?"

Will shrugged. At least her best friend was not a gun wielding lunatic. "How come you don't like it?"

"I don't want to avoid reality."

Sunshine made a sound that was like a seagull's cry. "I'm not avoiding reality, so called. I'm testing another reality."

"Oh, really? That makes sense." Jerusha rapped her fingernail on the handle of her spoon, clink, clink.

"Human reality is too confining." Sunshine passed the bong to Nitin who eagerly accepted it and clamped it to his mouth for a long toke.

"How can we know what other realities are through the chemical alterations of THC?" Jerusha picked up the spoon and stared into the concave reflection at its head. She seemed a trifle bored by this conversation. Maybe it was a recurrent one.

"But we can," Sunshine took a piece of bread and began to tug fingernail sized bits from it, which she popped in her mouth.

Nitin lowered the bong and rested it on his thigh. "Yes, we can. The chemical reacts with our internal human chemistry and changes us, just for a while, so that we can be other than what we are. Your alcohol is the same." He waggled a finger at Will and Jerusha's glasses.

"You had some too." Will nodded at the glasses in front of Nitin and Sunshine. "What was different about the wine?" Will tried to shovel through the refuse in his mind for an accurate word. Was transformation the word? "The chemical transformation of alcohol didn't give you a different perceived reality? Did it?"

"No, it's quite different."

They argued, with Will assuming a dominant voice as the opposition to Nitin and Sunshine, while Jerusha turned in her chair to face Will more directly. Sunshine finally said to Will, "Well, why don't you just try some, and then you can make an informed decision? You have your own take on all this, but you can't get ours until you've tried it." She shook the bong over the table. "Well?"

Will leaned back. Cornered, he cast a glance at Jerusha, whose green eyes were on him already. She said, "I've tried it."

So she was okay with him doing this? It was illegal. How could she approve? "You've only done it the one time though. You're not just going to let me do it on my own. Are you? Don't make me the sacrifice for greater understanding. That's kind of low."

They had a stare off. She lost, reached for the bong, took a quick puff, a half breath really, and shoved it at him. "Puff the magic dragon, asshole."

Well, he could no longer refuse. Trapped, he took the bong to his lips and inhaled.

"Look at him go!" Nitin slapped the table. The evening wafted by, and the scientific debate was set aside. Everything seemed looser, more humorous. Their talk rambled on, but Will could hardly recall from one moment to the next what they had just discussed. When Will caught sight of his watch, the hour was late. "I should get going." He rose and his chair tipped with a bang to the hard wood floor.

"How did you come here?" Nitin leaned to spy the fallen chair but had to grab the table to stabilize his weight. "Uh oh, I'm stuck."

"My bike."

"Ooh, I think he has to stay the night, Jer." Sunshine giggled. She snatched at Nitin's sleeve and, hand over hand, tugged him upright. "Wee!" When her boyfriend was vertical her head crashed on his shoulder.

"Stay the night?" Will asked. The room was dipping up and down and it felt like he stood on a foam pad. "Wow," he said in recognition of that altered state. "I still feel human. Ha! You were wrong about other realities."

Sunshine's eyes were closed as she snuggled against Nitin's larger mass. He too had his eyes closed, his head lolled back so that he faced the ceiling.

Jerusha stood. "I think the debate was a deception to get us to smoke. Come on." She took him by the hand, and led him from the table. Where was she leading him?

"What about them?" Will indicated Nitin and Sunshine.

"They're fine where they are. When they wake, they'll go to her room."

As they turned down the one hall in the house, he asked, "Where are we going?"

"To bed. Aren't you tired?"

"Yeah." He did not know how he felt actually. They went through the first door they came to, and Jerusha snapped on the light. Her bedroom was impeccable. There was a bed, nightstand, desk with chair, dresser, a calendar tacked over the desk, and a few framed photos and posters. Everywhere, there were stacks of books, yet they seemed organized and neat because she had placed all the Penguin trade paperbacks in one stack, all the Vintage Internationals together, and so on. This made those stacks of books, potentially unruly, regular and tidy. Jerusha went to the dresser and took out a set of flannel pajamas.

"I'm going to go change and brush my teeth. Sorry, I don't have an extra brush for you."

"It's okay. I didn't get to brush my teeth when I was in the field in Afghanistan. I'll survive one night without brushing. I don't know if you'll survive my breath though."

"I could survive a night without your debating though."

"My what?"

"Your debating. You always seem to do that."

"I guess."

"That's all you have to say about that?"

He nodded.

"Okay." She nodded to close out the inquiry. "I have some mouthwash."

"Better than nothing."

"Give me a minute to change then you can rinse while I brush."

A few minutes later they were in her room. Will's mouth felt quite clean. He had spotted some floss and used that in addition to the mouthwash. Jerusha shut the door. "Hop in." She gestured to the bed. "I'll give you the side toward the wall. That way you can't escape." She gave him a smirk that made him weak kneed. Were they going to have sex? He blinked and worked to make the floating room come to a standstill. "Well?" She put her hand on the light switch. He yanked back the covers and dropped into the double sized bed. He lay on his back. The lights went out and she was there, beside him, in the sudden darkness. He seemed to bob about in space. "Good night," she whispered. I guess they would not have sex. He waited for sleep to grab him. Sleep was not long in coming.

In the night, he woke and found he was face to face with her. Her breathing was regular. Moonlight outflanked the curtains. The room no longer pitched around as if the floor was balanced on the head of a pin. He had an irresistible compulsion to touch her. Would she smack him if he touched her? There was, of course, only one way to find out. Cautiously, he reached for her. Should he first touch her face or arm or waist or hip? He brushed his fingers across her cheek.

Instantly, she moved, wriggled closer to him and let out a sigh. This time he trailed the pads of his fingers along her jaw. Her head tilted back as it lay on the pillow. He kissed her. They moved to each other, struggled against the fabric of clothing. A brief pause ensued as she tracked down a condom from the bathroom. Slightly awkward, they attempted to adjust to the unfamiliarity of each other's movements. They succeeded for a few minutes anyway.

Jerusha feverishly scratched the pen at the top of the page. Nothing. The pen was dry. She spiked the pen in the wastebasket by her desk. That was a rare example of frustration, she interpreted of her action. Why had she done that? As she opened the drawer of her desk to procure another pen, there was a double rap on the door.

"Uh hunh?" What did Sunny need? Jerusha really had to get this idea on paper before it evaporated.

Sunshine came in. "Hey, so, I was getting a condom from my box last night and—what do you know—there was only one of these little God sends left. Hm. Now, who could be borrowing them to have sex without asking?"

Jerusha twisted in her chair, but looked at a clutch of pens she had brought out from the drawer.

"Who do I know who might be shagging? I'm not sure. Can you help me think of someone?" Sunshine asked with a bite of playful impertinence in her tone.

Jerusha selected a black ball point pen from the brace of others and tossed the unnecessary ones into the drawer again.

"It can't be my girlfriend Jerusha, who lives in the same house with me. She would tell me if she was getting lucky. Of course, she would."

"Shut up. It was me." Jerusha twisted the whole way around. Sunshine stood with her empty box of condoms.

"No." Sunshine put a hand to her chest.

"Yes."

"And how many times have you and the battler done it now?"

"Too funny."

"Well?"

"A few."

"And?"

"What?" Jerusha turned back to the beckoning book and her notebook.

"Is he big?"

"Oh God." Jerusha leaned her head into one propped hand and sought the spot in the text that had inspired her with something, some brilliance, some erudition, forgotten at the moment.

"Is he like a rabbit, a dog, a horse, or a bull?"

"I need to get back to work."

"When did this start?"

Jerusha sighed in aggravation. "When he was here for dinner."

Scrape, tick, scrape, tick. What was Sunny doing now? Jerusha twisted now the opposite way in her chair. The sound was from Sunshine scraping the box of condoms along her jeans and then giving it a quick rap at her hip. "That's very interesting. I knew you wanted to help him be more peaceful, but I didn't realize that you had to put your body on the bed to complete the task."

Jerusha swung around to face her studies and to show Sunny her back. "That was a low comment."

"You're not going to give me any details?"

"No."

"All right then." Sunshine's feet padded across the carpet until she was right behind Jerusha. A kiss descended on the crown of Jerusha's head. "I only hope and pray that he's good to you."

"He is."

"Good." Sunshine squeezed Jerusha's shoulder. She turned to leave.

Before she got out of the room, Jerusha called, "I'll buy us another box of condoms."

Sunshine giggled. "Better get the family size. You two have been hitting it hard."

Two weeks later, the four of them went to Walnut Canyon to see the Anasazi ruins built into the cliff sides. These were not the large multi-story dwellings of Chaco Canyon, which were quite famous. Natural rock shelves and overhangs provided the floors, ceilings and back walls. Stones were used to wall in a fairly small room. Both Nitin and Anderson ducked when they stepped within the perimeter of one such single room abode. As the four of them hiked along the single trail, Jerusha moved to the edge of the trail that dropped hundreds of feet into the canyon below. She hated heights, always, but she felt compelled to go to this place that frightened her to death. Every time she caught herself holding her breath, she made a sharp exhale and inhale. Breathe. She could do this. It was not as if she was on a high wire. She was on firm ground. She trembled. Stop, she commanded her body, but her body refused to obey and went right on shaking anyway. Keep going. She could do this. They were nearly half way around the mile long loop.

She set her foot down. Her whole body rolled with the motion of the loose stone. She reached out with both hands. In front of her face, the chasm appeared with dark green firs perched on yellow boulders. Her hands clutched at nothing, air. There was nothing for her to grasp or to brace against. She fell. Then she snapped about. She swung. The firs and yellow stones and boulders swung and whipped by, going right to left. As she came back over the path, her shins cracked against something hard. The toes of her boots gouged the hard packed dirt. She spiraled on her belly on the yellow dirt and the gray and red rocks. Finally, everything stopped. All she heard was her heart and her own whimpering and gasping. She clawed at the firm pathway.

"Are you okay?" His voice.

Her body contracted and she balled up onto her side like a dead thing. "Jerusha?" He grasped one of her shoulders, and his body shadowed hers. "Are you okay?"

She nodded as she shuddered. Pain stabbed from her shins up her body with the length of swords. The sun came back and made her raise a hand. Where had he gone?

"Jerusha!" Nitin shouted.

"Baby, are you all right?" Sunshine scrambled over to Jerusha's inert body. As she squatted and leaned over Jerusha's face, she brushed her own wild hair behind her ears. "Talk to me. Are you okay?"

Jerusha slowly twisted. She planted her hands and raised her upper torso. Nitin knelt on the opposite side of her from Sunshine, who grabbed Jerusha, a hand on each of her quaking shoulders. "It's okay. You're safe," Nitin said.

Finally, after craning her head to see past Sunshine, she found him. Anderson had collapsed onto the path, his back against the canyon wall. She gazed into his eyes. His face was emotionally flat. He didn't seem to be breathing. That broad chest of his didn't seem to be in motion, as if he was not breathing and had no need. She swallowed drily and nodded. "I'm fine," she said.

"You were very lucky." Nitin patted one of her arms. "Anderson has very fast reflexes. Amazingly fast." He sounded overawed, and he raised his face to view Anderson, who slouched there as if he was at total peace with the world, as if he still had yet to take a breath. "I hardly saw what had happened before he pulled you back from falling. Really amazing."

"Come here." Sunshine tugged Jerusha into her arms even though they were facing the same direction. She wrapped her arms across Jerusha's chest and squeezed. That made it difficult to breathe. Jerusha gasped and clutched at Sunshine's arm to loosen that bound.

A couple with two boys trotted up. "Oh, my God. Are you okay? That was incredible. He saved your life," said the wife as she skidded into a squat beside Jerusha.

"Hey, you saved her. Let me help you up." The husband threw his hand in Anderson's face. Anderson blinked, refocused his eyes on the proffered hand, and decided to take it. The man easily jerked him to his feet where Anderson swayed and filled his lungs. "Wow!" The husband patted Anderson on the back and turned to his son. "Take a look at him. He's a hero."

Anderson cocked his head to one side and his jaw gaped. "I'm not a . . . hero."

"Yes, you are, man. That was incredible."

"No, I'm no hero."

"How can you say that?" the wife asked. She and Sunshine now had Jerusha by an arm each. They helped her rise from that yellow dust. Jerusha's eyes were fixed on him. "Most people couldn't have reacted that fast," the wife said as she shook her head.

"Boys, look at him. Did you see how quickly he caught hold of her?"

One of the boys, probably eight years old, his blond hair without a distinct part hanging over his forehead to his eyebrows, said, "He was like a ninja." He whipped his hand out as if to snatch something in flight past him. He opened his hand to find it empty. "I couldn't even see him move he was that fast."

"Yeah, a ninja," said the older boy, maybe eleven years old and with his sandy hair parted neatly on the right but cut longer, nearly to his ears. "Hi-ya!" He too sliced an arm through the air, but his fist stayed shut the whole arc of his swing as if his action was a punch and not a catch.

Watching the antics of the boys made Jerusha want to hide her face. With a glance at her, Anderson shook his head. His eyes dropped and his jaw swung open again. Her eyes followed his gaze. The shins of her jeans were dark and bloody. Neither pant leg was ripped cleanly, but there were frayed patches and the fabric was dark. He rushed over, knelt in front of her, and placed a hand on one of her knees. "Can you walk? You're bleeding."

"Oh, my God." The wife put a hand over her mouth.

Sunshine leaned forward, spied the dark spots, and gasped. "Oh, honey, we need to get you out of here."

"We should carry you." Anderson said. The soldier took command. He spun around. "Don't stand and talk. Help her onto my back."

"Are you sure you can carry her that distance?" Nitin asked. "Maybe we could support her together?"

"No, it's fine. In the army I humped a hundred pounds of rifle, ammo, food, and gear over Afghanistan's mountains. Jerusha isn't much heavier than that. The hard part will be those steps going up. I'll need you to stay behind me to make sure I don't lose my footing. Come on." He motioned to the women. "Get her on my back. I can do it. We can't risk her walking if she has a fracture. Come on, Jerusha. Put your arms around my neck, and I'll wrap your thighs up with my arms. Mind her shins." Gingerly, Sunshine and the wife loaded Jerusha on Anderson's back. He stood and shrugged his shoulders to adjust her into a secure grip. Jerusha locked her hands around his neck. "Ready?" he asked her.

"Yes," she whispered in his ear. She became aware of how broad his back and shoulders were as she clung there. He felt more like a rock that breathed than a person. Anderson marched.

"Maybe one of us should go get a park ranger," the husband offered.

"No time." Anderson bent forward to keep her weight ahead of his feet, which gave him additional momentum. Every step made Jerusha cringe. She bit her lower lip to prevent any yelping.

"But a ranger could help."

Luckily, the accident had happened on the return leg of the trail, which was nothing but a big loop. He took about ten minutes to soldier to the foot of the stairs that led to the rim of the canyon, the national park tourist center, and the parking lot. Anderson paused. Jerusha now tasted blood in her mouth from where she'd bit her lip too hard. "Nitin?" Anderson said.

"Yes."

She gazed up the twisting stone staircase. There was metal railing on one side. If needed, could he use that for stability? "Nitin, old friend, I want you right behind us," Anderson said. "Keep a hand on her back to support her. Okay?"

"I will."

"Good man."

"All right. Here we go. You ready?" He turned his head and tried to eye Jerusha.

"Mm hm." He could probably hear the pain in her voice.

"Almost there. Just hang on," he said.

He had to hurry. She was in a hell of a lot of pain. Her shins throbbed. She was aware of the sticky blood that was on her legs and made the fabric of her jeans chaff. As they trooped up the steep stairs, tourists stopped where they were when they caught sight of them to gawk. Eventually, two rangers from the park service met them about twenty yards from the top.

"What happened?"

Anderson was struggling by this point. She felt a constant trembling in his body like an electrical charge. "Can't we get... to the top... and then discuss... this?" He gasped.

Finally, with that whole entourage of witnesses, Anderson mounted the last step. There was a boulder, about waist high, a reddish brown color, close by. Anderson staggered to it and tottered around.

"All right. Down we go." Nitin was by their side. As Anderson leaned back, Nitin steadied Jerusha atop the boulder. For her part, she unlocked her hands from around Anderson's neck and whipped her hands back to snatch at Nitin's shirt in order to feel steady. Anderson rose and stumbled away. His back was soaked with sweat. He bent over, braced his hands on his knees, and panted with a sudden plunge of exhaustion. Looking around, she saw the tourists assembled, along with that family that had the two boys who had followed them here, and even the park employees, and they all applauded. Anderson hung his head and closed his eyes. Why did there have to be all these people around? Jerusha doubled over and clutched her knees as if with her hands she could halt the pain from knifing along her nerves to her brain.

A few park service staff attended to Jerusha. They tugged up her pant legs and taped gauze pads to her shins. Anderson asked if she could move her feet and lift her legs. She did, but she winced and coiled up her face with pain from each effort. After the consultation of everyone present, whether their opinions were requested or not, it was decided that Jerusha should go to the hospital for x-rays. Nitin and a park ranger carried her to the car. She expected Anderson to sit in the back beside her, but Sunshine leaped into the opposite side of the backseat before the ranger and Nitin finished placing her inside. Nitin drove while Anderson sat shotgun. Anderson twisted in his seat. "Are you okay?"

She would not take her eyes from him. How had he reacted so quickly?

"You just want to go home. Don't you?" he asked.

She nodded. Would he countermand the orders of the others who wanted to fuss and fret and force her to get x-rays she neither needed nor could afford?

"We just need to make sure there's no fractures. Better safe than sorry. Right?" He winked. What was that strange bit of bravado about? He faced forward. "As soon as the doctor makes sure that nothing's broke, we'll get you home."

Sunshine started up. "Oh, honey, I was so scared. Weren't you scared? You look so tired. Come here. Come on, just lay up against me. There, there. I can't believe it all happened. It seems like a nightmare now." Sunshine prattled.

Will jolted awake. He had dozed off. He glanced at Nitin who drove and continued to watch the road. They were in Flagstaff again. Will rubbed his face and twisted so that he could see her. Jerusha lay against Sunshine, who, thankfully, was now quiet. Jerusha's face was toward the window on her side. Her features were still drained of expression. Had she been traumatized? Was she scared that badly? Had she never come that close to dying before? He craned his neck to spy her shins. The jean legs were both rolled up to her knees. The gauze bandages had spots of maroon in their centers, though it didn't seem to be spreading. He glanced at her face and found her eyes on him again. He smiled. "Are you hanging in there?"

Sunshine stroked Jerusha's head as if she protected a child from nightmares. Jerusha was mute and lay still. Only her eyes blinked.

"Honey, are you okay?" Sunshine's hand stopped at the peak of Jerusha's brow. "Talk to us."

"I'm okay." Jerusha's voice was very thin. When they reached the hospital, Sunshine was the one who accompanied Jerusha to the exam room to see the doctor and have the x-ray. Will and Nitin sat in the waiting room until they realized how hungry they were. They found their way through the maze of identical corridors to the hospital cafeteria. After they sat, they talked very little until they were nearly finished with their victuals. Nitin broke the silence. "Were you afraid?"

"No. Not until after."

"Why not?"

"I didn't have time to be."

Nitin took a bite of his red delicious apple and pondered this. Will scraped the inside of his yogurt cup with his plastic spoon to collect the last of the blueberry yogurt. "You just reacted," Nitin said from around the chunk of apple in his mouth. He wiped at the corner of his mouth with his sleeve.

"Yeah." Will set on his tray the empty yogurt cup with the spoon sticking from the top.

"You didn't think about what to do, you just did it."

"I guess." Will became suspicious of where this conversation was going. He eyed Nitin. "Why?"

"Is that what you did to Davis? He made you angry, so you just acted?"

"Ah."

"What's that mean?"

"I was wondering where you were heading with that."

"Well?"

Will shrugged. "I guess so."

"So you can beat someone one day and then some other day you save a life?"

Will swallowed drily.

"I see."

"In fairness though, I didn't like Davis from the moment I saw him." Will was compelled to admit.

"Hm. What about me?"

"You?"

Nitin's eyes went wide and he jerked forward, folded his arms on the table, and leaned into the space between the two men. "Yes, me. Did you not like me from the first moment you saw me?"

Will swallowed again and looked at his bottle of water that was half full or half empty, depending on your point of view. What was his point of view? It used to be the half empty point of view. Now? "I don't remember. I remember when all of you came into the café that day, but I don't remember what I thought about you. Maybe nothing."

Nitin made no movement. He seemed quite close to Will because of how pugnaciously he sat. His eyes were very dark brown. On his cheeks above his beard, Will saw what were either large pores or pockmarks from teenaged acne. Just like his own. Will reached and dug a fingernail into one of his pockmarks. "I wasn't threatened by you," Will said.

Nitin's eyes narrowed without comprehension.

Will nodded. "I saw how Davis looked at Jerusha. I knew he liked her. I liked her, and I didn't want the competition. I think that more than anything is why I beat him up."

"Because you were jealous of him."

"Yeah. You're the only one that I've told. The fact is that I'm an outsider. You, Sunshine, Jerusha, Davis, and all your friends, well, I mean, you're a group. You have things in common with each other. You're all in school, you date each other, some of you live together, and so on. Who am I? I'm a stranger. I've got no connection with any of you. And the truth is, I only wanted a connection with one of you."

Nitin sat back, crossed him arms over his chest, and said, "Davis liked her. She never reciprocated as far as I've ever heard, and, believe me, if she had, she would've told Sunshine, who would've told me." He pulled a strange face and dug into one of his front pockets to pull out his cell. He pushed a button and read something, a text from Sunshine, Will suspected. "They're out. We need to go."

They rejoined the girls in the ER waiting room. There were no fractures, but the swelling and bruising were substantial. The ER staff had swapped the bandages and also applied cold compresses inside the wrapping. Jerusha sat in a wheelchair with an irked expression that pinched her face to the right. As the two men strode up, she growled, "Stupid hospital rules."

Jerusha insisted on wheeling herself out, her strong willed self had returned. Nitin went ahead for the car, and by the time he pulled up at the sliding doors, the effort to roll out there, a distance of fifty yards, caused Jerusha to slump. Will understood that the adrenaline was long gone.

"Can you get in under your own power?" Will leaned and swiveled the footrests up. "Or do I need to lift you?"

She glared at him, mustered her strength, and pushed out of the wheelchair with both hands braced on the armrests. She tottered for a second. Both Will, on one side of her, and Sunshine, on the other, raised their arms to take hold of her in case she tripped or collapsed. She regained her balance. With her face twisted in pain, she scraped forward to the car door that Will opened. She wobbled around in place until she could sit back into the seat. A puppy like whimper escaped her tight lips. It was the most pitiful sound Will had heard in a long time.

They drove to Sunshine and Jerusha's house. When they arrived, Jerusha accepted help. Will carried her in his arms. His back stiffened at this renewed demand to transport her. Her legs dangled to one side, but her upper body was close. She had her thin arms around his neck, and her face was beside his. He felt the warm moisture of her breath. His guts knotted, and he became aware of his body. Her body seemed tiny in his arms. He focused on the door, which Sunshine opened the door, and Will carried her over the thresh hold. In another circumstance this would be romantic. They decided that she should be put to bed. The doctor had given her Tylenol with codeine at the hospital and a prescription for more. Her head lolled as he laid her on the mattress. He slowly extricated his arms from beneath her limp form. Her green eyes were murky like an algae laden pond. As he straightened, he paused to grin and brush her cheek with the back of his hand. Did her mouth pull into a smile, ever so slightly? She was so soft that he had to force himself not to caress her more. Why did she have to be soft, when she acted as hard as nails?

Sunshine was at the foot of the bed. She had watched him, but Will didn't care. Jerusha had probably told her about them. And he was tired of hiding everything. That touch was hardly something to feel guilty about. It's not as if he had touched her in an improper way, or as if Jerusha had not seen him do it.

"I'm going to change her. She can't stay in those bloody clothes while she sleeps," Sunshine said.

"I should be going." He turned and went out the door.

As he pulled it closed behind him, Sunshine said, "I'll be out in a moment."

Will delicately shut the door. He went to the living room where Nitin sat in the big easy chair and rubbed his palms over the thighs of his jeans. Nitin asked, "Is she all right?"

"She's wiped out. She was almost asleep when I put her down." Had Sunshine meant for him to wait for her to come out before he left? Did she have something to tell him?

"Where's Sunny?"

"Changing her. She said she couldn't stay in those messed up clothes."

Nitin stroked his beard then slapped his knee. Those hands were always in motion. "Care for a drink? My nerves need one." Will declined, and Nitin rose and went past Will to the kitchen. "Are you sure? Don't your nerves bother you?"

"My nerves are fine."

"Really?" Nitin returned with a glass of red wine. Passing Will, he slapped him on the shoulder. "Ha. I guess you're made of sturdier stuff than I." He laughed. He sat again and quickly guzzled half the glass while his eyes shut. "Ah." He reopened his eyes. "I'll feel better after the second glass."

"I was a soldier. Remember?"

"Ah, yes."

Someone caressed the back of Will's deltoid. He half twisted at the waist. Sunshine said, "You really like her."

"Yes, from the first."

"I couldn't have saved her like you did." Her glance traveled to Nitin and his wine glass. "And neither could he. I guess that's the flip side of the coin that's you."

"What do you mean?" Will wanted to go. He was so exhausted. He inhaled sharply and then let it whisper back out.

"You can be so violent, but you can save someone too. You put your life at risk. What if she had been farther out or if you had slipped on the same rocks she had? Then you both would've been gone." She paused and let her eyes float to his face. "You never worried about that. Did you? No, you didn't. You acted. We stood by and you acted.

You saved her." She rushed into him, was against him, and had her arms around him. It was a hug. Will stood with his arms half raised, uncertain what to do. Nitin's eyes were awkwardly on them. "I'll always be grateful to you. And I hope I can help you in return."

Will stood within her embrace like a tree. Finally, she stepped back. "Uh, thanks," he said. "I should go now. I'm wiped out. And my back kills." He rubbed the small of his back with one hand.

As he turned to go, she smiled with tears on her cheek. Had he finally won over someone from Jerusha's circle?

The following evening, after he left work, he decided to pay the patient a visit. On his way, he pedaled past a Safeway supermarket and decided that he should not arrive at her house empty handed. He locked up his bike and, with the urgency that had impelled him since the clock hit four and his shift ended, strode into the bustling grocery store. What should he bring? Flowers seemed wrong for some reason. He imagined coming in her house and handing her dead things, for that was what the flowers in grocery stores were. Snipped from their roots, the flowers tried to stand tall in black buckets of water, but they were like naked, unarmed soldiers who were so busy in their attempts to cover their privates that they became ridiculous. He breezed past the florist section of the store anyway, to confirm his decision. Adjacent to the floral section were the aisles of wine, beer, and spirits. Pain killers and alcohol were a peculiar combo. No, he moved on. A "get well" card? No. He paused in the middle of an aisle and set his hands on his hips. His heart snapped about in double time tempo. An irked shopper flashed him a nasty look as she scraped her cart past him. A four year old girl with smudged cheeks complained that they never had Oreos and that she would die without them. A dessert for Jerusha? He suddenly broke from his anxious trance in the aisle's center, and whipped past the shopper with her still berating child, who yammered "Oreos, Oreos" over and over. God, kids are the death of sanity. Will smirked. In the bakery section he picked through "single serving," plastic shell containers of cakes until he selected a German chocolate cake with its field of grass-like coconut in brown sugar and pecans.

He was in the checkout line when the same woman with her Oreo pleading girl came up. There was a man in front of Will. The sales clerk swiped one after another of his items over the laser scanner. Will had been entranced by the red streaks in the scanner, but as the woman approached, he twisted at the waist and received a look of annoyance from her. What was this woman's problem? What had Will done to her? He forced a pleasant smile. The woman's head jerked, and she riveted her unhappy gaze on the magazines for sale. Will had done nothing to her. He had only partially blocked the aisle before. She had still squeezed past. Was it the annoyance she felt at having to make room for him? Is that what it was? He surveyed the other checkout lanes and saw so many people with the same expression. Was the world only inhabited by these people who were hypersensitive to the impingement upon their personal sphere by other people, strangers? So much anger in this world. Why? Will came to the clerk, who whipped his German chocolate cake over the scanner where the red lasers read the bar code of black lines, and she said in a monotone, "Did you find everything you needed?"

"Yes, I did." Will handed her a ten dollar bill.

She told him the total in the same monotone. When she had his change in her hand, her flat voice intoned what the amount of his return was. She handed it to him. Will accepted his change and said thank you as he took his cake out of the plastic bag that she had shoved it into as part of her routine. "I don't need the bag, thanks. It's just something that wrecks the planet."

She halted as she began to pick up the first of the woman's items, a blue package of Oreos. Will had broken the tempo of her routine, confronted her with a break in the habits of her job. She blinked. "Okay." Her voice had a sense of bewilderment now instead of her typical monotone.

Will left. He smiled at the ease with which he had woken that one sleeper. If only he could pop other sleepers like that clerk out of the tracks of their daily drudgery, would the world be better? When he reached his bike, he pondered if he could've nudged that woman shopper with her Oreo begging child out of the rut of her day too. He leaned on the handlebar and stared back at the Safeway. Would it be worth it, to wake her? He zipped the cake into his backpack. How could he wake her? He slung the pack onto his shoulders. He should get going. He had to see Jerusha. He wanted to examine her wounds. Why had she been so close to the edge? Was she going crazy? Was it a weird way to commit suicide? Jerusha didn't seem the suicidal type though.

He hit the street, Route 66, and recalled how Jerusha had behaved like a tightrope walker as she went right along the edge of Walnut Canyon. Will didn't know what to make of her actions. Ten minutes later he bounced the bike over the lawn and up to Jerusha's porch. He leaned the bike against a support, took the cake in one hand, and thumped the door with a snap of his wrist that was harder than he meant. Who would answer it?

Sunshine let him in and shut the door. "I think she's had her nose in one book or another the whole day. Before I left this morning, she asked me to bring her book bag to her. Oh, and I did leave her some lunch."

"That was kind of you." Will smirked. He stood in the middle of the living room, almost where he'd been the night before when she hugged him. He looked to the kitchen.

"Ooh, what's that tasty treat?" She spied the plastic clamshell in his hand.

"German chocolate cake. Sorry, it's not vegan."

Sunshine came closer and spied the thick coconut topping. "I might have to set aside my morals for a bite. That won't hurt me."

Will hid the cake behind his back. "I can't allow you to do that. Think of the cows that suffered to have their milk taken and the chicks that were never born because the eggs were taken from the nest before fertilization. You can't set aside your morals just like that. And for what? Cake? No, no, no." He waved a hand between them. "I won't let you do it."

"Oh, you're so cruel. Fine. Take your cake and go to your love." Sunshine covered her face with both hands and faked a sob.

"My what?"

Sunshine dropped the act immediately. "Oh, come on. I know."

"You, uh, you know what?"

"Play all you want, but I know how you feel about her. It's obvious now." She left the room, headed for her bedroom. "Anderson's here," she called into Jerusha's room as she passed. At the end of the hall, she paused as she went through her door and gave Will a coy glance. Then she was gone.

Will came down the hall. Was this how most people were, full of banter and insincerity? It felt good until he tried to lie about his feelings for Jerusha and was ferretted out by Sunshine. With his knuckles, he rapped the doorframe to Jerusha's room. She sat propped against several pillows. Two pillows that belonged on the couch were beneath her calves to elevate them. Just as Sunshine had said, Jerusha's face was concealed by a book. On her lap was that notebook where she wrote quotes, notes, and ripostes towards all the books she read. She lowered the book.

"How's our patient?"

"Sore." She laid the book face down on the bed.

"Whatcha readin'?"

She glanced at the spine. "Roland Barthes."

"Never heard of him." Since she had not invited him in, he entered her room anyway, figuring that such hospitality was unnecessary now at this stage in their relationship. "I brought you something. It made Sunshine want to give up her morals." He came to the bedside and offered her the cake. "It's German chocolate."

"Thank you." She accepted the cake and smiled at it. She hefted it. "It's more of a two person cake, wouldn't you say?"

He shrugged and explored the depths of his pockets with his empty hands.

"Why don't you go get two forks?"

He left and a few minutes later returned with two forks and two small glasses of milk. He raised the milks. "I thought we needed something to wash it down. I almost grabbed some of Sunshine's weird 'milks.'" Even with the two glasses in his hands, he wiggled his fingers in the air to denote the quotes for the fakery of Sunshine's tastes in beverages.

She had the plastic clamshell opened and the room became redolent with coconuts and pecans. He set the milks on the nightstand, handed her a fork, and eased down onto the edge of the bed. The mattress, and Jerusha with it, listed with his weight. She reached out for support, and Will shot from the bed.

"Sorry," he said. He took the chair from her desk and brought it over.

After they each had a few bites, Jerusha said, "Delicious. Where'd you get this?"

He said and then switched to an event that had been on his mind since it had occurred at work that day. "Today," he began without preamble. "I had to deal with this lady, a customer, older, probably in her sixties, who wanted to put up shelves in her bathroom. She had a tough time understanding the mechanics necessary to anchor the screws in the wall—you know, so the screws stay in the drywall—and I went through it three times. Each time I got a little more frustrated." To demonstrate he held his left hand at chest level, then at his neck, and finally at eyebrow level to mark the mounting frustration. He took a bite and let her think of the situation.

"Did she see that you were annoyed?"

"I hope not. Each time I started over with my explanation, I took a deep breath or two, and I tried to be patient."

"That's good."

"Yeah." He shrugged and reached for his milk. After he rinsed some of the sticky sugar and caramel from his teeth, he said, "I don't think I'll ever be a good Buddhist, if that's what you're hoping for." He cut free more cake with his fork.

"That's not quite what I'm hoping for." She licked the topping from her fork. He watched as she drug the utensil across her tongue, first, right side up, then upside down. It might be wrong to watch her do that with the kind of fascination that he felt, but he could not resist.

"So what is it?" he asked before he ate what ought to be his last bite of cake. The sweetness was overwhelming. His stomach wanted to rebel in favor of the leftover chicken with rice and beans he had in his fridge. He laid his fork on the nightstand. "That's it for me."

"I guess maybe we could've split it three ways." She laid her fork atop his. "What it is, is that I want you to be a whole and well human being."

"That's all?"

"Yes."

"Why were you on the edge like that?" he blurted.

She turned away, looked at the book, the wall, her legs, her book again, and shrugged. "Careless, I guess."

"Bullshit."

She shut her eyes. He wouldn't let her lie or deflect him. She knew why, or at least, she better know why. "I . . . I just . . ."

"I remember last week you were reading that book, and you shared that quote with me about how you go to the places that scare you so that you become awakened and force yourself to face your fears, your mortality, and the path of enlightenment. You told me how that path never ends because there's no safe spot, no terminus. That's the gist. Right? So you tried to be an acrobat. You tried to put yourself right on that edge. What you were doing wouldn't awaken you. It would kill you. Where's the enlightenment in that?"

"I got too close." There were tears in her eyelashes like rain in spider webs. "It was an accident."

"I don't quite buy that."

"What?" She threw her arms out and looked around as if she sought support from someone else in the room.

"Oh, cut the BS." His voice rose to crush the challenge of her denial. "You put yourself right on the edge every step of the way around that canyon. That wasn't accidental. You couldn't have been anymore purposeful if you'd tried."

"So you're saying that I wanted to kill myself?" Her voice vaunted into defensive positions.

"I don't know. I don't understand you at all. I don't believe you either." He shook his head and turned away. "How do you think it looked to Sunshine and Nitin and me? What are we supposed to think? Do we need to keep your belts, razors and shoe laces away from you?"

"Oh, come on."

"Do we need to keep you under twenty four hour surveillance?"

"This is ludicrous. Why don't you just get out."

"Make me. What are you going to do? Push me out?" He glared at her. There was no way for her to enforce her will. She was powerless. "Good luck with that." He taunted her by raising his eyebrows.

She clawed at her comforter in impotence. "Get out."

"No. You want me out you're going to have to get up and put me out."

Her arms quivered with the necessary strength. She made the effort to lift her legs, to pivot, and to put them to the floor, but he planted his hands on her knees. She ground her teeth and winced.

"That hurt?"

"You son of a bitch."

"No, I'm an orphan. I'm no one's son."

She jerked and bucked as hard as she could to throw his hands off, but, when she did, one of his hands slipped and ran over her bandaged shin. Jerusha cried out.

Immediately, Sunshine was in the door. "What the hell is going on?"

"You know what?" Will snarled. "I'll leave, but you owe her and I an explanation." He stepped away from the bed. "If I had to go and apologize to every one of your friends for what I did, then you owe her, Nitin, and I an apology for pushing the limits of reasonableness, while you tried to be an acrobat a few hundred feet above a rocky canyon floor. You owe us, goddammit!"

He panted and waited, with one finger of one hand pointed at her like a duelist, who had his opponent dead to rights. Jerusha quivered and there were tears in her eyes, maybe from when his hand accidentally brushed her wound. Sunshine came to Will's side. Was she going to push him out, expel him from the house for hurting her friend? Any second she would turn on him, but Sunshine's gaze never shifted from Jerusha. Sunshine crossed her arms beneath her heavy breasts, and, finally, she said, "Well? Let's hear it. We all saw you doing it, now tell us why. After that you can apologize for scaring the shit out of us and almost getting yourself dead."

"You're siding with him?"

"You could've killed him, if he'd held onto you and you went over. You owe him your life." Sunshine leaned on one foot and tapped the other with outright irritation.

Jerusha sagged. "I'm sorry." She blinked a few tears away and rolled her head back so that she could use gravity to control her tears. "I was trying to scare myself. I never liked high places. My heart was in my throat that whole time. I kept forcing myself to face my terror, but I was clumsy and overwhelmed by my fears of falling. I was too busy looking at the long fall that I didn't look at the solid ground I needed to step on."

"So it was all just a dumb experiment?" Sunshine's jaw and arms hung. Will thought she might smack her friend upside the head in retribution, and he mentally prepared himself to restrain her.

"You aren't going to do that again, are you?" Will asked. He knew that had been the motive, but hearing Jerusha say it made him think how foolish it was.

"No." She was red with embarrassment.

"Buddhists aren't risk takers. What you did was wrong. Don't go looking for scary experiences. Just stick to the ones you meet in the natural course of your life. Besides, I thought I provided enough scary moments for you. Right?" He nudged Sunshine, whose eyes went wide as she slowly twisted to face him. "Too soon?" he asked.

Sunshine smiled awkwardly at first but the ice there melted and she grew tender. "Maybe."

He was up at six. He went to his closet and took two twenty pound dumb bells out to the living room area. She listened as he panted in rhythm to his efforts. Finished, he dressed for work. She feigned sleep, curled on her side. Through the fuzzy slits of her eyelids she saw him dress in jeans, a polo and the red vest of an Ace employee. She could not believe she was going to do what she was going to do. She heard him prepare his breakfast, eat, and clean the bowl, spoon and cup. He ate healthily. That was something she liked about him. He returned, stood over her for a moment, then kissed her brow. She stretched, pretended to awake, and smiled at him.

"I have to go."

"All right."

"Don't forget to get to class."

"Like I would."

He seemed to have more to say, but he turned and left the room. She heard him scoop up his keys. "Bye," he called.

"Bye."

Then he was gone. She whipped the comforter and sheet off and sprang from bed. She went to the closet first. On the floor, there was a pair of combat boots and a huge back pack. She rifled through the various pockets of the pack. She did not know exactly what she was looking for. She suspected a gun. He said that he wanted to be a better man but if he still had a weapon, like a gun, then he could revert to that older self any time. There was nothing incriminating in the pack. Next up, were a few shirts and jackets on hangers. She brushed her hand over the sleeves. The shelf at the top of the closet had only a single item. It was a gray plastic case with a pair of latches that popped loudly when she pushed them. She gave a start at the sound and glanced around the room. Of course, there were no witnesses. It was silly to look, but she felt like a spy, a criminal. She slowly laid back the lid. The black pistol gleamed at her. She dared not touch. Or could she? She dug her fingers between the hard plastic and the cool metal. It was heavier than she thought it would be. She laid it down and closed the case. Despite political protestations that guns didn't kill people, people kill people, Jerusha had a different point of view. People killed people because tools like Anderson's pistol made it so easy. Wielding a sword required skill, more skill if your opponent was well trained. All you had to do with this pistol was point and pull the trigger. Aiming required some skill, she supposed, but a bullet, once fired, travelled a specific trajectory and struck whatever lay in its path. There was no skill once it left the barrel. As she returned the case to its place, she wondered why he still had it. If Will was paranoid of a break in, he would never reach the weapon in time to defend himself. If he was scared enough, he would sleep with it under his pillow. Instead, it was at the top of his closet, the only item on the shelf, as she discovered when she patted about and came up with a hand caked in dust. Why have it at all? For almost a half hour, she went through the contents of the rest of the apartment. There weren't a lot of personal possessions and all of them were benign. She dressed and left for class, taking an apple and a yogurt cup with her to eat.

Later, as they sat at the café by campus, she with a pile of library books and her notebook, he with a book by Chogyam Trungpa that they had picked out at Bookmans a while back, she asked, "When you were in Afghanistan, what kind of weapon did you use?"

His face folded in bewilderment. "An M-4 rifle. Why?"

"Nothing else?"

"Grenades, knife." He shrugged.

"Not a pistol?"

This made his face bunch up. "No. Officers carried side arms, not enlisted men like me."

"Oh." She nodded. Then why did he have a pistol? She leaned into her books.

Paul invited all the employees to a party at his house on a Sunday evening after the store closed at five. Everyone was in the backyard. The spring night was reasonable, temperature wise, because the day was a Flagstaff-warm sixty and sunny. The sun set in a bloom of orange and the sky was cobalt with one or two stars just visible.

Will and Jerusha, who had taken the night off from the diner, arrived at five thirty. Most of the staff was there, those who came directly from work simply had to doff their vests and they were indistinguishable from the others. Paul was positioned at the two gas grills and two large coolers filled with ice and beers. On the grills hamburgers and bratwurst sizzled. On a nearby patio table stood great Tupperware bowls filled with salad, refried beans, chili, tortilla chips, salsa and tamales. The beans and tamales came from Maria, who was a cashier at the Ace. She and Paul had been dating for quite some time. Will introduced Jerusha to his coworkers as they moved around the crowd. Will made sure to include as part of his introduction of her that she was a grad student at NAU. He was proud of her for that. It sounded ridiculous, but he knew that this set her quite apart from the rest of this crowd. He was envious of her learning and wished that he could go back to school. How he could ever do that was a mystery since he had no social security number for Anderson Williams. How many doors were closed to him because of what he had done? How many jobs were unavailable to him? He could just flat out lie about his background, but that seemed impossible. How would he ever feel secure? No, he would be stuck in small, wage paying jobs all his life. That was depressing. He knew he was better and smarter than what was needed for these crap jobs. Jerusha could have the world. He was imprisoned in the evil of his past. So he made sure to prompt Jerusha to tell everyone what she was studying and what she planned to do.

Finally, they made it to Paul. He'd already had a few beers because he was all smiles and grand gestures and a booming voice. Jerusha sat nearby, in a plastic lawn chair away from anyone, her legs and arms crossed tightly. He should not force her to stay too long. This was not like her group of friends who would discuss books, politics, modes of alienation, and so on. He smiled at her when her eyes lit on him. She gave him some warmth and courage with a strained smile that said she was only here for him. No, these people, his coworkers, were only interested in gossip about who was with whom or about the basketball season or baseball spring training. Will was stupefied by it all too. Will said to Paul, "Why do you drink so much?"

"What you talkin' 'bout?"

"Come on."

"Why you care? Hm? You ain't no boss to me."

Will shrugged. "Fair enough. I suppose I'm just trying to understand. I want to know what reason you have for putting so much away every time I see you."

"This ain't no way you're gonna be adopted by me."

Will grinned. "You never tire of that one do you?"

"I gotta look out for my lil orphan Anderson." Paul flung an arm over Will's shoulder.

"Why do you always joke about that?"

"We blacks gotta tack care of ya'll crackers."

Will cocked his head and his eyes worked to penetrate the cloak of inebriation that Paul wore. "It's because of your son. Isn't it?"

Will could not have sobered Paul up any faster if he had simultaneously pumped his stomach and dunked him in Arctic waters.

"Let's not go there." Paul waved.

"Do you miss him?"

"What? Who?"

"Your son."

Paul turned to the grill and began to flip burgers. The grease dripped and exploded on the flaming coals.

"When was the last time you saw him?" Will asked.

"A long time. Two years. He probably wouldn't recognize me. He'd refuse to hug me probably if I tried to pick him up."

"You can change all that."

"Yeah."

"If you do nothing, that's the worst."

"Why you always so serious? You act like everythin' is a matter of life and death. That's how you is, man."

Will looked at the open beer in his hand. He drank. Paul rolled the brats on the spokes of the grill. He jammed the spatula beneath burgers and conveyed them to some buns waiting on a plastic square plate set on the grill's side tray. "Who's red eye for more burg eyes?" Paul forced a guffaw.

"I guess," Will began and twisted to glance at Jerusha, whose eyes were fastened on his face to await his answer. "That's how I see the world, how I see life and death, how I am."

"It's depressing. Cut it out."

"Right." Will went and sat next to Jerusha, the only one here who understood him at all. They watched Paul as he perked back up, drained a beer, opened another, and guzzled half. A few takers came for fresh burgers and Paul began to smile and joke with them as he had before Will talked to him. They stayed only half an hour after that, long enough to let Will drink his two beers, his minimum and his maximum. She drove home. He slouched in the passenger seat with a palm at his chin, each of his fingertips grinding into a pockmark.

She said, "You can't be disappointed when people refuse to see the truth about themselves."

"He's in a lot of pain. That's why he drinks."

"I know. It's obvious to you and me, but he doesn't see it. Probably not, anyway. It'd be worse if he did see himself clearly and still drank like that. That would be a terrible way to fool yourself."

"Yeah."

"You didn't think that you were going to make him change by talking to him at a party, did you?"

"I don't know. Yeah, maybe."

She reached without taking her eyes from the road and patted his knee. "Gentle, slow pressure works well on everything. Think of erosion, massages, erecting a pyramid, and many other events, they all take time and persistence. Think of your own slow change."

Will turned from the window and dropped his hand. She was right, of course. He had not changed overnight. He could not expect Paul to change in five minutes. He was being stupid. Keep at it. He does need help, unquestionably. Will could do it.

They were seated on her bed, and he kept blinking and his eyes tripped around, unable to find a rest. Maybe she could have delivered the news better, but, no, she had blurted it out, without preamble, without decoration. Her anxiety, the wild pulse, and the occasional shivers that made her wrap her arms around her torso, had forced her to shoot the news out at him.

"What?" he said.

She was prepared for his shock. She had beside her the evidence, and she handed him the white plastic stick with its blue chemical mark. His eyes steadied, and he stared. He did not reach for it. The blue symbol, a plus sign, caused by the chemical reaction was unmistakable. He stood and stepped away, spun, slapped his forehead with one hand, and said, "But we used . . ."

"Yep." Her eyes switched from him to the first indication of new life within her. She already knew what she would do. She had taken one test and then a second because she could not believe the first, but as she became convinced by the identical markers, she knew that she would have the child and raise her. She believed the baby was a girl, a miniature Jerusha.

"It could be wrong." His hand worked hard at his forehead as if he might tear the flesh from the bone and then he would be released from a future that he had never dreamed of before.

She pulled forth the second test with its identical chemical reaction mark. "Nope. I already scheduled an appointment with my doctor."

He tripped back a few steps until he banged against the window. "Oh. Uh. Uh hunh." He tried to swallow, but the fact choked him, and he had to clear his throat with a cough. "Wow. Hm."

She took a deep breath. "Look, I know this wasn't something we were trying to do or ever talked about before, but I want to make this clear. Are you listening?" She noticed that his eyes were doing that rapid bounce again as if he was a dreamer with his eyes open. His hand that had tried to rip the skin from his brow now pulled and clutched at the short hairs on his head. "I'm going to have the baby," she said with all the firmness that she could summon. Inside, she felt weak.

His eyes rolled and appeared to be suddenly engorged. He groaned. "I . . . I . . ." His head whipped about in a panic. "I'm going home." He dashed out.

After she heard the front door slam, Jerusha crumbled onto her mattress. She drew her legs in, wept, and her hands came to her belly. "Can you hear me? I'm your mom. I'll always do the best things for you that I can. The best morally and spiritually."

When he escaped Jerusha's house and staggered into the greater world outside those close, feminine walls, he had no clue where he should go. By the time he reached the end of the walkway though, he knew he had to get home. He set off with great purpose and swift steps. There was no wind and within only a few steps he was warm despite wearing only a t-shirt, jeans, and Chuck Taylors. He cut through campus.

His parents had died nearly two decades before, and his relatives had their own children to hand over to the bastions of higher learning. When was the last time he spoke to any of them? He resumed his march toward home. More than a year? Was it that long ago that he last phoned his paternal grandparents? What about any others? It was longer since he spoke to his maternal grandparents.

He sprinted across streets and dodged the heavy foot traffic of the students. The urge to arrive at his apartment was overwhelming. He imagined how he would enter and find himself among the comfortable stacks of his books, planted like potted trees around the few pieces of furniture he possessed. His woods that he now resided among had leaves that never fell. His woods had seeds that only planted and grew in the furrowed soil of his brain. Perhaps he was the 21st century equivalent of Thoreau, a Thoreau reincarnated in an era of dwindling wild nature, a Thoreau who now had to stroll among man's need to order in concrete, bricks and asphalt. Maybe he was, or maybe he was not. He wanted to get to his domain. He raced to Milton Avenue. He charged across the five lanes and threaded the roaring, squealing, radio booming, tire sucking traffic as it rolled off I-17 or I-40. That rush to movement, to go, go, go with the velocity of an engine in its glorified and ingenious combustion of gasoline would be exhilarating to his troubled spirit.

No, he had to get home. Only a few more blocks. He kept his stride long and his shoulders low. The rods of his arms rammed the air in tempo to the piston-like movements of his legs. He commanded his body to breathe easily, and his lungs obeyed the order. He mounted the first step to head for his second floor apartment. One foot on the step, one foot on the sidewalk, he put his hands to his hips and leaned over. Suddenly, he felt fatigued and breathless. Jerusha's news. He had managed during the journey home to suppress that news from his consciousness, but now it was there like the world on his back. It was no such thing though. Right now, he could not see the burden on his back unless he had a microscope and could peer into Jerusha's uterus. That would not last. The burden would grow, grow, grow, and be born.

With one hand on the rail, he scraped his shoes up the stairs one by one, when he habitually took them two at a time. The baby—there was the word he had shunned from his mind by the ever quicker pace of his return home—would be born, grow, sit, crawl, eat solids, tie shoes, get dressed in the mornings, and mature. The baby—oh, holy shit, he was a dad with a baby eight months or so from coming into the world and into his arms and into his sight—the baby would grow, grow, grow until he or she would stand beside Will very nearly eye to eye and ask, "Dad, were you happy when you heard the news that I was going to be born?"

Will gained the second floor, and he swayed and felt lighthearted. Was he happy? What did he feel? How could he be a dad? Wasn't he too young? No, not at all. He was twenty seven. He was unmarried. That did not matter. His hand crossed from his hip to his gut and hoped that he would not begin to swell, that there was nothing growing inside of him too. Ludicrous. He was the man. He lifted his gaze from an examination of the texture of the landing's floor. He found his door eight feet away. He lurched across those eight long feet, suddenly, oddly, afraid to enter his comfortable home. Why? Inside, there would only be the safe place of his own humble studies and his few healthful needs. He extracted his keys from his pocket, opened his door, slipped inside, shut the door, and went to the couch. As he passed one of those stacks of books like a small tree in his idealized world, he let the keys fall. Meant to land and stick there, the keys slid off the smooth paperback cover and clunked on the hard carpet. At the couch he dropped onto the cushions. He sprawled, face up, eyes on the white, textured ceiling. He became still, and he was aware that somewhere in his head there was a hurricane of thoughts swirling around where the news of a baby sat like a lidless eye that stared at him without rest. He did not dare to encroach on that activity, he lacked the courage.

The phone rang where it sat on the coffee table between his notebook, in which he copied parts of books he liked, and a book titled *Shambhala*. He scooped up the phone as it rang again.

"Hello?"

"Hi," Jerusha said.

"We're having a baby."

"Yep."

"Sorry, I left like that."

"I would've left too when I found out, but I couldn't get out of my uterus."

He smiled. "That's an image. Like walking out of a house."

"Only I can't walk out of it, and there is a life growing there, a life living there."

"Yeah."

They were quiet.

"Can you come over?" he asked.

Fifteen minutes later, he let her in. Her book bag slipped from her shoulder, and thudded on the floor. She had about an hour and a half before she taught freshman comp. He shut the door. She stood there only a few feet from the door and waited for him to act or to speak. It was his turn. She had no options, she was set onto a path. Would he join her? That was all he needed to declare, all that she needed to hear. He tied her up in his arms as if he intended to never let her leave. He had her arms pinned to her sides. In short order they breathed in unison, long and deep inhalations followed by comparable exhalations. She laid her cheek on his shoulder.

"So, what do we do? And I know that we're having a baby. I mean, about us," he asked.

"I don't know. I don't want to get married just because we're having a baby."

"But shouldn't we provide a family for our baby? I don't want our child to be bounced around from home to home like I did."

"But your parents died."

"Yes, but I'm talking about after that."

She shook her head and closed her eyes. "I know. I know what you went through, but, if we got married because we were having a baby, I would always suspect that the only reason you were with me was because you felt obligated to raise our baby."

"I love you, and I want to be with you."

They peered into those clichéd "windows" of their souls. He had never said that he loved her before.

"Do you really?" she asked.

"I have for a long time, though I don't think you love me like that. That's why I've never said it. I think you love me with Buddhist compassion and not with spouse-like passion."

She wiggled a hand up between their pressed bodies, and she stroked his jaw. There were a few acne scars along his jaw line, as well as up across his cheeks. He had lived a hard life, and he was only twenty seven. The one thing she knew that he yearned for, even if he did not say so, was to feel the comfort and love of a family, one that he never had to worry about being sent away from. His brown eyes were rounder than usual, and he seemed truly anxious about her answer, prepared to be distraught by her refusal. She did not want to be responsible for crushing him, but she never wanted to lie. Did she love him? Did she love him with the passion that he both wanted and needed and not just the compassion that he strictly needed? She said, "I think I love you too." She nodded and sent her hand around to stroke the other side of his jaw. Her knuckles and fingers trailed along more acne scars. "I know that I miss you when you're not by my side. I know that I'm challenged by you and that you help me to grow and be a better person. I know that the experience of you is one that I'm daily grateful for. I know that I've been my happiest in the last few months when I'm in your arms. I know that after we make love, I'm filled with so much light that I feel I might turn into a sun." A tear slipped from the sphere of one of her eyes. His hold on her slackened, and she raised her other hand to cradle both his cheeks in both her hands. His eyes were wet and red and his whole body trembled. She wondered if he could handle this. Was this what he wanted to hear? Was she telling him the truth? She nodded her head. "Yes, I'm telling the truth." It was as if she answered the question behind his eyes and that release caused the tears. She caught them on her fingertips. Her flesh drank each tear as it parachuted along the scarred contours of his face. "Yes, I love you. Yes, I mean the love of passion." She kissed him, violently, she assaulted his anxiety. "Yes, I do. Yes, I do," she gasped between the explosions of their lips plunged together.

They sat in the breakfast nook just off from the kitchen that evening. Their dinner dishes lay on the table. Anderson's eyes began to dry out as he could not blink from the words she had just told him. Finally, the agony of the burning and itching of his eyes did make him blink. Jerusha swallowed because of how her words had struck him into suspended animation. He hardly seemed to breathe. She felt compelled to say something, words that might ameliorate his shock. "I know we've never talked about this. I'm sorry. I guess I should've told you sooner." She shrugged in her inadequacy to reanimate him.

His eyelashes fluttered like hummingbird wings. "No, no, no." He shook his head.

Well, this was going badly. In one day she had waylaid him with two life changing facts. "I've made these plans. I had to send my applications in all the way back in the fall. I selected which universities to apply to before I met you even. I can't change my direction now. My spot is reserved and my financial aid is arranged. No matter what is different between us, I'm going," She put her hand to her belly. What she had just said came out more forcefully than she had intended. Why was she being such a bitch? She had just clubbed him over the head with the news that she was moving in two months, and she acted as if she expected him to take it all in stride.

"Uh, that's not, uh, that's not what I'm asking you to do. No. You see, I'm just, well, I guess that I'm in shock."

"Well, I'm sorry."

"It's not you. I should've thought about you graduating and what you would do then. I know what happens."

"Where, uh, where are you going? What university? Which state?"

"The University of Arizona in Tucson. There's two professors that teach there who I want to study with."

"I graduated from there."

She nodded. "I know."

"Tucson. I haven't been there in, whew, a while, I guess."

"Since you graduated?"

"That's about right. Well, no, I stayed for a month or so after that."

"I won't go until the end of July."

His hand rose and he picked at one of those pockmarks in his face. He was caught in the skeins of his thoughts. What would he say? She could offer the temporary solution of more time together. With his hand, the one that had picked at the acne scar, he brushed back through his lengthening hair. "I don't have any ties here," he said.

"What?"

"There's nothing to keep me here in Flagstaff. Do you see what I'm saying?"

"Yes. No. Wait. What are you saying?"

"I can move too."

"You want to move in together?" She wondered if he meant that. Did he? No, that was not where they were. No, no, no. Were they?

"No, I just thought that I'd move down to Tucson. I'd get my own place. We could, uh, continue as we are now. There would just be a change of venue. You see?"

It was her turn to blink. She nodded. "I guess. That's up to you."

"I'm pretty sure that there's a few Aces down in Tucson. I can ask Paul to write a letter of recommendation for me." He nodded in approval of his own idea.

"I thought the job market sucked."

"Well, yeah, but, I don't know, maybe I'll be lucky."

"Didn't you sign a lease for a year?"

"Well, yeah, but I'm sure there are escape clauses and so on."

"You were just putting roots down here."

"So?"

"Won't it bother you to sever them? For instance, your boss Paul? You guys go for drinks once a week, at least. Do you want to give up that friendship?"

Anderson slid out of the nook, paced back and forth for a moment, and said, "These are a lot of objections you're putting out to keep me here. Is it because you don't want me to come with you?"

"I didn't say that. Did I say that?" She put a finger to her sternum.

"No, but you were trying to convince me that it was I who didn't want to go."

"That's not it at all."

"Then what is it?" He paced again. His serpentine head leaned ahead of his body, and, when he came to the extent of his circuit, his head swung around first, and tugged the rest of him along. She did not like this. What was it that he wanted from her? She rolled a shoulder and waved a hand in a vague gesture. "So you want to go too?"

"I want to be there when our baby is born." He pointed to her belly. Both of her hands cradled her still flat belly. "And I want to be with you. If you're in love with me the way you said you were earlier then what objection could you have to me going along?"

"None." How could there be any objection on her part? She loved him. He was the father of her baby. She had to do the right thing not just for her but for her baby. It was possible to be a single mother but to create a baby required two, a mother and a father. There is no immaculate conception. She was no amoeba who could reproduce on her own. In his face, she perceived yearning, love, resolution and fear. Those emotions were what a father should have. "None at all," she restated.

They became speechless. Nothing had changed, or else everything had.

It was their going away party. Most of the crowd had gone through their hooding ceremony as part of matriculation with a master's degree throughout the prior week. The debauchery which began after each department's ceremony culminated in this complete blow out at Sunshine and Jerusha's house. The kitchen and front living/dining room were filled to capacity so the party also grew into both the back and front yards. There was a quartet playing some hybrid of rock and folk music out by the back fence. In the front yard a fellow strummed his guitar and sang the blues. No one knew how but more alcohol arrived with every moment. The smell and smoke of dope drifted over their heads. Paul had wandered into this alien crowd searching desperately for Will, who spotted him as he came through the open front door and came up to him. They hugged and smacked each other's back. The graduates made a bit of room for them grudgingly. Paul handed him a box wrapped with light blue paper and with baby bottles printed on it.

"You didn't have to bring me anything."

"Oh, it's not for you. It's for your baby." Paul's eyes stuck to the gift now in Will's hands. "Open it."

Will slipped his thumb beneath the flaps of wrapping paper taped on one end. He tore the paper and let it drop to the floor. Paul tried to catch it, but Will shook his head and gestured for him to let it lie. Will opened the small box. There were clothes inside. Will hesitated. He plucked one corner of a tiny onesie that was white and had an American flag printed on the chest. Will settled that onesie on the lip of the box. The other onesie was camouflaged. Will slowly smiled at the sight of these tiny stitched fabrics that seemed too small for a living being to wear.

"Thanks."

"Maria and I picked them out. Well, she suggested baby clothes. I picked out which. Thought it'd be good to remind everyone of your service."

"Thanks." Will was less proud of his stint than Paul was of his own, but the gesture was significant, a sign of their common past. "Jerusha thinks it will be a girl."

"So?"

"I don't know if she'll want to dress her daughter in fatigues."

"Tell her it's for July Fourth and Veteran's Day. It's to honor her dad." Paul slapped him on the upper arm.

Will stuffed the baby clothes into the box again. "What about you? When are you going to get in touch with your son?"

"I, uh, did." Paul picked at a thumbnail.

"You did? When? You didn't say anything."

"I sent him a Memorial Day card."

"I didn't know they made those."

"Yeah." Paul now stuffed his hands in his front pockets. "I found it at Walgreen's. It was just a quick note."

"And?" Will hoped like hell that Paul had heard something back.

"Well, I called the next week. It wasn't a very long call, maybe five minutes, including when I talked to my ex and told her I planned to keep calling and writing. I told her once a week I'd call. We agreed to make it Sunday afternoons."

"Did she give you any trouble?"

"She didn't sound happy, but she went along with it."

"She's just skeptical because of the past. Prove to her you're going to follow through, and then she'll come around."

"Yeah, I hope you're right."

"Wow. That's all great. I wouldn't worry about how long the conversation was. How old is your son?"

"He's five. Yeah, I knew the talk would be short. It'll mostly be me asking a question and him answering with a yes or no." Paul took a deep breath, withdrew his hands from his pockets, rubbed them together and then tucked his hands into his back pockets.

"Hey, so he'll talk about his toys or something. That's important for a kid," Will said.

"Thomas the Train. That's what he likes."

"That's good to know. I'll bet you didn't know that before you called. Did you?"

"No, I didn't know anything. I've been a shitty dad." His chin nearly pegged his chest as his head sank.

Will clamped a hand on his shoulder. "Maybe, but now you've got the chance to not be a shitty dad. You know why? Because you made the effort to write and call him. Now keep it up. Okay?"

"Yeah." He took a deep breath and raised his head. "So are you excited? About the baby, I mean."

Will's hand fell from Paul's shoulder. "I don't know. I'm terrified, I think, more than anything else."

"Don't want to fuck it up?"

They exchanged looks. "Right." Will nodded and glanced through the crowd of Jerusha's friends to find his love.

"You'll be fine. You take everything too seriously. Why would this be any different?"

"I guess not."

Paul laughed for the first time. "Ha! Come on. You worry too much."

"I know."

"Are their wedding plans?"

"Not right now. Though we decided to move in together. We thought it might work out better financially and when it comes time to care for our baby."

"That sounds like a marriage."

"I wouldn't know."

"I've been married." Paul teased. "If you're sharing a bed, a house, finances, and a child, well, that's a marriage."

Will nodded and glanced at Jerusha whose eyes were already on him. They smiled at one another. "Don't tell her." He looked back at Paul.

"Oh, sure I won't. Do you really think she hasn't realized it yet though?" Paul's eyes were also on Jerusha. He gave her a little wave.

"I don't know. Sometimes I think she wants to keep me at a distance and at other times I think she wants to always have me by her side."

"That's how women are. Who knows what they want? I'm pretty sure they don't know themselves."

Will's head bobbed as if he accepted Paul's sagacious advice at face value, but the truth was, in Will's estimation, she was scared of what he might do. She vacillated between wanting to be rid of him, and wanting to aid him to be a better man. Which impulse would be victorious? She could not waffle between those poles indefinitely. One would hold sway and the other would regress from her mind until it vanished totally. Where would that leave Will? Would he have what he wanted and needed? Or would he have what he deserved?

Eight months ago they had made love and now they were one month from bringing a baby into the world. Will shook his head at the thought. Jerusha opened a can of black beans, drained the preserving juice from the can into the sink, and dumped the load of dark pill shapes into the stainless steel saucepan. Their act of love was a new human being coming into the world. Will eyed Jerusha as she made dinner. The physical act of love was really the physical act of reproduction. And, also, her physical body was not designed solely to attract him, though it strongly did, it was to function as a home for a gestating baby. Her hips wider than a man's were to support the baby in utero and to allow for the passage of the baby through the birth canal. Her breasts were not for him to fondle but for a baby to feed on. Her body went well beyond the sense of the beautiful and moved into the sense of the functional. All this seemed ridiculously obvious, but it struck him as an epiphany. He sat at the dining room table and followed her with his eyes. "Do you need help?" he asked.

"No." She stirred one saucepan and checked beneath the lid of another. Truthfully, he did not want to help anyway. He wanted to let that epiphany wash through him and cleanse him of his old prejudices. Her hair was longer. He did not recall if or when she might have announced that she would grow it out. It must have been when she told him that they were going to be parents. She had begun to wear a bit of makeup, just some of that stuff on the eyelashes or that skin color stuff on her face, meant to make a woman prettier, to accentuate one thing while it deemphasized something else. So women confused their own purpose. They strove for the beautiful, the physical mystique of Helen of Troy—who was part Goddess, so there was little hope for any woman to attain such an ideal, such an eternal status—and forgot about the actuality of their physical selves. To complicate that, as even Jerusha rebuked him occasionally for such a lapse, many women desired to be known and loved for the person, intelligence, and spirit they believed to be their interior selves. Oddly, women emphasized a duality of mind and body.

Will took his Ace vest off and hung it off the back of his chair. It had been a long busy day at work. Several times he had found a quiet corner, took a few deep breaths to cleanse his body of the tension, and then returned to work. Being assistant store manager was not easy. Too many belly-aching employees came to him with 'so-and-so said such-and-such' that he had to deal with daily. Why could people not get along without being policed?

"Anders?" That was her new nickname for him. "Can you get the strainer, please?"

He rose, went to the back of the kitchen, and took down the strainer from the line of hooks drilled in the wall about six feet up, beyond her reach. He handed the strainer to her. She took it, held it over the sink and drained some pasta from a pan. He was happy that she had agreed to move in together. She would need his help more and more as the birth came nearer. Should he broach the subject of nuptials again? Soon, maybe.

"Should I get out of your way?" he teased.

"Yep. I can do this on my own." She waved the steam from her face.

He slid past her but trailed his fingers across the small of her back. Yes, she could do it on her own, and he would allow her to believe that she had accomplished dinner solo, but he knew that his help had gone into it, minimal though she permitted it to be. Were two better than one? He sat again at the table, cupped his chin in one hand and resumed his observation of her. Living together was a continual compromise, from his putting the toilet seat down so she did not fall in—why would anyone sit without looking first?—to her acquiescing to his having a beer with dinner—just because she no longer drank did not mean that he had to be a teetotaler too and it did not impair his ability to do yoga and meditation with her in the evening. He simply enjoyed the taste of an ale or lager with his meal.

She brought dinner to the table. As she ferried the meal to the awaiting pot holders, he set plates and utensils for them. "Water or milk?" he asked.

"Milk."

He poured her a tall glass of milk for the Vitamin D, calcium and protein that would aid their son's growth. He also pulled out a Samuel Adams Winter Ale from the fridge. They sat and ate. She appraised him on the progress she had made on her thesis while at the U of A's library that morning. Piles of books lay on the trunk they used as a coffee table in the living area. He listened, asked questions, and contemplated her ideas.

After dinner, they both read. She attacked the stacks of library books, and he cracked open a copy of Thich Nhat Hanh's *Peace Is Every Step*. Just after eight, Jerusha announced the need for a break. They did yoga for half an hour and then another half hour of meditation. Will took a shower after that. When he came out, Jerusha was in bed with one of her books and her notebook, pen poised in one hand above its lined pages. After he dressed in a fresh pair of boxers and a t-shirt, he was irresolute about what to do next. Reading did not appeal. He wandered down the hall to the baby's room. Yesterday's blue jay blue paint job was dry. With the light on, he studied the walls to locate any scantily painted patches. He found a few. He popped the paint can open, took a brush with a two inch head and concealed the white primer paint with the blue jay color. To ventilate the sharp smell, he opened the two windows. Next, Will hung framed pictures in the places where Jerusha had indicated a preference for them yesterday while he painted. They called this nesting, this need to prepare the place for the baby to inhabit. Jerusha was the mother bird and he was the papa bird. The idea made him laugh. When the pictures were hung, he clicked off the lights and went back to the bedroom. Jerusha was, as he knew she would be, asleep, still upright with the pillows propped against the wall since they had no headboard or footboard. He marked the page of the library book then closed it and her notebook. Laying those on the nightstand, he smiled at her. It was better if he did not disturb her. She would lay herself flat when she was ready. With the light off, he slipped under the covers too. Lying on his side, he nestle a hand along her thigh. She was there, his fingers comforted him. For a time he listened to her breathing, the soft puffs of her exhalations. He tried to match his breathing pattern to hers, but that felt like hyperventilation, too fast and shallow for him. He lapsed into his own rhythm. She was his, he was hers. Everything was all right.

The next morning, a Sunday, the first of his two day weekend rest, he stamped his feet into his combat boots and laced them with quick jerks. They had both awoken late. With breakfast eaten, he knew he had to get to work. He wore a long sleeved Henley beneath a flannel shirt and his jeans. This would keep him warm enough to dig the holes for the two apple trees and one walnut tree that Jerusha and he had picked out. They were to be delivered between eleven and one today. He would have to work fast to dig those holes. Jerusha thumped into the bedroom. She wheezed as she came around the foot of the bed.

"I just put the dishes away, and I feel exhausted, absolutely wiped out. Jeez." When she landed on the bed, he bobbed for a moment.

"You okay?"

"Yeah." She swiveled and lifted her swollen feet onto the mattress. With great care, she lowered her torso and groaned. "Ugh. How do women do this more than once?"

"Maybe because the baby's so worth it." He reached behind him blindly and contacted her belly. He rubbed small circles there. "Is he up?"

She closed her eyes, listened and monitored the baby within her, and said, "I think he's asleep. Last night I think he was working on his punches. I thought he would burst straight out of me."

"Not much longer."

"I'll miss having him with me all the time." She ran her hands back and forth over the half globe of her belly.

"It's not fair." He turned and propped one knee on the mattress. "I still haven't really met him yet. I want to know what color his eyes will be, and his hair too. Is he going to look like me? Will he be like me? I just want to know." Her hand caught his before he pulled away. She guided him to a spot near her ribs. There he felt a foot moving around. Very tiny, barely the length of one of his fingers, the foot brushed back and forth as if counting time. He wanted to call him by his name. "We still have no name."

"That's not true. We have ten. Why do you have your boots on?"

He told her.

"Today." She sounded wistful with the memory of the arrival of their fruit bearing trees, as if this was a mystical day on the calendar.

"Between eleven and one."

"Right." She sounded far away, far even from her own words.

He pulled his hand away from where the tiny foot ticked like a small second hand on the clock. Her head rolled just to the right of center, and her breathing fell to a shallow whiffing sound. He rose as softly as he could. He spied the air vent over the door as he stepped lightly to exit the room without waking her. How long could he keep that secret?

He came out of the house into cool sunshine. He fetched his shovel from the garage and went behind the house. The places for the trees were marked yesterday by Jerusha. Will set to work. The holes had to be fairly large, and it took him close to half an hour to dig each. He sweated despite the cool air. It was around ten when he completed the task. He drove the shovel into the mound of loose soil beside the last hole. With his fists on his hips he stared into the excavation. Several inches down the soil turned very dark gray, almost black. He wished that he knew something of geology so that he could define what was there. Was it clay? Or something else, a richer loam perfect for trees? He had not thought Arizona fertile enough for fruit bearing trees. Over the years he had passed orchards of one sort or another in parts of the state. Maybe Jerusha knew the local geology.

He returned to the house. She was up again, seated at the dining room table with a spread of books, some from the university library, some of them hers.

"You're up." He went to the kitchen, took his coffee cup from breakfast, rinsed it with water from the faucet, and refilled it with coffee. "Want some?"

"No, thanks. It gives me heartburn. Thinking about certain foods is almost all it takes." She wrote on note cards then stuck them into the book that she was studying. "Did you finish the holes?"

"Done." He leaned against the kitchen entryway and drank. "How long did you sleep?"

"Just a cat nap." She pored over a page. Her hand flattened the text so that she could spy the words in the middle.

"Hm." He came forward, took one of the few unopened books, laid farthest from her, and read the spine. "Is this required or research?"

She continued to read for a moment, and he knew that she had heard him and would answer when she could. He balanced the hardcover book in his left hand, while his right sought the table of contents.

"Which?" She glanced up. He held the book vertical so she could read the spine. "Oh, that one I dug up for this paper."

"Ah. How is it?"

"Haven't gotten to that one yet. What are you going to do now that you're done with that project?"

"Find another."

"Always on the move." She sounded as if she was older and wiser than him, his mother. Well, she was wiser, anyway.

"Idle hands do the devil's work," he said.

"I don't think that's the exact wording."

"I'm going to install the garbage disposal." He turned from her. The sink was new stainless steel, with two basins, and a matched, stainless steel faucet with an extension sprayer, which, he purchased and installed with his last paycheck. The garbage disposal was this paycheck. Next paycheck remained undecided. The trees were from Jerusha's account.

"Really?" She raised her eyes from the text and gave him a beaming smile.

"Yep." He sucked on his black, bitter coffee.

"Ooh, I can't wait. How long will it take?" She bent to the text once again.

He shrugged. "An hour?" He wasn't certain. He had never installed one before. It looked easy enough by the instructions that came in the box, and the how-to description that a coworker offered him also seemed straightforward. He gulped the last of the coffee in two long draughts.

Back in the kitchen, he opened the box and slipped out the cylindrical garbage disposal. He opened the cabinet doors below the sink, took the plumber's wrench, turned off the water line, and disconnected the pipe to the sink's drain. The job lasted only thirty minutes, mostly on account of Will's need to turn the water on several times to insure that there were no leaks. The task accomplished and his pride assured, he carried the box and instructions to the recycling bin. It was only ten forty five. What could he do now? There were numerous projects around the house, but which could he do in the time before the nursery guys arrived with the trees? He saw the low-flow shower head on the kitchen counter. Stay busy, he ordered himself. He snatched up the package and his wrenches and went to the bathroom. That job lasted a whopping two or three minutes but only because he had to go for his plumber's tape from his tool box to wrap the threads of the pipe and watertight the connection. What else could be done? Days off from work were always tough. His need to be occupied was a defense against seeing the nasty parts of his life, but, since he did meditation, he knew he faced his demons while most people fought to hide from them. Did that make him enlightened? Well, more than most, but he would never be the Dalai Lama.

When the nursery's flatbed truck, with the three saplings strapped down with mover's straps, arrived, Will was watering the tomato plants after he had finished the bell peppers and squash. Neither man was familiar to Will from when he selected the trees two days ago. The nursery must keep delivery staff separate from sales staff. Will kept his fists closed and his elbows flexed as he explained to the two men that they could pull the truck around back if that would make it easier. "Only, mind the vegetable plants."

The delivery men nodded in unison. One was Mexican, the other probably a Pasqua-Yaqui or a Tohono O'odham, the two local tribes. Both were an inch or two shorter than Will, but they appeared quite muscular, probably resulting from their jobs rather than hours spent in a gym. The pair climbed back in the truck and Will strode ahead of them into the backyard. When they hopped out a second time, now in the backyard, they had gloves. Both wore jeans with untucked t-shirts. Were they at all cold? They seemed to not be. Will tugged off his flannel shirt and pitched it onto the back porch, and he shoved the long sleeves of his Henley to his elbows. The Tohono clambered onto the flatbed. He called to Will, "This is the walnut. Where's it go?"

"The farthest spot." Will pointed. He crossed his arms as he watched, a surge of uselessness grabbed him. The pair were quick. How long had they been at this? Will, whose confusion at not having a purpose was acute, went to the back step which led to the porch, and sat to witness the men at work. When the third tree went into its hole, Will jogged inside, found his fold of cash, and raced to the men as they began to shovel the soil over the roots.

"Hey, guys," Will said.

The two brown faces rose to inspect him. Sweat shone on their brows and upper lips.

"Here." He handed one of them a ten and the other two fives. "Thanks for all the hard work. Also, ah, do you mind if you stop now? I want to fill in this last hole."

The two men exchanged glances and shrugs.

"Okay."

"Your tree."

"Thanks. It's just that watching you work while I had nothing to do was frustrating. You see, I don't like not working. I need to do things, always. Okay?"

The pair shrugged. Will felt embarrassed that they did not fathom such guilt. They would gladly have watched him work while they sat by.

They removed their gloves, went to their truck, and drove away. Will went inside. Jerusha was in the kitchen.

"How about some lunch?"

"Not yet. I'm going to finish the last hole myself. It won't take long."

"Okay, but I'm going to eat now."

"That's fine."

"Did you want a sandwich for later?"

"Okay."

"What kind?"

"Whatever you're having." He was in the bedroom when he shouted his final response. There was a simple chair in there that he drug over to the doorway and stood on. He used the flat head driver on his Swiss Army knife, which he pulled from his pocket, to undo the two screws from the air grate over the door. He gripped the grate between his thighs. Reaching into the vent, he ducked his head to spy down the hall. She was still in the kitchen. He heard a dish or something scrape into the new sink. But how much longer? Hurry. His hands closed on the cold steel. He pulled free the pistol and tucked it into the front of his pants. Into the vent, his hands groped for the other metal objects. He found them. He shoved the two clips into his back pockets. He placed the grate over its rectangle hole and finger tightened one screw then the other. He set the head of the knife's driver into the slot and twisted the red handle until it was tight, one then the other. He dropped from the chair and slung it over to its place though he set it lightly to the floor. He dashed to the back door, passing her at the table as she luckily sat with her eyes on the text even as her mouth closed and chomped away at her sandwich. He bolted out the door and jumped from the back porch several feet into the yard.

He ran to the final tree. It was the apple tree on the right. He squatted, and his hands went to his gut where the cold metal dug uncomfortably. The barrel bore into his groin. The pain caused him to shift and switch the bearing of his weight from side to side. He craned his head over his shoulder to spy on the house. Though the back porch was empty, he could not see into the windows where the reflections of the backyard prevented his ability to sight her. What if she was watching? He could not let her witness this. He required this solitude. Un-witnessed and unknown to the whole world, Will was about to carry through a deed that would bury his old self. The sapling's bundle of soil and roots was centered in the large diameter of the whole, and there was space. He sat on the edge and tucked his feet as well as he could into the space left between dirt and packed soil which held the tree's roots. Now the barrel of the pistol gouged into his lowest region. He had to get it out of there. He drew the pistol and flung it like a dead thing into the hole. His disgust twitched a sneer onto his face. He leaned back and shoveled his hands into his pockets where he found and brought out the two spare magazines. As he flipped them into the hole and they spun end past end, he caught sight of the still loaded brass casings tipped by copper slugs. Get away from those. He scrambled up and stood uncertainly. Could he do it? He had to. Bury them, bury the old you. Bury William Anderson Cooper. He scuffled to the mound of dirt and snatched the shovel. He threw dirt over the metal corpses. He threw dirt on his friend Rand. He threw dirt on his past. The side where the metal would rust in peace he overfilled so that he had to relocate some to the other side to even it all out. He lifted and dumped, again and again until the earth contained the precious roots. Finished, he tottered back a few steps and stood with the shovel in both hands parallel to the earth. How long until the tree bore its gala apples?

"Are you done?" Jerusha shut the door behind her and came down the steps. He eyed her slow, weighted progress. Since her eyes were on him, he nodded. She said, "Good. I'm still hungry. So how about that lunch?"

He smiled though he neither felt like smiling nor like eating. She radiated heat and goodness as she approached. His heart did not beat faster but, rather, stronger. His heart throbbed and the rest of his being oscillated to that beat. She gained his flank and reached and patted his shoulder. She gazed about the yard. "Well? Are you going to come inside and eat with me?"

He swallowed hard. Through his shirt he felt the solar heat of her essence radiate toward him. He did not trust his voice to emerge so he drummed his head twice to the marching beat of his heart.

She furrowed her brow and tilted her head to gain the right perspective on him. "What's wrong? You're not going crazy . . . are you?"

She had edited a word from that question. He knew what it was: "again." He relinquished the shovel to gravity's impartial pull because it occurred to him only when he heard the word she had not spoken that he held that shovel like a rifle, a weapon of defense and offense. She backed away a step, but he followed, closed the distance, and got in front of her. Both of his hands went to her belly and framed the boy gestating there. He said, "I love you. And when he arrives I'll love him too. I don't have a heart that can touch everyone, but what I have is all for the two of you."

She smiled and leaned her head on his shoulder. He kissed her on the brow. He had a family now, one he had made himself. He would never be alone again. This was his home, his land, his garden, and his apple trees. Everything was good for him now. For a tender moment they stood by the apple tree until she patted his back and led him to the house.

Anderson and Mason

They pulled to a stop at the curb. Agent Sammy Rialto said, "I hate this."

"This is a part of the job." Special Agent Christopher England shut off the car. "He's the last one, anyway."

"That's cold."

"So is life."

"God, you're depressing. I should take you to the hotel and fuck you until you die with a smile on your face."

"Do I smile when I come?"

"No." She opened the door and stepped out, her sly smile hidden from his view. They trudged to the door of the corner house set back from the street. The front yard was done—or not done—in the style of Tucson's desert landscape. Cholla cactus and mesquite trees formed a wall at the front edge of the property. They took the walkway to the door.

They were in Tucson, Arizona. The suspect, David Raskin, a recent graduate of the University of Montana, had embarked a few weeks earlier on a campaign of terror that swept south from his native state all the way to this city in the Sonoran Desert. Sammy and Christopher had been in pursuit from the get-go. The eerie similarity to the murders three years prior had everyone in law enforcement believing that the lost Plato Warrior, the one who had survived a Montana bar gun battle that left twelve dead, including the Plato Warrior Randall Krieger, had reemerged to continue his reign of terror. The MO of philosophical questions on note cards was the same, though the handwriting was different. The prevailing hypothesis was that William Cooper had altered his handwriting to conceal his identity. The loudest dissenting voice to this opinion was Christopher, who believed, correctly as it now turned out, that this was a copycat.

David Raskin travelled to the University of Arizona, the very school that Randall Krieger and William Cooper attended and graduated from. He entered a classroom, seemingly at random, and opened fire with two pistols while he shouted his one question: "Why shouldn't I kill you all?" No one in that first classroom escaped unscathed. When he moved to the classroom across the hall, he found it locked. He shot it open, entered, and repeated the process. Unlike many mass murderers, Raskin worked methodically. He did not practice the spray and pray method of shooting. He aimed, and he missed rarely. Since he stood in the doorway and thus blocked the one exit, the teachers and students could only try to smash the windows and leap past the jagged glass still in the frames to safety. A few students did make it out. The others were gunned down. After he expended his last full clip of ammunition, Raskin took from his pocket a hollow point bullet. He slipped it into the open chamber of one of his nine millimeter Glocks, pressed the slide release, put the pistol to his head and said his last will. "Why shouldn't I kill myself too? It's all the same." The hollow point bullet ripped the back of his head off when it exited.

They knocked on the front door, were allowed entrance by a somber faced man, who asked them how he could help, though he hardly raised his eyes to either look them in the face or check their offered identification. Sammy and Christopher sat on the couch across from the grieving husband, who pulled over a dining room chair, and sat on it slightly off center, his knees together, his hands flat on his thighs.

"We have a picture of the Plato Warrior suspect. Would you mind looking at it?" Sammy led this interview. Christopher seemed drained from the investigations of the last two days. She half stood and extended her arm with the file photo, a DMV picture blown up to a 3X5. The husband took the photo, but his arm flopped to his lap as if he did not have the fortitude to peer at the face of his wife's murderer. His head bowed and he gazed at the photo for a long time. His expression slowly altered. He scowled and narrowed his eyes more and more. Was that hatred? Did he remember the suspect from somewhere?

"Have you seen him before?"

The husband shook his head in slow motion. Voices came from elsewhere in the house. The husband stared at the photo. His jaw clenched and unclenched.

"We're sorry to ask these questions now, Mr. Williams, but we need to learn all that we can about this man."

"He's dead though," the husband said.

"Yes, but we have reason to believe that he once worked with another killer."

"Another? Who?"

"A man named Randall Krieger."

The husband blinked. He reached and wiped at his eyes. Sammy did not relish these interviews with grieving families.

Christopher sat mute but watchful, his eyes never straying from the husband.

"Who's that?" The husband blinked again.

Sammy reached to retrieve the photo. "He was one of the Plato Warriors, as they were known in the press."

"Plato Warriors," the husband repeated with detachment. "Wasn't that a few years ago?"

"The end of two thousand eight."

The husband nodded, began to hand back the photo but gave it a fresh glance. Sammy took the top of the photo, though she did not pull it free from the husband's grasp.

"Do you recognize him?"

He shook his head. "He's young."

"He was twenty four."

"What was his reason?" He released the photo, and his hand plopped into his lap. With rapidly blinking eyes he contemplated his hands in his lap. Did he want revenge? Did he imagine holding a gun and shooting David Raskin? Or maybe strangling him? There could be no revenge against a murderer who was already dead.

Sammy sat on the couch again and slipped the photo beneath a paper clip on her legal pad. Christopher cocked his head. His study of the husband became intense, and, if it was her, Sammy would have wilted. As it was, the husband did not raise his eyes, and, though he stopped blinking, he still concentrated on his hands, his fingers now flexing deliberately.

Abruptly, Christopher said, "He was motivated by a radical ideology."

Sammy expected the husband to ask what that meant. Instead, he said, "Which was what?"

"He had a handwritten manifesto in his pocket."

The husband took a deep breath. "He was at war with the world?"

"That's how he saw it. Yes."

"Why?"

"He believed that it was the duty of humans to dominate each other, violently if necessary. This kid believed." Christopher leaned both hands on his knees and his eyes sharpened. Why was he telling the husband all this? So far this was closely guarded information.

Someone had leaked the existence of the letter but the contents were secret. "We humans have a biological imperative to be violent."

Sammy leaned forward, peered into Christopher's face to get his attention, and flipped her hand up to ask silently why he had divulged this much. Christopher's eyes darted to her for a moment, narrowed to indicate that he knew what he was doing and jumped back to his scrutiny of the husband. The expression on Christopher's face was the same as she had seen when he dealt with suspects not with witnesses, victims, or the families of victims.

Christopher said, "What's your take on that?"

The husband's eyes rose for the first time since he had sat down after showing them in and offering them a seat on the couch. From one of the bedrooms there came laughter and clapping. The husband glanced in the direction of that sign of life. He smiled with obvious affection and pain. "My take? He was a fool."

"Why's that?" Christopher sat back, laced his hands together, and seemed to expect an illuminating lecture.

The husband turned back to them. "He sounds like he studied too much Nietzsche in college. He became enamored of Zarathustra. Western philosophy was always about inflating the ego, elevating the human race as close to god as possible."

"I guess you don't buy into that?"

"No."

"Your wife was working toward a Ph. D. wasn't she?"

"That's right."

"What about you?"

He shook his head. "I have a bachelor's. That's all."

"You aren't drawn to the academic life?"

"Not for me. If I tried to don wings like that, I'd just burn up as I tried to soar to the sun."

"I see. That's the Greek myth of Icarus that you're alluding to. Isn't it?"

"Yes."

"Well, you sound pretty well read for someone who doesn't want to earn any degrees."

"Being educated and obtaining degrees doesn't mean that you're enlightened. The Dalai Lama says that we have more knowledge, especially scientific, but less wisdom. I think what he's pointing to is that we know better how the universe works, the mechanics of stars and the biology of animals, but we're clueless about existence and how to live it."

Christopher nodded appreciatively. Sammy felt clueless. Where was this going? She was supposed to conduct the interview, and now Christopher had hijacked it to discuss philosophy. What the hell? She folded her arms irritably.

"Are you Buddhist?" Christopher asked.

"More than anything else, I guess."

"You seem to know your way around Western philosophy though."

"That's part of my cultural inheritance, part of the education I was given by society."

"I didn't take philosophy in college. Did you?" he asked Sammy.

"No, and, as interesting as all this is, I think we may be getting off track." Sammy said tartly. She tapped her notepad with her pen. To the husband she asked, "Had she told you about any threatening emails, letters, or phone calls."

"No."

"What about calls where the caller hung up?"

"No."

"Have you noticed anyone hanging around your house or neighborhood?"

"No."

"Did your wife attend U of A for her Masters?" Christopher interrupted.

Sammy did not round on Christopher this time because the question was on topic.

"No, she went to Northern Arizona University."

"That's in Flagstaff?"

"Yes."

"What about for her bachelor's?"

"Arizona State."

"She went to all three universities in this state?" Christopher chuckled, though it was not his natural laugh. What was he setting this husband up to answer? Sammy wondered.

There was a burst of laughter from down the hall, which drew the husband's attention.

"Who is that?" Christopher asked. "They sound like they're having a good time."

"My son and friends of the family with their son." He looked at them for only a brief moment before his eyes jumped to Sammy's right. She followed his gaze to the bookcase beside the couch. To see what he did, she had to twist and crane her head. It was a framed photograph of his wife holding their son, who in the photo was a newborn.

"Did your wife—it's Jerusha, right? Did she ever mention a Randall or Rand?"

"No."

"Will or William?"

The husband shook his head as he turned to look in the direction of the continuing sounds of play.

Christopher leaned and cocked his head. This brought him almost on top of Sammy. "Does he look familiar?" he whispered to her.

Sammy stared at the husband as he sat in profile. He was an ordinary looking man in a number of ways. His hair was a bit long for Sammy's tastes, brown but with gray coming through. He had a muscular build, was of average height. There were acne scars on his cheeks. He had the lines from both sides of his nostrils diagonal to either side of his mouth. Wrinkles crinkled the outer corners of his eyes. As she took all this in, she reconsidered her initial assessment and decided that he seemed old for his age which she had assumed to be about thirty. "No," she whispered back.

Christopher sighed and straightened up. "Do you know who William Cooper and Randall Krieger were?"

"You said one was of the Plato Warriors. Who was the other?"

"They both were. Did she ever talk to you about the Plato Warriors?"

The husband shrugged. "Maybe when we first met. It would've been in the news maybe."

"Which was when?"

"January of O-nine."

"This was at which school?"

"NAU. Northern Arizona."

"You were a student there too?"

"No, I worked at an ACE Hardware up there. In fact my boss there is one of the ones who is back there." He pointed to the source of the laughter.

"How'd you meet then? Your wife, I mean."

"At the diner where she worked part time." The husband checked his watch.

"Is it almost time for the memorial?" Sammy asked. Christopher did not seem to be getting anywhere with this line of questioning.

"Yes. Excuse me." He rose, went down the hall and spoke for a few moments.

"Who do you think he looks like?" Sammy whispered to Christopher as they sat alone in the living room.

Christopher's brow furrowed. "I've been trying to place him as soon as he answered the door."

Sammy waited. Christopher pondered the possibility as he looked at Sammy's legal pad. "Who?" she pressed.

"It's like seeing a ghost. It's him but not him."

"Him who?"

"I don't know. I feel like I should know this man, but I can't place him in any context."

"An old friend or a classmate?"

"I don't know."

"Another case?"

"I don't know."

"Someone you saw sometime?"

He shook his head in resignation. "Forget it. Whoever he is he's no one to me."

"He might be."

"I could rack my brain all day and come up empty headed."

"Maybe, maybe not."

"You don't have that feeling do you? Kind of like déjà vu?"

"No."

"It's so strong, but I just can't get a grip on it."

Sammy shrugged. They were going in circles, and she had attempted to be helpful. Footsteps approached from down the hall. Out came the husband holding his two year old son followed by an African American man, a boy who must be his son, and a Mexican American woman who was fairly short and thick set.

"If there's nothing else, we really need to go. I'm sorry that I probably didn't give you any leads." The husband rubbed his son's back.

"You helped us narrow down the possibilities. That's always a big help." Sammy closed her pen and stood. Christopher followed suit. They made their condolences and their goodbyes to the husband, son, and friends as they walked out of the house and to their car. When Sammy shut the car door, she asked, "Still can't remember?"

"No."

"So should I just forget you and your déjà vu?"

"I guess."

"All right."

Anderson closed his car door and his body convulsed. His hands trembled with seizure-like force. Oh, holy fucking shit. It was all he could think as he watched the two FBI agents drive away. He wanted to puke. He wanted to piss and shit all over himself and curl into a ball. Had he done it? Had they believed him? Could they not recognize him? How was that possible?

In the back seat, strapped into his car seat, Mason began to flip through an Eric Carle board book. "Zee-ba. El-phant. Pole Bear." Anderson cranked the engine to life, and he backed out of the driveway. Waiting in their car, idling on the side of the street, were Paul, Maria, and Eric. When Anderson stopped the car and shifted from reverse to drive, he paused and searched for other cars on the street with drivers whose eyes were hidden from sight by large sunglasses. He saw no one. Were they watching him? Did they have a reason to watch him? Was he suspicious? If they had recognized him, those two agents would have drawn their guns to arrest him. They would have cuffed him and led him away from Mason. No such thing happened. He was still free. He took his foot from the brake, allowed the transmission to turn and pull them slowly along. He leaned and turned his face upward to spy any circling helicopters. Nothing. He applied the gas and the car lunged forward. He would be late for the memorial. That was fine. He did not want to go anyway. After he drove past their car, Paul pulled away from the curb and tucked in behind Anderson.

Jerusha's parents demanded the memorial. The day of the shooting, they flew into Tucson, were chauffeured to a Sheraton hotel, and once the rental car was delivered, began to prowl about Tucson. They popped in at the house whenever they pleased, without calling ahead. Twice that Anderson knew of, they found no one at home. They finagled a deal to rent one of the conference rooms at the Sheraton for the memorial. To create an invite list, they pestered Anderson for names of the professors Jerusha was close with, her fellow Ph. D. students, and the students from her classes. To this last request, for the names of her students in her classes, Anderson listened with mute pain and a sharp tightening in his throat.

"Well, the class she was instructing at the time are either dead or in the U of A Medical Center all shot up." His voice was like a barrage of artillery that surprised even him. He glowered at them. Both Liebgotts blanched.

Mr. Sheldon Liebgott wore a jacket, button up shirt and slacks at all times. His glasses were thick, and Anderson had a fantasy of smacking those specs off Mr. Liebgott's face so that he could see the mole eyes beneath blink blindly. He was in his fifties and had a paunch that dropped over his belt. He was a defense attorney, and, though Anderson did not inquire as to who his defendants were, he loathed the man's sanctimonious airs. Anderson, in order to lessen the violent contractions of his heart, avoided eye contact and argument with Jerusha's dad as much as he deemed prudent. He endeavored to take two or three breaths before he answered any questions, but that response to their request for the students' names and phone numbers had burst out without any reflection. Was his true self in those words, the self with that other name? He needed to check those inclinations and meditate on who he truly was.

Anderson breathed twice to cleanse his head of the animosity. "Anyway, I don't know any of her students. I never met them, and, if she had a list of their names and numbers, or even email addresses, I wouldn't know where to look for them. Frankly, I wouldn't want to invite them anyway."

"Well, maybe you don't, but we want to learn about her life. She kept us in the dark." Mr. Liebgott said as he pushed his glasses up on his nose.

"We've never met out grandson until now." Mrs. Harriet Liebgott had a stronger voice than her husband, though her whole frame shook as she spoke. Was it from anger? "Nor have we met you."

Anderson uttered no response. He had never once cross examined Jerusha about why she never made contact with her parents. It was not his place. While he yearned for parents to love him, she yearned to cut loose from hers completely. Over time, she divulged hints that she despised their "carefree, luxurious lifestyle" that was "morally and spiritually bankrupt." To Anderson those phrases rang dully because they were borrowed, inserted into her views as stand-ins for her own memories of, and tangled emotions toward, her parents. When Mrs. Liebgott said, "Nor have we met you," he had the impression that she, and most likely Mr. Liebgott too, believed that their estrangement from their daughter originated with Anderson. What ignorant shits! There was the old, angry side of him again. Anderson needed to tamp that voice of hatred. What was between Jerusha and Mr. and Mrs. Liebgott did not include Anderson or Mason.

"We want as many of our daughter's friends and coworkers— everyone she knew, as far as possible—to have the opportunity to say goodbye to her." Mr. Liebgott blinked as he tried to stare down Anderson.

Mrs. Liebgott said in her violent tremors, "And that includes your family. Are they here? We want to meet them. I assume they knew their daughter-in-law and grandson unlike us."

"I'm an orphan," Anderson's voice retained its explosive edge. The Liebgotts said nothing. "I have no family." Anderson felt the compulsion to add.

"We know what the word means. We do not need it defined." Mr. Liebgott jammed his hands on his hips.

"We've come here to celebrate our daughter's life not to be insulted by . . . you." Mrs. Liebgott peered up and down at him as if he was a piece of excrement.

Anderson wanted to bite off his own tongue and spit it into their faces as a way to let them know he was finished talking to them. As it was, he clenched his jaw shut so defiantly that his whole body vibrated with his rage. Where was all this emotion coming from? Breathe, dammit! He inhaled deeply and folded his arms in front of him.

In the end, the Liebgotts were forced to go to the English Department so that they could glean the information they desired. That initial interview was on the first morning of the Liebgott's stay in

Tucson. No conversation after that had been any more pleasant. Now, the hour of the memorial had arrived. Anderson sat at a round banquet table in a corner of the large conference hall. Also at the table were Paul, Maria, and Eric. Paul's son Eric drew cars and people in a notebook. As he finished a picture he colored it with Crayolas from a pack of sixteen. Mason's diaper bag had been filled by Maria and Anderson with toys and books to entertain the toddler for the duration of the memorial, which was nothing more than a party for the Liebgotts to show themselves off and insinuate their presence into the minds of anyone Jerusha knew. Anderson thought he now understood Jerusha's act of turning her back on her parents. They seemed devoid of any substance. Their sharply tailored clothes, practiced smiles and studied absorption in whatever their current interlocutor was employed at or able to offer the Liebgotts were what they brought to the room. Perhaps it was a charade, like a mask a tragedian donned for a while in order to be host for this party of their calling, and later they doffed that mask as the curtains in their minds fell to reveal them restored in their hotel room, nothing but a pair of grieving parents. Or it was not an act at all. This lack of personality was not skin deep but emanated from the cells through the whole of their beings.

No one approached the somber table where Anderson sat.

"You don't have to stay." Anderson gestured to Paul, Maria, and Eric. "This is horrible."

"We're here for you," Maria said.

"Yeah, that's right." Paul thumped Anderson on the back.

"Come off it, man." Anderson shook his head. "I don't want to be here, so I doubt that you do."

Maria and Paul exchanged looks. "Well," Paul said.

"We're here to support you in . . . this." Maria waved to the rest of the room.

"I don't know anyone here." Anderson's eyes gave the room a once over then settled on Mason. "I'm here because I feel this need to have Mason here for them." At this, he shoved a hand in the direction of the Liebgotts. "And they're not even checking in on us or sitting with their grandson they've never met before and over whom they made such a stink about. Like that work shop toy set that you saw in his room, they bought that yesterday. You know how much that was?"

"Probably a pretty penny." Paul shook his head.

"Try a pretty fifty dollar bill. I doubt they even checked the price when they bought it. Anderson knocked on the table like a judge pounded his gavel.

"Probably not."

"They lugged it in the house, opened it, and then just stared at it. There it lay on the floor out of the box, and they just stared at it as if they couldn't believe that it didn't come out of the box already built and ready to play with. I just sat on the couch and waited for it. I knew what had to be going through their minds. I knew what they would ask me. It would come any second. And you know what?"

"What?"

"You'll love this. Guess."

"What?"

Anderson shook his head. Breathe a second. He was letting emotion and suffering carry him off. Just one more breath. "They looked at me with helpless, childish eyes to do what they didn't dare ask me to do. They couldn't put it together themselves, and they saw that I knew they couldn't." Anderson crossed his arms and leaned into his seat back. "So I just sat there and waited. I'd be damned if I would bail them out of the jam they were in. The best part was that Mason didn't seem to give a damn. He played with the stuff as it was, in the plastic bags, and he fooled with the box."

"So when did you put it up?"

"After a few minutes, Jerusha's parents began to fidget and stammer out some bull excuses about having to meet someone or do something. I said, 'okay.' And they left. After that I put it together. It only took a few minutes. I just can't believe that Jerusha came from . . ." Anderson spied the Liebgotts approaching. "Them."

"We need Mason." Mrs. Liebgott put out both hands and went straight for Mason.

"What?" Anderson blinked. "You need him for what?"

At the sound of his name Mason looked at Mrs. Liebgott, but, as she bore quickly down on him, he scampered from his chair into Anderson's lap. "Dada."

Anderson wrapped him in his arms and tucked him close to his body.

"We have people who want to make the acquaintance of our grandson." Mrs. Liebgott walked in her shaky way around the table.

Anderson again wondered if she had Parkinson's or some other malady. "Give him here."

"Dada."

"Hey, what's the matter, boy-O?" Anderson leaned his head away so that he could peer into his son's face. Was he scared?

"Dada." Mason clung by his chubby arms to Anderson's neck.

Mrs. Liebgott put her hands on Mason's back but at a sharp glance from Anderson she proceeded no further in disentangling son from father. Instead, she looked to her husband who waited on the opposite side of the table. Husbands and wives have vast nonverbal communication relays that are designed to seal off others in favor of the united front of a couple. Mr. Liebgott entered the campaign from his flanking position while Mrs. Liebgott maintained the physical pressure of a direct assault.

"Look here, Anderson, he is our grandson and you can't deny our rights to him." Mr. Liebgott said more, but Anderson only heard that first sentence which blared and irked of legality and proprietorship.

"Fine." Anderson curtly interrupted the fine argument of the lawyer. Mrs. Liebgott infiltrated her fingers into Mason and Anderson's embrace to pry him loose. Mason now wrapped his legs around as much of Anderson's torso as he could, determined come hell or high water to not be parted from his Dada. "No. I stay. Dada," Mason squealed.

Heads in the room turned. Both Liebgotts flinched and took a step back. Their heads turned with smiles meant to assure the guests that nothing was amiss. Public embarrassment was the way to control these two.

"I think his stranger danger trumps your need." Anderson rose. "Paul, what time is it?"

"What? Are you going to time us, limit our custodial rights?" Mr. Liebgott shook his soft fist in the air as if he spoke from an imagined platform of strength.

"No."

Paul consulted his Timex analog watch, probably the same he had worn since his days in the Persian Gulf War, and announced the time with a tone of unequivocal authority.

"What I propose is this." Anderson repositioned Mason so that he was to one side, which also disrupted Mrs. Liebgott's feeble hold.

"It'll soon be naptime. We'll go around and meet whomever you want as we make our way to the exit."

"Both of you?" Mrs. Liebgott seemed aghast at this counter offer. Perhaps they wanted to disavow any connection to Anderson. They would simply introduce their grandson as Jerusha's without the benefit of a husband and father. It would be like a twenty first century immaculate conception, imagined and sanctified by lawyers.

Anderson's jaw ached but unlocked enough to say, "Yes. I'd be glad to meet your acquaintances." He forced a small, firm smile.

Mrs. Liebgott's eyes rounded into shock and turmoil. She bodily faced her husband, who gave a weak shrug to tell her there might be no other way to arbitrate this situation. Paul and Maria both stood. Paul laid a hand on Eric's shoulder and leaned down to whisper in his son's ear. Eric said, "Okay." He gathered his crayons and worked to reload them into their box. Anderson took Mason's diaper bag from the chair back, but, before he could swing it onto the opposite shoulder from his son, Maria stepped up and took it with a smile. "Let me."

"Thanks."

"Anytime." She rubbed his arm and hung the diaper bag on her shoulder.

The Liebgotts led the way, each of them twisting to look back at their grandson who gripped Anderson so closely that they were cheek to cheek. Perhaps they wanted to ensure Anderson's compliance with the strategy of Mason's exhibition to the newly created Tucson connections that the Liebgotts wanted to foster. As they wended through the throng, the cumulative lack of sleep from the last two days crashed on him. He had nothing left. In his arms, Mason felt like an elephant. The noisome fumes of lady's perfume made him reel. His whole body bucked with the throbbing of a violent headache. He became nauseous. Any second he might pass out. What a cluster fuck that would be! Imagine the faces of the crowd. Would there be gaping mouths, dilated nostrils, doughnut eyes? Who would rush to his fallen form? Who would mill about and go on tiptoe to witness the humiliation of a man? What man would want to faint whether there was a crowd of one or one million, even if the only witness was his own conscience? No, he would not faint. Even if he had to pinch himself or slap his face he was not going to lose consciousness. Never. His tongue swelled in his mouth, threatened to choke him, but he swallowed and forced his esophagus open. His lips parted, not slack, but cracked to suck at the fortifying air. He did not faint. The queasy feeling rolled back into his stomach and hid there, lurked like a leopard in the lair. The pulsations of his headache dropped to above his left ear and drummed there while awaiting another chance to retake the territory of his temples and eyes.

They twisted and skirted through the crowd. Anderson clung to Mason as if he was a life buoy, while Mason clung to Anderson like a climber to the mountain's summit. In their trail came Paul, Maria, and Eric. At last, they broke out of the last introduction before the door. They rushed out of the Sheraton and into the omnipresent Tucson sun. Anderson pulled up his quick march when he hit the curb at the end of the red awning flanked by two valets in uniforms with silver name tags pinned to their breasts. Anderson swayed. No, no, no, do not pass out. How would he make it home? Breathe. This time, his mouth stretched and gobbled the air like a man hungry for life. He had to be well enough to drive so that he could get Mason home. The only protector for Mason was him now. Pull it together.

"You all right?" Paul clapped a hand on the back of his neck.

"Mm." That was all the sound Anderson could get out.

"Do you want us to drive you?" Maria asked.

Anderson shook his head.

"You don't look okay. You look like you're about to drop." Paul released his neck.

"I can drive our car, and you drive them in theirs," Maria said to Paul.

"Give me your keys." Paul put out his hand. The stern face of an NCO would not accept Anderson's refusal.

Maria reached for Mason, who now left Anderson willingly. Without the burden of his son, Anderson slumped. Paul caught him by an arm. Anderson dug in his pocket and came up with his keys, which he slapped into Paul's landing field of a hand. They went to the cars and got in. Paul drove Anderson and Mason. Anderson wanted to lean his head against the window, but it was blistering hot and the heat radiating off it made him want to puke. He twisted and leaned against the seat, seeking a cool slipstream from the A/C vents.

"When was the last time you had a good night's sleep?" Paul asked. "'Cause you looked like the ragged end of nothin'."

"I don't know. Before." He meant before Jerusha died, and he assumed that Paul would recognize that. Anderson shut his eyes. He listened to the car engine rev, shift, and slow. His body swayed according to the turns they took, the accelerations, and the braking. He jerked awake when they lurched over the pothole in his driveway, the crater on the left side that he always caught when he pulled in and which Paul had done the same, too. Maria pulled in after them. Paul shut off the car, hopped out, went to the back door, and worked to free Mason from his car seat. Okay, you're home, Anderson tried to motivate his body, I know you're whipped, but you have to get up. Paul could not carry him. The back car door shut. Anderson watched his son toddle off at speed to the front door. Mason was on a mission. He probably wanted to play with that tool set. The Liebgotts had been right that such a toy would be what a boy would want. Anderson's door opened.

"Come on."

Anderson struggled to rise and was tugged back into the seat.

"Your seat belt." Paul pointed.

Feeling more than a lot stupid, Anderson punched his thumb into the orange button. "That was dumb."

"I'm not sayin' a thing." Paul had a full face smile.

Anderson sighed. Paul's hand reached inside, and, with Anderson's hand in his, he tugged him from the car seat. "There you go. Now let's get you in the house, in your room, and in your bed. All right?"

"Okay."

The nausea forced him to claw at the top of the car door for support. Paul took Anderson's arm, slung it over his shoulders, and caught him under the opposite armpit with his own arm. As he lugged Anderson away, after they cleared the car, Paul horse kicked the door shut. They buddy walked to the house, through the open dining/living room, into the hall, and to his room. "Now, you kick off your boots, get on that comfy looking bed, and sleep for a few hours. Don't worry about Mason. He's in better hands than you are." Anderson kicked off his boots after he shakily unlaced them. The door clicked closed. Paul was gone.

Anderson turned on his side and curled his legs to him. He stared at the empty field that was Jerusha's half of the bed. She was no longer there. She never would be. He imagined reaching his arm around her small waist and nestling his hand between her breasts. He could almost feel the B cup weight of her small breast on his hand, but his hand lay empty on the comforter. Why? Why her? Why did she have to die? Was it because of him? Was her death the unbelieved-of-God's retribution for his sins? Was this his kharma? What if that chance meeting with that man-child those three or four years ago had ended with Rand and Will killing him? Would that have saved her? She did not deserve an early death. According to the rules of engagement that Will and Rand created years ago, she had plenty of moral consciousness. There was not a stupid cell in her. She could not be found lacking on any question that kid had dreamed to ask. There was no way. She could have argued him into a corner where the only way out would be for him to blow his own head off. So why was she dead?

So that man-child had ignored the rules that Will and Rand had created years ago. In the end though, Rand had ignored the rules too. Their principles, those high minded ideals that originally illuminated them, fell away, and they were replaced by some savage impulse to fill the earth with the dead. How did it come to that? When had the transformation occurred? Was it wrong to kill on principle? Yes, but how did killing due to principle lead to killing with no consideration at all? If that seemed like an inevitable metamorphosis of men like Rand and the man-child—though tagged in newspapers, television, and the internet every few minutes and with those FBI agents telling him the name this morning, Anderson could not keep the name of Jerusha's killer in his head—then why had he, William Anderson Cooper, newly reborn as Anderson Williams, not undergone the same? What prevented him from losing—or was it abandoning, since he was not sure which it truly was—his principles? But he had lost something else. If Rand and that other guy had lost their sense that there were people who deserved life and there were people who deserved death, a fundamental distinction between right and wrong, good and evil, justice and injustice, Will had lost the sense of his self. He recalled the wandering in the snow, the same wandering in the mountains that he endured after he returned from war. There had been, in both cases, a vast blankness, an area ablated within his head that only slowly refilled, and as it did only then could he rejoin the company of humanity, raise his eyes to take a peek at their faces. What had he lost, what gained? He could not advance any answer for that first case, that time in the Rockies after his return stateside from the ruin of the ravaged nation of Afghanistan. The time and the man who emerged were as remote to the man now as the suggestion of a God to govern the slaughter of humans for obscure, God-ordained reasons. What of this last time when he wandered nameless in the wilderness? What had he gained? He had a new name. His hair had changed to gray at his temples. His beard, when he neglected to shave on the weekends, sprouted white on his chin. He meditated daily. He did yoga daily. He was a father and a husband. His patience for the foibles of others, though tested daily and stretched, never ruptured. He did not, even in his head, demand that they change. He never announced in his head that he accepted people as they were because the acceptance was total and undeclared. He felt love for two others and knew their love in return. He created his own family.

He closed his eyes. Breathe in and breathe out. He saw Mason's round face as he plunged into the depths of sleep.

He woke up. She was not there. He clawed the empty half of their bed. Tears came. She was never going to be there again. His knees drew into his stomach. He clutched her pillow and smothered himself. Death, please, come. Heart, you can stop. Lungs, you can deflate and refuse to expand. Blood, no more pumping along your veins. Just all of you stop. She was no longer with him. What was his purpose? She had been everything to him. Why has his heart not stopped? Why do his lungs keep pulling air in and pushing it back out? Why is his blood still thumping around in his body? Why can he not just will it all to stop? The pillow was not thick enough to do the job. Somehow air, a miniscule amount to be sure, slipped through the fibers of the pillow. He slung the pillow away, and it flumped against the wall before whispering to the floor. He automatically gasped for breath. If he still had his pistol, he could just blow his life out like a candle. Languidly, he sat up and leaned back on his arms, his hands behind him. There were other ways. He once killed people in other ways. Remember? When the name was William?

His chin sank to his chest. What thoughts were these? Would she approve? No. His gun and his knife, his old name and his old self were all buried. They were no more. And she was responsible for that. Could he let her down? What about all the meditation, yoga, books she chose for him to read, the compassion she showed him, the sensitive and forgiving ear she listened to him with, the love making, and the looks of caring and understanding she shone on him? Thanks to her he changed. He exercised the Buddha's teachings. Thanks to her he tread the path of enlightenment. He no longer forced people to change by terror and the promise of death. Was he going to waste all that by killing himself?

He swung his legs off the bed and sat on the edge. He heard laughter from beyond the door. He checked the time on the alarm clock placed on the nightstand by his side. It was a little after seven. Had he been asleep that long? Almost five hours? He had not slept much in the last three days. Does anyone ever sleep much when a close relation dies? No, of course not.

He rose and made his way out into the family room. At the dining room table there was a plate, silverware, and a napkin laid out for him. The rest of the table was clear. On the TV an animated movie was playing. Mason leaned on the end of the sofa with an open mouthed smile on his round face. On the rug, Eric lay on his side with his head propped by a hand. Paul and Maria sat on the sofa and held hands. They made a pleasant picture of a family. None of them had seen Anderson.

"What're you watching?" Anderson asked. All of them spoke at once. From the entrance to the hall, Anderson half way crossed the room to where Mason stood before he squatted and extended his arms to invite his son to come to him. Mason charged with fists pumping at chest level right into him. If the boy was any bigger he might have bowled Anderson over. Anderson stood and repeated his question so only Mason could hear. The boy repeated the title with a two year old's elisions.

"Is it good?"

"Yah." Mason craned his head to see past Anderson.

"Is it funny?"

"Yah."

They sat in the easy chair. All five of them focused their attention on the movie, or, at least in Anderson's case, attempted to do so. What really fascinated him was Mason. He was so tiny. Eric, only about five years older, was huge by comparison. Eric could feed himself, maybe not cook, but he could get a bowl of cereal and pour milk in it. Eric could dress himself, brush his teeth, take a bath, and play on his own. Mason could do none of that. He needed someone to be responsible for him, to rear him, to teach him to be a man.

The movie ended and the Dolphys said goodnight.

"Let's get together for breakfast." Anderson pumped Paul's hand.

"Sounds great. Where do you want to meet?"

"Just come here. Everybody likes pancakes, right?"

It was agreed that the Dolphys would return at eight o'clock. When Anderson closed and locked the front door after the departure, he tickled Mason's belly and said, "That's it, bud. It's bedtime."

He was surprised the boy was awake at this late hour anyway. After all the bedtime preparations such as brushing teeth, changing his diaper, and putting on his pajamas, Anderson gave him a piggy back ride to his bed. The toddler bed was so low to the floor that Anderson's back twinged with pain to stoop so far. All the yoga he did would not make those deep scars vanish. Mason leapt from his dad's back and rolled around on the mattress. "Hey, hey. Now calm down. It's bedtime, silly boy." Anderson could not stifle a smile at his son's antics.

"Read," the boy insisted.

"Read?" Why not? They had nothing else to do tomorrow. "Oh, all right."

They read another Eric Carle book, this one about a crab. He kissed his son good night. As he stood at the light switch by the door, he took a last look at his son. Mason lay with a small knit blanket over him. Curled on one side, he had his eyes closed and pretended to sleep even though he smiled. For Anderson, his son was the most cherished person in the world to him now that Jerusha was gone. He pushed the switch slowly down, knowing that he had to do it, but he savored every second that he could see his boy's face. The light was off. The dark startled him. Anderson went to the living room where he sat on the couch in silence and stillness. When enough time passed, he rose, turned the lights off, and tiptoed back to Mason's room. If the boy was awake he would have protested the sudden total darkness, so Anderson figured. He must be asleep then. Anderson crept to Mason's bed and sat on the edge. He felt obligated to Mason. And, for some unfathomable reason he had to say something to his son, despite his immaturity and inability to comprehend, and never mind the fact that he slept.

Anderson said, "There will be lots of hard times ahead for both of us. I know better than most what the worst things that can happen to you are. Maybe because of that, maybe with all my experiences of the rotten parts of being a living human, I'll be able to guide you through it better than other dads. Yeah, maybe. I know that I'm all you have." He brushed Mason's round cheek as he lay asleep. Then he recommenced to whisper to him. "But you're all I have, too. That means that we have a responsibility to each other. Mom is . . . she isn't with us anymore. That's a hard fact. I don't know if there's a heaven. I always doubted it, and still do now, but I know that she would want us to work together. She'd want us to keep together and never let each other down. That'll go both ways. Eventually, I'll be old and decrepit and then I'll need you to care for me." He patted Mason's thigh beneath the blanket. "I'm going to tell you something I've never told anyone before. It's something I've buried, a whole chunk of me that I don't like, that I hate really—I want that to be a word you never use—and that made me go crazy for a long time. It was only because of mom that I managed to change my direction in life. Who knows where I'd be otherwise. She saved me. I don't know why she did it. I wasn't anybody to her. I wasn't even a friend at first. She retrained me. You might say that she reprogrammed me to be a new man. Maybe the other man, the one that I'm so ashamed of, maybe that man is completely gone. So if he is gone, it's only because of your mom's compassion, patience, and knowledge. You see . . . ." He stopped and swallowed on his dry tongue. How had his mouth become so dry? He felt choked. He tried to swallow again. What he had to say needed to be said. "I was a man who killed people. I had a friend, named Rand, and, maybe it was his idea at first, but I certainly went along with it. We decided to start a war against every other person on the planet. We thought we could be the judge of everyone else. We could ask every person a question that would show how smart they were, how much they thought about life, and whether or not they were conscientious. Maybe Plato's words to the effect that the unexamined life was not worth living was part of the impetus. If we didn't like their answer—and we did cross examine these people that we met for quite a while—then we killed them. We shot them. We were judge-executioners. We thought we knew everything. I knew more than Rand at first. I taught him how to fire a pistol. I taught him how to stab with a knife. That was me. Maybe the initial idea was his, but I was the planner. I was the trainer, the one with the know-how. I still thought I was a soldier. I'd been to war and maybe I thought that what he and I did could be a new war, one that we fully understood, one that made more sense, and one that we controlled unlike that war in Afghanistan where I fought. I'd like to tell you that I was naïve, that I was tricked, that I didn't really know what I was doing, but those would all be lies. I would be deceiving you, if I told you that. I already knew what it was like to kill another person. I knew what a real war was like. I'm going to tell you that I'm someone who can't easily be forgiven for all that I did because I understood what I was doing. Maybe Rand came up with the initial idea, but it was me who sat there in our living room, listened to him, and thought it was a good idea. Don't ask me how I could do such a thing, how I could believe that murdering people would somehow make the world a better place, but I did. I hope you never think such a thing. I'll do my best to dissuade you. I'll give you history, philosophy, Buddhism, and my own personal experience. I'd rather you hated me than ever dreamed of following my example. Maybe because every war that was ever fought by every nation or kingdom always exhorted the soldiers and families of the soldiers that this would be the last war, the war to bring eternal peace, that's why I did the things I did. I don't want you to believe that I'm excusing myself. I'm not. I'm trying to take as much responsibility as I can. We, Rand and I, thought that if we got rid of the stupid by killing them that would help the world. We questioned everyone we met who would stop to talk, and we asked, for example, 'What is the good life?' or 'What is the meaning of life?' The answers we got were mostly pretty bad. Most people just don't have a clue about anything. A lot of people just give answers they were taught by school or church or movies or governments. They never really think about how those answers related to the world, how if you believe one thing, it follows that you must believe other things. That's logic at work. People never consider how everything is connected. For most people, they just accept what comes to them, and if they do rebel, they don't really have a vision of what an alternative would look like, what it would be, how it would work and affect others.

"I do remember two people who gave incredible answers though. One was this nervous, little guy that kind of reminded me of Hume Cronyn in *Shadow of a Doubt*. He was a professor of something I can't recall. He said that we have to be able to account for everything that we've done. He kept track of all the minutiae of his existence. I'm in awe of that kind of dedication to recording our existence. It was the other person that I think might have the greatest impact upon you and me. You see, she was a mother of three girls. Of all the people that I've met over the years, she's the one I keep running into again in my mind. Maybe I don't remember her right, but I think of her as one of the most beautiful women I ever saw in person. Sure, those Hollywood actresses are hot, but they aren't real, not the way this woman was. She had these bright blue eyes, the color of the Pacific Ocean. Her hair was blonde and hung half way down her back like a downpour of sunlight that you might see as it slips between storm clouds." Will smiled in the darkness at his own poetic vision. Mason rolled on his side, and, for a time, Will sat quite motionless. His smile remained. He put his hand on Mason's back. The tiny respirations were a comfort. The quick flutters of his heart were a joy. Finally, reassured that Mason was asleep, he went on. "That mother, I think of her a lot. I know I said that, but it's the case. Her daughters all looked like her. She had strong genes. We asked her what the purpose of life was. I think that's what it was. It was something like that, anyway. Her answer was that she had the responsibility to her daughters to teach them, protect them, and raise them so that they would be good people who did good in the world. I think she understood what most people never do. It's easy to be a parent. A few minutes of sex at the right time of month, and, Bingo, nine months later you're a mom and dad. You may love your children, you may want them to go to the best schools, wear nice clothes, have all the best material items that maybe you had or didn't have when you grew up, and you give them everything you can, and you have them go to church or whatever, but through all this, well, despite it really, you forget one crucial aspect of life. You neglect something. Probably most people think it's covered by going to church. Maybe they're right. Maybe church does answer the question, though it's not so much a question really as it is an underlying frame— a skeleton might be the right image—that you put your life on top of to give your life its shape. Yeah, that's maybe it. Without a skeleton you're just a puddle of life, shapeless like an amoeba." He chortles. "Amoeba. 'Stimulus, response, stimulus, response, that's all you ever do.' That was the punch line of a cartoon. It's so true though. And that's what people are like who don't have that skeleton. They think it's there because they're alive but they haven't got it. When everyone around you looks just like you, your perception is that you are the norm, the way you ought to be. It's only when you see someone come along with a skeleton in them, with that totally different shape from yours, that's when you see what a person is really like. Of course, you resist that. You refuse to see that the person with a skeleton is really a person because you're so accustomed to people who are just puddle-people. This mother though, she grasped that idea of a skeleton, the metaphorical one that I'm talking about. She had one, and she was going to help give her daughters skeletons too. She told us that, as soon as she found out she was pregnant, she studied up on how to be a mother. She read books. She wanted to be ready. So she got through the difficult stage of infancy, when you focus on the baby surviving. You have to know how to feed, burp, change their diapers, and know what to look for if they're getting sick. She taught them sign language at first so that they could communicate their wants and needs to her and their dad. As they got older she worked to teach them the alphabet, colors, numbers, and nursery rhymes. The crucial thing was that whenever one girl would do something to hurt, make fun of, or shout at one of the others, the mother taught them that they had to be nice to each other because they were family and someday the three sisters would be all they had as far as family went. Mom and dad would be gone. Grandma and grandpa would be gone too, because they were even older than mom and dad. The three sisters would have to look after each other. As the girls got older and were in school, the oldest in third or fourth grade and the youngest in preschool, she widened the circle of who the sisters should take care of and look after. They had pets. 'Look after you pets' became 'look after all pets and animals.' 'Look after your sisters' became 'look after your friends, look after your classmates, look after those that are younger and smaller.' 'Look after plants in the house' became 'look after the plants in the yard and then the plants in the world.' 'Only Connect.' Everyone was connected, everything was connected. She said that 'only connect' came from the novel *Howards End*, which she read and felt such a, well, connection to when she read it for school. She wanted to teach her girls that they were keepers for the world. They had the minds to understand the interconnectedness of it all. They had the bodies to do something good for the world. That was their purpose. It was her purpose, her daughters' purpose, the purpose of all people. I remember that Rand was quick to ask why. I thought it sounded right, but he, the cynic, didn't buy it. She said that because we as humans have the brains and bodies to do it that made us the biological recipients of the duty to do it, to be responsible for the world, to see how it was interconnected, and to do good and not harm because we knew that difference, we apprehended the meaning and function of the values. That's another responsibility that I'm going to teach: you need to teach others. Yes, caring for other beings, having compassion for them, that's the Buddhist conception of it, is important, but you must also pass it along. I will teach you all I know. I will empty myself in service to you. My hope is to raise you above what I am, not in the usual way of financial rewards, the way so many parents want their children to have greater wealth and material comfort with more TVs, cars, computers, and a more spacious home, but a greater knowledge, understanding, and compassion for the world."

He lay on the bed, beside Mason, and stared at the blinds, which seemed to glow as if some angelic presence stood outside the house. No such thing was true. Tonight was a full moon and the sunlight the lunar surface reflected was transformed into a haunting silver light, as it had done since the moon bound itself to the earth when the solar system came to have its current placements and dimensions, and it continued to do when lava rose from the tumultuous cracks in the crust to create continents, and when there were only creatures in the seas, and when dinosaurs thudded and pounded out their heavy bodied lives, and when mammals scurried and survived, and when humans barely distinguishable from apes began to gesticulate, utter words, and find mysteries and laws that caused them to wonder and believe. Yes, the full moon and its light were a permanent fixture in the minds of humans even as mysteries yielded to scientific knowledge and the laws were rebelled against for the sake of vanity and novelty. So were the ancient truths lost? Were those things that humans knew long ago of no consequence to Anderson and Mason? No, the Buddha had lived over two thousand years ago. This was hardly ancient in consideration of the vast time frames that the solar system was measured by, but for humanity's earliest written documents, its first efforts to commune with those who were not yet born and to inscribe into a medium presumed to be more indelible than the soft gray tissues of the brain lodged within our crushable skulls, this was as deep within Time with a capital T as it was possible to proceed. *The Torah*, the *Testaments* of Christianity, the *Tao Te Ching* and *I Ching* and other texts of China, the Nile River Valley, the Middle East, and Mesoamerica were the earliest, tenuous links to what laws and beliefs humans lived by long ago and which they continued to live by now. Did that mean that those ideas were the best? Did that endurance mean that those ideas were the only important ideas humanity had to offer?

Anderson closed his eyes. His ken was reduced to the abyss as deep as the universe behind his eyelids. Could he offer to humanity something more enlightening than what those ancients had bequeathed? He doubted that he could. Creation was not that important, though its primacy seemed unquestionable to most people. Survival and endurance, or maybe a better word in the case of ideas, continuance, were the supreme acts of life. If, to prove the point, a planet, person, or thought is born only to be extinguished before it can nourish and sustain further life only then did it prove to be meaningless. In that vein, it was not Anderson's or Mason's or anyone else's duty to fashion new modes of thought that would boggle and enthrall the minds of future generations. No, the issue of importance was the inheritance and subsequent transmission of ideas that proved to be valuable in life after life. Eyes closed, Anderson nestled his hand once more along Mason's respiring back. "That is what I will do," he said. "I will pass it along. That is my pact, the pact that all people need to make because it is what survives of us over the distance of Time. We must be humble enough to see that as individuals we are motes, but as the whole of humanity we are something great." Anderson smiled. He slept. He was baptized in the endless currents of life and Time as One.

Made in the USA
San Bernardino, CA
07 May 2014